Berkley Books by John L. Campbell

OMEGA DAYS

SHIP OF THE DEAD

DRIFTERS

CROSSBONES

CROSSBONES

AN OMEGA DAYS NOVEL

JOHN L. CAMPBELL

BERKLEY BOOKS, NEW YORK

BERKLEY

An imprint of Penguin Random House LLC
375 Hudson Street, New York, New York 10014

This book is an original publication of Penguin Random House LLC.

Copyright © 2015 by John L. Campbell.
Penguin supports copyright. Copyright fuels creativity, encourages diverse voices,
promotes free speech, and creates a vibrant culture. Thank you for buying an authorized
edition of this book and for complying with copyright laws by not reproducing, scanning,
or distributing any part of it in any form without permission. You are supporting
writers and allowing Penguin to continue to publish books for every reader.

BERKLEY® and the "B" design are registered trademarks of Penguin Random House LLC.
For more information, visit penguin.com.

Library of Congress Cataloging-in-Publication Data

Campbell, John L. (Investigator)
Crossbones : an Omega days novel / John L. Campbell.
pages ; cm
ISBN 978-0-425-28375-2 (trade)
I. Title.
PS3603.A47727C76   2015
813'.6—dc23
2015014518

PUBLISHING HISTORY
Berkley trade paperback edition / September 2015

PRINTED IN THE UNITED STATES OF AMERICA

10 9 8 7 6 5 4 3 2 1

Cover art: pirate ship by Shutterstock/Alexeye30; ship by Shutterstock / HES Photography.
Cover design by Diana Kolsky.
Interior text design by Laura K. Corless.
Title page art © iStockphoto.com/trigga.

This is a work of fiction. Names, characters, places, and incidents either are the product of
the author's imagination or are used fictitiously, and any resemblance to actual persons,
living or dead, business establishments, events, or locales is entirely coincidental.

*This book is dedicated to the men and women
of the United States Coast Guard.
Their quiet and steady devotion to duty not only
saves lives but keeps the wolf away from the door.
We owe these professionals our gratitude.*

For Linda, whose courage continues to inspire me every day.

*And for my brother, Louie.
I wish you could have seen this. I'll miss you.*

ACKNOWLEDGMENTS

As always, this book would not have been possible without the skillful editorial talents of Amanda Ng. She's become as invested in the characters as I have, and that makes me work harder. Thanks also go to Jennifer DeChiara for her ongoing efforts, and to my family and friends for continuing to believe. Finally, my warmest gratitude goes out to the readers who have journeyed with me through this series. You make me want to be a better writer. Thank you all.

CROSSBONES

A CRUEL SEA

ONE

Elizabeth drained the last sip of her coffee and quickly washed the mug, drying it with a dish towel and placing it carefully back among the ordered rows in the cabinet beside the sink. The kitchen clock read 6:45 A.M.

"Ready, shipmate?" she called.

A *meow* answered her from the living room.

Liz was dressed for work: a dark blue shirt and matching pants with the cuffs tucked into black boots. The name over her shirt pocket read *KIDD* in black letters. At fifty, she was trim and lean, a runner who worked to keep herself fit, something she was finding more difficult as the years rolled on. Still, she didn't suffer from the loose skin at the throat—*turkey neck*, people called it—many women her age developed. She was toned, her skin weathered by sun and elements, with deepening crow's-feet at the corners of her eyes. Those eyes were dark and clear and, other than reading glasses, required no correction. Liz looked forward to passing her annual physical fitness qualifications with ease.

She pulled a dark blue baseball cap down over a bristle of short hair the color of steel. Most people, she knew, assumed that she didn't care for having men in her personal life. The hair, her profession, the absence of a husband, and even the cat contributed to the stereotype. Those people were wrong, and she had even been married briefly, it just hadn't worked. She had a spouse nonetheless, an incredibly demanding one, and to which she was utterly devoted.

"Okay," she said, crouching in front of a pet carrier and sticking her fingers through the grille. "Ready to go for a ride? You need to be a good boy while Mommy's gone."

A black-and-gray-striped cat pushed its head against the fingers and meowed.

Liz slung a black nylon laptop bag across her chest, then picked up a heavy blue sea bag in one hand and the cat carrier in the other. Outside, she set her load down long enough to lock the front door, and then put her gear into a dark gray Camry. The cat carrier went onto the passenger seat, where she strapped it in tightly with the seat belt's shoulder harness.

She loved this town, and had lived here three different times in nearly thirty years, and it would be where she retired. Her tidy little house with its immaculate lawn sat in the suburbs of Rainier Valley, south of Seattle. Bright blue skies and clouds still tinged pink from the sunrise soared overhead. Though she didn't yet know it, the world was already ending this glorious summer morning, and she would never see her little house again.

Liz backed into the street and in her side mirror saw one of her neighbors, a young woman, out for a morning jog along the sidewalk. At the house next door, Mr. Fulton, in pajamas, a robe, and bare feet, lurched down his driveway toward his morning paper. The man suffered from both gout and a heart condition, and the way he moved told Liz he was having a particularly difficult morning. Liz threw them both a wave—the jogger returned it, Mr. Fulton did not, as he was a consummate grump—and pulled away, headed to work.

She had already turned the corner and so couldn't see the jogger and Mr. Fulton reach the end of the old man's driveway at the same time. She also didn't see Mr. Fulton wrestle the jogger to the ground, rip out her throat with fingernails and teeth, and begin to feed.

A s the Camry made its way west, winding out of residential neighborhoods and heading toward the more built-up section of the city near the water, the cat in the carrier beside her settled in and quieted. He was used to this routine. Liz wished she could take him with her, but that just wasn't possible.

She would have preferred leaving him home where he was comfortable, but that wasn't possible either. Chick, who lived in the small basement apartment of her little house, wouldn't feed him. He wouldn't water plants or do yard work, either, and she had to employ a landscaping company to keep her lawn and shrubs squared away during her prolonged absences.

No, Charlie "Chick" Kidd wasn't one for domestic responsibility. But he was her brother, her only sibling, and despite his many flaws she loved him and was happy he had accepted her offer to share the house. Chick was coming home today after being out for three weeks, and though her own job would keep her extremely busy, she hoped they could make time to see each other for dinner before she had to leave.

The lights and blare of a siren came on fast as an ambulance raced toward her. Liz pulled quickly to the shoulder, and as the vehicle passed, a string of unhappy yowls came from the cat carrier.

"Steady," Liz said, "it's just a medic."

Before she could pull back into the road, a squad car appeared, screaming after the emergency medical vehicle. The cat was not pleased, and let her know it. Liz reached across and put her fingers through the grille of the cat carrier. "It's okay, kitty, Mommy's right here." The cat ignored the fingers and made a noise that was more groan than meow.

The quickest way to work at this early hour would have taken her up onto I-5 near Seattle-Tacoma International Airport. As she approached, however, she saw the flashing blue and red lights of police and fire vehicles, so many that it indicated a major accident. A river of stopped motorists was stacked up behind it with car doors standing open and people moving slowly through the traffic jam. Liz bypassed the on-ramp before she could become stuck herself and took an alternate route. She cut left, then right, and passed under the freeway, traveling across the industrial district before turning north on Route 99, also called Alaskan Way. She could follow it all the way to work, and the many traffic lights were still preferable to sitting still for who knew how long while the accident was cleared.

The day was bright and clear, a contradiction to what most people believed about Seattle: that it poured every day. The heaviest precipitation ran from November to January, and although it was usually cloudy and did experience frequent mist and light rain, August was typically warm and dry, just like today. In her rearview mirror, Mount Rainier—simply called The Mountain by locals—dominated the southeastern horizon. Through her windshield, Seattle's skyline rose with the iconic Space Needle standing against a bright blue background. It was a beautiful day to be a Seattleite.

She continued north, passing the Pacific Maritime Institute on her left. A block farther on, she slowed and came to a stop behind several cars lined up behind a tractor-trailer standing in the road. Its emergency flashers were blinking, and the cab's driver door stood open. After a few moments the cars ahead of her eased around it and continued on their way. Liz did the same, and as she passed she saw the cab was empty, the driver nowhere in sight.

"Hell of a place to break down," she said.

The cat meowed its agreement.

She arrived at her turn and made a left. The view ahead made her catch her breath and smile. There it was, *Joshua James*, its snowy white hull brilliant in the morning light, black masts and antennae towering above. Although it had yet to receive its markings and have the big 754 painted on its bow, the vessel was more beautiful than any she had ever seen. It would be her last sea command, and what a way to finish a nearly thirty-year career of serving aboard cutters. There was still some debate about whether the ship would remain here in Seattle after commissioning or report to a new home in Charleston, South Carolina. Certainly Liz preferred it remain here, but she wouldn't complain about relocating to Charleston for a few years. She wasn't part of the decision-making process; the Coast Guard would cut her orders, and she would report wherever they sent her without complaint.

Liz slowed as she reached the base gate and a young man armed and wearing camouflage stepped out of the gatehouse with a clipboard. The striped barrier was down and a red and white sign set in the clipped grass off to the right read *MARSEC LEVEL 1*—out of three—with the words *SIGNIFICANT RISK* beneath it. The sign had displayed this message for some time as a response to recent threats from foreign terrorist groups. Guarding against those threats was, to a great extent, Liz's responsibility, and the reason *Joshua James* and her sister ships had been built.

As Liz brought the Camry to a stop and rolled down her window, the sentry looked at the base pass in the windshield, checked his clipboard, then snapped off a crisp salute. "Good morning, Captain."

"Petty Officer," she said, giving him a nod. When the sentry stooped to look inside the vehicle, Liz patted the pet carrier. "House cat, one each," she said.

The sentry allowed a trace of a smile and looked again at his clipboard. "Ma'am, I have orders to direct you to the base commander's office immediately upon your arrival."

"Very well," she said, and the sentry saluted again as the barrier rose and the Camry pulled through. He watched her car for a moment, then stepped back into the guardhouse and picked up the phone.

Half an hour later, the young sentry squinted at something out in the road in front of the guardhouse. He lifted a pair of binoculars for a closer look.

"Holy shit," he whispered, reaching for the phone again.

Every line was already lit.

Liz parked the Camry in a visitor's space in front of the base administration building, then grabbed the cat carrier from the front seat. On the way up the steps, she returned the salutes of two enlisted men exiting the building. Once inside, she immediately tucked her ball cap into a cargo pocket and headed up the main corridor, boots thumping the tile in a measured cadence, the pet carrier hanging in her left hand.

Down another corridor she stopped before a door with *James Whelan, Rear Admiral* stenciled in black letters on frosted glass. She smoothed her uniform blouse and went in. Beverly, the base commander's secretary, was at her desk in the outer office.

"Good morning, Liz," the woman said brightly. She was a few years younger than Liz, thicker and wearing a yellow dress, eyeglasses hung around her neck on a chain. "I see you brought a friend."

Liz set the pet carrier down on a chair. "I'm going to leave Blackbeard with Dottie Carr over at the Base Exchange to watch him while I'm out. Is it okay if I leave him with you while I talk to the skipper?" She jerked a thumb at the door to the inner office.

The secretary smiled. "He's no trouble at all," she said, coming around the desk and crouching in front of the pet carrier. "Are you, Blackbeard?"

The cat began to purr and rub his head against the grille. He knew Beverly.

"They're waiting for you," Beverly said, rising.

Liz frowned. "Who is *they*? It's not just Whelan?"

Beverly shook her head. "You didn't know there was a meeting?" She seemed flustered. "I just assumed . . ."

Liz gave her a smile. "Not to worry, Bev." She rapped hard on the door frame twice, then let herself in.

The office of Base Seattle's ranking officer was carpeted and done in rich, dark wood paneling and bookcases. The admiral's desk sat before blinds that were mostly closed and was flanked by the American flag on one side and the Coast Guard colors, known as the Service Mark, on the other. Photos, awards, and framed certificates covered the walls. A conference table lined with padded leather chairs dominated the room. Liz caught the scent of the admiral's aftershave at once. *Too much Old Spice.* His grandchildren insisted on giving it to him every Christmas, he had once told her.

The admiral rose from his desk as she entered. He was thickening around the middle, wearing a light blue tropical uniform shirt, the breast heavy with ribbons, and he smiled when he saw her, but Liz noticed at once that it was forced. Standing near the conference table, a stack of manila file folders on the polished surface before them, were a male Coast Guard officer and a thirty-something woman in a tailored gray business suit.

Liz came to attention. "Captain Elizabeth Kidd, reporting as ordered."

The admiral came from behind the desk and shook her hand. His grip and his eyes were warm, but he looked tired. "Good to see you, Liz." He put a hand on her shoulder and gently turned her to face the two others, who had stopped talking and now stared at her.

"This is Lieutenant Commander Chamberlain of Coast Guard Investigation Services," the admiral said, "and this is Special Agent Ramsey of the FBI's Seattle field office."

The visitors did not offer to shake hands.

Liz's radar was up, and the lines around her mouth deepened. The two investigators appeared to be waiting for Liz to ask, *What's this all about?* She hadn't risen to command by being predictable, and remained quiet.

"Let's take a seat." Admiral Whelan took the chair at the head of the table and gestured for Liz to sit beside him. The two investigators sat down across from her.

Whelan cleared his throat. "Liz, Lieutenant Commander Chamberlain and Agent Ramsey are here because of a situation involving Charlie. This is going to be difficult, but I trust in your professionalism and will expect your cooperation."

"Chick?" Liz said, looking at her superior officer. "What happened? Is he all right?"

Whelan nodded, and then the Coast Guard investigator started. "Captain Kidd . . ." He smiled and shook his head. "Captain, is it true you're a blood descendant of the famous pirate?"

Elizabeth knew this was simply the young man's attempt to break the ice and establish rapport. She had no shame about her ancestor, quite the opposite, actually, but it was the smirk she didn't care for. It put an edge on her voice. "You didn't really come here to discuss my lineage, did you, Mr. Chamberlain? Do you have some official business?"

The young man reddened.

Agent Ramsey took over, her voice clipped and businesslike. "Captain, I'm going to explain some details to you that might help move this conversation forward. At first, they will seem quite sensitive. The facts are not in dispute, however, and the case is bulletproof. We would not have come to you at this point were that not the case." She folded her hands on the table. "I'm going to be candid with you out of respect for your service to this country, and in the hope you will in turn provide full disclosure."

The FBI agent rested her hand on a file as she spoke, not opening it. She knew the case well. "Your brother, Senior Chief Charles Kidd, is the suspect in a joint FBI, DEA, and Coast Guard investigation involving drug trafficking and multiple homicides. His ship just arrived at the base, and he is being taken into custody as we speak."

Elizabeth stared at the female agent, stunned by the allegations and unable to speak. Admiral Whelan reached out and gripped her arm for reassurance.

"Our evidence," the agent continued, "establishes that on June twenty-seventh of this year, Mr. Kidd was involved in a narcotics transaction just off the Washington coast, using his own boat. He murdered three foreign nationals during that transaction. A fourth survived, a witness to the homicides. As it turns out, that man was a DEA informant."

Liz processed the words as the CGIS officer and her commander watched her. There was no notable change of expression on Liz's face, but inside was a storm of scattered thoughts and emotions. Chick, a murderer? Drug deals? Yes, he had his own boat, and when he wasn't at sea with the Coast Guard, he often went away for days at a time by himself to go fishing and camping. He had a temper, to which anyone who knew him could attest, and he wasn't the most polished person in the world. He'd barely hung on to his Chief's rate, drawing the occasional disciplinary action for conduct. There were other issues as well, troubles during his childhood, but these had never seemed to manifest as more serious issues in his adulthood. Not really. A murderer, though? Not a chance.

"Captain," the FBI agent said, "Senior Chief Kidd resides with you in your home in Rainier Valley." It was a statement, not a question.

Liz nodded. "He lives downstairs."

Now the agent did open her file, and read off the address. "We'll be executing a search warrant there this morning. For both residences."

Both residences, Liz thought. She pictured men in black tactical gear and others in Windbreakers with yellow FBI and DEA letters on the back, storming her home as if Osama bin Laden himself might be inside. It would be a circus, the media would show up, and Elizabeth Kidd's name—and profession—would be spoken on the air in the same sentences as *drug trafficking* and *murder*.

Oh, Chick, what have you done to me? Whether it was true or not, regardless of the fact that she had known nothing about it, Liz had no illusions about what this would mean for her career, her command. The look on both investigators' faces said they believed she was in this thing up to her eyes. And what if they found something in Chick's apartment? Upstairs or downstairs, it would remove any doubts about her complicity.

There was a long silence then, except for a ringing phone in the outer office.

"James," Liz said, turning to her commanding officer, "I can't believe this about Charlie, and *you* can't believe I had anything to do with murder, or *anything* illegal."

The admiral's eyes were guarded. "Elizabeth, I don't know what to believe."

Her heart broke as he said the words.

"The best thing for everyone is for you to cooperate and tell the truth," the admiral said.

The officer from Investigation Services slid a legal pad and pen toward her across the desk. "Ma'am, we'll require a detailed statement from you, to get your initial position on record."

Her initial position on record so they could pick it apart for comparison once the real questioning began. She wondered if she should ask for a lawyer. *Probably.* But then what could possibly make her look more guilty than asking for one and staying quiet?

The phone kept ringing outside, followed by a thump against the wall. No one seemed to notice. All eyes were on Liz.

The female agent pulled a phone from a jacket pocket, looking at a text. "The senior chief has been taken into custody without incident," she said without looking up. "They have him at the dock right now." Then she rose, already dialing and moving toward the office door. "Excuse me," she said, stepping out.

The secretary's phone was still ringing. *Answer the damn thing already, Beverly,* Liz thought. She looked at the pad and pen before her, at the impassive face of the Coast Guard investigator, then at her commander.

"Admiral, what is this going to mean for me?" She already knew the answer but needed to hear the man say it.

Whelan frowned. "Captain, you'll be beached and placed on administrative duty until this matter is resolved."

Liz's heart fell even further at the man's official tone. "My ship . . ."

"Your XO will take command for now." The admiral looked away.

Until you find a new captain to replace me permanently. Her Coast Guard career was finished. A loud bang from the secretary's office made Whelan look up in annoyance. "Mr. Chamberlain, go see what that's about."

"Aye-aye, sir." The investigator crossed the room and opened the door.

Special Agent Ramsey was waiting on the other side.

Her charcoal suit was darkened and wet, both hands were bloody, and her once-neat hair looked pulled and disheveled. Red smears covered her mouth and cheeks, and her head hung low and forward. The FBI agent's eyes were a milky yellow.

With a snarl, she caught the Coast Guard investigator by the shoulders and sank her teeth into his Adam's apple, ripping it out in a red spray. Chamberlain let out a gurgling cry and went down with the agent on top of him. The woman held the man's head in both hands as she tore back into his neck.

Liz bolted to her feet, knocking over her chair, but the admiral just sat there, hands splayed across the table's polished surface. His mouth was working, but no sound was coming out. In the distance, beyond the frosted-glass door that led from Beverly's office to the corridor, came a high-pitched screaming.

The admiral stood abruptly then, and Agent Ramsey's head snapped up at the sudden movement. She let out a low growl and bared her teeth, rising in a crouch over the dead Coast Guard investigator. Blood was soaking into the carpet around his body. The admiral seemed to be trying to anticipate which way the woman would go around the table, left or right, so he could move in the opposite direction and keep the barrier between them. By now, Elizabeth had backed into the room near her commander's desk, ripping aside the blinds to get at the catches that secured the tip-out windows.

The creature that had been Agent Ramsey didn't go left or right. Instead, she scrambled right up onto the conference table and scuttled forward on hands and knees, making a throaty, croaking sound. Admiral Whelan wasn't quick enough, and was standing there with his hands raised when the dead FBI agent lunged off the table and took the older man to the floor.

Still tugging on a window latch that would not give, Liz heard the attack behind her, heard James Whelan choking on his own blood. She turned to see Agent Ramsey straddling a man who had been not only her commanding officer, but her friend for more than a decade. Even as the woman savaged him, those dead, yellow eyes stared up and locked on the only remaining living thing in the room.

The creature—Liz could think of no other word for it—was between her and the door. She would never get by it. She also sensed that should she try to get out in the other direction, the thing would pull her down before she got halfway out the window. If she could open it at all.

Liz clenched her teeth. It was time to take the battle to the enemy.

On the wall among the admiral's many commendations and framed certificates was a chrome-plated anchor about the size of a hammer, affixed to a polished walnut plaque. Liz snatched it off the wall and put all her lean muscle into prying the object off the wood. It came away with a ripping sound, just as Agent Ramsey scrambled to her feet and attacked.

Liz had no thoughts of how what she was seeing could even be possible; she only saw a combat problem that needed resolution, something that required the cool precision that had put her in command of the USCG's finest boat, and she moved on instinct.

In the span of a second she judged the distance and swung, the chrome anchor heavy in her hand, arcing overhead in a flash. One bladed end hit the woman's head right at the crown and sank up to the anchor's central shaft with a crunch of bone and a burst of red. The thing that had been Ramsey shuddered and dropped immediately to the carpeted floor, Liz ripping the hammer-sized anchor free as the woman fell.

She looked down at James Whelan and saw that he was beyond help, just as another croak came from across the room. It sounded almost as if there were a question mark at the end of the sound. Lieutenant Commander Chamberlain was sitting up, legs stretched out before him, his uniform soaked red. He was facing away from her and croaked again, turning his head right and left.

Back from the dead? This went beyond bio attacks and into the realm of horror movies. Without hesitation, Liz strode to the sitting officer and buried the anchor in the top of his head. He sagged and was still, and as Liz wrenched her weapon free, she realized she had found the enemy's vulnerability. She would be sure to exploit it.

Special Agent Ramsey was carrying a nine-millimeter Sig Sauer in a hip holster under her jacket, with two full magazines in leather pouches beside it. Liz took it all, shoving the spare mags in her pants pocket.

A moan came from the outer office, followed by a metallic rattle and the terrified hissing and screeching of a cat. Liz ran out to see Beverly, her yellow dress torn and bloody, down on all fours shaking the pet carrier and trying to pry open the grilled door.

"Leave him alone!" Liz snarled, pressing Agent Ramsey's Sig against the back of Beverly's head and blowing brains and skull fragments across the office wall. She picked up the carrier, holding it so Blackbeard could see her face. "Mommy's here, handsome."

Blackbeard made an unhappy wail but pressed his head against the grille. She gave him a scratch.

"Time to go," she whispered.

A groan came from behind her, and as she spun she saw James Whelan standing, his throat torn out, his face and uniform red. The man's once-warm, brown eyes were glazed and malignant, and he reached for her.

Liz put a bullet between his eyes.

Then she cracked open the outer door, checked the hallway, and ran. The blood-sprayed cat carrier was in one hand, the Sig in the other, and the chrome anchor was tucked into her back waistband. Screaming echoed in the hallways, and thrashing shapes could be glimpsed beyond open office doors, but her only objective was the building's front doors and the parking lot beyond. As she burst into the morning sunlight, a single word repeated silently in her head.

Charlie.

TWO

Elizabeth Kidd's gray Camry raced through the streets of Base Seattle, hitting speed bumps too fast and jarring both woman and cat. Blackbeard's carrier sat on the passenger seat again, this time sharing it with a bloody chrome anchor that was staining the upholstery. Liz wanted to turn on the news, gather information, but she would soon be at her destination and needed her full attention on the road.

A Humvee with a flashing light bar on its roof blasted across an intersection ahead of her, quickly disappearing up a street to her left, its siren rebounding off warehouses. As she passed another admin building on her right, she saw a pair of bloody guardsmen lurching across a lawn toward the entrance, while in a second-floor window above them a woman in civilian clothes leaned out, screaming for help. The beat of helicopter rotors came from somewhere above, and the base siren was going off.

Liz had to slam on the brakes as a civilian worker in gray coveralls, hair matted to his head by blood, staggered into the road in front of the Camry. The man slapped wet, red palms onto the hood and glared at her through the windshield. Then he began pawing his

way up the side of the car toward the driver's door. Liz didn't wait
for him. She accelerated and left the thing behind.

A turn took her between a large machine shop and a yard of
storage containers, and she swerved to avoid two men in camouflage running with rifles. At the next intersection she hauled the
Camry right, then tensed and cried out as the front bumper smacked
into a woman crouching on all fours in the road. The impact sent
the woman's body into a chain-link fence, limp as a rag doll, and the
Camry bounced over the shape she had been feeding on with a sickening crunch.

There were masts ahead, black antennae and radar panels rising
behind the roofline of a building. The docks were close, and she
gunned the engine.

As the Camry burst from between two buildings and raced onto
an open expanse of concrete, Liz saw a pillar of smoke rising over
the base to her right, followed by the sight of an orange flash screaming low over the rooftops, a Coast Guard Dolphin helicopter. Ahead,
Joshua James stood tied to the docks, several figures running on
deck. Berthed just beyond it was another cutter, older and much
smaller than her own, the *Klondike*.

Charlie's ship.

Midway between the vessels, parked on the concrete that led to the
dock, another Humvee sat with its light bar flashing on the roof. The
Coast Guard emblem was on the driver's door, and at the back, black
lettering read *PORT SECURITY* and *K9*. A pair of uniformed bodies
were facedown on the pavement near the hood, and two others, men in
green camouflage wearing pistol belts, were hammering at the Humvee's side windows, leaving bloody smears.

Liz drove right at the Humvee and slid to a stop only yards away.
The two law enforcement guardsmen turned at the sound of screeching tires and limped toward the new arrival as Liz jumped out with
the FBI agent's handgun. Liz could see at once that their faces were
slack and dead, horrific wounds visible through torn uniforms.

"Charlie, get your head down!" she yelled toward the Humvee, then opened fire. The Sig barked five times before both creatures went down with shots to the head, one stray bullet sparking off the Hummer's front rim, another punching a hole in the driver's door. Liz ran to the vehicle and jerked open the rear door. "Chick?"

Charlie Kidd, wearing his blue uniform without the ball cap, slumped in the backseat with his hands cuffed behind his back. "Jesus, Sis, you trying to kill me? Get these damn things off."

"Shut up and get out," Liz said, unclipping keys from one of the men she had just dropped, opening Chick's handcuffs as he slid out. An enraged German shepherd barked incessantly in the back of the Hummer.

"What the fuck is going on?" Chick demanded, rubbing his wrists and looking at the dead men on the ground. "Those guys got jumped by two of their own, went down firing, then a couple minutes later were back up and trying to get at me. What the hell?"

Liz didn't answer. She was looking at what could only be described as a brawl on the gangplank of *Klondike*, half a dozen coasties fighting each other hand-to-hand. Other men and women in bloody uniforms were staggering away from the older cutter and making their way toward *Joshua James*. Off to the right, a dozen more figures were shuffling across the pavement, heading toward the dock.

"Gather weapons," she told Charlie, staring at the approaching dead, simultaneously repulsed and yet curious at their broken, relentless gait. They were people—monsters—some kind of abomination that fed on the living. It wasn't possible, but here it was all around her.

Charlie Kidd, eight years his sister's junior, began relieving his former captors of their weapons belts. He was not a tall man, but he compensated with a broad chest, a thick neck, and powerful forearms a strangler would envy. Chick's face was broad like the rest of him, his nose crooked from a tavern fight that had once cost him a stripe. He retrieved an M16 rifle from the front of the Hummer, along with a bandolier of magazines.

Liz was at her Camry, grabbing Blackbeard's carrier, shoving the bloody chrome anchor into her sea bag, and then throwing the duffel's strap across her chest. Behind her, the cries and barking of the German shepherd wouldn't stop.

"Let that dog out," she shouted to her brother.

"Fuck that, it was there when they busted me." He belted on one of the pistols, a Sig Sauer forty-caliber with a twelve-round magazine, the standard sidearm of the Coast Guard and a weapon with which he was more than proficient. "He'd go right for my balls."

"Asshole," Liz muttered, slamming the Camry's door and hustling across the pavement. "Move it, Chief!"

Charlie gripped the rifle and hurried after her.

An electrician's van was parked on the dock near the gangplank to *Joshua James*, a civilian in his forties standing nearby, looking confused and trying to use his cell phone. On the deck at the top of the gangplank, a pair of Coast Guardsmen stood gripping the rail, watching their captain run toward the ship, followed by a man she had just set free by shooting two other men.

Liz knew the electrician, one of the civilian contractors working to move her ship closer to commissioning. "Mr. Leary," she said as she passed him, "get aboard, if you please."

When the man didn't move, Chick yelled, "Assholes and elbows, mister!"

The electrician jumped, then hurried up the gangplank behind the captain, the senior chief following. On deck, the two enlisted men snapped off salutes, eyes wide. Liz handed the cat carrier and her sea bag to one of them. "Take these to my quarters." To the other she said, "Is the XO aboard?"

"No, ma'am. Ensign Liggett is the watch officer."

Liz looked down at the concrete expanse beyond the dock, where trucks would line up to move equipment and supplies aboard the cutter before sailing. There were no trucks, only a Humvee ringed with fallen bodies, and beyond, figures shifting toward them with that sickening, lifeless gait.

To her brother she said, "Raise the gangplank and prepare to cast off."

Charlie Kidd grinned. "Aye-aye, Sis, and thanks—"

Elizabeth was on him in an instant, grabbing his shirt in both hands and hauling him in nose to nose. "Do not *think*," she said tightly, "that being related gets you a break. You sank my life and my career. Now you will snap to, or I'll put you back on the beach personally." She gave him a shake, her voice low and coming through clenched teeth. "Do you read me, *Chief*?"

He nodded. "Yes, ma'am."

She shoved him away from her. "Prepare to get under way." Then she ran across the deck and disappeared through a hatch. At the gangplank, Charlie Kidd stared after her for a moment, then looked at the young seaman standing nearby.

"You heard the captain, deck ape! Raise the gangplank. Unless you want them aboard." He waved at the slumping figures closing on *Joshua James*.

The seaman leaped to his task as Charlie Kidd went in search of crewmen to untie the ship from Base Seattle's dock.

Liz quickly went up a steel ladderway, through a floor hatch, and onto the bridge of her cutter. The only person in here was a twenty-year-old, two-stripe seaman. He stiffened immediately, startled at her appearance.

"Captain on the bridge!" he shouted to no one.

Liz slammed a fist on a large red button, setting off the ship's general quarters alarm. She picked up a microphone handset, stretching out the cord as she went to the port windows. Down on the dock, dozens of figures in Coast Guard uniforms had nearly reached the ship's hull where it pressed against the wharf. Out beyond, an orange helicopter hovered slowly over the base, stirring the smoke of a burning building. Liz's eyes were drawn to the flashing lights of a fire truck, its crew turning a high-pressure hose not on the flames, but on a mass of people stumbling out through the building's front door. The people were smoking, and a few had hair that was on fire.

She keyed the mic. "This is the captain speaking. All stations, make ready to get under way. Ensign Liggett, report to the bridge."

Out on the forward deck, she saw her brother and two other seamen hurrying along the port side, casting off the heavy ropes that tethered *Joshua James* to the dock. Looking left, she saw with satisfaction that the gangplank had been raised and secured.

The dead reached them at last, pushing themselves against the white hull and hammering at it with their fists.

A vibration in the deck plates traveled up through her boots as the twin 7,400-kilowatt diesel engines fired and began warming up. Two young men ran up the ladderway and onto the bridge, a helmsman and a quartermaster second class who went immediately to the navigation gear.

"Mr. Waite," Liz said to the QM2, "let me know as soon as we're under power."

The quartermaster acknowledged, ordered the helmsman to stand by, and then called the engine room for information. Liz removed her cap from its cargo pocket and pulled it squarely onto her head, the bill low and at the perfect regulation distance above the bridge of her nose.

A woman of twenty-two entered the bridge next. Amy Liggett was fair and smooth-skinned, her dark hair pulled into a tight bun under her blue ball cap, her uniform stiff and new. *Joshua James* was her first assignment after graduating with honors from the Coast Guard Academy in New London, Connecticut. She had a bachelor's degree in engineering, a commission as a Coast Guard ensign, and next to zero operational experience.

"Captain," she said, moving to her commanding officer.

"Who and how many aboard?" Liz asked.

The young officer flipped to a page on her clipboard. "Twenty-two, ma'am. Third shift. Plus yourself and two others." Amy had already heard about the shooting on the dock, and about the man her captain had freed from Coast Guard custody.

Third shift, Liz thought. *The smallest, and for the most part, most inexperienced crew.* Not too much happened in port overnight, so the bare minimum of personnel was scheduled. It would include six civilian contractors, four engine room personnel, three watch standers for the bridge, and a scattering of others, mostly technical ratings. Less than a quarter of the cutter's full crew of ninety-nine enlisted and fourteen officers.

"Any other officers?" Liz asked without much hope. The third shift schedule called for only one—an officer had to be aboard at all times—and the overnight duty, at least in port, went to the most junior.

"Yes, ma'am," Liggett said, making Liz turn. "Lieutenant Commander Coseboom slept aboard last night."

The captain nodded. Boomer was having marital troubles, a small blessing for *Joshua James.* "Is the master chief aboard?" Again, hopeful.

"Negative."

"Who is senior enlisted man?"

The young woman hesitated, seemed unsure of how to answer at first, then looked at her sheet. "Chief Newman."

Newman, Liz thought. *Maritime enforcement specialist and a boarding team officer. Solid. But Charlie still outranks him. Damn.*

"Captain," said the quartermaster, "all crew are at battle stations. Engine room reports we are at full power and ready to get under way."

"Very well, Mr. Waite. Stand us off from the pier. I'll conn us out."

Base Seattle's main pier held only two cutters at the moment, *Klondike* and *Joshua James*, along with a cluster of much smaller patrol boats. The cutter was nose-in and would have to back down the man-made channel, past *Klondike* and out into the Duwamish Waterway before it could turn and put its bow toward Puget Sound. The quartermaster gave commands to both the engine room and the helmsman, and the big ship eased away from the pier. As it moved off, corpses that had been hammering against its hull toppled into the water.

"Mr. Coseboom to the bridge," Liz said into the microphone. Boomer was an experienced officer, and she would need him, especially since there was barely enough crew to get under way. She stepped to the communication gear and switched on the Guard channel, a restricted, military-only radio frequency. Rapid chatter poured from the bridge speakers at once.

"Miss Liggett," she said to the young woman waiting beside her, "I want a report on the following: fuel status, fresh water levels, name and specialty of every civilian on board, magazine levels and weapon systems readiness, a full inventory of light arms and galley stores."

The younger woman scribbled furiously on her clipboard, her hand shaking. "I . . . I think . . ."

Liz took her by the shoulder, and in a low voice said, "Steady, Amy. A lot of that information will be in your watch orders." She tapped the clipboard. "I already know that most of those things will be either low or nonexistent, but we need an accurate accounting."

"Yes, ma'am." Her voice was quavering, and she fought to control it.

Liz softened her voice even further, so that no one else on the bridge would hear her. "Maintain your bearing. Be a role model for the crew. They're going to be scared and confused, and they need to see calm, confident officers. You know my expectations."

The younger woman took a deep breath and nodded, and Liz gave her shoulder a reassuring squeeze before sending her off. *Joshua James* had moved slowly into the center of the channel, and Liz gave the command to reverse at four knots. A new vibration in the deck signaled the change, and the cutter began to back up, slowly coming alongside *Klondike* on the port side, still tied to its berth. Liz returned to the bridge windows to inspect the other ship.

The dead were swarming across the cutter's decks, hunting the living.

Liz keyed the microphone. "This is the captain. Stand by to commence rescue operations."

THREE

One of two Short Range Prosecutors—SRPs—aboard *Joshua James* launched at speed from the stern ramp of the cutter, its water jets throwing up a fan of spray. Seven meters long, the rigid, inflatable boat hooked around the vessel and blasted back up the channel toward *Klondike*, LCDR Coseboom at the helm with three other men aboard. In the bow, a Coast Guardsman crouched with the M16 Charlie Kidd had taken from the port security Hummer.

There were people in the water ahead and more leaping from *Klondike*'s deck or simply toppling over the rails with reaching arms. The men in the SRP saw a female petty officer try to scramble over the railing, only to be pulled back by dead shipmates before she could make the leap to the water.

Boomer slowed as he neared the other cutter, taking a moment to think. Some of the figures were swimming away from the ship; others were struggling to stay afloat, splashing and waving their arms. A few sank almost immediately, not even attempting or unable to swim. These had ashy faces and snapping teeth.

"Be careful what you pull out of the water," he said to the two men standing at the SRP's edge. "Only the living, understand?" He was a little surprised at himself, at how easily he had accepted that the dead were rising. But that brought on thoughts about his wife in their little apartment, and the stupid argument that had caused him to storm out and spend the night on *Joshua James*. He should have been with her.

The young crewmen aboard weren't so accepting, their faces revealing their overall shock, but they nodded at the order. Boomer angled the SRP to bring them closer to the swimmers, careful not to get too close to the cutter's hull. He didn't want one of those things dropping into his boat.

The guardsmen cast out their lines and started pulling survivors from the water.

Joshua James, still reversing at an agonizing four knots, had nearly reached the mouth of the channel, where it would back briefly into the Duwamish Waterway, then steam almost immediately into the sound. Elizabeth was impatient to engage forward propulsion, aching for open water where she would have some maneuvering options. This was like backing slowly down an alley, and she felt vulnerable. She used a pair of binoculars to watch the rescue operation taking place off the bow. Boomer seemed to have it under control.

On the radio, the Guard channel was crowded with impossible horrors and unthinkable events, monotone voices mixing with panicked cries for help and even screaming. Mass riots were tearing Seattle apart, the police were being overwhelmed, and civilian casualties were staggering. Chaos, confusion, and miscommunication reigned, but the commonly repeated fact was that people were returning from the dead and killing the living.

Sea-Tac airport had been closed to nonmilitary traffic, and any airborne civilian flights were being diverted. National Guard units were being mobilized to defend hospitals. Fires were erupting throughout the city and suburbs, and the population was being ordered to evacuate, though to where was unclear. North of her position, the naval base in Everett, where *Nimitz* berthed when it was home, was locked down and reporting attacks by ground forces.

What ground forces? Liz wondered.

A lone destroyer had managed to sortie from Everett an hour earlier and was now cruising just offshore of the city, raking the waterfront with its five-inch gun in an attempt to "suppress aggressors."

Liz stared at the radio. *The Navy is shelling Seattle.* She shook her head.

An order came down from National Command Authority. It was transmitted in the clear, but it had a genuine authenticity code, as Liz confirmed with a plastic snap-card from a small safe below the communication gear. NCA announced that the United States had been placed under martial law and all military units were to consider their country under attack by foreign aggressors. Biohazard protocols were to be observed, though *Joshua James* was currently unequipped for such measures, and every unit was to prepare for strike operations. *Joshua James* had just become a ship at war.

Liz switched over to the Coast Guard channel, bringing up the microphone. Before she could speak, the airwave buzzed with an official-sounding voice.

"*Joshua James*, this is Base Seattle Command. Acknowledge."

"This is USCGC seven-five-four," Liz said, "Captain Elizabeth Kidd, commanding."

"*Joshua James*, you are ordered to return to port immediately."

Liz made a face. "Base Seattle, our pier has been overrun, and we are engaged in rescue operations for *Klondike*. I am preparing to maneuver my ship." There were going to be a lot of civilians in need of help, she thought. Why would Command order her back during a crisis?

The voice came again. "Negative, seven-five-four. Return to port immediately."

The bridge crew looked at their commanding officer, then at each other. Out the thick front windows, Liz saw LCDR Coseboom's small craft racing back toward *Joshua James*. She couldn't see any more figures in the water near *Klondike*. There was plenty of movement on the decks of the smaller ship and the docks beyond, however, staggering figures, none of them living. Did Command think she was going to return her ship to *that*? She had a responsibility to her crew.

"I cannot comply with that order, Seattle Command," she said, shocked to hear herself utter words she had never before even considered. But then nothing like this had ever happened in her nearly three-decade-long career. "We are at wartime conditions, and I will preserve this ship." The voice on the radio began to repeat its demand, but Liz snapped over to the Guard channel again, cutting it off.

The close, heavy thump of rotors approached above the ship, making the deck thrum. A black helicopter dropped into view twenty-five yards off the cutter's bow, its cockpit level with the bridge windows. A yellow star and the letters *DEA* were stenciled on the fuselage, and a man in body armor holding a sniper rifle could be seen at an open side door, clipped into a harness.

A loudspeaker mounted to the helicopter's belly blared over the chop of rotors. "This is DEA flight zero-three. *Joshua James*, heave to and prepare to be boarded."

Ensign Amy Liggett hurried down a passageway, clipboard in hand. Earlier, nearing the end of her overnight watch, she thought she'd been tired. No longer. Adrenaline and the sudden appearance of her commanding officer had erased all traces of sleepiness, but those weren't the only reasons.

The crew was using the word *zombie*. People were attacking and *eating* one another, and the crew was looking to her for answers she didn't have.

Having the captain aboard made things better. The woman was a career veteran who knew her business, and she was gifted with a cool decisiveness Amy could only envy. But then, what of the captain? Crew members had told her they'd seen port security take a man off *Klondike* in handcuffs and put him in the back of a Humvee, someone a petty officer said he recognized as the captain's brother. Then the captain had shown up, shot down two guardsmen, and brought the man aboard. Now he was loose on the ship and barking orders.

It couldn't be true, could it? Just scuttlebutt, people misunderstanding things amid the chaos. And what was really happening? Zombies? Please! Her little brother back in Virginia was a zombie freak, devouring anything that had to do with the walking dead: books, movies, and video games. It was kid stuff, fun, yes, but not real.

Now they were at battle stations, leaving Base Seattle with less than a quarter-strength crew. They were unprepared for a cruise of any length in a ship not yet commissioned. They were just now transitioning from builder's trials to acceptance trials, and the cutter hadn't yet received its Coast Guard markings. Many of the ship's systems either hadn't been fully tested or weren't working at all. Actual readiness was many months away.

Amid all the questions and unknowns, there was only one certainty, and that was her fear. Amy had never been so scared in her life.

"Steady," she chastised herself. An officer had to be locked down and in control, even when all she wanted to do was cry. "There'll be none of that," she growled at the empty corridor, turning a corner toward the armory.

The door was open.

She slowed, suddenly wary, and looked inside. The lights were on, illuminating a room that was, as it should have been, mostly empty. To the right stood vacant rifle racks, where the M4s, M14s, and shotguns would be, once they were delivered. Beneath these were numerous empty slots for handguns, the forty-caliber Sigs. Regulations at this point of the trial process authorized only three: one each for the captain, XO, and chief of the boat. There they were, snug in their slots. Spaces for rifle and pistol ammunition were all but empty, again as they should be.

She looked around. The M240 medium machine guns weren't due to arrive until just before commissioning, and ammo for the ship's heavier weapons—what was aboard, anyway—would be secured in the magazine one deck below. Four rail-mounted fifty-caliber heavy machine guns had arrived ahead of schedule, along with their crates of belted ammo, and stood against the far bulkhead.

Why didn't things look right? She started counting. *One . . . two . . . three . . .*

"Uh-oh," she whispered.

Liz moved to the front of the bridge, holding the radio handset and still on the Guard channel. "DEA flight zero-three, this is *Joshua James*. That is a negative, do not attempt to board. We are on a war footing per National Command Authority, and we *will* enter Puget Sound."

The response from the loudspeaker came as if those aboard the helicopter weren't monitoring the military traffic channel. "Coast Guard Cutter, heave to at once." The sniper in the helicopter's door raised his rifle and sighted on the bridge. "Captain Elizabeth Kidd," the speaker boomed, "you have unlawfully seized a vessel of the United States and are harboring a federal fugitive. Surrender your vessel immediately."

Liz gripped the handset so tightly she thought the plastic might crack. "Flight zero-three, do you even *know* what's happening at Seattle Base?" *It was insane. Everything was coming apart, they were in the middle of a national security crisis, and the DEA was worried about Charlie and Elizabeth Kidd?* "Flight zero-three, we are—"

The sniper fired, the bullet sparking off the steel just above the bridge windows with a loud ping. Liz and the crewmen ducked.

"This is your last warning," the loudspeaker blared. "Stop your vessel now."

"Cease fire!" Liz shouted into the mic. "Do not—"

The chopper banked left and roared over the ship toward its stern, flying over Coseboom's SRP as the officer prepared to come around to the cutter's boat ramp for recovery. The DEA bird hung in the air, then pivoted to face the ship's stern, and then four men in black with assault rifles rappelled from its doors, two on each side. All four descended an even twenty-five feet on their lines and hung there in the air.

On the water, Boomer completed his turn around a ship that was backing toward him. He couldn't think about helicopters now, or about what the loudspeaker had said about his captain, though all other eyes on the small boat were looking up. He had to concentrate on lining his boat up with the narrow, alleylike gap that was the cutter's boat ramp.

Above, the DEA helicopter moved forward, the four men beneath it swinging backward as a group. Seconds later the chopper flared and hovered, a maneuver that now swung the four men forward and low over the flat, eight-by-fifty-foot flight deck, where they would unclip and drop onto the vessel.

Liz dropped the mic and headed for the ladderway on the run. "Mr. Waite has the conn," she yelled as she disappeared down the metal stairs, leaving command of a vessel nearly as big as a Navy frigate to a midlevel enlisted man. Her boots pounded the steel decking as she ran aft down the passageway. The DEA would board

at the flight deck, she knew. Liz had worked enough joint operations
with them to know their tactics.

She had to get there before they boarded, had to reason with
them when they arrived, before any of her people could be hurt.
Two-thirds of the way along the passage, Amy Liggett charged up a
ladderway to the left and started running behind her captain.

A moment later they both heard the thunder of a heavy machine
gun.

At a range of one hundred feet, a storm of fifty-caliber bullets
shredded the helicopter's cockpit, both pilots and the sniper in
back. More bullets raked across the fuselage, rotor blades, and engine
cowling. The weapon, designed to go up against armored vehicles,
knocked the thin-skinned aircraft out of the sky. It crashed into the
channel and went down fast. As it fell, the four men still attached to
it by rappelling lines were snapped away, their bodies slamming
hard against rails and steel protrusions before being dragged beneath
the surface by their tethers.

Still reversing, *Joshua James* crept past the point where the helicopter had gone under, the surface boiling with bubbles and oil.
LCDR Coseboom's SRP roared up the boat ramp a moment later,
and the officer and his small crew immediately began helping the
handful of *Klondike* survivors up onto the deck.

Elizabeth Kidd and Amy Liggett burst through a hatch and onto
the aft deck that sat atop the ship's twin helicopter hangars, overlooking the flight deck and boat ramp below. Directly ahead of
them, Senior Chief Charlie Kidd stood behind an M2 heavy machine
gun set in a pintle mount, the deck around him littered with fifty-
caliber shell casings. Liz slowed as she reached him, her face revealing her horror.

"You *did* do it," she whispered. She didn't mean the helicopter.

Chick turned to his sister, giving her a salute and a lazy smile. "Captain, boarders have been repelled."

Liz glared at him, then looked over the side to where pieces of honeycomb rotor blades and other debris were floating to the surface amid a spreading oil slick. "Secure that weapon," she hissed.

On the lower deck, Lieutenant Commander Coseboom, half carrying a *Klondike* survivor, was calling for a medic. "See to that," Liz said, directing the order at the young ensign beside her, but still staring at a point in the water where seven men had just lost their lives.

The bridge was quiet when she returned, QM2 Waite calmly giving orders to the helmsman as *Joshua James* finished backing into the Duwamish Waterway, preparing to engage forward propulsion. The enlisted man glanced at his commanding officer, who was standing off to the side, hands on her hips and looking up at the bulkhead above the bridge's front windows. Despite her presence on the bridge, his command of the conn had not yet been relieved, so he ordered a course that would take them northwest into Puget Sound, calling for seven knots.

Liz stared at the bold, black letters stenciled above the windows, stark against the white bulkhead. *Honor. Respect. Devotion to Duty.* The Coast Guard's core values. Then she looked out the starboard side, thinking about what she had seen and done in Admiral Whelan's office, about the DEA helicopter and its loudspeaker, and once again seeing her brother leaning on a smoking machine gun.

Her entire adult life had been dedicated to her country, her crew, and saving lives. Now, in the course of a morning, Captain Elizabeth Kidd had broken out a federal prisoner, fired upon and killed agents of a sovereign nation, and unlawfully seized an American military vessel: all acts of aggression against her own country.

The word for that was *traitor.*

"Mr. Waite, advance to flank speed and keep us clear of that destroyer to the north," she ordered. As she looked out at the gray surface beyond the bow of her cutter, she thought about how quickly things and people could change, and wondered at what new changes lay ahead.

FOUR

January 12—San Francisco Bay

Father Xavier Church worked the heavy bag, slowly circling on the balls of his feet, throwing punches in combinations. He had already skipped rope until sweat plastered his shirt to his broad back, and twenty minutes on the speed bag had the muscles in his arms and shoulders burning. Soon he would begin running laps around *Nimitz's* flight deck.

He worked the bag harder than usual, fists slamming into the leather and dense padding with thumps that could be heard all the way across the gym. He was worried, and feared for the friends who had lifted off from the flight deck in Vladimir's Black Hawk only yesterday: Angie, Skye, and Carney. He prayed for their safe return from Chico, prayed they would find Angie's family safe and whole. Yet he couldn't help but think that their chances would have been better had he gone with them.

In his middle forties, Xavier's dark brown face was a graphic example of man's capacity for violence. A scar split his visage down the center, from hairline to chin, and a trio of pale claw marks gouged one cheek. Behind the damage were dark eyes that were both watchful and weary with responsibility. Taking *Nimitz* from the dead had come at a substantial cost; friends had been lost and children orphaned. Xavier felt the absence of every life.

His fists hammered the bag, and he blinked away sweat as he struck, still dancing in a circle. He threw a powerful combination to the center and then a roundhouse high on the bag, hits that would have put a heavyweight on the canvas. Xavier winced as the grenade fragment deep in his thigh twitched, but he gritted his teeth and worked through the pain. Doc had managed to remove all of the other pieces of metal, and now only the one remained, too deep to reach without risking nerve and tissue damage. She hoped movement and time would work the piece closer to the surface, where she could get at it with a simple incision. Doc said it would be a painful process, and she had been right.

A balanced diet from the aircraft carrier's galley, combined with an exhausting and disciplined workout regimen, had returned the priest to fighting shape, hardening the wide V-shape of his boxer's physique. He still limped after exercising, or if he overdid the walking when he was out with the hunting parties, searching out the dead in the carrier's miles of passageways, but it couldn't be helped. There was always so much to do, and Xavier wouldn't allow himself to be slowed down.

He gave the bag a final, powerful hit, then crossed the mat to where a towel was draped over the back of a chair. A pump shotgun leaned there as well. Xavier mopped his head and face, then hung the towel around his neck. He was tightening his shoelaces when a man walked into the gym.

Calvin was older than Xavier by about ten years, but now he looked senior by at least twenty. A gray ponytail hung down his back, and he was dressed in jeans and boots. A sleeveless leather vest revealed lean, muscled arms. The man had ten days of gray stubble on his drawn face, and the lines at the corners of his eyes, put there by sun and laughter, had deepened from grief. He looked pale, and his eyes no longer gleamed with mirth. Calvin carried an assault rifle, a big knife, and a woman's wedding ring hung from a thong around his neck.

"Sorry to interrupt, Father," he said.

Xavier finished tying his shoes and stood. It had been only two days since he last saw Calvin, but he was nonetheless startled by the man's appearance. He looked washed out. "Are you feeling well, Cal? Getting enough sleep?"

The man shrugged but didn't reply. He tapped a legal pad he was holding. "I wanted to give you some updates. I can come back if you're busy."

Xavier frowned. Even the man's voice was diminished, no longer booming and gregarious, and he now spoke only of business, never about his family. Xavier would see him moving quietly through compartments and passageways, usually alone and rarely speaking, tending to the needs of those on board; ensuring they were fed, properly quartered, had enough clothing, and were staying healthy. The only thing he seemed to speak about with any passion these days was his constant reminder to remain watchful and stay out of the unsecured areas of the ship.

He'd lost his wife and brother within hours of one another, followed by more than half the members of his traveling hippie family during the taking of *Nimitz*. Like Xavier, he bore the weight of that, but in his case, it had devoured him. *Ghost* was the word that came to Xavier's mind when he saw his friend. Pale, silent, lacking any spark of life.

"Grab a seat," Xavier said, indicating the chair.

Calvin didn't take it. "I won't be long." He looked at his pad. "Yesterday's hunt bagged four drifters down in engineering. No casualties. Chief Liebs thinks they're coming in from the bow."

Xavier's frown deepened. It was something he and the chief had discussed at length, both of them frustrated by the lack of a solution. The aircraft carrier's forward decks remained a nest of zombies, mostly in the lower areas. The survivors had tried to contain them, but *Nimitz* was a rabbit warren of passageways, ducts, and connecting compartments, and somehow the dead were slipping into the rest of the ship. Not in great numbers, he conceded, but even one of them in a supposedly secure area could be disastrous. The only way they would ever be safe was by hunting down every last walking corpse, and that was a task not without peril, especially in the bow.

"The doc reported a slip on a ladderway that caused a twisted ankle, and one bump on the head that needed stitches."

"Knee knocker?" the priest asked. Calvin nodded. Knee knockers were the oval-shaped openings for hatches in corridors and compartments, designed to strengthen the ship's overall structure. The lower portion rose six inches above the floor, while the arched top was lowered, requiring ducking. Passing through them at any speed required timing and kept Rosa in practice with her needle and thread. Both men had visited her for such injuries, angry at their own clumsiness.

"How is Maya?" Xavier asked, interested in her health, but more interested in getting Calvin to speak about his family.

"She says the pregnancy is normal and on schedule," the hippie leader replied, speaking as if Maya were a stranger and not his first-born.

Xavier tried again and smiled. "You're going to be a grandfather. How's it feel?"

Instead of answering, Calvin began a terse, bullet-point report on food supplies, fresh water levels, the status of repairs for various ship's systems, an overview of training as everyone learned new skills, and the usual *no results* in regard to their attempts to reach the outside world with the aircraft carrier's communication gear. He spoke of crop conditions. Last fall, Vladimir had set his Black Hawk down in the parking lot of a Berkeley garden center, and an army of hippies had raided the place for seeds, tools, fertilizer, and bags of potting soil. A small farm was created on the hangar deck, close to one of the aircraft elevators so it could get sunlight. The winter crop was surviving. Many on board were hoping they would find some goats or even a couple of cows out there, and sling them under the chopper for the ride home. Xavier grinned every time he pictured a dairy cow clopping through a space that had once held jet fighters.

Calvin wrapped up his report by stating there had been no excitement to speak of, just another couple of routine days for the survivors on *Nimitz*. It was just the way the priest liked it.

"Cal," Xavier said, his voice soft, "we can talk any time."

"I know."

"About anything. If you're feeling . . ."

The hippie raised a hand and gave his friend a gentle smile, but his eyes warned him off the topic. They had been here before.

The priest nodded. "You know where to find me."

Calvin left without another word, departing as silently as he had arrived.

Xavier's sneakers thumped on the rubberized coating of the flight deck as he ran, a Windbreaker zipped up to his neck with *U.S. Navy* across the back. It was California, but it was still January, and a chill wind was pushing in from the bay, giving him resistance as he ran. There were no aircraft up here, of course, nothing to interfere with his circuit of the deck's perimeter. He was alone, the only other person in sight a single lookout high on a superstructure catwalk, bundled against the wind.

Nimitz was facing east, nose-in toward western Oakland, and stuck fast to a silt bed in the shallows about a mile offshore. The aircraft carrier tilted slightly forward and to the left, the result of a damaged hull that had taken on water. It had been torn by rocks and bridge supports as the great ship cruised unguided through the waters of the bay in the opening days of the plague, and many of the lower, forward compartments were flooded. The tilt was enough to notice when walking or standing, but not uncomfortably so. After what they had gone through in order to make this a sanctuary, complaining about *anything* seemed obscene.

His heart rate and body temperature climbed as he hit his stride, running down the port side of the ship, toward the stern. Behind and across from him, the superstructure rose at the edge of the flight deck like an eight-story building, bristling with antennae, radar dishes, and air defense missile batteries. From here, the view north looked much as it always had, the flat expanse of the bay touched by wind and sunlight, darker smudges of land beyond, too far off to reveal any detail. Bridges still crossed the water, and gulls still swept through the air.

As he approached the stern, however, the view changed, and left no question about what had become of their world.

The Bay Bridge still teemed with the dead, their slow-moving shapes continuing to empty out of San Francisco and into Oakland, even after all these months. Beyond stood the ruins, where clean glass towers had once risen over the hilly city, where streets once hummed with the vibrancy of life. It looked gray now, burned and crumbling, wind sweeping through shattered windows and blowing clouds of ash before it. A city of the dead.

The priest pounded across the stern and headed forward once more, up the starboard side. Another dead city lay ahead, closer than San Francisco, but no less ruined. Fires had done more damage here, spreading from the waterfront industrial areas and fuel tank farms, charring entire square miles of urban area. Oakland looked black, and the occasional gust of wind would kick up clouds of ash that drifted across the city like little coal-colored sandstorms.

Xavier knew the fires would have done little to impair the dead. They would still be shuffling the avenues, charred and blackened, endlessly searching for the living.

Alameda was closest in view, and the dead there could be seen with the naked eye, at least a hundred thousand of them packing the expanse of airfields at the old naval air station. The priest didn't know what had drawn them there, why they stayed and didn't just wander away, but there they remained. From a mile out, the abandoned airfield resembled an open-air concert for a major rock band, a sea of heads and shifting bodies.

Xavier had completed two full circuits of the four-and-a-half-acre flight deck when he heard the hydraulic whine of an aircraft elevator rising from the hangar deck. He looked over to see one of *Nimitz*'s Seahawk helicopters come into view from below, and as soon as the elevator stopped, a low, flat tow vehicle driven by a bearded man pulled it out onto the flight deck. A pair of figures, one a woman in blue coveralls with her dark hair whipping in the breeze, the other a man in a green flight suit, followed the aircraft off the elevator. Xavier threw them a wave and kept running.

As he passed the towering crane and the garage door that boasted the *World's Smallest Fire Truck*, he saw a figure step from the wide hatch at the base of the superstructure. The other man looked around, saw him, and waved him over.

Xavier slowed to a brisk walk, puffing and rolling his arms as he started his cooldown. Time to put his administrator's hat back on.

FIVE

Evan and Maya walked across the deck holding hands, following after the haze-gray helicopter marked with *NAVY* and the number *2* on the tail, to where it had been towed. Evan was of average build, and his once-collar-length black hair was now neatly trimmed in a military style. In his midtwenties, he wore a flight suit with the legs bloused into boots, a survival vest, and the Sig Sauer Calvin had given him snugged into a shoulder holster under his flight jacket. Maya, just twenty, wore blue coveralls that didn't do justice to her slim figure, though she swore she was developing a pot belly. Doc Escobedo assured her she was only now entering her second trimester and wouldn't be showing for a while. A small, .380 automatic handgun was tucked in a pocket of her coveralls.

The bearded hippie unhooked his little tow vehicle from the helicopter's nose, gave Evan a thumbs-up, and motored back to the elevator. Maya moved close to the aircraft in order to get out of the wind, pulling Evan's hand as she brushed blowing hair from her face.

"Two hours, right?" she signed. Maya had been deaf and mute since birth.

Evan made sure he was facing her so she could read his lips. His signing was improving every day under her tutelage, but he still made mistakes, and so he spoke whatever he signed. "Two hours, maybe less. Up around San Pablo Bay, then back down."

She nodded. "Where's Gourd?"

"He knows we're flying." Evan checked his watch. "He'll be here; you know Gourd." She smiled, and a look into her sapphire eyes made Evan's heart flip, as it always did. He placed his hands on her belly. "I love you."

She grabbed one of his hands and pulled it up to her breast. "And I *want* you. Being pregnant makes me horny."

Evan gasped in pretended shock. "What would Calvin think?"

"My dad knows how this baby got in here." She grinned and kissed him as Evan wrapped her up in his arms. When they parted she said, "You be careful."

He winked. "Always."

Another man in a flight suit trotted across the deck carrying a pack in one hand and an M4 rifle in the other. He was one of Calvin's hippies, also in his midtwenties, and had earned his nickname from the shape of his body while growing up. He was one of the survivors from the Alameda pier evacuation as well as the battle with the dead on *Nimitz*'s open-air fantail. Vladimir Yurish had identified the young man as a potential pilot candidate and begun his training. He was behind Evan in the process but learned fast. Since reaching *Nimitz*, he had shaved his beard, buzzed down to a crew cut, and hit the carrier's gym. He no longer looked like a gourd, but the nickname had stuck. Evan was happy about that, as no one seemed able to remember the man's actual name, and Evan was too embarrassed to ask.

"Take your time," Evan called. "Really, it's all about you."

"Wiseass," Gourd grumbled, giving Maya a peck on the cheek and putting his gear in the chopper. "You're starting to sound like the boss."

"Nyet!" Evan yelled, putting on the thick accent. "That is to compare Baryshnikov to MC Hammer!"

"Who?" said Gourd, climbing into the right seat of the cockpit. "Hey, are we going, or are you two gonna hug and kiss away all our flight time?"

"This aircraft," Evan said, still using the accent, "will depart when the pilot is ready, and not a moment sooner." He kissed Maya again, then crouched and kissed her belly through the coveralls. "See you soon, little one."

Maya walked to the superstructure, then stood and watched as the helicopter's turbines heated, the blades began to move, and then as the wheels finally left the deck. She stood there as it climbed and headed east, not going inside until it was out of sight.

*N*imitz, this is Navy zero-two," Evan said into the helmet mic. "We are airborne." He received an acknowledgment from the aircraft carrier as he rose toward the east.

The SH-60 Seahawk was essentially the Navy version of the Black Hawk. It carried some different equipment—a rescue winch, dipping sonar for sub hunting, and the capacity to carry torpedoes— but it was for all other purposes the same aircraft, a fact that made the process of training rookie pilots easier for Vladimir. The only real difference was that the Seahawk had a hinged tail for tight storage, a design with a mind toward a carrier's limited space.

Vladimir had checked Evan Tucker out for solo flight three weeks ago with the understanding that he had much to learn and would require a great deal of practice before he could call himself proficient. "The most important thing to remember," Vlad said, "is that when you crash due to stupidity, you do it in the water where you will harm no one else."

Evan had been going up once a day since his solo flight, mostly small trips, practicing his turns, hovering, climbing and descending, and of course, landing. Longer flights tested his navigation skills, like today. With only two helicopters flying, there was no worry of running out of the JP-5 aircraft fuel on which they ran. Millions of gallons remained in the carrier's fuel bunkers, and any leaks—piping compromised by gunfire—had been repaired by Chief Liebs and his handful of men wearing hazmat suits. That same crew had also safely disarmed the nuclear weapons Brother Peter had rigged for detonation. The televangelist, firmly in the grip of misguided religious zeal fueled by lunacy, had been intent on using the nukes to incinerate the ship and all aboard. Father Xavier arrived just in time, preventing their annihilation by killing the madman with his bare hands. Evan knew that brutal—though necessary—act still weighed heavily upon the priest.

"So where are we going, Gourd?" Evan knew, of course; he had been the one to create their flight plan and had the same plastic-coated map strapped to his thigh as his co-pilot. It was Gourd's job, however, to keep them on their planned flight corridor.

"Due east," the former hippie replied over the helmet intercom. "Cross Oakland Middle Harbor, locate the expressway, and come left zero-nine-zero. Then we follow Interstate 80 north." His voice was developing the same businesslike tone familiar to aviators all over the world.

"Roger that," Evan said, smiling. The clean-cut young man in the right seat had come a long way from the casual wayfarer he'd been. They both had. Evan went from a lone biker wandering the highways of America, trying to write a novel, to an accepted member and then leader of a traveling band of hippies riding out the apocalypse on the road. Along the way he had made and lost friends, had fallen in love, and was now soon to be a father.

The Seahawk climbed to five thousand feet as he leveled off, quickly crossing from water to land—*feet dry*—as it overflew industrial Oakland. A wide ribbon of elevated concrete was ahead, the multilane expressway packed with derelict vehicles. Evan began a slow left turn as he neared it, then lined up the nose of the helicopter with the metal graveyard below and flew north at an easy 140 miles per hour. Like the Black Hawk, the Navy bird could go much higher and much faster, but Evan was cautious. As the Russian frequently reminded him, he was an amateur, and dead pilots were of no use to anyone. Evan kept it simple, concentrating on his controls and cockpit readings, letting Gourd do the sightseeing.

There wasn't a lot of detail at this altitude, but it was clear to see that the world had died. The old world, anyway. Much of the urban sprawl of Oakland had been consumed and blackened by fire, and many of the motionless vehicles below were charred. Nothing moved. Nothing they could see from up here, anyway. But the dead were down there. Earlier, lower altitude flights revealed that the highways and streets were packed with what could only be estimated as millions of bodies, a slow-moving swarm of the undead. Vladimir setting down and waiting while the hippies scavenged for farming supplies was both a testament to the man's nerve and an affirmation of his insanity. *Not this kid,* Evan thought. He liked it fine way up here.

Evan made a correction to account for the twenty-knot crosswind coming off the bay, descended to three thousand feet, and kept the Seahawk moving north up the highway. They were flying over Richmond now, with Berkeley to the right. Starboard, he reminded himself. To port was the flat surface of the bay, sunlight burning through an overcast sky in places to touch the water with golden fingers.

Gourd was fiddling with some dials, grunting in frustration. "I still can't get the air radar to work in this damn thing."

"Are you afraid we're going to run into another aircraft? Evan asked, seeing endless, empty skies all around them. "I don't think that's likely."

"The boss expects me to know this by now," Gourd said.

Evan chuckled. "A few months ago you were wearing tie-dye, smoking weed in a van, and wishing your mother had named you *Moonbeam.*" He laughed at his own humor. "Give yourself a break."

"I would, but he won't."

Evan couldn't argue. Vlad was a stern teacher with high expectations. Personally, Evan liked the man's methods, sarcastic or not. He thought he learned faster as a result. "Look," he said, "if you're going to play with something, get the weather radar online. We're more likely to run into a storm than a plane."

"Roger." Gourd began playing with a new set of dials next to a scope, and Evan kept them pointed north.

Xavier followed Petty Officer Second Class Banks into the superstructure, then up the back-and-forth metal stairway that climbed through the center of the eight-story tower. Banks was an operations specialist, a carrier's jack-of-all-trades, one of the five Navy men the group had located and rescued during the assault on *Nimitz.* One of that five hadn't survived the dead.

"Pat was doing his daily sweep of frequencies," Banks said as they climbed. "He thinks he heard something." Patrick Katcher, also known as PK, was a Navy electronics technician who, like everyone else, performed many different jobs aboard ship. One of them was learning the carrier's complex communication equipment in the hopes of making contact with other survivors.

"What was it?" Xavier rubbed his thigh. The jump rope, boxing and running, and now this climb had caused the grenade fragment to shift.

"It's hard to tell, the audio isn't great. He recorded it, so you can decide for yourself."

They emerged on the bridge level, one deck below Pri-Fly, the primary flight control station. The bridge was empty, though Xavier saw a young man through the windows, standing on an outside cat-walk with a slung rifle, looking through binoculars. It was Stone, the seventeen-year-old who had transformed from boy to warrior. Banks led the priest through a hatch and into the comm center behind the bridge. Katcher sat before an intimidating console of screens, digital readouts, and keyboards, listening to a headset with his eyes closed.

"PK, it's the skipper," Banks said, and the tech looked up, gesturing at an empty swivel chair beside him and handing the priest a second pair of earphones.

The electronics tech pointed to a screen with several horizontal colored bars. "I was scanning the frequencies like always, listening, transmitting and then listening again. As usual, nothing but dead air. But here . . ." He pointed to the digital colored bars. "See for yourself. There'll be some static at first."

The tech hit a playback button and Xavier listened, watching the screen. As the man had explained, the hiss of dead airwaves came through the priest's headset for a moment, followed by Pat Katcher's bored voice. "USS *Nimitz* transmitting in the open. Any copy, please respond." The colored bars jumped as the voice spoke, then settled into a barely perceptible waver, and the hissing returned.

The colored bars twitched again, and Xavier's eyes widened. The tech hit the pause button. "Did you hear it?"

The priest nodded. "I thought I heard the word *Reno*."

Katcher smiled. "That's what I thought too. Listen again."

Once more the recording played, and Xavier strained to hear. The contact was brief, only one and a half seconds during which time the colored bars registered some kind of disruption in the frequency. There might have been other words, or just different pitches of static, but he was certain he heard that single word, spoken by a living voice.

Xavier took off the headset. "It's definitely contact. Have you—"

Katcher frowned. "I've been transmitting over and over on that frequency since it happened. But that"—he tapped the screen—"was all I got."

"Where could they be?"

The younger man tipped back in his chair, sighed, and ran his palms over his face. "Anywhere. The Bay Area, out to sea, an aircraft. It could actually be from Reno, Nevada, or it could be on the other side of the world."

The priest shook his head, not understanding.

"I think we got lucky with a satellite," Katcher said. "One that was still working just happened to be in exactly the right position at the time of transmission. I can't be sure, it's just a theory." He made a disgusted noise and looked around the room at all the high-tech gear. "I don't know how to use ninety-five percent of this stuff, or I'd give you a better answer."

Xavier clapped the man on the shoulder. "You did great, PK, and you're learning. It's cause for hope, so keep at it."

The tech smiled and returned to his transmitting. Xavier was rising from his seat when Stone, the bridge lookout, stuck his head through the hatch.

"Father, there's a boat headed this way."

SIX

Flashlights danced through the black corridor as the laughter of children and the sound of running feet reverberated off steel bulkheads. Three shapes ran through the darkness, sneakers sliding to a stop outside a door labeled *SAFETY MEETING*. The door opened, and flashlights darted about inside, revealing rows of chairs, a conference table, and two freestanding dry-erase boards.

Nothing moved, and nothing would as this was a secure area. But they still weren't supposed to be here, and wasn't that part of the fun?

In seconds they were inside, a boy and a girl climbing atop the conference table and cavorting like ninjas, filling the air with high-pitched *hee-yahs!* The other boy went to one of the dry-erase boards and began drawing a dripping, lurching zombie, then a kid firing an enormous laser cannon. Red and black markers zipped across the white surface, showing the creature's brains blowing out the back of its head. A dialogue bubble over the kid's image read, "*Suck this!*"

The girl's name was Wind. She was eleven and an orphan, having lost both her parents during the taking of *Nimitz*. The nine-year-old boy on the table with her was Denny, the child who had come into the Alameda firehouse with Tanya, Margaret Chu, and Maxie, and was now the only one of that group still alive. The artist was ten-year-old Michael, Calvin's youngest son who, along with his brother, endured childhood diabetes. He knew he shouldn't be here, not because the bow was off limits—it was—but for a deeper reason. He shouldn't *be* here because he had nearly been devoured during the battle of the fantail, when he'd fallen with a twisted ankle and a corpse grabbed hold of him. Only the fast and savage actions of his oldest sister, Maya, had saved his life.

It should have given him a cautious respect for the threat the dead posed, but that incident was months ago, he was ten, and kids quickly grew numb to horror.

"Look!" Michael shouted, putting his flashlight beam on the drawing.

"Gross," said Denny.

"Is that supposed to be you?" Wind asked.

"Yeah. Cool laser cannon, huh?"

"I meant the other one," she said, then stuck out her arms and did a stiff-legged walk across the table, head cocked to one side and groaning. Denny immediately did the same.

"Ha-ha," Michael said, then wrote the word *Wind* on the board with an arrow pointed at the zombie's rear end. He laughed and added the word *break* in front of her name. "Now it's perfect."

Wind leaped down from the table and darted across the room, swiping a sleeve at the drawing and smearing it as she went past. "C'mon," she yelled, headed for a door across the room. Denny ran after her. Michael made a face at what had become of his drawing, then followed.

The door opened onto another dark passageway, and the three kids ran down it, bouncing from wall to wall, flashlight beams jerking across the ceiling.

"I'm a *craaaazy* person!" Wind shouted, rebounding off a wall.

"*Craaaazy!*" parroted Denny.

Michael bounced off a door. "A *looonatic!*"

More laughter and screeching, and as they neared the end of the corridor their sneakers splashed through a puddle of water. They slid to a halt, Denny running into Wind with a grunt, and the laughter stopped.

Michael shone his light on the floor, revealing a long, narrow puddle streaked with green and yellow, along with a distinct, wet boot print. The water smelled bad, and in fact the entire corridor reeked. The puddle and boot print went in the direction from which they had come, so he tracked his light back along it, turning to see its origin. The gore-streaked water came from the head of a ladder-way that descended into darkness. An even more repugnant odor came from that opening in the floor.

Denny pointed. "That's—"

Wind clamped a hand over his mouth. "We know what that is," she said, her voice soft. Then she looked at Michael, who stared back with wide eyes. "We need to go."

Michael nodded. They weren't supposed to be in the bow, they all knew it, but the grown-ups had been clearing this area, hadn't they?

Was *it clear?* Michael wondered. *Who, exactly had said that it was? Had anyone said that, or was that just what he wanted to hear, not wanting to give up the coolest playground in the world.* As he stared at the trail of slime on the floor, more thoughts leaped at him. *The three of them were unarmed. How many drifters had come up from below? Who else knew they were up here playing in the bow? His dad was going to kill him for being here.* Michael was suddenly certain that the grown-ups would have marked the areas not yet cleared. *Had he and the other two kids simply not seen them? Had they cut through some compartments and missed them?* His heartbeat accelerated.

"Back the way we came," he whispered to Wind, who nodded. Flashlights panning ahead of them, the three children moved back up the corridor, keeping to the balls of their feet and avoiding the water on the floor.

A moan echoed somewhere in the darkness, and the children froze. *In front of them, or behind?*

"Go, go," Michael hissed from the back of the little trio, waving them forward. Wind hesitated for a moment, peering into the darkness, then gripped Denny's hand and crept forward. Michael panned the light behind him to see an empty corridor and closed hatches. They went slowly at first, and then Wind picked up the pace, hurrying along and pulling Denny. A moment later she was running, a wail of panic starting low in her chest and rising.

"Wind, wait, don't!" Michael called after them, worried that her cry would draw attention, that she would run straight into—

—the dead thing lurched into the hall from a doorway on the right, only feet in front of the two running children. In the glare of a flashlight Michael saw a rotting blue uniform, patches of hair clinging to a gray scalp that was sloughing off the side of its face, and yellow eyes. It was still dripping and reeked of seawater. The thing snarled with blackened teeth and reached.

Wind screamed and fell, sliding into its legs, Denny piling up behind her. Liquid drooled from the thing's open mouth as it dropped onto the little girl.

"No!" Michael cried, swinging the flashlight and bashing it in the temple. The blow made a spongy sound. The creature jerked, head snapping up, eyes glaring into the light. "No!" the boy shouted again, and hit it once more, harder this time, rocking its head to the side. Beneath it, Wind kicked furiously and scrambled past its legs, dragging a wailing Denny with her. They got to their feet behind the drifter and began to run.

The thing started to turn in pursuit, but Michael bashed it again. "Over here, ugly!" When it turned back to face him, Michael back-pedaled. "Over here!"

The creature began to crawl quickly toward him, then struggled to its feet. Michael quickly judged the width of the hallway, knew he would never get past it. He backed up instead, drawing it in, away from the echoes of Wind and Denny's running feet. The thing snarled, pale fingers hooking into claws, took two jerking steps, and then broke into that obscene gallop they had all seen the dead do just before they took down prey.

Michael turned and ran.

He didn't get far. In seconds he was back at the point in the corridor where they had first encountered the puddle. Closed, oval-shaped hatches stood to the right and ahead, and on the left was the stairway from which the thing had originally come. Michael reached for a hatch handle, then heard the squishing of waterlogged flesh galloping in boots, splashing as it ran through the puddle. He would never get the hatch open before it was on him.

There was no choice. Michael bolted for the top of the stairway just as the creature reached him, leaping down four and five steps at a time into the darkness below.

Michael's abrupt scream rose from the stairwell.

The dead thing followed him down.

Waiting room's empty, Doc," said Tommy, poking his head into the curtained ER cubicle. Tommy was one of the hippies who had helped take back sick bay and now worked there as an orderly while studying to be an EMT. His beard was gone and he felt more comfortable in scrubs now.

Rosa looked up from the patient notes she was making, sitting on a rolling stool and using the exam table as a desk. She wasn't tall, but even without makeup and with her hair pulled into a ponytail, she was a very attractive woman. Beneath her scrubs and white doctor's coat was the full figure of an exotic dancer, remnants of another lifetime.

"I'll clean up next door and then hit the books, if that's okay," he said. The doc had just finished stitching up a lacerated forearm. There were a lot of sharp edges on this ship.

"Sure," she said. "What are you working on today?"

He raised his eyebrows. "Today? Doc, I've been on the pulmonary system for four days. I didn't know there was so much to learn about a person's insides. I thought being an EMT was, like, stabilizing, and patching people up."

Rosa smiled. "You need to know how it all works on the inside before you can fix the outside."

"Off I go," he sighed, then paused before leaving. "Doc, you look beat."

"When am I not, Tommy?"

"This place is quiet. Why not grab a meal, maybe a nap? I got this."

Rosa scratched another note on the chart. "I'll get to it."

The man shrugged and let the curtain fall back into place. As he walked away, his voice called, "Don't make me rat you out to Father X, Doc."

"Up yours, Tommy," she called after him, smiling. It wasn't a threat without merit. The big priest was forever after her about pacing herself, reminding her that she wouldn't be able to tend to the needs of others if she didn't look after her own needs, and other assorted nagging remarks along that vein. *Father* was the right title. Rosa didn't know what she would do without him.

It was more than his gentle (and sometimes not so gentle) guidance that drew her to him. He had a particular strength, something Rosa desperately wanted to possess. He knew what it was to be responsible for others, understood the fear and constant worry that went along with leadership, the frustration of never being able to do as much as you wanted. Even after her time spent serving as a Navy corpsman in combat overseas, and as an EMT on San Francisco's streets, she had never felt the same, sometimes unbearable weight of responsibility as she did now. In both those lives there had always been someone to turn to, backup waiting if things got too intense. Now, in this new life, this new world, there was only her; not nearly a doctor, but counted on to be just that.

Rosa left the cubicle and dropped the patient file in a plastic wall holder. Tommy was seated at a desk nearby, face pinched in concentration as he used a highlighter to work over a medical book. She pulled a different chart from the same wall holder and scanned it, standing near the desk and not looking up.

"Name the anatomical features of the respiratory system in mammals," Rosa said.

Tommy grumbled but closed the book as she expected. "Trachea, bronchi, bronchioles, lungs . . . that's it."

"And diaphragm."

"Right, diaphragm."

Still reading the chart, she said, "The process by which oxygen and carbon dioxide molecules are passively exchanged?"

"Diffusion," Tommy said, "and before you ask, it takes place in the alveoli air sacs in the lungs." He grinned triumphantly.

"The respiratory system, in Latin."

"Ah . . . *systema . . . resp . . . respiratorium*. Did you use a lot of Latin riding the ambulance, Doc?"

"You'd be surprised. But it's part of being a professional. The *real* reason is that it makes you sound smart, so your patients won't catch on that you're about to kill them with your lack of skills." *Oh, no, I'm starting to get snarky like Vlad.*

Tommy snorted. He was used to it. "You're such a peach to work with, Doc."

She threw him a wink. "Good, because the peach would like you to list the anatomical terminology of the entire respiratory system, top to bottom."

Tommy swallowed. "I don't know it all."

"Tell me what you know."

He drew a deep breath. "Frontal sinus, sphenoid sinus, nasal cavity..."

She nodded slowly, looking at a simple stitch job on a lacerated shin. Those damned knee knockers. She would have to do a follow-up in a couple of days to ensure the stitches had held, and that the antibiotics were keeping away any infection.

"... oral cavity, pharynx, epiglottis, vocal fold..."

It was also time to do an A1C blood test on Calvin's boys. Their father had done a good job monitoring their sugar levels and giving them the proper doses of insulin, but they were growing, and as their bodies changed, so would the treatment. Her greater worry was that the insulin Calvin had on hand, as well as the supply aboard the ship, would not last forever. Rosa had been staying up late researching its manufacture, discovering that she had all the raw elements as well as the equipment to make it right here in the medical lab. Fears of getting it right, though, and risking injection into a child, kept her awake long after the research was done for the night.

"... thyroid cartilage, cricoid cartilage..." Tommy was touching points on his throat and chest as he spoke, using his body as a mnemonic device. Everyone did something different, and whatever worked, worked. The doc remembered that when learning the names of all twenty-seven bones in the human hand, she had turned it into a song.

"... trachea, apex..." He split his fingers into a V and touched his breastbone. "... main bronchi right and left..." He sighed. "That's all I got, Doc. I start getting jumbled when we get into the lungs."

Rosa sat on the edge of his desk. "For the *most* part, you only have to learn one side, because the other is just like it. There are exceptions, though. The left lung has the cardiac notch, for example."

Tommy was taking notes. For all his grumbling, he wanted to learn.

Rosa smacked his shoulder with the patient file. "You're doing great, and you got them all in order, didn't miss one until the lungs. They'll be calling *you* Doc before you know it."

That gave her a smile. Tommy was about to say something when the double doors to sick bay banged open, and two crying children rushed in. Their sobs rose in volume as they saw the adults and ran to them.

Rosa dropped to her knees and collected both in her arms, and Tommy was by her side a moment later, a first-aid kit in his hands appearing as if by magic, looking the children over for injury. And more importantly, bites.

Both kids were talking loud and fast between the sobs, pointing back at the doors. As soon as they said the word *zombie*, something hard came into Tommy's eyes and he set down the kit, snatching an M4 assault rifle from where it leaned against his desk. He snapped the charging handle, dropped to one knee between the children and the entrance, and aimed the muzzle at the double doors. He hoped a survivor didn't come pushing in. If so, he was so tense they would die before he could stop his trigger finger.

"Shh, slow down," Rosa said, looking them over as well. She didn't see blood or bites, thank God, but both would need a full exam just to be sure. Her mind didn't allow her to consider what would come next if indeed they had been bitten.

Denny was crying too hard to be understood, but Wind was trying to get herself under control and managed to speak between deep gasps and tears. "We were . . . playing in the bow . . . I know we . . . shouldn't be there. . . ." More sobs, and Rosa rubbed her back.

"You're not in trouble, honey. Just breathe and tell me."

Wind sucked in a pair of shaky breaths, rubbing her palms at her eyes, and told Rosa what had happened.

"Tommy," Rosa said softly as the girl spoke, but the orderly was already up and moving. "Did it get him?" she asked the girl.

"I didn't see. But we heard him scream, like he was a long way off."

That wasn't good, but it didn't mean the boy was dead or bitten. "Can you show us where?" the doc asked. Denny shook his head emphatically, so Rosa gave him a hug. "I want you to go straight down to the mess hall, find Miss Sophia or Big Jerry, tell them what happened. Can you do that?" He nodded. Rosa was confident that the spaces between here and the mess hall several decks below were safe enough for the boy to travel alone. For now, anyway.

Wind wrapped her arms tightly about herself as if to still her own shaking. "I'll show you," she said in a small voice.

"Nothing will hurt you, honey, I promise." Rosa looked in the girl's eyes, and Wind gave her a little smile. Tommy reappeared with a bright orange backpack for Rosa and another like it already on his back. He handed her a pistol belt with her Glock and spare magazine pouches. As she strapped on the weapon, she found herself wishing for boots and fatigues instead of sneakers and scrubs. There was no time. Rosa shrugged out of the white doctor's coat and grabbed a pair of Maglites from the desk.

"Let's go," she said, leading them out of the sick bay.

Denny didn't make it to the mess hall.

Alone and frightened, he heard a metallic bang from somewhere up ahead in the empty passageway he was traveling. Stifling a sob, he looked around quickly, then darted into an unoccupied crew berthing compartment. Far in the back, he crawled beneath a bunk, curled into a ball, and started to cry softly.

SEVEN

USCGC *Joshua James* was a Legend Class Maritime Security Cutter, the very latest design and the fifth of its class, with four others already in service and more in various stages of the building, design, and funding process. The Legend Class was intended to replace the much older Hamilton Class cutters, and the upgrade was laughably overdue. The United States Coast Guard was operating some of the oldest naval vessels in the world; of the world's forty largest navies and coast guards, the USCG had the thirty-eighth oldest fleet.

The term *cutter* referred to any Coast Guard vessel sixty-five feet or more in length, with an assigned crew and accommodations for their extended support. The National Security Cutter was not only the biggest boat the USCG had ever put in the water—418 feet long—it was capable of a flank speed of twenty-eight knots, had a range of twelve thousand nautical miles, and could stay out for sixty days without replenishment. Its state-of-the-art radar and navigation systems, combined with a lethal weapons package, were testament to the fact that the cutter had been built to ninety percent military specifications. The design made it a more valuable asset to the Department of Defense, and although the Coast Guard carried out a wide variety of missions—environmental and fisheries protection, drug interdiction, and search and rescue—the new class of cutter was primarily intended for the role of maritime security and patrol, interception, and counterterrorism.

It should have been the perfect boat for the crisis unfolding around them, Elizabeth thought. Unfortunately, as she was quickly learning, *Joshua James* was so inadequately outfitted and crewed that saving lives, including those already aboard the ship, might be an impossibility.

Liz and her two officers, Ensign Amy Liggett and LCDR Coseboom, were gathered in a small office just below the bridge, down the central passageway from officer berthing. Amy was giving the briefing, almost all of it bad news, and Boomer sat stone-faced, occasionally looking at his commanding officer with eyes that were difficult to read. The cutter was steaming northwest, with Mr. Waite at the conn.

"Our supply trucks would have been arriving throughout today," Amy said, "so most of what should be aboard for the cruise is not." The cruise she was talking about was the ten days at sea that *Joshua James* had been scheduled to depart for the following morning. As part of the acceptance trials, it would have meant a full crew, a fully armed and supplied ship, steaming off the coast of the Pacific Northwest while contractors and technicians completed projects and went through a lengthy list of systems testing. "Almost everything is at a minimum, Captain," the ensign said.

"Stores?" Liz asked.

"The galley can feed about twenty people for three days. I already ordered half rations to extend that."

"The right decision, Amy," Liz said.

"Fresh water is a problem," the young woman went on. "The contractors report that the desalinization unit comes and goes, and it was on the testing schedule to find and work out the bugs. We have five cases of bottled water aboard, less than a three-day supply for current crew levels."

They wouldn't last long without food and water, Liz thought. It would have to be a priority. "Systems readiness?"

The ensign turned a page on her clipboard. "The bunkers for the diesels and gas turbine are full, and we're topped off with JP-5. Diesel and turbine engines, as well as the propulsion system, are functioning at one hundred percent. Surface search radar is also performing at one hundred percent." Amy swallowed, knowing this was the end of the good news.

Liz saw the look on her officer's face. "Continue."

"Air search radar, fire control, and electronic warfare systems are not fully functional, and the antimissile countermeasures are not functioning at all." Amy went on to list another dozen systems that were not yet working: air conditioning units, warning systems, IT and medical equipment, galley appliances. All of it was to have come online through the natural course of the acceptance trials.

"Weapons systems?" the captain asked.

Amy shook her head. "The Bofors fifty-seven-millimeter gun is capable of firing, but there is no ammunition on board. The twenty-millimeter close-in weapon system is reported as functioning and was on the testing schedule for this cruise. Ten thousand rounds are aboard."

"Air operations?" Liz said, her frown deepening.

"Nothing, ma'am," said the other woman. "We have zero out of two Dolphin helicopters, no pilots or rescue swimmers, no crew aboard with aviation-related ratings. We have two MQ-1 Predator drones." One was intended as a disposable unit upon which they would test the twenty-millimeter close-in weapon system, the CIWS. There were no technicians aboard qualified for launch and operation.

Seated at the small table beside Elizabeth, Coseboom simply tapped a pencil slowly against the surface.

"Light arms?" asked Liz.

Amy answered without hesitation. "Four M2 heavy machine guns, approximately eighteen hundred rounds. One M16 assault rifle, one hundred twenty rounds. Five Sig Sauer P229s; three from the armory, two brought aboard during the action at the pier, along with whatever firearm the captain brought aboard. Approximately one hundred rounds."

Elizabeth looked at her watch. She would need to return to the bridge soon. "Tell me about *Klondike*'s survivors."

It was Boomer who spoke. "We pulled seven out of the water. Three were injured, and Amy took them to sick bay. The other four were whole, and we put them to work." He gave their ranks. None were officers.

"And where do we stand on crew?" Liz directed this at the ensign.

Amy turned another page. "Five civilians: two plumbers, two electricians, and one IT tech. For enlisted personnel we have two engineers, a machinery tech and the main propulsion assistant, three bosun's mates, two food service specialists, one electrician's mate, and one electronics tech." She rubbed at her tired eyes. "We have a quartermaster, a damage controlman, a helmsman and Petty Officer Vargas as our operations specialist." She cleared her throat. "Chief Newman is ranking . . . except for the senior chief who came aboard with you." Amy didn't look at her captain as she said this, but Boomer fixed her with a stare.

Elizabeth turned to meet the man's gaze. "Very well," she said, "Lieutenant Commander Coseboom is now executive officer and will assume all the responsibilities of the gunner's mates, as well as his own law enforcement and boarding party duties. Petty Officer Vargas will stand in as electronic warfare department head. Amy, you now run not only propulsion, but all of engineering." She pointed. "I want those contractors working to get everything online as soon as possible, do you understand?"

"Yes, ma'am."

Liz stood. "Everyone is going to have to wear many hats to take up the slack for absent crew."

"And our *guest*, Captain?" Boomer said, standing as well.

"Senior Chief Kidd will become acting department head for the deck division," Liz said. "His rate also makes him chief of the boat."

Amy nodded, but Boomer just stared.

"That will be all," Liz said, and Amy scooted out of the office.

"Liz," said Coseboom, catching the woman's arm before she could go. "I need a word."

The captain closed the door and faced her new XO.

Amy Liggett returned to the bridge and gave out the assignments as she had been directed, then spoke to the quartermaster. "Where are we, Mr. Waite, and where are we going?"

The QM2 pointed to a spot on a digital chart table and said, "I've turned us due west, with Seattle to our stern, and we are making flank speed along the approximate route of the Bainbridge Island Ferry." He gestured out the bridge windows. "It's getting pretty crowded out here."

Amy looked at the surface navigation scope to see that it was clustered with shapes. A glimpse out the windows showed that the sound was rapidly filling with vessels of all sizes, from behemoth Japanese car carriers and oil tankers to freighters, tugs, container ships, and hundreds of smaller craft, both charter and private. Most were heading away from the city, and many were turning north. There were plenty of low-flying aircraft as well, mostly police and news helicopters, but small civilian planes as well. An orange-and-white Coast Guard C-130 buzzed low over the sound, flying north to south.

As she watched, a local news helicopter appeared from the rear and paced the cutter less than fifty yards out, a cameraman sticking his lens out through an open side door. Amy had a frightening moment as she imagined the bird being cut apart by fifty-caliber gunfire, but no weapons went off, and after a minute the news chopper banked away in search of something more interesting.

"My intention is to close on Bainbridge Island, then come north," the quartermaster said. "The captain wanted to stay clear of that destroyer on Seattle's waterfront."

Amy looked at the man for a moment, but he added no speculation as to his commanding officer's order or meaning.

On the overhead speakers, the military-only Guard channel was choked with traffic, units talking over one another, giving situation reports, commanders giving orders and calling for immediate support. The Navy destroyer from Everett reported that it had moved slightly north and was now just off the Port of Seattle, its guns providing cover fire as civilian evacuees streamed in, trying to get aboard anything that could float. A National Guard unit on shore providing security for that evacuation first called for medevacs, then began demanding an airstrike, and finally went off the air. There were no transmissions directed at *Joshua James*.

"Keep that destroyer on your scope, Mr. Waite," Amy said, "and report immediately if it changes position." She hadn't allowed herself to think much about what the captain had been accused of, and she tried very hard to block out the thought of a DEA helicopter and its crew being destroyed. The way she knew how to do that was to immerse herself in her work, and follow orders.

But it was impossible to completely still the worries and questions racing through her mind. Disobeying orders from Base Seattle and killing federal officers was criminal, there was no getting around it. But they were a warship now, and wasn't a captain's first priority keeping that vessel and crew safe until it could be properly deployed? That was what she had learned in New London. Permitting hostile boarders from any nation didn't fit well with that responsibility. She imagined what would happen if a U.S. Navy ship tried to board an American nuclear submarine without permission. The sub commander would slam a torpedo into it and send it to the bottom, regardless of what colors it was flying, because his first mission was to keep his boat secure.

The captain's actions had been justified. Of course they had. As for keeping away from the destroyer? Hell, that was just common sense. Right now there was a hot-shit warship commander out there, already weapons-free, raging with adrenaline and testosterone and just itching for a little surface combat. *Joshua James* wouldn't last thirty seconds against a destroyer and wouldn't have time to make its case. No, the captain knew what she was doing, and Amy would follow her as a good officer should. That decision made the young woman feel better.

"Plotted and tracking, ma'am," Waite said, pointing to a contact indicated in red on his screen. "It's USS *Momsen*, a guided missile destroyer." He scowled for a moment, looked out the bridge windows, and called to the helmsman. "Come left twenty degrees."

The helm acknowledged and the ship leaned slightly left. Amy looked out to where the quartermaster was pointing. Ahead and to their right, less than a mile off, was the *Wenatchee*: four decks high and 460 feet long, a Jumbo Mark II class ferryboat a full forty feet longer than *Joshua James*. The white monster was capable of carrying 2,500 passengers and over two hundred automobiles as it made its thirty-five-minute trips back and forth between Bainbridge Island and downtown Seattle each day.

Wenatchee was off course, still steaming at full power and leaving a wide wake, but deviating from its regular, decades-long route at a sharp angle. As Amy lifted a pair of binoculars, she saw why.

The dead were aboard, and they were slaughtering the living. Corpses galloped after fleeing people on the open-air decks, tore into crowds huddled against the barrier chain on the bow, and pulled screaming faces away from wide, scenic windows. Ensign Liggett did not hit the alarm and order rescue operations, and the quartermaster looked away from the horror without saying anything.

"Keep us away from her," Amy said quietly.

"Aye-aye, ma'am," Waite replied, giving the appropriate orders to the helm.

The young officer watched the ferry until it passed out of sight on the starboard side, her heart racing as she saw what the dead could do and how they went about it. Then she looked forward again, to where the quartermaster had brought them back onto their original course.

Not my call to make. Besides, attempting to rescue those people would invite nightmares aboard, and that was irresponsible. "Steady as she goes, Mr. Waite."

Bainbridge Island loomed before them, and the quartermaster ordered the turn that would take them up its eastern coastline.

What's on your mind, Boomer?" Liz said, folding her arms and leaning against the hatch frame.

"Your brother," the man said at once. "The helicopter. What the DEA said before he chopped them out of the sky. Making him chief of the boat."

"I don't have time for all this, and you know it."

"Make time . . . *Captain.*"

Liz pursed her lips. "Very well, *Commander.* Since you're now my executive officer, I'll explain myself to you, this time. Don't get used to it. As my XO, I expect and demand your support, are we clear?"

Coseboom nodded.

Liz ticked off a finger. "I don't know *what* those things on the dock were, but they were already dead, so I didn't *kill* anyone. I rescued a shipmate in peril, which I would do again for any of you." Another finger went up. "We are a ship at war, and I will not permit it to be compromised by anyone, regardless of their claims. Were his actions extreme? Perhaps, but that will be decided by appropriate command levels at a later date."

"You *are* appropriate command levels, Captain."

She went on as if she hadn't heard him, raising a third finger. "Senior Chief Kidd is the ranking enlisted man aboard, and a veteran of deck operations, something otherwise lacking aboard this ship. His assignment is more than justified."

Now she stepped away from the hatch frame and closer to the other officer. "We don't know if we're at war, facing plague, or right in the middle of the End of Days. Mr. Coseboom, you heard the reports on the ship's condition and crew deficiencies the same as I did. We're less than a quarter strength, and that will mean hardship: long watches with very little rest. We need every capable hand, and all the experience we can get."

Coseboom nodded slowly, and Liz softened her voice. "Boomer, the ship needs you and so do I. There's no telling what this is all about, or how long it will take before things get back to normal. Until that happens, I will command this vessel in a manner I believe serves the mission."

"And what is that mission?"

"Right now," Liz said, "preserving ship and crew. We're going to make for Port Angeles up on Ediz Point. I'm hoping we can fill out our missing stores and crew there."

Coseboom took a deep breath. "They'll have heard what happened at Base Seattle. There's bound to be trouble."

She nodded. "And if there is, *we* will deal with it. Understood, XO?" She extended a hand.

Boomer looked at the hand, then shook it. "Yes, ma'am."

"Very well." She moved to the hatch and stepped into the passageway. "I want sidearms issued to all three officers, Chief Newman, and Senior Chief Kidd."

Coseboom started to say something, but Elizabeth left without waiting to hear what it was.

EIGHT

Seaman Recruit Moses Thedford sat on a metal stool in the cutter's tiny, four-bed sick bay, twisting a damp rag nervously in latex-gloved hands. Just nineteen years old, he was not trained for boarding parties or even as a bosun's mate, yet there he had been with a rifle in the bow of the commander's Prosecutor, hauling aboard *Klondike* survivors. Neither was he a medic, yet here he sat watching over three wounded crewmen from that ship, possessing the same medical skills as everyone else aboard—or less. And why? Because he was a one-stripe nobody, ensuring that he would be shit upon by everyone with more than six months in the Coast Guard. The other reason, he knew, was that he was a cook, and therefore everyone thought he'd have nothing better to do.

Wait till you motherfuckers want to eat, he thought, twisting the rag.

He could just as easily have said it out loud, because no one could hear him. The three men in the sick bay beds were sleeping, one of them tossing fitfully with fever. The other two had what looked like serious wounds, one at the neck, the other at the inner thigh, and Moses along with two of his shipmates had done their best to stop the bleeding and bind the wounds. It seemed to have worked, but who the hell knew? His shipmates had run off to their stations as *Joshua James* completed a turn and engaged forward propulsion, leaving Moses alone with no idea of how to care for these men.

He was tired, close to coming off third watch and thinking about his rack back in the barracks when the world went ass-up, and it looked now like this was all the crew the cutter was going to get. It meant there were no medical officers, no med techs, not even an EMT-trained rescue swimmer. It meant endless shifts ahead for everyone aboard.

No one to watch these men but poor Moses. I should have stayed in the Bronx and taken the auto body job at Terrell's. The Coast Guard sucks.

Moses thought about the wounds. He wanted to believe that their flesh had been torn by protruding pieces of metal on *Klondike*'s railing, but he had seen what was happening up on the cutter's decks, had seen the way those things attacked. Moses knew bites when he saw them. And it was clear to him that either ISIS or Al Qaeda had set off some kind of biological weapon, a bug of some kind that turned people into rabid maniacs. Dead people, though? What bullshit. He'd attended countless training classes concerning bio attacks, but not one about the living dead. In the Coast Guard there was a manual for everything, and if there was one about zombies, he would have seen it. No, it had to be ISIS . . . or ISIL, depending upon who you talked to. Both meant *bad guys.*

One of the men, the guy with the neck wound, made a rattling sound from his bed at the other side of the room. Moses Thedford remained on his stool, gripping his rag tightly. The man wasn't moving. What should he do now? He looked at the intercom phone on the wall. Should he call an officer? He immediately rejected the idea, knowing the conversation would go something like this:

*Sir, this is Seaman Thedford in sick bay. One of the injured men
   just made a noise.*
Did you check on him, Thedford?
No, sir.
Then unfuck yourself and go check.

Of course an officer wouldn't curse at him, he knew, but a chief
or a petty officer might, and either way Moses would come off looking like an idiot, probably drawing some shitty work detail as punishment for being stupid. Slowly, he got off the stool and moved to
the side of the man's bed. His eyes were closed and his face was
turned away, but the young Coast Guardsman saw at once that the
man's pillow was drenched with blood, his neck bandage wet and
sagging.

Shit, he bled out! Moses lifted one of the man's eyelids; cloudy
and no reaction to light. When he pressed his fingers against the
neck, there was no pulse. *Oh, shit, it's gonna be my fault.* He turned
to the man in the next bed, the one with the leg wound, and saw this
one staring blankly at the ceiling, his chest unmoving. Moses ripped
back the blanket to look at a thigh bandage dripping red, soaking
the mattress beneath. *Bled out.*

"I already fed the dog, Ma!" the third *Klondike* man screamed,
squirming as his feverish head sought a cool spot on the pillow.

The scream made Moses jump. "Shut up!" he yelled. Then he
went for the phone, knocking over the metal stool. The feverish
guardsman shouted, "It's David's turn!"

Moses punched the button for the bridge. He didn't care if
he pissed off the captain herself. This was *not* his job, and *not* his
fault.

Behind him, the dead man with the neck wound sat up in his
bed.

. . .

Liz stayed on the bridge long enough to check their position and course, see where the Navy destroyer was and that it appeared disinterested for the moment, and to wait for LCDR Coseboom, who arrived a minute after she did. Boomer sent Amy off on the task of arming key crew members per the captain's directive, then took command of the conn as Liz left again. She told him to have Chief Kidd report to her quarters.

Liz's accommodations were spacious by warship standards, especially for a boat this size. There was a couch that folded down into a rack, plenty of storage, a private head, and a drop-down desk with a wall safe mounted above it. She'd stored Special Agent Ramsey's pistol and spare magazines in there, preferring to use the smaller variant Sig employed by the Coast Guard. Her room had no porthole—this wasn't a cruise ship—so she snapped on a light above a small table and a pair of chairs. A low *meow* greeted her.

"Blackbeard," she said, letting the cat out of the carrier from where it rested on one of the chairs. The black-and-gray-striped animal meowed long and loud as she picked it up, then began to purr and rub its head against Liz's chin.

"Mommy's got you," she said, scratching the cat behind the ears. It leaned into the rub. "Now we really are shipmates." She chuckled. "Yes, I'm happy to see you too." She looked around her quarters. What was she going to feed him? Coast Guard galleys didn't stock cat food, and she certainly hadn't packed any in her sea bag. That was when she realized she had left her laptop in her Camry on the dock. Well, there was nothing to be done about it now, and it wouldn't have helped feed her cat, anyway.

"We'll figure something out," she said, as Blackbeard turned a circle in her lap and curled up, still purring.

After several minutes there were two sharp raps on the door. "Come," Liz called. Charlie entered, his broad, squat frame filling the doorway. He closed the door behind him and stood at attention in front of the table, eyes fixed on the bulkhead behind his sister. "Senior Chief Kidd, reporting as ordered."

In her lap, Blackbeard hissed and jumped down to hide under the couch. "Stand easy, Senior Chief," she said, and her brother did, clasping his hands behind his back. "Are you wondering why you're not in irons, Chief?"

"It's not because I'm your brother. I know that cuts me no slack."

"You're alive *because* you're my brother, Chick. I could have left you in that Hummer." She gestured for him to sit. "We'll talk later about what the FBI told me."

"Sis, I—"

She cut him off. "Save it. We'll talk about it later, because at this point it's moot. The helicopter is another matter."

Chick leaned forward on the table. "What was I gonna do, let them take your ship away? Put you in cuffs right beside me in the back of that helicopter? Not gonna happen."

"Oh, you did it for me, did you?" She shook her head.

"We're at war," he said, "and people die in war."

"Do not lecture me on war, mister." The undeniable fact was that his actions had kept her in command, but at the cost of seven lives, men with families. Her crew had families too, though, didn't they? And no matter what was happening to them back on land, they would want to know their loved ones were safe out on the water. Unfortunately she couldn't provide the same reassurance to the men and women aboard. Seattle was in chaos. It was confusing and frustrating, made more so because her sense of duty was at war with her need to look after her younger brother, something she had once failed to do and that had exacted a heavy price on both of them. *Am I still atoning for that sin?*

"My biggest worry right now," she said, "isn't downed helicopters or even that Navy destroyer out there. It's the crew. They don't know *what* to think, and that's because of you." She leveled a finger at him. "My XO is the Law Enforcement Division officer, the top cop on the ship, and he has some serious objections to one Senior Chief Charles Kidd not being in custody, much less being made chief of the boat." She explained her decision and told him he would be running the deck division. That had been Charlie's job aboard *Klondike*.

"You'll have next to no staff," she said, "but you'll still have to make it work."

Chick nodded. "We'll be squared away, Skipper."

"Also because of what you've done," she continued, "my crew is in turmoil and no doubt questioning my decisions. I'll deal with that, but it leaves you as the only one I can absolutely count on to have my back. I need to be able to depend on you, Chick."

"Without question," he said.

"And you will *not* engage in further combat action without orders."

"I understand."

Two sharp raps came at the door, and Liz told the visitor to enter. It was Amy Liggett carrying two sidearm belts of Sig Sauers and spare magazines. Another was already belted around her waist.

"That will be all, Senior Chief," Liz said, standing and buckling on the weapon. Liz asked the young woman to find some food and water for her cat, and then all three dispersed, the captain heading for the bridge and what would be the longest watch of her career.

Moses Thedford didn't get to make his call to the bridge, and didn't get the hatch to the passageway open before the creature that had been a *Klondike* survivor was on him. His last conscious thought, as blood shot from his severed artery and the creature worked in deeper with its teeth, was that he should have stayed in the Bronx.

There were four of them in the compartment now, three *Klond-*

ike men and Moses, his dark skin already turning ashy. Two of the creatures stood facing different bulkheads, a third wandered back and forth in the narrow space between the beds, and the thing that had been Moses stood with its arms limp at its sides, head cocked over, swaying and staring at the hatch. Occasionally there would be sounds on the other side, and Moses would let out a croak, but for the most part he was still, staring at the steel oval that kept them in this room.

It would be hours before one of Moses's dead hands finally came up slowly and reached for the handle.

Many had called it the *Emerald City* and *Gateway to Alaska*, a place known for its jazz, poetry, alternative music, its iconic Space Needle, the Seahawks, and the Mariners. With 3.6 million people in the metropolitan area, Seattle's real estate was among the most expensive in the country, in part due to the high-paying corporate presence of Amazon, Microsoft, and an assortment of biomedical companies. It was a diverse, tolerant, progressive city.

It was dying fast. Many of those millions of residents would be dead by the end of the day, and that number would multiply exponentially as the plague spread. Uncontrolled fires began devouring neighborhoods and quickly spread to the thousands of square acres of dry forest waiting at the city's outskirts. Before long, a heavy smoke would hang in the streets, but it would only impair the living who were trying desperately to get out. Smoke didn't bother the dead.

On the bridge of *Joshua James*, Liz and Boomer plotted their course north. They would maintain flank speed and steam directly up the sound, putting as much distance between themselves and the Navy destroyer as possible. On that topic, Boomer gave a softspoken opinion.

"They must have bigger problems. They should have been all

over us by now. How hard would it be to launch a Navy helo out of Everett and put a torpedo into our side?"

Liz grunted noncommittally. The same thought had occurred to her, and so she had privately taken aside Petty Officer Vargas, the man now in charge of their electronic warfare system down in the Combat Control Center. Her orders had been to have the twenty-millimeter CIWS loaded, and use the fire control radar—when it decided to work—to track, identify, and target any aircraft within their threat radius. If an airborne attack was detected, Vargas was to be standing by for the order to engage. If a Navy helo *did* come at them, her intention was to spot it and destroy it before it could put a torpedo in the water.

Getting easier and easier to kill U.S. helos, isn't it, Liz?

She went back to the chart, noting that their course would take them up beyond Kingston, and then they would bear northwest for a time past Whidbey Island, continuing through Puget Sound. A right turn would take them into Possession Sound, the home waters of the Navy base at Everett, which wasn't an option. Their northwest course would eventually put Marrowstone Island off their port side before they finally turned west into the open water of the Salish Sea and the Strait of Juan de Fuca. *Joshua James* would slow then, approaching the Coast Guard Air Station at Port Angeles cautiously, monitoring radio traffic and perhaps sending in an SRP for reconnaissance.

"I estimate five hours if all goes well," said Boomer.

"Which we know won't happen," Liz replied, "but it's a plan for now."

Beyond the thick bridge windows, the sound had grown even more chaotic. At nearly 10:00 A.M., the surface traffic was dangerously congested with vessels of all types, most disregarding all water safety rules in their race northward. Liz found her ship in the center of a waterborne rush hour, and no sooner had Boomer given his time estimate than she had to order the cutter to slow, keeping pace with the vessels around them in order to avoid a collision. It might not be a bad thing, she realized. Perhaps *Joshua James* would become lost in the clutter.

Many ships tried to radio the Coast Guard vessel or signal from their decks, but Liz ordered radio silence and gave no response. In another life, even yesterday, she would have been communicating and working to bring order to the madness. But this was a new life, and though her heart ached to help the frightened civilians all around her, it wasn't safe to bring any of them aboard a ship that might be attacked by the U.S. Navy at any moment. The other consideration was that she didn't have enough stores or clean water to support her crew, much less refugees. No, for now she had to carry on. Things would be different after they resupplied at Port Angeles. Then she would come back here and start saving lives.

Off the starboard bow, a sport fisherman got too close to a maneuvering freighter and they collided. Fiberglass shattered and the sport fisher went under as the big, rusty ship plodded on. Yellow spots appeared in the water as life jackets bobbed to the surface.

Joshua James steamed north without slowing.

NINE

The Ediz Hook was a curving sliver of land extending into the Strait of Juan de Fuca. It sheltered a deepwater harbor for the small town of Port Angeles, boasting a population of only twenty thousand, resting in the shadow of the Olympic Mountains. The town had an airport and a ferry service to Victoria, British Columbia, and other than a small tourism trade, it survived because of industry: logging, oil tanker berthing, and commercial fishing. It was also one of the last American communities before this part of the world turned into either Canada or the Pacific.

Port Angeles held little interest for Liz Kidd, who was standing on her bridge and observing the view ahead through binoculars. It was the Coast Guard Air Station out at the tip of the Ediz Hook that drew her. Air Station Port Angeles was a logistical support center for several cutters operating in the area and would have just what *Joshua James* needed. Liz had served on a small cutter here once, back when she was a young lieutenant, junior grade, and she knew the base well. Getting in quietly, however, would be impossible. They had company.

Slowing down to mix with the flotilla of vessels trying to escape the Seattle area had masked their transit—no officials, including the Navy, had discovered them—but the reduced speed added three hours to their journey, causing them to arrive just after 6:00 P.M. Most of the smaller craft around them had peeled away toward marinas hours ago, thinking to find safety on one of the many islands in Puget Sound. The biggest ships, the tankers, freighters, and containers, steamed on around the cutter, eventually angling either toward Canada or out to sea. A dozen vessels, private craft as well as two commercial fishermen, followed *Joshua James* at a close distance, no doubt believing the cutter would lead them to a safe harbor.

As Liz ordered her ship to a dead stop, two miles from the air station, the tiny flotilla with her did the same, drifting into a staggered line off her port and starboard, expectant faces looking toward the big, white Coast Guard vessel. Liz had long since stopped listening to their radio calls for information.

"Nothing in the slips," Boomer said, standing beside her with his own binoculars. The pier that served the air station was completely empty of Coast Guard vessels, or any others for that matter. "Nothing on the runway, and the helo pad is empty too." From here they could even see into the open, cavernous aircraft hangar. The three MH-65 Dolphin helicopters stationed there were gone.

Every coastie is out doing their job today. Except me. Liz keyed the radio mic. "Air Station Port Angeles, this is Coast Guard Cutter seven-five-four. Acknowledge."

No response, and sorting through the chatter on the Guard channel told them none of it was coming from the air station. Still, she tried to raise them several more times, each time with negative results.

"Helm," she called, "ahead seven knots, come to zero-two-zero." The helmsman steered the vessel toward the air station as twin diesels pushed *Joshua James* through the water. Most of the small craft around her took that as a positive sign and raced ahead to the marina at the edge of the small town to the left. They didn't have much choice, Liz knew. Most would almost be out of fuel by now. One of the two commercial fishermen didn't like the look of it all and turned north to strike out for Canada, but the second hung on and followed the cutter.

Liz summoned her officers and section heads, handed the conn off to Mr. Waite, and gathered her people at the back of the bridge for a quick meeting.

"I'm going to bring us alongside the long pier," Elizabeth said. "Mr. Coseboom will lead the shore party." She looked at the man. "While you assemble your team, I'll draw you a map of the base so you won't get lost. Priorities are food, water, arms, and ammo, collecting any coasties you find. If you can make a second trip, some of the contractors will go with you so we can identify and obtain any systems equipment they need."

Boomer nodded.

"Deck division," she said, looking at her brother, "will mount the fifties and provide cover to the operation." Then she looked at Amy, now going on twenty-four hours without sleep. "Engine room and propulsion needs to be standing by to get us off that pier fast."

Everyone said they understood.

Liz looked at Boomer again. "If you encounter the dead, remember that head shots put them down. I want this operation executed fast and without casualties, people. You have your assignments."

The officers and brand-new section heads dispersed, and Liz moved to her quartermaster. "I want to get into that harbor and then come about to one-eight-zero before approaching the pier, so we end up bow-out to sea."

The quartermaster watched his digital charts and gave commands to the helmsman, and *Joshua James* moved into the sheltered waters of the Ediz Hook.

. . .

Lieutenant Commander Coseboom was bright, and he had a quick, tactical mind. He and his shore party had been on the base for only a few minutes before it was clear to him what had happened. The crisis erupted in Seattle, and Air Station Port Angeles sent all three of its birds and every vessel they had south to assist, emptying the base of all but administrative and service personnel, and probably a tiny security detachment.

Like everywhere, the dead appeared in the small town across the water, and the civilian population, those that hadn't gotten out on boats, packed the road that traveled the length of the hook, passing through the bird sanctuary and seeking refuge on the only military base around. There would have been no way to hold them back; the base gate was nothing more than a sentry box and a pair of wooden traffic arms.

The dead followed the exodus.

And caught them.

Air Station Port Angeles now crawled. Through the spaces between buildings, sluggish figures could be glimpsed moving in large groups along the runway. Others, many in uniform, staggered across the closer lawns and parking areas.

"We're moving to Warehouse One," Boomer told the eight men with him, "fast and quiet." Only he, Chief Newman, and a bosun's mate were armed, and the bosun held their lone M16 rifle.

An ocean wind blew across the base, cool and salty, making the colors snap atop the flagpole in front of the administration building. The shore party had run down the cutter's gangplank, sprinting down the pier and onto the base itself, angling to the right down a paved access road. Boomer took the lead, a forty-caliber Sig in his hand and a pack on his back, carrying a pair of bolt cutters.

Two corpses in mechanic's coveralls stumbled across a strip of grass and onto the access road, moving to meet the running shore party. Boomer stopped twenty-five feet from them, took the Sig in two hands, and fired three times, putting them down. The shots echoed across the quiet base. He'd seen enough during the *Klondike* rescue that the sight of other Coast Guardsmen in this condition— or shooting them, for that matter—caused him no hesitation. As his captain had said, the head shots put them down, and they didn't get back up.

The map Liz drew for them led the party to a warehouse about midway between the far helicopter hangar and the pier behind them, positioned right on the access road. Boomer hauled on a big sliding door mounted on rollers, running it open while the bosun's mate pointed the M16 inside. The lights were on, and nothing appeared to be moving among the high steel racks packed with crates. Forklifts were lined up to one side of the high-ceilinged space.

The officer looked at Chief Newman, who was also holding a Sig. "You know what we need. I'm taking three men and heading to the armory."

"Copy that," Newman said, pointing at the forklifts. "Take a couple of those." Parked beside the vehicles was an airport-style tractor attached to a string of flatbed carts, something to service large aircraft out on the runway. "I'm using that," the chief said.

Boomer gave him a thumbs-up and ran for a forklift.

Liz used her binoculars and tracked her shore party until they reached the warehouse. A radio to keep her in contact with her men now hung on one hip. On the forward deck below, her brother had mounted a fifty-caliber on the port side and was loading it with a belt of heavy rounds. He yanked back the charging handle to arm the weapon and pointed it toward shore. Three other fifty-cals would also be aiming at the base now, positioned at intervals down the length of the port side. She hoped they wouldn't have to use them.

The mass of a peeling, green-and-white commercial fisherman

drifted in off the port bow, coasting into one of the slips near the shore, its diesel stacks blatting smoke and noise as it reversed to slow itself.

"Goddammit," Liz growled. The fisherman ended up directly between the shore and Charlie Kidd's fifty-caliber. As she watched, four men in jeans and flannel leaped to the docks carrying empty duffel bags, running to shore and then heading in the direction her shore party had gone.

She was about to switch to the exterior PA system and order the fishermen to clear out when a muffled echo of gunfire floated up the bridge ladderway from decks below. *Gunfire? Who else aboard was armed?* She looked around.

Amy Liggett was not on the bridge.

Amy moved down the passageway, eyelids heavy, her body exhausted. Tired people made poor decisions, she knew. It had been Amy who put Seaman Thedford in charge of babysitting the wounded *Klondike* survivors, and then, in all the excitement, promptly forgot about him. *How long has this poor guy been waiting for his relief? He must be bursting to make a head call.* She was almost at sick bay when she realized she hadn't brought anyone to relieve him. *Stupid. Tired and stupid.* She would let him visit the head, then tell him to hang on just a bit longer until she could find someone to take his place.

Alone in the corridor, she came to a hatch marked with a red cross in a white circle and was reaching for the handle when it moved upward on its own. The door swung in.

"Moses, I'm sorry—"

Her voice and her breath caught as the young black seaman, now gray, gripped the open hatch frame with pale, blood-encrusted fingers and leaned out, gasping. He lunged, but the lower lip of the hatch caught him at the ankles and he collapsed face-first into the passageway.

Amy let out a shriek and stumbled backward, clawing for her sidearm as more corpses in bloodstained uniforms tumbled out on top of the former Moses Thedford. Heads turned, creamy eyes with pinpoint pupils seeking and locking on prey, and they scrambled to their feet, moving awkwardly toward the young ensign. All were croaking and rasping.

Of all the military branches, it was the United States Coast Guard that trained the hardest with handguns. In their law enforcement role, it was the weapon most commonly carried. Though still considered green in almost every area of responsibility, Amy Liggett had qualified as expert with the Sig Sauer P229. As she had been trained, she took a wide stance and a two-handed grip, then fired two shots in quick succession. The forty-caliber slugs took the *Klondike* survivor in direct center mass—also as Amy had been taught—and punched out his back without slowing him in the least.

Head shot, the captain had said, and Amy focused, raising her aim. She fired, and the round hit the crewman in the forehead, spraying gore into the faces of those behind him. The body crumpled. In the tight steel corridor, the pistol shots echoed, hurting her eardrums. She shifted her aim right and fired, blowing off a jaw and making one of the things stagger against the bulkhead, but not stopping it.

The three creatures were fifteen feet away and leaned into a sidestepping gallop. Amy turned and ran back up the corridor, but only twenty feet before she turned again and resumed her shooting stance. The Sig banged out four more rounds, and the remaining *Klondike* crewmen went down.

Five rounds left. Moses Thedford hopped toward her, arms flailing, mouth yawning as he let out a ghastly moan. Amy fired once, hitting Moses in the eye, blowing out the back of his skull. He collapsed.

She remained in her shooting stance, pistol trained on the open hatch down the hallway for a moment as she did the math, counting occupants. Then she advanced cautiously. Sick bay was a blood-splattered ruin, but there were no more bodies in here, moving or otherwise. When the sound of running boots came from the distance in the passageway, followed by her captain shouting her name, Ensign Liggett holstered her sidearm and leaned against the open hatch frame, resting her forehead on her arm.

"Clear," she called back. "And it's contagious, Captain."

Liz Kidd turned and ran back for the bridge.

Air Station Port Angeles had fallen almost exactly as LCDR Coseboom had guessed. When the dead began attacking and rapidly multiplying in the small town across the harbor, the residents who could went to the marina to escape by water. Most of them made it and put to sea long before *Joshua James* arrived, with Victoria, British Columbia, as their destination.

Victoria had fallen by the time they reached the Canadian city, and death was waiting for them.

The majority of Port Angeles's citizens made for the Coast Guard station, quickly clogging the access road and then abandoning their vehicles to go ahead on foot. The base was never meant to be particularly secure. Its remote location provided security, as its position at the end of a slender peninsula meant that a small armed detachment could hold back any moderate threat. The gate, such as it was, had never been intended to stem the tide of thousands of panicked refugees, and the civilian mass pushed in without resistance. The few guardsmen assigned to defend the gates weren't about to fire on their terrified and unarmed neighbors, and so the civilians poured

out onto the airfield. Once they arrived, however, they weren't sure
what to do next, and so most of them stayed on the airfield.

Like a wolf pack taking down stragglers at the back of a herd, the
dead followed the living onto the peninsula, taking down the slow
and steadily increasing their numbers. By the time the last of the
living were through the gates, there were the dead surging immediately behind. The five armed Coast Guardsmen on duty went down
firing, falling in minutes and then rising to join the horde soon after.

Before *Joshua James* was even on the horizon, the only living
beings at the air station were scattered pockets of frightened, hiding
refugees and a handful of Coast Guardsmen.

Corpses covered the runway, drifting without purpose and wandering slowly between the buildings at the west end of the base. Few
noticed the cutter gliding silently into the long pier, but distant gunfire, followed by the not-so-distant blatting of a commercial fisherman's diesels, got them moving.

Chief Petty Officer Newman, a boarding party team leader who
had a nose for sniffing out contraband and concealed drugs, was
well satisfied with what he and his small crew had accomplished in
a short time. All four flatbed carts were loaded with foodstuffs and
bottled water and he'd found a crate of foul-weather clothing, four
medical kits, a surgical kit, and perhaps the biggest score of all,
eleven cases of toilet paper.

He pointed to a young seaman. "You're driving," he said, spreading the rest of his men into a protective square around the tractor
and small trailers. Those who hadn't been carrying firearms had
managed to put their hands on fire axes.

The tractor engine fired and was pulling out of the warehouse
when two men with crew cuts and wearing flight suits almost ran
past the doors, then slid to a stop as they saw their fellow coasties.
Newman was startled and almost shot them.

"That your cutter?" one of them shouted.

"Yeah, and you're coming with us," Newman said.

"Goddamn right we are," yelled the second man, and the two new arrivals began sprinting ahead of the slow-moving tractor, heading for the big white ship at rest against the base's long pier.

The armory was small, far smaller than the warehouse, and that made sense to Coseboom. Ship crews needed a lot more food than they did arms and ammunition. He was glad he'd brought the bolt cutters, because as his captain had warned him, the stout, brick armory building was encircled with a high fence topped with razor wire, its gate chained and locked. The bolt cutters got them through and then into the building's roll-up bay door. Two of Boomer's crewmen drove their forklifts right inside the structure.

It didn't take the shore party's leader long to locate what they wanted, and in short order both forklifts were loaded with heavy pallets and smaller crates stacked on top.

"Commander!" one of his men yelled, a two-stripe damage controlman left at the fence as security. Coseboom ran outside to see him pointing. A mob of dead people were swarming from between two buildings and across a lawn that led to the access road. Another cluster was on its hands and knees on the grass, tearing at screaming, thrashing shapes. Boomer thought he saw bloody flannel and duffel bags. Passing left to right, two men in flight suits raced down the access road, heading for the docks.

"Haul ass," he barked to the men in the forklifts, then stood aside as they roared out of the armory, through the gate, and onto the road. "Don't stop for anything," Boomer shouted, then ran back inside. He returned a moment later with a pair of M4 assault rifles and several magazines. "We're their cover," he said, handing the damage controlman a weapon and taking off at a jog after the growling forklifts.

To their rear, a tractor hauling loaded trailers, ringed by four men, followed closely.

Because of the fishing boat directly across the pier from him, Charlie Kidd lost sight of the first forklift as it neared the entrance to the dock, and he couldn't see what was coming at the shore party from between the buildings. He could see to the left, however, and there the dead were surging in a wave across the lawns.

Letting off a string of curses, he swiveled the M2 in that direction and ripped off bursts of fifty-caliber. At once, the three other weapons mounted on the port side did the same, chopping into stumbling bodies, knocking them down. Chick saw most of them get back up, and even those with their legs cut from under them began dragging themselves across the grass by their arms.

He cursed again, firing shorter bursts, and tried to aim for the heads of the crowd. A few exploded in red and gray, but most of his rounds either slammed into dead flesh or sailed harmlessly overhead.

The first forklift came into view and shot up the dock toward the cutter. Then Chick saw the second take the turn from the access road too sharply. Its load shifted, and the weight, angle, and speed carried the heavy vehicle, along with its cargo, right off the dock and into the water, its screaming driver still gripping the wheel.

"Son of a *bitch*," Charlie snarled, and kept firing.

They were coming in too fast, Boomer saw, a dead horde crossing the lawns in a shambling wave. He and the damage controlman knelt and fired their rifles into the mass as the tractor and its loaded trailers hummed past behind them. He spared a look to see Chief Newman standing at the head of the dock, motioning the men on foot to keep up, and waving the tractor on. Once it was past, he turned to add pistol fire to the defensive action.

"Fall back to the ship," Boomer ordered, and the damage controlman took off at a run. The officer changed magazines in his rifle and trotted to the head of the dock, stopping next to Chief Newman. With fifty-caliber rounds rattling overhead, the two men aimed and fired, trying to be calm, making sure their shots hit the mark.

Back at the gangplank, both the tractor and the surviving forklift had arrived, and every available hand was racing off the ship to meet them, struggling back up the gangplank with crates and cartons. The sounds of the fifty-calibers dropped off as new ammo belts were loaded, and both Boomer and Chief Newman took turns reloading so that someone was always firing.

The horde pressed in, savaged bodies of adults and children stiffly, inexorably approaching. Thirty yards out. Twenty. Ten.

"Last magazine," Newman called, slamming it into his pistol.

Boomer slapped at a cargo pocket, finding it empty. "I'm out." He dropped the M4 and pulled his sidearm, risking a look back. The supplies and arms they had found were being loaded, but not quickly enough.

"They need time," Coseboom said.

"That's why we're here," Newman replied.

The two men lasted another two minutes, and then the swarm overtook them.

*N*o!" Liz cried, slamming a fist against the steel above the bridge window, watching her XO and chief go down. She snatched up the mic, switching to the PA. "Deck gunners, concentrate fire as they come up the center of the dock. Loading party, *get it done!*"

The dead were forced into a narrow channel as they swarmed up the dock toward the much wider long pier. At this range, with bodies packed close together, the storm of fifty-caliber rounds chewed them apart, blowing off limbs, tearing torsos in half, and detonating heads. Though many still lived in these new, mangled forms, they began to slide off into the water or pile up, forcing the newly arrived dead to crawl over them. The fifties kept up their fire.

Amy Liggett, sent to lead the loading party after her fight below-decks, radioed to her captain that all supplies and surviving team members were aboard, along with two new arrivals, and that she was raising the gangplank.

"Gunners," Liz said, her voice booming across the ship from exterior speakers, "maintain your fire until we're away." She called to the quartermaster, standing near the helmsman. "Mr. Waite, take us out of here, flank speed."

A moment later the harbor's water boiled at the cutter's stern, and the ship leaped forward, throwing up a white crest. It roared away from the long pier as the machine gun fire stopped, and the dead arrived to follow the departing cutter into the water, arms still reaching.

Liz didn't look to see if Boomer was among them.

They were just coming around the tip of the Ediz Hook, turning north, when the Guard channel buzzed with a transmission that made Elizabeth's blood turn cold. "Coast Guard seven-five-four, this is DDG ninety-two. Respond."

Liz snapped a look at her quartermaster, who quickly shook his head. "The *Momsen* is not on the scope, Captain. Maybe they're trying to draw us out, get a fix on our position."

"That destroyer has two helos," she said, picturing a pair of gray birds flying fast just above the waves, preparing to drop torpedoes. "Mr. Vargas," she said over the intercom, calling the operations specialist down in the combat center, "do we have any airborne contacts?"

"Captain, the air search radar is not online at this time," Vargas reported.

It was too close. Whatever was happening in Seattle, the destroyer had found the time—or been ordered—to hunt them down. There would be no going back.

"Mr. Waite," Liz said, dropping into the padded swivel chair with *CAPTAIN* stenciled on the back, "maintain flank speed and take us to sea."

An hour later, with the last strip of U.S. soil well behind them, *Joshua James* steamed into the vast Pacific.

TEN

Michael limped along a passageway, blackness all around him and the flashlight his only illumination. Jumping down the last four steps of the ladderway had landed him in a puddle of seawater and slime, and his right leg shot out from under him, twisting his ankle and making him cry out. There was no time to sit and cradle it, no time to cry. The dead sailor was already tumbling down the ladderway after him. Michael ran, moving in a painful, limping gallop, similar to the dead.

Choices of corridors presented themselves, most with the dark spots of open hatches running their length, none of them attractive. He went right, hobbling as quickly as he could, hearing the thing land behind him with a wet, crumpling noise.

God, it stinks down here.

His flashlight swept across walls covered in vertical piping and valves, cables and colored conduit overhead, and hatches with their purposes stenciled on them in white letters, going by too fast to read. He nearly tripped over a decaying corpse in the center of the passage, leaping over it and tensing for a gray arm to shoot up and grab him. It didn't—the body was long dead—but Michael came down his injured ankle with a flare of pain.

A moan traveled up the steel tunnel behind him.

At an intersection, Michael stopped and panned the flashlight in each direction, biting his lip at what he would see. All three passageways were empty. The moan came again, and that got him moving, to the left this time. Moments later his sneakers kicked several shell casings that rattled across the deck, and he slowed. A closed hatch to his left read *CAT SUPPORT 3*. A metallic *bang* came from behind him, accompanied by a moan. It was answered by another moan from the corridor ahead.

Michael worked the handle, prayed he wasn't stepping into a nest, and went through the hatch, closing it behind him. He held his breath and listened, heard only his own thudding heartbeat, and turned with the light. It was a workshop of some kind, with grinders and clamps bolted to metal tables, tall green bottles stored behind a chain-link fence with a *Flammable* sign on it, unlit fluorescent lights set in the ceiling behind wire mesh. An open hatch led into darkness on the right.

His light found a tool locker, and he eased open the metal door, careful not to let it swing into the wall. Inside was a confusion of equipment, the uses for which he couldn't begin to understand, but he saw the hammer and grabbed it at once. It had a long handle and a heavy head, flat at one end and rounded into a steel ball at the other. He gave it a practice swing and nodded. Also in the locker, clipped to one side, was another flashlight. After testing it, he shoved it in his waistband.

Cautiously, he approached the interior hatch and put his light through the opening. Another workshop was beyond, appearing much like this one, with yet another open hatch on its far wall, opposite where Michael was standing. Again, nothing moved.

Michael went back to a worktable and crouched behind it, peering around one end at the hatch through which he had entered. It was damp down here, and he shivered, his ankle aching. Everything smelled of the sea, and death. After months aboard the aircraft carrier, the ten-year-old had become accustomed to the stench of death, but down here it was different, sour, more *corrupt* somehow, though he couldn't quite articulate that word. *Extra* dead, he decided.

He was nervous about his flashlight beam but didn't dare allow himself to be completely in darkness, so he held the lens close against his stomach to reduce the glare. He was breathing slower now.

Wind and Denny had gotten out, he was sure of that. *They would tell a grown-up, and people would come looking for him, wouldn't they? His dad would come. He'd be pissed, but he would come. And maybe Father X too. How would they find him? It didn't matter, they would. All he had to do was stay put and keep quiet.*

He froze as there was the sound of something thumping against the outer hatch, followed by the creak of a handle being lifted.

Rosa and Tommy's flashlights cut through the darkness, Tommy in the lead with his light clamped against the forward stock of his assault rifle. Rosa held her own light, and the Glock in the other hand. Wind was pressed against her, gripping the medic's scrubs in two fists.

So far they had yet to encounter any of *Nimitz*'s former crew and had seen none of the slimy puddles the girl described. Wind led them to the safety meeting room, and had to bite back tears when she saw the picture Michael had drawn, and which she'd smeared with her sleeve. She wished she hadn't done that.

"Through there," she whispered, pointing across the room. Tommy advanced on an open hatch, poking his light and rifle muzzle down another passageway.

"You're sure, honey?" Rosa asked, and the girl nodded.

They went through, moving carefully down a corridor where voices at play had only recently echoed. Within minutes, they came upon a deck surface streaked with water and putrescence.

"It's seawater," Tommy said, sniffing.

Rosa wrinkled her nose. "They're coming up from flooded compartments."

"It almost got us right here," Wind said, near tears again. "Michael made it chase him that way." They moved slowly in the direction Wind was pointing. Soon they came to the end of the hallway, with its choice of two closed hatches and a steel ladderway that only went down. Streaks of water and gore, as well as the imprint of a small sneaker, led to the stairs.

A pair of moans, sounding close together, echoed through the passageways, their direction unknown. The three of them stood at the top of the stairs for a moment, listening, and the moaning came again, accompanied by the soft thud of something hitting a hatch or a bulkhead.

"Take her back, Tommy," Rosa said.

He started to protest but then caught himself. They couldn't take the girl down there, and they couldn't send her back on her own. This area was now active. "Let's all go back and bring reinforcements," he said at last. "More guns and lights, maybe a map."

Rosa knew he was right, even as she shook her head. "Wind said she heard a scream; he could be hurt. By then it could be too late." Not her brightest idea, but the urgency of finding Michael moved her forward.

Tommy wanted to say more, but he also knew it was pointless to argue once she'd made up her mind. "I'll come back with help. Don't go too far."

Rosa didn't respond and started toward the stairs.

"Doc," Tommy said, handing her the M4 and two magazines. He unholstered his own pistol. "See you soon."

Rosa nodded, and as the orderly hurried away with Wind now

holding on to the edge of his scrubs, the medic aimed the light and
the rifle into the darkness and went down the ladderway. There was
a mess at the bottom, a spread of water and a sticky, yellow substance. A rotting, gray ear sat in the puddle, along with a piece of
what might have been scalp with some hair still attached to it. A
dead thing had come down hard here, and the marks on the floor
indicated it had crawled to its feet and headed to the right. She saw
no fresh blood, a very good sign, and was even more relieved when
she saw a pair of wet sneaker prints headed in the same direction.

She advanced with her light and rifle leading, trying to move on
her toes and flinching each time her rubber soles made a loud *squeak*
on the metal floor, reminding her of the echoing noises made in a
school gymnasium. A closed hatch on the right was marked *CATA-
PULT ENGINE ROOM*, but she had no interest in it. The wet trail led
forward.

Rosa wanted to call out to the boy, the sound of her voice perhaps keeping him from moving deeper into the ship. She decided
listening was better, and following the trail. The darkness was like a
heavy blanket all around her as she moved through it, kept at bay
only by the beam of white light. More hatches went by, many with
only numbers stenciled on them.

A rasp came from behind her and she wheeled, putting the light
on the passage. The beam extended a long distance, but it revealed
nothing in the corridor. Turning back, she saw something lying on
the deck about twenty feet away and moved slowly toward it. A rotting corpse in a blue uniform, long dead. Streaks of water and gore
showed where a drifter had stumbled over it.

Rosa thought about all the water. The thing she was following
must be waterlogged, dripping constantly, the pressure of movement forcing liquids out of its tissue. Had it been submerged somewhere, and found a way out? Hundreds of *Nimitz* crewmen were
still unaccounted for, and the hunting parties had encountered only
a few of the creatures they called *wet ones*. Was the bulk of the dead

crew in these flooded areas? There had certainly been speculation. Rosa hadn't expected to be the one to prove the theory, and certainly not alone. She knew she was no hero, and she was frightened, her heart tripping at an accelerated rate. She didn't want to be here, but Michael didn't, either, and she couldn't leave him to face his fate alone, not a child, not anyone. She would bring him out.

The rasping came again, followed by a wet gurgle, and Rosa turned spun once more. There it was, a woman in khaki stained almost black, the front of her shirt torn away to reveal savaged gray flesh, and an open chest cavity where white bone gleamed amid wet, black organs. She was pale, like the belly of a fish, and her eyes were bulging white orbs. Lips peeled back, and she hobbled down the corridor toward Rosa.

The medic put the rifle to her shoulder and sighted, resting the green pips of the combat sight on the woman's head. She took a deep breath, thought about the coming noise, and then tensed on the trigger.

A boy's scream, Michael's, rebounded down the passageway behind her, making her jump. The shot went wide, the bullet whispering through limp hair at the side of the corpse's head, the gunshot echoing. The scream came again, and Rosa gritted her teeth, aiming, firing. A wet mass exploded onto the bulkhead, and the creature sagged to the deck. Rosa turned, searching the corridor, and saw an intersection up ahead. She ran for it.

Had he made a sound? Could it smell him through the steel, follow his scent? Michael put his flashlight beam on the opening hatch, his hand trembling as he crouched frozen at the end of the worktable. The waterlogged zombie that had been pursuing him from the start pushed the steel oval aside and stumbled over the knee knocker, white eyes reflecting the light. But it wasn't alone. A corpse that looked withered and mummified, dressed in coveralls, followed it in, with a third that simply looked rotten pressing close behind.

Michael bolted for the hatch to the next workshop, and the trio let out a chorus of moans. He heard them banging against tables as they hurried after him, and the boy raced through this new room, putting his light on the next open hatch, speeding toward it. He ducked and leaped at the same time, clearing the knee knocker and avoiding the low overhead frame as he burst into a third workshop.

A corpse came at him from the right, a withered thing with a ball cap still on its head. It growled and lunged, raking his shoulder with dirty, ragged fingernails. Michael screamed, felt his flesh tear, and dodged left, smacking his hip painfully into a worktable. The creature snarled and galloped at him, catching the back of his shirt in one hand, teeth snapping within inches of the boy's ear. Michael screamed again, jerking free.

There was an open hatch to the right, but yet another creature was coming through it, tripping over the knee knocker but quickly getting back to its feet. Hungry moans came from the middle compartment, and the trio stumbled through the hatch as the thing with the ball cap pawed its way down the length of a worktable. Michael's flashlight threw spastic beams of light, and in every direction were milky eyes staring out of dead faces, and snapping teeth.

To his left, one wall of the room was stacked high with eight-foot lengths of loose steel pipes, held back by canvas straps. Directly beneath the pipes was an open, black rectangle in the floor: another stairway down.

There were five of them in the workshop now, coming around both sides of the last table where Michael was, the ball cap zombie croaking and scrabbling up onto its surface. All were snarling as they closed in for the kill.

Michael let out a whimper and hurried down the stairway.

ELEVEN

Xavier looked down from the superstructure catwalk using Stone's binoculars. Passing under the Bay Bridge and coming toward the carrier's port side was a boat similar to the rigid inflatable boats carried on *Nimitz*. Its hull was gray with an orange-and-blue stripe, Coast Guard colors, and a man piloted the craft from a central wheel station. There looked to be fewer than a dozen people aboard, all but the helmsman hunched against the spray and wind beneath blankets and ponchos. A square, white piece of fabric flew from a radio antenna.

"Too far to see if they have weapons," Stone said, standing beside the priest.

The chief arrived on the catwalk a minute later, puffing from running up more than eight flights of stairs. He was a compact man, fit and with close-cropped hair silvering at the temples. Chief Gunner's Mate Liebs was one of the Navy men Calvin and his group had rescued from a dry-goods locker during the taking of *Nimitz*, and the man had since proven to be a dependable person to have around, now part of *Nimitz*'s leadership core and a skilled zombie hunter. He was also in charge of weapons training and overall ship defense.

"What do we have?" Liebs asked, and Xavier handed him the binoculars. After a moment the man said, "Well, we talked about this, didn't we?"

They watched the boat approach.

"Stone," the gunner's mate said, "find me a bullhorn."

"Aye-aye, Chief," the young man said, disappearing back into the bridge. He had become something of a right hand to the Navy man, carrying out any assignment without complaint, paying attention to what he was being taught, and growing increasingly proficient with a variety of weapons. It was clear to see the chief liked the boy.

"Yes, we did," Xavier said at last, gripping the catwalk railing and staring at the shapes huddled in the small craft. It had only been a matter of time, and the fact that refugees had not tried to make their way out here before now was a chilling reminder of how little human life remained in the Bay Area. Both men on the catwalk knew people would come eventually, though, and there had been not only discussions on how it was to be handled, but talk on a more philosophical and moral level.

The Alameda survivors had what anyone living in this postapocalyptic world would want: a fortress, one with high walls and ringed with water; a place with stockpiles of food and water; medical facilities and weaponry; and most importantly power. *Nimitz* was an island sanctuary where the dead could not reach them, or so outsiders would think, not knowing of the infestation that remained aboard. People who had survived this long would be no strangers to deprivation, fear, and death. To them, *Nimitz* would look like paradise. The question was, were they willing to share that safety, become part of a community of trust, and work toward a common goal? Or would they want to take it for themselves, preying upon those already aboard?

The simplest and perhaps safest solution was not to permit any-one else to enter their world. This was Chief Liebs's opinion, coming at the problem with a straightforward, military pragmatism. His strategy was difficult to argue with; it worked. But there had been argument—lively discussion was more like it, because those who had participated in the conversation trusted the others and respected their opinions. That talk had taken place in the admiral's conference room not long after *Nimitz* was taken, as the dead were continually being hunted down and life was taking on a semblance of normalcy.

"It's like Skye has said repeatedly," Chief Liebs said. The young woman to whom he was referring had been sitting on a leather sofa, leaning against Carney. "With the dead on board," the chief continued, "every one we destroy moves the odds in our favor. This is as simple and direct as that, math and logic. If we don't let anyone else aboard, we don't run the risk of inviting in people who will be hostile."

"You're so wise," Carney had whispered into Skye's ear. She gave him an elbow shot to the stomach.

"What if Angie had been like that?" Big Jerry asked, the rotund, former stand-up comic now turned ship's cook. He wore a black medical cam boot and a knee brace, souvenirs of the battle for *Nim-itz* that he would have for the rest of his life. "If she hadn't taken in strangers at the firehouse, a lot of us wouldn't be here."

Angie West, the reality TV star who'd saved so many lives with her knowledge of firepower and had become a leader within their group, was still in sick bay when the meeting took place, recovering from multiple, close-range gunshot wounds inflicted by the late TC Cochoran. TC had been Carney's murderous San Quentin cellmate and was now the *late* TC because of Skye's well-placed bullet.

"I know it's a hard line to take," said Chief Liebs, "but it's the simplest answer, and it's the only one that guarantees the ship won't be compromised."

"That doesn't make it the right answer, though, Chief," Evan said. He was sitting across the table, Maya close to him. "What Jerry said is true for all of us. Calvin's family took me in, Rosa took Father Xavier in, and we all sort of accepted one another that night when we came together on the airfield." He smiled at the Navy man. "You and your shipmates would still be trapped in a locker if someone hadn't shown you some trust, right, Chief?"

Liebs shook his head and grinned.

Xavier was at the head of the table. He'd been reluctant to sit there, as he didn't like the superiority it might imply. Everyone on board had either openly or silently placed him in charge, and the Navy men had begun calling him *Skipper*, a term of genuine respect given to officers by enlisted sailors and Marines. He'd come to accept the responsibility without complaint, but he knew he was no commanding officer, and this was by no means a dictatorship. Any decisions made would be agreed upon by the group. It was their lives at stake, and for many of them, the lives of their families.

The priest listened to the conversation, pleased with the thoughtful debate, and was once again reminded that these were good people gathered here with him. For that reason, it was even more important that they be protected, ruthlessly if need be, a thought that was at odds with his priest's calling and yet felt absolutely right to the man.

"If refugees come to us," said Rosa, sitting on Xavier's left and looking weary, "they could bring skills we don't have within the group. Another medical person, perhaps. Technical skills that could make this place run better."

"Perhaps even a person with rudimentary culinary skills," offered Vlad, and that got a laugh. Big Jerry put on a pretended hurt face, and the Russian flashed him a homely grin.

Rosa laughed as well. "Maybe we could find someone who understands high-tech communication better than we do, or an engine mechanic, a dentist even. God knows none of you want me in your mouth with steel instruments."

A few of them silently wished for a person with bomb disposal skills, someone who could safely neutralize and get rid of the nuclear weapons still down in the ship's magazines. Although Chief Liebs assured them the devices were safe, they all knew how close they had come to being incinerated by a madman, and the mere presence of those weapons on board was a chilling and frequent reminder.

"It doesn't matter what they know how to do," Rosa said, as the discussion about theoretical refugees went on. "We can teach them, and every pair of hands makes us stronger."

There was nodding at that, and even a shrug of acknowledgment from Chief Liebs.

"There's also the moral question," said Evan, and all eyes turned to the priest at the end of the table.

Xavier gave them a small smile and gestured back at the writer-turned-helicopter-pilot. "You brought it up, Evan. Morality isn't only for the clergy. You're just as qualified to speak on the matter."

The young man frowned at that but then looked at the group. "We've all pretty much agreed that this thing is global, and we've seen life *erased* right in front of us. I couldn't even guess at what the ratio of living to dead might be now. A hundred thousand to one? More, probably? How can we see that, see what's become of us as a species, and *not* try to protect our own? By that I mean the living."

The others listened, and Maya watched his face closely.

"We know the dead mean us nothing but harm, and they can't be reasoned with in any way. This," Evan said, making a gesture to include everyone in the room, "doesn't happen with them. There's no reasonable discussions, no questions about right and wrong. To them, a gathering like this isn't a rational debate where ideas are heard and respected, it's a buffet." He placed a palm on his chest. "*We're* the only ones who do that, living people. We have to save that whenever we can, seek it out and protect it."

Smiles greeted him around the table. Xavier said, "I sure hope you're still writing, Evan. You should write *that* down."

The young man blushed, and Maya hugged him.

"I feel much as Evan does," said Xavier. "He's more articulate than I am, and the only thing missing from his speech was a soundtrack." There was more laughter. "But I think he said it very well. If we're not going to try to shelter what life remains out there, but simply hide here and keep from dying, then what's the point? No one in this room is a selfish person."

Although there were plenty of seats at the conference table, Calvin had chosen to sit on a chair against the wall. He hadn't spoken until now, and when he did, his voice was as dry and hollow as a prairie wind blowing through an abandoned house. "Keeping our loved ones alive isn't being selfish. People died to get us this far. Let's not forget what they sacrificed so we could be safe."

Maya felt her heart break as she watched the words on her father's lips, and she squeezed Evan's hand.

"You're right, Cal," Xavier said, wanting to go to the man, but instead he remained seated. "And there will be others out there deserving of that safety. Everyone here has put themselves at risk for others. Some have sacrificed all," he said, looking directly at Calvin. "Now those strangers you fought to save are your family."

They were quiet for a while, and then Chief Liebs spoke up. "I don't disagree with anything that's been said here, and I don't think anyone is being naïve about the potential dangers. But what if it turns out that strangers we welcome in mean to do us harm?"

Xavier spoke in a flat voice that brought a chill to the room. "Then we destroy them."

Is that what we'll need to do now? Xavier thought, standing on the superstructure's catwalk and watching the boat come in. *Friend or foe?*

Stone returned with the bullhorn and handed it to the chief. Liebs looked at the priest. "Like we decided?"

Xavier nodded.

The chief waited until the tiny boat motored in closer, watching it slow. "That's close enough," he called, and the launch came to a drifting stop. He counted ten people inside, with no space for anyone to hide. "Where did you come from? How are you armed?"

The pilot of the launch looked up at the high superstructure and made a cutting motion across his neck, then extended his arms in an exaggerated shrug.

"They can't communicate back at this distance," said Xavier.

Liebs triggered the bullhorn again. "Move to the stern. Tie off at the swimmer's platform but do not get out of your boat. We'll come down to meet you. We'll want to see your hands when we arrive. No weapons, understand?"

The pilot nodded and gave a thumbs-up, then steered the little boat toward the rear of the aircraft carrier.

"Let's get into position," said Xavier.

Stone and Mercy, the hippie woman who not only had survived alongside Calvin during the capture of the carrier but had turned into an efficient killer, took their places on the ship's fantail. Here, on the vast deck that was exposed to the sea through a wide, rectangular opening, a place where jet engines had once been tested, they were able to aim their rifles down in an unobstructed view of anything approaching the swimmer's platform at the waterline below. If these new arrivals showed aggression, Mercy and Stone would fill their little boat with automatic fire. Using the handheld Hydra radios, they reported that the small Coast Guard launch was tied up alongside the thirty-two-foot Bayliner and police patrol boat still tethered there since the assault. Everyone was showing their hands, they reported, and none were holding weapons.

From within, Xavier opened the hatch to the swimmer's platform, the door through which their assault teams had first entered the carrier months ago. Chief Liebs, wearing body armor and aiming an M14 rifle, stepped slowly out onto the platform. Calvin moved out next, also in armor and pointing his Canadian assault rifle. Xavier joined them, leaving two armed hippies in the compartment to his rear.

The priest eyed the group in the boat. They were a wet, bedraggled bunch: six bearded men, three women with tangled hair, and a toddler sitting on one of the women's knees, crying. They all looked thin and were clearly malnourished. The launch pilot was the only one standing. He was short and broad, and it looked as if he had shaved his head with a knife blade instead of a razor. He wore a ratty blue turtleneck sweater.

"Who are you people?" Xavier asked.

The launch pilot spoke. "Former Coast Guard, mostly, with a few civilians we rescued."

"Where did you come from?"

The man gestured to the northwest. "We were on a cutter. The supplies ran out and there was a mutiny; the ship went down. We managed to get away in this."

Xavier stared at the man, who suddenly seemed surprised. "Oh, no . . . we didn't mutiny," the man said. "We supported the captain, but there were more of them. The ship went down just off the mouth of the bay."

"And your captain?" the priest asked.

"Murdered. We came into the bay looking for a safe place to beach." The launch pilot shook his head. "But the dead are everywhere, and there's no place to land. Then we saw this thing, saw your helicopter." His shoulders fell. "Please, we don't have anywhere else to go."

Chief Liebs and Calvin said nothing, and Xavier kept looking at the launch pilot. "Are you armed?"

The man nodded. "We have a rifle, two handguns, and a few knives. It's all on the deck of the boat, and no one is going to touch them."

The priest took a deep breath. If he went forward now, he'd be putting their plans to the ultimate test. He didn't care much to hear about a violent mutiny, especially not knowing on which side these people had actually been. But then would someone with harmful intentions even mention something like that? Wouldn't a simpler lie suffice and not put prospective new hosts on their guard? The story had a ring of truth, but how loud was that ring? If Xavier turned them away, what sort of man would he be? He looked at the crying child, his mother hugging him close.

"If you come aboard," Xavier said, "you'll all do exactly as you're told, and answer all our questions. That's the price just to get in. Staying will mean additional agreements."

"We will," said the launch pilot.

"Everyone will be strip-searched, one at a time, as you enter. Your weapons and all your bags and possessions will be confiscated for now."

"We understand," the man said. "We don't want trouble."

Xavier said something to Liebs, who stepped back through the hatch. Calvin remained on the platform, rifle aimed at the boat's occupants. The priest pointed to the launch pilot. "You first."

The man climbed onto the platform and approached slowly, arms still raised. Then he cautiously extended a hand. "Thank you."

Xavier hesitated, then shook it. "What's your name?"

The man gave him a smile. "Charlie."

TWELVE

When the Seahawk reached El Cerrito, Evan turned slightly north-west and began following the water's edge of South Richmond, dropping to two thousand feet and slowing to one hundred miles per hour. Gourd had gotten the weather radar working and reported a rain system heading in from the west. He said he saw no lightning strikes. Evan had flown in rain before, but only with Vladimir in the co-pilot seat. He might have to cut this trip short. Still, the front was a ways off, and he still had some flight time before it arrived.

At this altitude and speed, they both had a good look at what was below them. Most of Richmond had burned, and that was no surprise. The tank farms at its western edge had ruptured during an earthquake last fall, and with no one to control the outbreak of fire, the blaze set off row after row of fuel tanks. Winds from the Pacific pushed the conflagration east, where it devoured the industrial areas and rail yards before moving on to consume Richmond itself. Below and to the north, the city appeared as a blackened grid.

The Navy bird passed over Marina Bay, a place of charred docks, gutted multimillion-dollar homes, and no boats of any kind. Anything that once floated there had either sailed away or been scuttled by fire. The chopper crossed a stretch of water and then overflew a large peninsula neighborhood that the super-rich once called home, their mansions now enormous shells surrounded by charcoal lawns and burned trees.

"You ready?" Gourd asked over the helmet intercom.

"Ready for what?"

The co-pilot laughed. "To be a daddy, dumbass."

"I'm nervous," Evan said. "Diapers and formula aren't standard issue on aircraft carriers."

"Those are just logistics," Gourd said. "Maya can feed it, and any piece of cloth can be cut and folded into a diaper. People were having babies long before Huggies came along."

"I guess."

"You're still nervous, though," Gourd said. "I get it. I'd be scared shitless."

Evan thought about it. "I'm not worried about Maya; I know she'll be a great mom. And I'm not worried that the baby will be born with . . ." He trailed off.

"Be born deaf?" Gourd adjusted a knob on the weather radar. "And if it is, that'll be okay too."

"I know," said Evan. "That's not it. It's this world. What kind of life will it have?"

They were both quiet for a while as a dead community slid past beneath them, and Evan banked northwest again, still following the coastline. Finally Gourd spoke. "There's got to be pregnant women who survived out there." His voice was subdued. "Not many of them will have what we have. How hard would it be having a kid in *that*?" He waved at the windscreen. "What kind of life will that be, and for how long?"

"I'm not whining," Evan said, but still he felt ashamed. His son or daughter was going to be born in safety, under medical care, with both parents still living. It would be a better life than probably any child out there, he decided, and the thought was both sobering and sad.

"I know you're not," said Gourd. "I wasn't saying that. *I* feel guilty sometimes, thinking if I could trade places with some mother or family out there, let them live on the ship . . . I think the reason I took Vlad's offer to learn how to fly was so that maybe someday I could put my bird down somewhere and actually rescue someone, you know?"

Evan didn't know if that made him feel better or worse, but he was leaning toward the latter. Gourd knew him pretty well, and said, "Your only mission is to protect that family of yours, buddy. You put your ass on the line to make a safe place for them, along with a lot of other people. Don't be anything but happy about that." He slapped his friend's knee across the cockpit. "You're going to be a good daddy."

Better than mine, Evan thought, remembering the fights between him and his father in the years following his mother's death. Dad called him a loser who didn't want to work. Evan shouted that he didn't want a pointless, nine-to-five grind like his old man, wasting his life. Dad called him a bum. Evan said his father might as well have already been dead for how worthless his life had become. All words that could never be taken back, and the last words spoken between them had been in anger.

Will *I be a better father?* he wondered. *Was Dad that much of a shit?* The man had lost his wife of twenty-five years and was left with a son he didn't understand, and who *wouldn't* try to understand *him*. Evan once told Father Xavier that the end of the world had clarified things and put them into perspective. Now he realized it had clarified something else: *regret*. He would never have the chance to talk to his dad again, to say he was sorry for the things he'd said and done. If he truly was to be a good father, he would have to ensure that neither he nor his child left this world having regrets about the other, and there could be no unspoken words. Evan decided that if nothing else, that was a worthy task for a man.

The shattered, circular remains of petrochemical tanks swept past, and where rail lines wove through the industrial area, entire freight trains had been welded to the tracks by the intensity of the heat. Evan thought about the temperature required to do that and thought surely even the dead couldn't have survived those flames.

"So, Uncle Gourd," Evan said, brightening his tone, "are you ready to change shitty diapers?"

Gourd laughed. "Hell yes! Bring 'em on!"

"Oh, you're so full of shit."

"No, man," said Gourd, "I'm all in. For you and Maya? Anything. Babies bring joy, my friend."

"Wow," said Evan, "that is some seriously girly talk for a chopper pilot."

Gourd laughed again. "You know I'm still a flower child at heart, right?"

The Seahawk flew over the eastern end of the Richmond–San Rafael Bridge. It, like the highway that approached it, was snarled with motionless vehicles, a silent, dead river of metal that looked out of place against the beauty of the late-afternoon sun on the water.

"Hello," Evan said softly, slowing the bird.

"What do you have?" Gourd asked, his voice professional again.

"Port side, out where the bridge starts to rise in elevation so ships can get under it." He stayed over water and descended to five hundred feet, bringing the Navy bird into a hover and rotating left so the cockpit was facing what he had seen.

"What is that, a cargo ship?" Gourd asked, unzipping a breast pocket and pulling out a small pair of binoculars.

They were at least a half mile away. "I don't know," said Evan, "but it wasn't there when we flew up here last week."

"Maybe it broke loose of its mooring somewhere and drifted up against the bridge supports?" his co-pilot offered.

"Maybe," Evan said, but he didn't think so. The vessel was clearly *not* touching any of the supports. He worked to hold the Seahawk in a hover while maintaining altitude, the effort reminding him yet again that he was a long way from being a skilled pilot.

Through his binoculars, Gourd saw a ship sitting motionless, very close to the bridge, its bow pointed away from them so that the vessel rested perpendicular to the span. It also just happened to be positioned so that the wide strip of shadow cast by the bridge lay right down the length of the vessel. If they had been going any faster, they might have missed it. Gourd didn't believe the shadow concealment was an accident. It was even harder to see because someone had painted the ship black; not a professional job, but thorough enough to cover most of the hull and superstructure. Patches of white poked through in only a few places.

Gourd focused, seeing some movement on deck, and not the slow, stiff-legged gait he had come to expect from the dead. The ship had a sleek look to it, and that was definitely a helicopter deck toward its stern, butted up against a pair of hangar bays.

"That's not a cargo ship," Gourd said. "It looks milit—"

Evan caught movement. Something on the deck above the ship's helicopter bays swiveled, something tall and mechanical, something with a barrel. "Oh, shit," Evan breathed, throwing the chopper hard to the right. A string of red, glowing shapes reached out from the ship, and a second later Evan's bird was filled with a deep rattling and the sounds of tearing metal as rounds tore through the troop compartment and shredded the tail. The aircraft shuddered, still turning away, and Evan applied full power. Warning buzzers and flashing lights filled the cockpit as more tracers blurred past the windscreen, several thudding into the turbines overhead. There was a squealing sound, a *boom*, and smoke poured into the cockpit. The bird staggered in the air, now pointed and moving east, starting its fall.

"Mayday, mayday," Evan called on the *Nimitz* frequency. "Navy zero-two is going down, mayday, mayday."

The Seahawk spun, both turbines torn apart, the bird's plunge slowed only because of the blades still spinning with their own momentum, what Vladimir had called *autorotation*. The aircraft was going down at a steep angle nonetheless, crossing the shoreline now and headed inland, the ground rushing up fast.

"Navy zero-two, Mayday, Mayd—"

The Seahawk vanished into the burned ruins of Richmond.

Patrick Katcher sat in the communication center behind *Nimitz*'s bridge. His eyes widened as he heard the tense transmissions, and then he saw the blip on his radar scope that was Navy zero-two blink off the screen.

"Navy zero-two, this is *Nimitz*," he called.

Static answered.

"*Nimitz* calling Navy zero-two. Evan, come in."

No one answered, and the blip did not reappear on the screen. He reached for the intercom phone and made an all-ship announcement for Father Xavier to call communications *immediately*. He was going to have to report the unthinkable to the skipper.

Evan and Gourd had crashed.

HERE THERE
BE MONSTERS

THIRTEEN

January 12—Nimitz

They were gathered in the officer's mess, the new arrivals kept separated from the main mess hall used by the residents of *Nimitz*. Big Jerry had already brought out coffee, along with a hot chocolate for the toddler, and was now in back putting together soup and sandwiches. The refugees sat at two tables, wrapped in dry Navy blankets, drinking their coffee quietly. Xavier and Chief Liebs had pulled chairs close to them, while Mercy stood at a pair of double doors with her assault rifle slung around her neck. Calvin sat on a table midway toward the other entrance, watching them closely with his rifle across his knees.

"We tried to help people when it started," Charlie said. "We really did. But we had so few supplies, and there were so many people at the water's edge, everywhere we went." He looked down, shaking his head slowly. "We couldn't save them all. And we didn't find out about the bites until later, after we brought someone aboard." He looked up at Xavier. "We lost half the crew. They just kept turning, and we . . . we had to . . ." He looked down again. "They were our friends."

The priest watched him. Spending most of his life in poverty and crime-stricken areas, where everyone always seemed to be trying to get over on the other person, he thought he had developed a good nose for deception. He wasn't seeing any of that here, just a man reliving painful memories. But he had been fooled before.

"Tell me about this mutiny," Xavier said.

Charlie nodded. "We were out there for months, and putting in to shore to find supplies was dangerous, worse every time we tried it. We lost more people, and after a while we didn't dare go ashore anymore." He sipped his coffee. "The food and water ran out; people were hungry, angry, blaming the captain. A young female officer started it, started the mutiny. She promised the crew she would find them food. Lots of people sided with her, people with weapons."

"And you?" the priest asked.

"We tried to stop them," Charlie said, "tried to talk them out of it. The female officer killed one of us, a ship's cook, just a kid. She did it to make a point. Then the fighting started."

Not far away, Calvin listened closely, watching for signs that the man was lying or holding something back. Chief Liebs was watching closely as well.

"What happened?" Xavier prodded.

Charlie told them it happened fast, and was so confusing that he wasn't sure of all the details. There was a lot of gunfire, people running and screaming. He said he saw the female officer shoot down the captain, also a woman. "I killed a man," he said softly, looking up at the priest. "He was guarding the launch, and I shot him. He was part of the mutiny, but he was also a friend. I didn't have a choice." He took a deep breath and gestured at the others. "We took the launch and got out, trying to get away from the ship. Someone shot at us, but they missed."

"We heard an explosion," one of the women added, saying her name was Ava. She was the one holding the toddler, who despite the blanket and hot cocoa continued to squirm and whimper. "Something on board blew up," she said.

Charlie bobbed his head. "Probably the magazine. We saw the ship break in half, and then it sank fast."

Xavier looked at Chief Liebs for confirmation. The chief shrugged. "A magazine explosion could do that."

"We . . . we didn't go back to look for survivors," Charlie said. "We should have, I know, but we were afraid they might be mutineers and would take away our boat. We just kept going."

"And then you saw us?" Xavier asked.

"We saw your helicopter first. It was taking off. That's when we knew people were still on this thing." He looked into the priest's eyes. "Please let us stay."

Xavier pursed his lips. "It will have to be discussed. But you're safe here for now."

A speaker on the wall of the officer's mess urgently requested that Father Xavier call the communications center.

"Father?" said Charlie. "You're a priest?"

Xavier nodded as he rose and went to a phone. Liebs looked at Charlie. "What's your rate and rating?"

"Petty officer third, bosun's mate," Charlie replied. "You're Navy, right?"

Liebs nodded. "Chief gunner's mate."

Charlie extended a hand. "Nice to meet you, Guns." The use of the nickname made Liebs smile a bit and confirmed that if nothing else was true, the man was a seaman as he claimed, albeit a bit old to only be a petty officer third. Still, who was he to judge another man's career movement?

The double doors closest to Calvin pushed open, and there stood Tommy in his scrubs, wearing a backpack and holding a pistol. The orphan girl Wind was close at his side. The orderly saw Xavier talking on a phone, saw Calvin, and waved them over frantically.

Xavier hung up the handset, frowning deeply, and moved to speak with Tommy. Calvin joined them a moment later, and Xavier said, "Chief, I need you too." Liebs gave the new arrivals a long look. They were heads down, warming up and drinking their coffee, so he went to the three men.

"Comm reports that Evan's chopper is down," Xavier said, keeping his voice low. "He made a distress call, then went off the radar somewhere over Richmond."

Liebs cursed. "Did he activate his beacon?" the gunner's mate asked. "If so, we can find him. I'll go pick him up in a RIB boat."

"I don't even know if he's alive," Xavier said. "Can you handle this?"

The chief nodded and pushed through the doors, hurrying down the passage and taking Wind with him. This was no place for children right now.

The priest turned and gripped Calvin by both shoulders. "Michael is lost somewhere in the bow. Rosa has gone looking for him." That was as far as he got. Calvin swore, pulled free of the priest's hold, and shoved through the doors yelling, "Where are they, Tommy?"

"Cal, wait!" Xavier and Tommy both went after him.

I should get a fucking Academy Award, Chick thought, standing as soon as the men were out of the room. "Getting more coffee," he called, waving his mug at Mercy. Standing at the far doors, the woman began lifting her assault rifle.

Ava, the woman who had spoken to back up Chick's story, stood as well, still carrying the little boy and bouncing him as he continued to whimper. She walked toward Mercy.

"Sit down," Mercy ordered, swinging her rifle barrel toward the woman.

"You're going to scare him," Ava said, still walking toward her. "We're about to have a potty emergency. I need to take him to the bathroom."

Mercy's rifle wavered, and she looked back to the leader of the refugees. He had already disappeared into the back with his empty coffee mug.

"Please, he really needs to go," Ava said, stopping in front of Mercy. "Where's the bathroom?" Her right hand slipped under the blanket and crawled up under the boy's shirt to where she had taped an object to his back. The boy cried and tried to twist out of her arms. "Shh," Ava said, her hand closing on it. The crew of *Nimitz* had searched all of the adults, but nobody searched children.

Big Jerry looked up from a cutting board, where he was spreading mayonnaise on slices of bread. A package of ham slices was open beside him. Chick smiled as he approached, waving the empty mug. "Need a refill," he said.

The former stand-up comic smiled back. "Help yourself." He gestured to a big urn on a countertop.

"You folks have been really good to us," Charlie said, turning toward the counter but ignoring the coffee urn. Instead he plucked a butcher knife off a magnetic strip on the wall. Then he walked to the table, holding the knife low at his side. "That looks tasty," he said.

Jerry smiled again, then noticed the still-empty coffee mug in the man's hand. "You didn't get—"

Chick's right hand came in fast, and the big comic grunted, eyes going wide. "Hey . . ." he gasped, eyelids fluttering. Their faces almost touching, Chick gave him a grin.

Xavier caught hold of Calvin's arm in the hallway, his strength bringing the man to a halt. "Calvin, wait."

The aging hippie made a snarling sound and jerked his arm free. "Tommy, where *are* they?" he demanded again.

"They're in the bow," Xavier answered for him. "If you run off alone it's going to make things worse."

"That's my son."

"And we're going to find him," the priest said. "But we need to be smart, and go with a group." He looked at the man, at the new anguish stamped on his friend's face. "Maya needs to know about Evan. You should be the one to tell her."

Calvin's expression fell further as this new realization hit him. First Michael, and now his daughter would have to be told that her man, the father of her unborn child, might be dead. "Oh, God," Calvin whispered.

"We'll get through this," Xavier said. "I'll stay with you. We'll tell Maya, then we'll go get Michael and Rosa."

The hippie sagged against the bulkhead and put his face in his hands.

"Tommy," Xavier said, "go back into the officer's mess for a bit so Mercy isn't alone in there, okay?"

The orderly headed back down the hall.

"We're going to find him, Cal," Xavier said, taking his friend's shoulders once again. "Rosa might already have him. You know her, you know she'd give her life to protect him."

Calvin nodded, but when he took his hands away from his face, his eyes were filled with tears.

"Father . . ." Tommy's voice came from the mess hall doors, and Xavier turned to see the man standing there, his face pale. Xavier and Calvin went to him, and when they entered the room they saw that all the refugees were gone.

Except for the toddler, who was sitting abandoned on the floor and crying.

Mercy was crumpled against the wall in a pool of her own blood, next to the far doors. Her throat had been neatly slit by a straight razor, and her weapons were gone.

"Dear God," Xavier said, going to the child as Calvin knelt beside a woman he had known for years. Tommy just stared in shock. Then a moan came from the galley, and Big Jerry stumbled through swinging doors. He lurched into the mess hall, moving awkwardly in the knee brace. There was no color left to his eyes, and his apron was stained red. The worst of it was spreading from the point where a butcher's knife protruded, buried in his heart up to the handle.

Jerry made a croaking noise and started toward Xavier and the crying child. With a sob, Tommy used his pistol to put their friend to rest. By the doors, Mercy shifted and opened eyes that were cataract blue. Calvin used his big knife to finish her with a single, sharp thrust, letting out a sob of his own.

Calvin pointed the bloody knife at the priest. "You did this."

That was when the aircraft carrier began to tremble.

FOURTEEN

It was a foreshock, nothing compared to what was to come, but it was as strong as the quake that hit the Bay Area in 1989. Though it lasted only eleven seconds, its force was tremendous, and its violent tremor traveled up into *Nimitz* from the point where the bow of the ship was mired in silt at western Oakland's shallows. Positioned a little over a mile from the earthquake's epicenter deep under Alameda, the warship began to shudder. Everything shook, and the vibration swept through the ship. Anything not secured was thrown about, and many things that *had* been secured were shaken loose.

The foreshock was powerful enough to disrupt the silt bed that had held *Nimitz* to the bottom for so many months, and with a groan of steel grating against underwater rock, the current pushed the warship's bow loose and the entire vessel drifted sideways. It was at last free of the bottom, with steadily deepening water beneath its keel. Once again seawater poured in through the gashes in its hull, finding its way into forward compartments, and within minutes the aircraft carrier picked up another degree of list to the left and forward.

Untethered, and now at the mercy of the current, *Nimitz* began to move.

. . .

The dead were coming, thumping down the ladderway behind Michael as he ran down a dark passageway, gripping his hammer tightly, trying to keep the flashlight beam in front of him. His sneakers splashed through several inches of water, and each time he came down on his right foot, the twisted ankle caused a flare of pain that made him bite the inside of his cheek.

A short corridor to his left led to a hatch with *FORWARD BERTHING 4.07* stenciled above it. Milky eyes and a snarl waited at the hatch opening, and Michael kept going. Another short hall to his left, another berthing compartment from which came the sound of splashing. He let out a soft wail and ran on, the water to his shins now and slowing him down. From behind came a chorus of groans.

He turned right, then left at an intersection. The glare of his flashlight picked out a bloated, pale thing in a blue uniform hunching toward him, glazed yellow eyes reflecting the light. He backtracked and crossed the intersection, coming to a hatch marked *HANDLING GEAR*. Michael worked the handle and pushed through into a large chamber, where his light revealed seemingly endless coils of rope hanging on the walls, orange buoys, chains hung from hooks and still more rope coiled on the floor, these lengths thicker than one of his legs. There was water in here too, and he splashed through it, hurrying across the chamber, looking for a place to hide.

A figure moved awkwardly through the hatch behind him, its groan echoing in the room. Michael didn't dare to turn and put his light on it. He needed to find a way out, another hatch, a passageway, a ladder that would lead him up.

Something to his right rose from six inches of water, a woman with gray-and-white mottled skin, fluid drooling from her open lips. The flesh was sloughing off her fingers as she held on to a rope locker to help her stand. She gnashed her teeth.

Michael let out a cry and bolted left, away from her.

It was a stairway down to a forward magazine, an open rectangle set in the floor, just like the one he had used to get down to this deck. The space below was completely flooded, and the stairway opening was concealed beneath the six inches of seawater in the compartment. Michael ran into the opening without realizing where he was stepping, and plunged beneath the surface. His flashlight flew away, and he lost his grip on the hammer as he sank.

A pair of bloated corpses moved toward the opening from the chamber above.

Rosa was following the screams and came to a passageway with a pair of limping corpses in uniform heading for an open hatch on the left. She raised the M4 and fired, five times, six, seven before the pair went down. Without hesitating, she ducked through the open hatch and into a workshop.

Snarls echoed from an opening to her right, and she advanced with her light. Beyond was a second workshop, with another open hatch at the far side. A figure appeared in the light, a withered thing wearing a ball cap, and she shot at it, bullets sparking off the steel hatch frame before one found its mark. Shadowy movement came from the room beyond, and she went in.

It was a third workshop, one with countless lengths of pipe stacked and tied off against a bulkhead to the left. There were two corpses in here, both rotting and giving off a putrid stench, heading for a rectangular stairwell opening in the floor. Rosa fired again, the muzzle flash blinding in the black space, each echoing shot making her ears ring, the whine of a ricochet passing close by her head. Both creatures went down.

Michael had been here, she was sure of it. That was what had stirred up the dead. *Or had it been her earlier rifle fire?* No, she told herself, shaking her head as she switched out the M4's magazine for one that was fully loaded. *Follow your instinct. The dead were heading for that stairwell for a reason.* She did too.

Descending softly and cautiously, Rosa led with the light and the rifle muzzle, praying Michael wouldn't suddenly appear in its glare. She was wired so tight she might trigger a nervous shot into the boy without thinking. Midway down the steep risers, Rosa crouched and used her light to see what was below. There was a flooded passageway leading forward, ripples making her beam of light flicker on the surface. She raised the light and put it deeper into the corridor, picking out the backs of a pair of figures about twenty yards off, shadowy at the edge of her beam, facing away from her. They weren't moving, simply standing with their arms limp at their sides, heads tilted back and to the right.

They're scenting for Michael. Her hand clenched the rifle's pistol grip and she continued down. She was still on the stairs when the tremor rumbled up through her legs, growing in intensity, and then she was shaken right off her feet, thrown to the bottom and landing painfully in several inches of water, her flashlight bouncing away, throwing the area into pale shadows. A tremendous crash of metal came from above, and for a terrifying second she thought the ship was folding in on her. She saw a tangle of long, dark shapes tumbling down the stairway—pipes that had broken loose from the compartment above—and one shot at her like a medieval battering ram.

The medic jerked aside and tried to roll out of its path, sparing her body but unable to prevent the edge of the pipe from clipping her forehead. There was a flash of white and pain, and Rosa collapsed in the water, her unconscious form sagging against a length of pipe that had come to rest against her side.

The shaking went on, creating a deep grinding sound below, and then it ceased. Up the passageway from the motionless EMT, the pair of corpses that had been facing the epicenter lifted themselves from where they too had fallen. Heads turned toward the stairwell, and dead limbs began to move.

. . .

Rosa was on the pole again at the Glass Slipper Gentlemen's Club, white stage lights turning the crowd into faceless shadows, a Beyoncé song pounding from overhead speakers. She was in ridiculously high heels and peeled off first one side and then the other of her white doctor's coat, revealing her heavy breasts as the shadow crowd whistled and hooted. She did a turn on the pole and threw her head back, letting her long hair swing free.

Howls came from the crowd and she saw hands thrust forward into the stage lights, fingers clutching tens and twenties. *Money that will pay for school.* She executed another turn and coyly covered her breasts with one arm, then put her back to the pole and began sliding slowly into a crouch.

Shame was burning inside her, and only the heavy makeup prevented it from coloring her face. Not that anyone was looking at her face, she knew. The shadows moved, pushing against the edge of the stage as she slowly slid back up the pole. *It's for school. That's all this is.*

Then she thought, *A doctor's coat?* When had she ever used one of those in her act?

Jimmy's face appeared in the lights at the front of the crowd. Her EMT partner and former lover, a man she'd never really *stopped* loving. Gone now, turned like the rest. No, she didn't want him seeing this! He wasn't supposed to come to the club, they had an agreement. There was no color to Jimmy's face, and the ragged wound in his throat was colorless, like his eyes. *Oh, baby, you're hurt. You need a doctor.* She kept dancing. *Not much longer, honey, I promise. Another year at the most and school will be paid for.*

Rosa's mother appeared next to Jimmy. Even through the peeling and blackened skin, the expression on her face was one of hurt and humiliation. *No!* Rosa spun again, turning her backside in a slow circle toward the hands now turned gray and torn, still waving bills. *Mommy, you can't be here. You don't know about this.* Rosa began to cry, her tears making the heavy eyeliner run. Her mother said something, but Rosa couldn't hear it over the music.

A name came to her. *Michael. Was that one of her professors? No, he was Calvin's son. He was too young to be in the club.* But that wasn't right. He was lost and needed her. Her mother had vanished, but Jimmy began to climb onto the stage. So did the others, middle-aged men with rotting flesh falling off their bones, all of them waving money at her. *They're dead, Jimmy's dead, Michael's . . . no, he's alive, he needs me.* Rosa squinted. The lights were so bright. It was making her head hurt.

Rosa opened her eyes. She was lying in water, a cold length of steel pressed against her side, her head throbbing. In the muted glow of the fallen flashlight she saw a pale hand slide over the curve of pipe above her, followed by a fish-colored face with white eyes.

Her right hand went to her hip, found the butt of her automatic still in its holster, and jerked it free. She thrust out her arm and fired at point-blank range. The dead face burst open in a wet spray, and the zombie collapsed onto the pipe. She felt its stinking droplets on her cheeks. Another figure started over the pipe, and she shot this one too, holding up her other palm to shield her face from blowback. She hit the mark, and it slid back down the other side of the pipe.

A moment later she was on her feet and had retrieved her flashlight, splashing water into her face and wiping away the gore, praying she hadn't gotten any in her eyes or mouth. A wave of dizziness hit her and she fell to her knees in the water, supporting herself with one hand against a bulkhead to keep from going all the way down. Something warm ran into her eyes, and she wiped away blood, her fingers finding the gash in her forehead. *Had any of that thing's gore gotten into the wound?* When the dizziness passed, she panned the flashlight around, seeing a passageway that was empty for now. The ladderway above her was hopelessly choked with a snarl of steel pipe. There would be no exit by that route.

The medic took several minutes to bandage her head with supplies from the pack, swallowing a few pain relievers. The wound would need stitches, she knew, and was almost certain to get infected in this damp and rotting place, but there was no time to give it the attention it required. She crawled on her hands and knees in a circle, searching under the water until she found the M4. A quick inspection showed that instead of caving in her head, the pipe that had shot down at her hit the rifle instead, crushing it against the deck like a hammer on an anvil, bending the magazine receiver. The weapon was useless.

Standing now, waiting to see if the dizziness would return, Rosa aimed her light down the passageway again. It was the only way Michael could have gone. With her pistol held before her, the medic started down the corridor, shin-deep in seawater.

From somewhere in the distance came a deep, baritone gurgle as the crippled warship took on more of the San Francisco Bay.

Michael screamed as he plunged through the opening in the floor, then choked as he swallowed stagnant seawater. His arms flailed and he kicked violently, one hand rapping hard against metal, a foot connecting with something solid. He opened his eyes, but there was only darkness followed by the vicious sting of salt. He pushed off with one foot and propelled himself upward, through the stairwell opening. As his head broke the surface he sputtered, arms thrashing until he caught the edge of the opening and pulled himself against it, as if clinging to the rim of a swimming pool.

There was light coming from somewhere. He choked and spat, rubbing one fist at the burning in his eyes, straining to keep his face above the surface. His flashlight was lying submerged several yards away, glowing up through the brine, creating a sphere of gray in the otherwise black chamber. Michael started to pull himself out of the water but then froze.

Not three feet away, the bloated dead woman was facing him. Her arms were limp, and rivulets of water ran from her hair and mouth. The thing's head was tipped slightly back and tilted to one side. Michael tensed for the attack, but the creature simply stood there, unmoving.

The ten-year-old didn't understand what was happening but took advantage of the moment and moved hand-over-hand down the lip of the submerged stairwell opening, feet kicking free in the water below, until he reached the end farthest from the corpse. He planted his hands and prepared to lever himself up and out.

The foreshock hit the compartment, making the deck beneath his palms buck, and he let out a cry, trying to hold on. He felt his grip slipping, his body vibrating away from the edge. He kicked hard, hands scrabbling for a hold on the wet metal.

"Daddy, help me!"

The shaking stopped, and Michael was still holding on. He saw the woman's corpse turn its head and look at him with dead eyes, and water bubbled past her lips as she tried to make a sound.

Up yours! Michael planted his hands again to thrust himself clear. *I can outrun her, and maybe she'll fall into—*

Cold white fingers gripped his ankle from below and pulled. Michael let out a startled yelp and was ripped under into the inky depths.

FIFTEEN

Someone was stroking his face, light fingertip touches against his cheek. Evan's eyelids fluttered, and he winced at the change from dark to light. He turned his head toward the touches, and now the fingertips brushed his nose. His head was heavy, and he opened his eyes wider. Two fingers tapped at his face, an index and a middle, both encrusted with blood. The middle finger was badly fractured, bent at a forty-five-degree angle with white bone sticking out of a torn knuckle.

Evan squeezed his eyes shut and then looked again, not sure how to put together what he was seeing. He realized he was still belted into the Seahawk's pilot's seat, but the angle was wrong, crooked, and he was hanging against his harness. *Suspended. Sideways.* He willed his brain to work. The cockpit was lying on its right side, and so he, in the left seat, was suspended over the co-pilot. Below him, a man in flight gear with a red-smeared helmet had been crushed against the starboard fuselage, the instrument panel folding inward and pinning his legs at the hips. The man's right arm was bent back and lodged behind him, but his left arm was free, and it was this that reached up across the cockpit, fingertips barely able to touch Evan's cheek.

There was fresh blood on the left half of his friend's face, a growing splatter, and as he stared at it a drop of red hit the man's skin. Evan realized his nose was bleeding, dripping onto Gourd and driving the man crazy. *No, not a man, not anymore.*

Half of Gourd's face had been caved in, but the left side remained intact, pale and bloodless, and a murky brown eye rolled in the socket, looking up at Evan. Gourd gasped, and his teeth came together with a sharp click.

Evan closed his eyes, and the broken finger trailed across his forehead.

What happened? It came back quickly, the sight of the black ship hiding in the shadow of the bridge, a rear-facing gun firing at them, the Seahawk taking hits, going down, Evan unable to control it. He recalled an instant of seeing the ground rushing up at them, but he couldn't remember the impact. *Are we on fire?* His eyes snapped open. *No, just a smell of leaking fuel.*

He wondered how long he had been hanging in this position. It was uncomfortable, and his face felt heavy from the blood collected there. With a groan he lifted his head, moving it away from the groping fingers. Gourd let out a frustrated whine. *How badly am I hurt?* Evan looked around, seeing that his side of the cockpit had not folded like Gourd's, and he could see his legs and wiggle his feet. His right arm was wedged against his side, the gloved hand caught on a harness buckle. *Good thing too, or else it would have been dangling down into Gourd's face.* He wiggled those fingers, found they worked, and pulled his arm loose. His left arm was free, but when he tried to move it, a sharp pain raced up its length. *Broken wrist.* Evan shifted as much as he could. *Back feels okay, neck sore but rotating, breathing fine. Tell me I got out of this with only a fractured wrist and a bloody nose.*

But he wasn't out of this, he knew. He was still tangled in a downed chopper, hanging above a dead man, far from home. Drifters could be shuffling toward the crash site right now, he thought, but he was unable to see out of the spiderweb of fractured Plexiglas that had been the windscreen.

Another drop of blood smacked against Gourd's face, and the thing that had been his friend made a thick, huffing noise and pawed more frantically at Evan's face.

Think. What comes next? He had to get out of the wreckage. An image of Vladimir came to him, a scene of the two of them sitting on crates in *Nimitz*'s cavernous hangar deck, Navy zero-two parked in the background. Vlad loved his cigarettes, but he wouldn't smoke down here. The Russian was a fanatic about safety.

His mentor's voice spoke in Evan's head. *Listen to me carefully, Evanovich.* Evan always smiled when the man called him that. A Russian putting the *-ovich* at the end of a name made it a term of endearment. *You must understand that you are a* combat *pilot, and every time you leave this deck, no matter the reason, it is a* combat *mission. We are at war with the dead, yes? You must treat it as such. I will teach you combat survival. If your aircraft goes down over land, and you should somehow survive, you will be in enemy territory. This is no different than war in any other place. The enemy will seek to find your crash site, and this enemy does not take prisoners.*

The Russian had delivered the message without his usual sarcasm, and Evan hadn't forgotten it. That talk was the beginning of Vlad's survival training, and he was both particular and impatient with the details. Evan was forced to know every piece of equipment he carried, why it was important and how it was to be used. Vlad drilled him relentlessly.

I need to get clear of the wreck and activate my locator beacon. Evan unsnapped his helmet and took it off, hesitating for a moment before letting it drop onto his friend. Gourd grabbed it at once, pulled it to his mouth, and dragged his teeth across its surface, then

cast it aside and went back to reaching for Evan's face. Those fingertips were starting to annoy him now, and Evan batted the dead hand
aside. It came right back.

"Cut it out!" he shouted. It felt better to be angry with Gourd. It
covered up the sadness for his lost friend.

Evan was wearing a jumpsuit-style Nomex flight suit, designed
as an antiexposure garment. On top of this was a waist-length,
green flight jacket, and over it all was a bulky survival vest. How he
had complained about this thing, covered in pouches and gear, adding weight and bulk and making him feel like he was wearing a fat
suit.

Yes, it is a pain for your ass, Vladimir had said. *And no matter
what happens, you will never take it off. Not until your boots are back
on the deck of this aircraft carrier.*

First, he had to get out of his restraint harness. His left hand
went to the pouch where the webbing cutter was secured, a flat,
hooked tool made to slash through seat belts and parachute strands.
His hand stopped as soon as he touched it. *What would happen if he
cut himself free? Gravity would drop him right onto Gourd, and his
co-pilot would put him in a headlock and chew off his ear.*

He took a deep breath and reached his right hand beneath the
vest, inside his flight jacket, until it found the butt of his Sig Sauer
nine-millimeter. *I'm sorry, Gourd.* He pulled the weapon, batted the
reaching arm aside once more, and fired a shot into Gourd's helmet.
The arm dropped, and Gourd's head sagged to the side.

A moment later he had cut through the straps and was untan-
gling himself from the co-pilot's seat and the twice-dead thing still
belted into it. A glance into the rear troop compartment showed
that it had been torn in half and flattened, leaving no exit that way.
Instead he kicked out the broken windscreen in front of the co-pilot
and climbed out, gripping his pistol and holding his broken wrist
close to his body. It was throbbing, and the jolt of falling onto Gourd
hadn't made it better.

Hiroshima. That was the word that came to mind as Evan stood beside the Seahawk's wreckage and looked around. He remembered the photographs from textbooks in school: miles of destruction, piles of blackened rubble, and the burned trunk of an occasional tree. Everything was covered in black ash. He saw twisted metal skeletons that might have been fuel tanks or refinery structures, and to his right was a line of tanker cars that had detonated, their remaining carriages and wheels seared right to the rails. The only way he could tell this had been an industrial area in California was because it was marked as such on his map. Otherwise he might have been standing at the Hiroshima nuclear bomb detonation site on August 6, 1945.

Except then, the charcoal corpses had been frozen in death poses. Here, they were up and walking.

Evan saw them, only two at first and some distance off, but then he spotted three more moving in from the left, about a hundred yards off. They were hairless, sexless things without faces, crisped black and moving stiffly, pieces flaking off their bodies with each step. Why they didn't simply crumble to ash, Evan didn't know, but he sensed that no matter their condition, they would still be able to bite somehow, could still infect.

He withdrew a cell-phone-sized device in a hard, yellow plastic casing from a pouch on his survival vest, folded out the rubber antenna, and flipped the Activate switch. A blinking red light appeared on its face, and he tucked it back into the pouch, antenna protruding. The plastic-coated map showing their flight plan was still strapped to his right thigh, and he pulled it off, deciding his probable location. There, just north of the bridge and to the east, above Interstate 580, was Richmond's refinery and industrial sprawl. *Nimitz* was located twenty miles south, across the East Bay. He pulled a small compass from another pocket and took his bearings. The elevated concrete span of I-580 was to his south, and that would be his first waypoint.

A hollow moaning drifted across the charred terrain.

Holding his Sig and still cradling his wounded wrist, Evan looked back inside the chopper. Most of the aircraft had been torn away on impact and was nothing more than pieces scattered in who knew what direction. He wanted Gourd's M4, and the man's pack that would contain bottled water and snacks. He wanted the helicopter's first-aid kit. He found none of it.

Evan glanced at the approaching dead. There were no others in sight, but that could change. Ripping open another pouch on his vest, Evan pulled out a rolled length of fluorescent orange plastic, a signaling device that a Navy flier downed in water would use to show his position, clipping one end to his flotation vest and streaming the rest out across the surface. Using the survival knife attached to the vest's right shoulder, he cut a sufficient length of streamer and fashioned a sling for his broken wrist. The pressure came off at once, and he sighed.

Time to get moving.

He headed south, stepping carefully over cracked brick and cinder block as his boots kicked up a cloud of ash. A broken wrist he could deal with, but a broken ankle would be a death sentence.

Evan stopped suddenly, feeling foolish, and reached for the vest pouch containing his combat survival radio. Vlad would have cursed him blue for forgetting.

The flap was open, the pouch empty.

It had been there! He remembered the weight. Evan turned back toward the Seahawk's fuselage, thinking it must have popped out during the crash. The nearest trio of drifters was less than fifty yards away. *Still time.* Back at the cockpit, he climbed through the open windscreen once more and started searching. It was difficult with only one hand, and not being able to see out the windows made him nervous. Every heartbeat was like the tick of a clock.

He looked in the space where his legs had been, under the pilot's seat, all around the dead co-pilot. Then he stared at where the instrument panel had collapsed, crushing Gourd's legs and hips into its hollow. If the radio had bounced in there, then it was gone. He'd need power tools just to excavate the corpse enough to check, and he had neither the equipment nor the time. Evan was turning away when he stopped, wanting to scream at his own stupidity. Gourd had a vest too. He reached for the pouch, but saw that it, along with most of the man's right side, had been crushed and pinned under metal, including the place where Gourd's survival radio would have been.

Evan closed his eyes and took deep breaths, forcing himself to think. He still had time. Gourd wore a sidearm, and—no, he wore it on his right hip, and that was pinned as well. There would be other things he could use, though, and he reached for more pouch flaps.

A growl came from outside, and Evan scrambled back through the opening, bringing up the Sig. The trio was close now, but another creature covered in soot was limping along the side of the Seahawk. The charred skin of its face was peeled back to reveal gray bone and teeth, empty eye sockets, and something black and wet lurking behind them. It lunged. Evan stumbled backward and fell, the creature landing atop his legs, its skeletal fingers clawing at his groin. The teeth sank into his thigh—

—and bit into something metal.

Evan screamed and shoved the Sig against the top of its skull, pulling the trigger. The head disintegrated in pieces of bone and a tar-like substance that spattered across the front of the chopper.

Are those its brains? Evan wanted to vomit.

A rustling noise came from his right, and Evan looked to see that not ten feet away, a black ball of a head was rising from the cinders, narrow shoulders following, nearly skeletal arms levering it out of the black powder. Teeth clicked as it tried to stand, and beyond it two more lifted themselves out of their camouflage, cinders sliding off their backs and heads.

Oh, Christ, they're under the ash.

He scrambled to his feet and started running south, now far less worried about a twisted or broken ankle, searching the ground ahead of him for hidden shapes. Behind him the trio and pair shifted direction to follow the running shape. The creatures climbing out of the ash did the same.

Evan forced himself to slow to a brisk walk and not to give in to panic, knowing even at that pace he was still faster than the opposition behind him. After a few minutes his breathing and heartbeat began to settle, and he suddenly realized that this was the first time he had been alone since the first two weeks of outbreak last summer. Since then he'd always been surrounded by people who cared about him. There had been terror, and many times he'd been convinced he was about to die, but he had known he wouldn't die alone. There would be someone there to mark his passing and ensure he didn't come back as something terrible. If he was pulled down by the dead out here in this wasteland, no one would ever know. Did they know he had crashed? If so, he might be dead to them already.

That made him think of Maya. He saw her crying, her belly only now starting to swell with his baby. It caused an ache in his chest.

I'm coming home, Maya. To both of you.

This resolve made him walk faster.

Ash kicked up by his passage across the destruction quickly coated his gear, clothing, and skin with a thin film. It also got into his nose, making him snort and cough, causing it to start bleeding again. There was an acidic, aluminum smell to it, sharp and unpleasant, and it tasted coppery in his mouth. He knew that refineries all across America produced more than just gasoline, and most of what they made—along with their waste—was toxic to humans. *What the hell am I breathing in right now? And do my lungs hurt from exertion, or something more insidious, invisible and lurking in the air and ash?*

Evan stopped to rest for a moment, looking around to make sure he was alone in these blackened fields. The drifters following him were no longer in view, but he shuddered at the thought of what might be lying beneath the surface, right underfoot. He took a moment to wipe at his eyes and trickling nose, wishing for a bottle of water, settling for a stick of gum from a flight jacket pocket.

He pulled a stubby, steel bottle from a thigh pocket, and turned it to see the impressions of teeth from where the creature had bitten him. The bottle was topped with a mouthpiece like a scuba diver would use, mounted beside a valve and a small pressure gauge. Vlad had called it an *emergency egress device*, two to five minutes of bottled oxygen for fliers who went down in water and would need to escape a submerged aircraft. Evan took a single pull from the bottle, sucking down sweet air, and twisted the valve closed. It made him feel better at once, convincing him that there *was* some bad shit in the ashes out here. He told himself he would use it sparingly.

Moving once more, he walked across a warped metal sign lying flat on the ground, the word *Chevron* still visible beneath an oily black film. He checked his map. The Chevron refinery was large enough that it was marked on the map, but that was farther east from where he thought he was. Had he strayed off course? He doubted it. The Chevron plant was a greater distance from the crash site than he could have walked already and the sign could have been blown here in the firestorm.

Richmond. Chevron. Why was that familiar? Then he remembered the girl he had spent a week with in Sacramento before he went to Napa, an activist and a hippie wannabe who might have fit in pretty well with Calvin's people had she not been so angry all the time. She had once ranted about the Chevron plant in Richmond and how an accident in 2012 had filled the air with sulfur trioxide, a poisonous gas. Evan had commented that it sounded like the Union Carbide accident in Bhopal, India, back in the eighties, and the girl had then gone on about *that*. She'd been pretty annoying, and the only reason he'd hung around for an entire week was that she was a freak in bed. At least now the Chevron plant wouldn't be poisoning anyone else.

Untrue. That shit is on the ground now, in the air, on your skin, he thought.

Evan took another quick breath from his oxygen bottle. *How badly would it suck to escape zombies, a madman with a nuclear weapon, and now being shot down, only to die from chemical poisoning and bleeding lungs?* He chewed the gum harder.

He was less than a mile from the elevated concrete span of I-580 when the weather front Gourd had seen on the radar finally arrived, and it started to rain. Evan tipped his head back and wiped at his face and arms, scrubbing fingers through his short hair, opening his mouth and then spitting. Rain had never been so welcome.

It not only washed the grime from his uniform and gear, it began to expose skulls in the ruins around him, most of them partially covered in what at first appeared to be burned chicken skin, but then was recognizable as scalp. More than a dozen of these figures began to rise around him in a circle. Their blackened skin was taut against their frames, making them appear almost skeletal. Evan froze, raising his pistol and turning in a circle. They were everywhere, maybe two dozen. He tracked the Sig, looking for the thin point in the crowd, preparing to shoot his way out of the encirclement. Beyond the ring of corpses, he saw more of them pulling themselves up from the cinders. The rain caused black rivulets of soot to slide down their bodies.

The creatures didn't rush him. Instead they shifted in place until they were all facing south, and their heads tipped back slightly. One made a cracking sound as the head broke free of the charcoal spine, the body collapsing, the head falling and rolling away. They made no other noise, and a breeze passed through them, carrying away black flakes of skin.

Evan was stunned at their behavior, but not frozen. He ran

between them, bumping two aside and expecting reaching arms and snarls, getting neither. He aimed for the elevated freeway, skirting left around a giant crater left by an exploding petroleum tank, avoiding a pair of burned drifters at the crater's right edge.

The earth began to tremble, growing in power, and then hurled the running pilot to the ground. Evan landed on his chest, his broken wrist smashing hard against a fragment of brick and making him cry out. The ground bucked beneath him, and Evan clawed for a hold, certain for one crazy moment that he might be shaken right off the earth's surface and flung into the sky.

There was a dull cracking sound beyond him, and he lifted his head to see a section of Interstate 580 wiggling in slow motion, like a piece of partially cooked spaghetti. About three hundred yards from where the interstate would feed into the Richmond–San Rafael Bridge, the elevated roadway began to tip to the right, spilling cars and trucks over its rails and down into the ruins. The vehicles struck in a string of distant, metallic crunches, kicking up a black cloud. The highway continued to twist, dumping more cars and then collapsing in place, adding concrete dust to the rising cloud of ash.

Evan was both horrified and awed, and he couldn't look away.

The earthquake ran its brief course and then stopped, but I-580 continued to collapse in sections for another full minute. When it was over, there was only the pattering of rain on the ground, the sounds of feet shuffling through ash, and the cries of the dead. Even looked back to see that the drifters were moving again, several dozen black shapes now, locked in on the only living thing within this field of destruction. He didn't have the bullets to deal with them. Not even half of them.

Evan turned back to face the highway. He picked out a point that hadn't collapsed, a place he could use to move under and past the structure, and started moving again.

The dead followed.

SIXTEEN

September—The Pacific

The crew of *Joshua James* managed to stretch their food supplies until the end of September, nearly six weeks at sea steaming in wide figure eights across hundreds of miles of ocean. The bottled water ran out quickly, but the civilian contractors aboard *Joshua James* managed to get the desalinization unit working—for one day—and that got them through. The crew functioned on half rations throughout it all, and drinking water grew too precious to use for bathing. At the end of six weeks, the men and women aboard the Coast Guard cutter were a thin, haggard bunch.

Two days after leaving Port Angeles, Liz had mustered all hands on the quarterdeck and held funeral services for Lieutenant Commander Coseboom, Chief Newman, and the seaman who had died when he accidentally drove his forklift off the dock. Also honored were Seaman Thedford and the three *Klondike* crewmen who had turned and had to be put down. Elizabeth wore her whites and read a Bible passage as she committed their memories, if not all their bodies, to the sea. Ensign Amy Liggett was subsequently named ship's executive officer.

Despite the losses, there had been a positive outcome from their raid on Port Angeles. In addition to the supplies and arms, they had picked up two new crewmen. Lt. Riggs was a helicopter pilot, and although there was no such aircraft on board, he had the basic skills needed to prep, launch, and fly their Predator drones. He was also a much-needed addition to the officer corps. Petty Officer Third Class Castellano was a rescue swimmer, and thus a trained EMT. *Joshua James* had its medic.

Liz made it clear to the crew that they could not return to Seattle because of the chaos and could not attempt to contact any other elements of the U.S. military because of "false information and mis-understandings," finally citing the need for security. She did not offer an explanation as to what any of that meant. She also informed them that their standard lifesaving mission had been changed to one of national security. They were now a warship awaiting orders from the proper authority. Again she did not elaborate. She did state that their objective, above all others, was to preserve ship and crew.

Too little food, long watches, not enough crew to handle the workload, and decreasing hygiene led to low morale, despite the efforts of most of the officers to maintain positive attitudes. It was a difficult fight to win. Everyone aboard knew they had lost people, perhaps *all* their people, and they were powerless against forces they did not understand. Then there was Charlie Kidd, who took a harder approach with the crew, demanding they suck it up and do their jobs, maintaining order through threat and intimidation. Amy Liggett brought her concerns about Chief Kidd to the captain.

"If we lose discipline, Amy," Liz had said, "we lose the ship. I won't allow it. The chief of the boat will handle the enlisted crew as he sees fit." That had been all the captain had to say on the matter, and Amy hadn't brought it up again.

They monitored the radio, listening as the world quickly fell apart. Cities toppled like dominoes across the United States, the largest population centers going first. The plague was everywhere, all-consuming, and they learned about how it spread and what it left behind. All the while *Joshua James* drifted silently and alone in the northern Pacific, avoiding contact with all other vessels, and not responding to any radio transmissions, whether directed at them or not. Anyone trying to hail the lonely ship assumed it was crewed by the dead and moved on.

Liz listened throughout the weeks as the military tried unsuccessfully to stem the tide of the infected, and the government hurried to implement plans, only to see them fail or come apart almost at once. Units were overrun, bases were lost, and the Navy ships that had managed to escape to sea or were already out when it happened went off the air one by one. Commanders broadcast that there had been undiscovered suicides aboard that quickly spawned infectious nests, and apparently these spreading threats eventually consumed their ships, for the situation reports ceased one by one. The carrier *Ronald Reagan* was operating far to the south for a while but fell into radio silence either because it had been lost or because its captain had dropped off the grid and was hiding, as Liz was. More than one ship reported mutiny before going quiet. After a while there were no more planes in the sky, and captains who had docked their ships in nearby Anchorage, Alaska, soon reported that the city had fallen before they went off the air. There would be no sanctuary to the north.

The civilian news was only on long enough for those aboard *Joshua James* to hear about their country and hometowns being devoured by the dead, each crewman praying their loved ones had somehow survived but knowing it was a thin hope. Morale got worse, and eventually Liz prohibited anyone but the officers from listening to the radio.

Joshua James experienced three suicides of its own: two civilians (a plumber and an electronics technician) and one female seaman from the engine room. The contractors obtained a pistol and ended their lives in a murder-suicide, shooting themselves in the head. The seaman, however, slashed her wrists and bled out quietly in her rack. She rose and killed two other crewmen—both *Klondike* survivors—before Charlie Kidd followed the screams and put bullets in all their brains. Elizabeth tightened restrictions on the firearms after that.

Subtle grumbling began among the crew, increasing complaints and suggestions that the ship should put into the nearest port and permit each crew member to decide for themselves whether they wanted to leave. One of the most outspoken of these voices was a two-stripe seaman from the engine room named John Henry.

After holding a brief Captain's Mast, the nonjudicial punishment hearing of the Coast Guard, Navy, and Marine Corps, Elizabeth had the boy secured in an emptied-out maintenance closet and put on quarter rations. He remained there for four days before Liz decided he was subdued enough for her liking.

On the last day of September, Liz was in her quarters, Blackbeard curled up and purring in her lap as she sat at the small table making notes in her captain's log. Two sharp knocks came at her door, and she called for the visitor to enter.

The door opened, and Seaman John Henry rushed in, slamming his shoulder into Liz's chest, knocking her back against the bulkhead as the cat screeched and ran for cover. She grunted and tried to push him off, but even though the boy looked like a filthy scarecrow, he was still much bigger than she was, and he had leverage. Liz grabbed for the sidearm on her hip, but Henry hissed, "Don't," and pressed a steak knife to her throat. Liz stopped moving and took her hand away from the gun.

Henry pulled it from her holster at once, still pressing the serrated edge of the blade against her windpipe. He smelled foul—they all did—and his skin was jaundiced, cheeks and eyes sunken in dark hollows. The young man's eyes were red from crying.

"I want to go home," he said.

"I understand, John," Liz said, speaking slowly and careful not to move against the steak knife. "We all do."

He shook his head. "Not you! You just want us to float out here until we die." He shook his head. "I want to see my mom again. You won't let me."

"That's not—"

"Shut up!" he screamed, his breath sour. He had the shakes and looked ready to cry again.

The hammer of a pistol clicked in the open doorway. "Put your weapons down right now, Seaman." Amy Liggett, looking as dirty and unkempt as the wild-eyed Coast Guardsman, was in a shooting stance and aiming her sidearm at John Henry's back.

The boy glanced at her. "I'll cut her throat. I'll do it." He moved the blade, and a red line appeared on Liz's throat. The captain winced and hissed. "Drop that pistol and kick it to me," Henry said.

"Don't you do it, Ensign," Liz growled, and Henry pressed the knife harder, making her close her eyes and grit her teeth.

"Now!" the seaman yelled, sliding the knife.

"Stop!" Amy cried, placing her pistol on the deck and holding her hands out to her sides. She kicked the weapon toward the young man, and he kicked it under the captain's folded-down rack.

"You can't keep us out here like this," the seaman said, his face close to Liz's. Blood from a two-inch slice trickled down her neck as he moved the blade to her jugular. "Call the Navy. Give them our position." He nodded. "I'll surrender to them when they arrive."

"I will," said Liz. "But I'll need the frequencies."

"Bullshit," he snarled. "Just call them."

"I can't," she said, pressed hard against the bulkhead. "In time of war the frequencies change. The wartime freqs are locked in my wall safe."

Seaman Apprentice Henry was nineteen, a machinist's mate from the engine room and not versed in communication protocol. He was also young enough to believe that for the most part, officers knew everything. It sounded reasonable to him. "Open it," he ordered.

Liz moved slowly, Henry now pointing Liz's own pistol at her stomach, the knife blade still at her throat. Liz turned to face the safe, and Henry shoved the pistol against her spine, moving the steak knife to rest against her right cheek, the tip near her eye.

Liz spun the combination and opened the door.

She reached in, gripped the butt of Special Agent Ramsey's pistol, and turned violently. Startled, John Henry pulled the trigger, but she had spun away and the bullet merely kissed the skin at the small of her back. He jerked the steak knife, however, and opened the right side of Liz's face.

Liz let out a scream and pistol-whipped the young man in the temple. He collapsed, and she immediately kicked the fallen pistol away from her attacker's limp hand. Keeping the FBI agent's weapon pointed at the man on the deck, Liz stepped to the intercom phone. "Chief Kidd to the captain's quarters on the double," she called, "and bring a pair of handcuffs."

Then she looked at her XO still standing in the doorway with a stunned expression on her face. The captain's right cheek hung in a bloody flap against her jaw, and her uniform blouse was quickly turning red. "Amy," she said, her voice low, "you surrendered your weapon and put us both in jeopardy. Don't *ever* disobey me again."

Amy reddened, and her voice came out in a whisper. "Yes, ma'am."

"Now call the medic," Liz said.

That same evening, Liz was back in her quarters, the door now locked. Petty Officer Castellano, the rescue swimmer, had put twenty-seven stitches in her cheek to close up the flap of skin, starting her on a series of antibiotics and giving her a Percocet for the pain. A large gauze bandage covered the right side of her face. Castellano told her that it would scar badly without the attention of a plastic surgeon. She had grimaced. Small chance of finding one of those. She put the Percocet in her safe, next to Agent Ramsey's pistol. It hurt like the devil, but the pain was a reminder of several hard lessons she had learned today.

Seaman Henry was handcuffed and back in the maintenance closet, an armed guard posted outside. Throughout the ship, the crew was subdued and barely spoke. Perhaps something good could come of this, she thought, highlighting passages in a manual open on the table before her.

She sat back and sipped a cup of coffee, black with a pinch of salt, Navy style. Her cheek throbbed, but she wouldn't take the painkiller. Now more than ever, she needed a clear head, for there were decisions to be made that would affect everyone aboard ship.

Her eyes drifted to the bulkhead across the room. Three frames hung there: the certificate of her commissioning as a Coast Guard ensign, her diploma from Cornell certifying her master's degree in engineering, and the portrait of an old-world man in a high collar and powdered wig. It was here that her eyes settled.

This image of William Kidd had hung on the wall of her dorm all through the academy, had been in any office she occupied when not on sea duty, and had decorated her quarters aboard every ship upon which she had served since she was an ensign. Her ancestor. None of Elizabeth's known relatives had been sea captains, and so she felt a special connection with the man. But oh, the crap she had taken in school, and then as a junior officer. She'd kept her chin up through it all. Even today, with her current senior rank, people meeting her for the first time had trouble saying *Captain Kidd* without a smile or smirk.

That generally happened only once.

Liz had learned everything she could about the American pirate, both the man and the legend.

William Kidd was a Scottish sea captain who, upon returning from a voyage to the Indian Ocean, was tried and executed for piracy. Most historians agreed that Kidd was a poor pirate, if he was even a pirate at all. They speculated that much of his legend was fabricated by people seeking to benefit from his disgrace, and the man's insistence on clearing his name was what ultimately led to his downfall.

William married Sarah Bradley Cox Oort, a young lady in her twenties, already twice a widow and considered one of the wealthiest women in New York. It was believed that her wealth was what drew Kidd's enemies into a conspiracy to defame him in order to justify seizing her fortune.

The captain was originally commissioned as a pirate hunter and privateer and set sail in the *Adventure Galley*. But Kidd was unsuccessful at both pirate hunting and finding French prizes, and members of his crew, angry at this lack of success, frequently deserted the *Adventure Galley*. Still he carried on, despite being branded a *pirate*.

Liz tapped thoughtfully at the rim of her cup with a pen, looking at the painting. The title wasn't completely without merit. He did take several small ships, and whether they were truly French or merely convenient was in dispute. Additionally, Kidd may not have been a pirate, but he was certainly a murderer, as he had struck and killed a crewman who insulted him for refusing to attack a Dutchman.

Eventually, William was lured into Boston, his enemies proclaiming that all had been a misunderstanding and forgiveness awaited. Kidd and his wife were immediately imprisoned, their family fortune seized. Although Sarah was released to spend her days in poverty, William was shipped to England, tried for piracy and murder, and executed. After his death, Kidd's body was placed in an iron cage and hung over the Thames to rot, displayed as a warning to others. He was fifty-six.

Elizabeth sipped carefully at her coffee, trying to move her face as little as possible. Once, before the world had gone mad, she'd been planning to write a book about her ancestor, something to pass the time after she retired. That no longer seemed likely.

Most people knew nothing about William's lackluster career as a pirate, but they had heard the tales of his treasure, and that was what caused the legend to grow and live on. Indeed, some of what he had hidden was found on Gardiner's Island while Kidd was still alive, and was dug up and sent to England. Rumors of vast riches persisted through the centuries, however: tales of gold bars, Spanish coins, and jewels, all hidden away by a genuine American pirate.

Liz smiled, and scratched Blackbeard behind the ears. The cat had appeared silently and unnoticed in her lap, the way cats often did. She stared at the painting. Hidden chests of coin were of small interest to Liz. Her affinity, especially now, was for the man and the troubles he had faced: a captain who believed in honor and duty, falsely accused and unable to defend himself, cast in a role for which he did not ask and threatened by the betrayal and disobedience of an undisciplined crew. The parallels couldn't be sharper.

Of course he hadn't had to contend with the walking dead, she thought, sipping her coffee too quickly and wincing. Blackbeard looked up and meowed softly.

Two sharp knocks came at her door, and Liz moved to it, drawing her pistol. "Who is it?"

"Ensign Liggett, ma'am."

Liz checked the peephole to ensure Amy was alone, then let her in. "Take a seat," she said, returning to her chair. Blackbeard had gone to hide under the bed. "What can I do for you?"

Amy looked at the bandage on her commanding officer's face and flushed. "I want to apologize for my earlier actions. I never should have put down my weapon. I should have listened to you."

Liz gave her a nod, her voice coming out tightly because talking hurt. "I'm confident you understand. As far as I'm concerned, that aspect of this incident is behind us."

Amy thanked her. "Ma'am, may I ask why I'm still executive officer when Lieutenant Riggs is senior to me by two ranks?"

"Because he's part of the air division," Liz said, "and therefore cannot be the XO of a seagoing vessel. Is there anything else?"

The younger woman hesitated for a moment before speaking. "Captain, what are you going to do with Seaman Henry?"

"I'm going to hang him, of course."

Amy blinked, then stumbled over her words. "How . . . why, but . . ."

"It's mutiny, Amy," Liz said. "Article ninety-four of the UCMJ. The penalty is death." She pushed her copy of the Uniform Code of Military Justice across the table, the book open to the section she had been highlighting.

Amy took a deep breath. "I'm aware of the article, ma'am."

Liz nodded again. "You're right out of the academy; the lessons should be fresh." She gave the girl a lopsided smile. "Go ahead and make your case, Ensign. As my executive officer you should be prepared to disagree with me and articulate your argument. In private, of course," she added.

"Yes, ma'am. Captain, a charge of mutiny or sedition requires a conspiracy, an acting-in-concert. Seaman Henry acted alone."

"As far as we know. Go on."

Amy tapped the book. "Such a charge requires a review by the Judge Advocate General's office. . . ."

"They are unavailable."

"At the very least," Amy went on, "a general court-martial. He's entitled to a fair trial, representation by counsel, and a chance to cross-examine witnesses."

Liz reached out and closed the book. "Very well spoken, Amy. Your file said that you received high marks in legal studies, and it shows. Well done." She steepled her fingers. "You were present in this very compartment earlier today, and witnessed the events, yes?"

"Of course."

"Then you saw Seaman Apprentice Henry attempt to overthrow a lawful authority, and commit both open rebellion and violence against a ship's captain. It's mutiny."

"But the conspiracy . . ." Amy started.

Liz cut her off. "Semantics, and we don't have that luxury. It's mutiny. Any person who is guilty of mutiny shall be punished by death. He's guilty. He'll hang."

The younger woman started to say more, but Liz lifted a hand. "Amy, I've let you have your say, and I've explained my decision. I needn't remind you of our precarious position, not only with this vessel during a crisis, but as heavily outnumbered officers. There must be discipline, and the crew can *never* be permitted to think it is even *possible* to rise up against the officers. I'm certain that concept was explained to you at the academy."

"Yes, ma'am."

"Good. And you will support me, in this and in all things." It wasn't a question.

Amy looked down. "Of course."

"Very well, you may take your leave. And tell Senior Chief Kidd I would like to see him."

The following morning, the entire crew of *Joshua James* was mustered on the quarterdeck. Seaman Henry stood to one side, handcuffed and under the watchful eye of Charlie Kidd. Amy Liggett read a brief recount of the incident, the formal charges, and the decided penalty.

No one among the ranks of the crew spoke, and even the remaining civilian contractors lined up alongside them remained silent. There was only Amy's voice, and the sea wind across the deck. Seaman Henry was given the opportunity to speak, but he simply kept his head down and cried.

Senior Chief Kidd hanged the nineteen-year-old from a radio

mast, and the crew was dismissed. When the dangling boy turned a few minutes later, Charlie shot him in the head, cut him down, and heaved the body overboard.

Liz and her brother stood alone by the rail of the forward deck for a while, looking out at the sea. A line of dark clouds was on the horizon, heralding an approaching storm. "This crew needs supplies and some hope," Liz said at last. "I'm taking us to the Oregon coast, and we'll see what we see."

SEVENTEEN

Portland had been out of the question. It was too close to Seattle, and an equally large urban center that would have suffered the same levels of destruction and infestation. Liz wanted someplace small, unobtrusive, and remote. She found it in the southern Oregon town of Brookings. Seven miles north of the California border, the little seaside village had—before the plague—only six thousand residents, a tiny community living off logging, fishing, and tourism.

Joshua James approached the mouth of the Chetco River at a creeping speed. Every pair of binoculars aboard was in use as the crew scanned the small town, and below in the combat center, Mr. Vargas monitored the screens for the cutter's zoom-capable exterior video cameras. The forward fifty-seven-millimeter gun was armed and ready (they had managed to salvage twenty shells from the armory at Port Angeles), and all four fifty-caliber guns were mounted and crewed.

"Take a sounding, Mr. Waite," Liz said, looking out the bridge with binoculars of her own. The Chetco River split the town in half, with its two harbors on the right. Liz had little hope that either one could handle the cutter's twenty-two-foot draft, though the river might. They wouldn't get far even if it did, though. The bridge for US 101 crossed the waterway only a mile in, barely high enough to clear the ship's bow, much less the superstructure.

"Captain," the quartermaster replied, "the river mouth has a thirty-one-foot-deep channel that is wide enough to handle us. I wouldn't try getting in much farther than a ship's length, though."

It would be enough. "Helm, all stop," Liz ordered, and the deck vibrated as the ship reversed briefly, bringing the vessel to a halt. "Let's take our time, people."

Every crew member on the bridge continued looking out the windows.

Liz wore a blue wool pullover that desperately needed washing, and her ball cap was pulled down over greasy hair. She'd tried to make her deodorant last, but she knew she didn't smell good, and she itched constantly. The men aboard—except for the young ones— were bearded as she'd relaxed the grooming standard out of necessity. Liz had never wanted a shower so badly in her life.

At first she was surprised to see boats in the two Brookings marinas. There weren't many, but they included a handful of sail and power craft, along with several commercial fishermen, including one that looked big enough to handle crabbing in the unforgiving Alaskan seas. She thought about the waterborne exodus from Seattle and realized that the presence of boats here wasn't that unusual. This was the kind of place people would run to, for the same reasons Liz had selected it: quiet and remote. That also meant an increased probability of living people still being here, not necessarily a good thing.

"Starboard watch, any movement at the CG station?"

"No, ma'am," a young seaman reported, "not even the dead."

USCG Station Chetco River sat on a peninsula just to the south of the river's mouth, a single, flat structure with an attached lookout tower. Its docks were on the far side in the lower marina, out of view. According to the hard-copy manuals in her quarters—the digital files were locked in a network computer system that still wasn't working—the station was thinly manned but had a trio of forty-seven-foot motorized lifeboats, known as MLBs, and a pair of launches like those carried on *Joshua James*. Armament would be minimal, nothing heavier than a medium machine gun, and the base had no air station.

This close to shore, the big white cutter attracted a lot of attention, and she wanted to tuck it away somewhere. The river mouth was calling to her, but before she put her ship someplace with no room to maneuver, she wanted to be certain the area was secure, or at least controllable. So far, the dead they had seen along the waterfront were scattered and few in number.

"XO, Senior Chief, on me," Liz said, moving to the starboard side of the bridge. Both Amy and Chick joined her. "We're going to launch two shore parties," she said once they were all together, "five crewmen each. Objective one is to seize the Coast Guard station. Objective two is the commercial docks and buildings across the harbor. We will recon the hillside to port from the ship. Once I'm sure we're clear on all sides, I'll bring the cutter in." She was more confident in the chances of her shore parties now. Before he was killed, LCDR Coseboom had ensured that plenty of M4s, handguns, and ammunition had been loaded aboard the forklifts. Half of it made it to the ship. The people she put ashore would be well armed.

"If the cutter is on the river," Amy said, "how could the dead—"

"I'm concerned about the living right now, Miss Liggett. This place is remote enough that there may be civilian or military survivors in there, all of whom are sure to be armed. This vessel is a prize worth taking."

Amy nodded.

Liz went on. "Don't worry about scavenging right now; this is purely a security mission. However, make a note if and where you locate food supplies and water. Keep an eye out for fire engines, especially pumpers, as well as bottled water trucks."

"Rules of engagement?" Chick asked.

"The dead are fair game," Liz said. "If you encounter the living, and they make a hostile act, you are clear to engage. You'll both have comm with the ship, and we can support you with the Bofors gun or fifty-calibers as needed. Questions?"

There were none.

"Then assemble your crews and let's get this done. We will not have a repeat of Port Angeles. Everyone comes home. If you encounter strong opposition, living or dead, you are to fall back to the ship, understood? Dismissed."

Liz used the ship's PA to inform the crew that shore parties would be launching, and all watches and weapon positions were to remain vigilant. Then she ordered what crew there was left to report to the bow with rifles.

It was strange to be on land. After more than six weeks at sea, Amy still felt the swaying motion in her body, despite the fact that there was concrete under her boots.

She and her crew of four had taken one of the Prosecutors and motored into the mouth of the river, turning right and passing the commercial fishing docks, heading into the south marina. Almost at once they'd come upon the high, corrugated metal enclosure for the Coast Guard station's vessels. Only one remained, a forty-seven-foot motorized lifeboat tied to its moorings, a sleek, gray boat capable of vaulting over ocean surf and heavy waves. It had both an enclosed cockpit and a top-deck steering station and was essentially a massive power boat. Amy had trained on one at New London.

They moored their SRP inside the shelter, across from the much larger craft, and made their way up a wooden stairway before moving out onto the station's grounds. Amy led with her pistol in hand, the four men behind her armed with M4s. Normally a boarding party would have been fully outfitted with tactical gear and helmets, but that equipment hadn't yet been delivered to *Joshua James*. She hoped they might find some here but knew it was a long shot. It was usually the cutters that did the boarding. This station's mission was probably more attuned to lifesaving and fisheries protection.

It started to rain as the team moved down a sidewalk toward the station's single building, a spread-out, one-story structure painted white, with a three-story lookout position that resembled a traffic control tower. Overgrown lawns extended to either side as the group closed on the building, stacked up in a single-file, tactical formation. Amy's heart was thumping as she tried to remember her training.

"Seven-five-four, this is Team One," she said into the radio mic clipped to her shoulder. "Mooring is secure. We are advancing on main building from the northeast."

"Copy, Team One," came the reply.

As they reached the building's corner, Amy stopped and took her bearings. To her right was a short open lawn bordered by the harbor on two sides. Out to her left she could see the access road leading to the station, and the entrance to an RV park that appeared filled to capacity with motor homes, cars, and recreational trailers. The corpse of a teenager in cutoffs walked stiffly across the road and disappeared behind a big brown-and-white motor coach. Amy cautioned herself that the presence of so many RVs meant either lots of frightened, desperate refugees hiding within or lots of dead things trying to get out.

To her immediate front was the lawn between the station and a parking area crowded with vehicles. A black Charger with *Brookings Police* on the door sat at the curb. Nothing moved, the breeze coming off the Pacific making the colors snap atop the flagpole out front.

"Team One advancing to main building," Amy reported quietly. She led her men past the building toward the entrance, weapons aimed at the windows they passed, and then they were facing double glass doors. "Breaching," she told her radio mic, and they went into an empty, tiled lobby.

One of the expectations of a Coast Guard officer was to be able to lead boarding parties and conduct searches, going aboard everything from small pleasure craft to the big oceangoing freighters and container ships. The purpose of the boarding was almost always to look for migrants and contraband: drugs and illegal arms. Occasionally intelligence would direct them to a counterterrorism op. Amy had learned how to move a team through the close quarters of a ship, a maze with plenty of places for bad guys to hide, ever aware that someone might pop out of a hatch with an AK-47 on full auto. The training had been both intense and fun, but it had been *training*. This was her first live mission, and she had to watch out not only for armed aggressors, but also for things that *bit*. Dead things. Her heart hadn't slowed, and now she was sweating.

She motioned her team down a corridor to the left, and they began a room-to-room search. It smelled bad in here. Rotten. They found a mess hall with a kitchen—which smelled a different sort of rotten—small offices and a meeting room, separate berthing for both men and women, as well as heads and showers. Rusty blood smears in one shower told them someone had died in here but had since moved on. Otherwise, there were no other signs of violence in this half of the building, and no occupants.

Amy checked in over the radio and took her team back to the lobby, then started toward the other side of the station. More offices, a briefing room, storage for the gear needed aboard rescue craft—life jackets, rope, rafts, and boat safety equipment—and then they came upon the small armory. It was open and empty except for a pump shotgun and several boxes of shells. It looked to the young officer as if the coasties who had gone out in the station's other vessels had armed up before leaving. She understood now why the place was so empty.

"Seaman," she said, snapping her fingers to get a bosun's mate's attention. "Take that weapon and the ammunition." The young man immediately slung the shotgun across his back and stuffed the boxes of shells into a nylon satchel. Amy keyed her mic. "Armory secure and empty."

At the back of the team, one of the *Klondike* men was watching the rear as he had been trained and saw a man in dark trousers, dress shoes, and a light blue shirt covered in service ribbons come through a doorway they had just passed. He wore short gray hair, and a pair of commander's insignia was pinned to his collar. His shirt was darkened on one side, and a chunk of his neck was missing, blackened at the edges.

"Ensign," the seaman hissed, and the team pivoted as the corpse groaned and began a quick sidestep toward the bosun's mate.

"Engage!" Amy yelled, bringing up her pistol, but the crewman in front of her was quicker and triggered a three-round burst, hitting the dead man in the throat, jaw, and nose. The body dropped. "Stay in formation," Amy ordered, moving to the bosun's mate at the rear of the stack, grabbing him by the strap of his ammo harness.

"You're our rear security, and you engage on sight. Don't hesitate!" Her voice was a tight growl.

"Aye-aye," he said, and nodded.

Amy looked at him for a moment, then softened her expression and patted him on the shoulder. "We're all tense." Then she looked at the corpse and keyed her mic. "Seven-five-four, this is Team One. We just had contact with a Whiskey-Delta." Her captain had decided that until something better came along, they would simply be called *Whiskey-Delta* for "walking dead," while the living would be referred to as *Limas*. "It's down, no casualties." Then she noted, "I think we just took out the base commander."

Joshua James acknowledged, and Amy pressed forward. The only part of the station they hadn't investigated was the lookout tower, and as soon as they opened the door at its base, which was a single communications room, they were hit by an oily, nauseating stench. Across the room, near a spiral metal staircase that led up into the tower, a bloated green Coast Guardsman turned and began trundling toward them. Its eyes were white with pinpoint pupils, and it was so swollen that its uniform had begun to split at the seams. Gases erupted from its body in a *blatting* sound as it lurched, and Amy thought for an instant that she could hear it sloshing.

The seaman behind her, the same one who had shot the base commander, stepped past her and fired another burst. The creature *exploded*, painting the walls and equipment with a sticky green-and-black grease, and then the *real* smell hit them.

Amy gagged, and the rifleman beside her vomited, joined two seconds later by one of his shipmates. The young ensign managed to keep it down for a moment, until she thought about the powdered scrambled eggs she'd had this morning. Her breakfast came up in a heave.

In the center of the room, what was left of the green coastie flopped about and snapped its teeth, as something in the tower above started down the stairs and let out a long wail. Amy shot the exploded dead thing in the forehead, spat, and wiped her mouth on her sleeve. "Let's finish this," she said, and started up the stairs to kill whatever she found.

While Team One was still entering the sheltered Coast Guard mooring, Chick's crew motored up to the commercial docks, a high pier set in front of a warehouse. There were no vessels here now, and the SRP tied up at a low wooden walkway with a stairway at one end. The crewmen spotted movement among the barnacle-encrusted pilings and aimed their rifles into the shadows under the pier.

Water sloshed against wood and concrete, causing a figure in a yellow rain slicker to bob up and down. The surf turned it over and they saw a picked-at, gray-white face with one colorless eye, mouth open and trying to gargle out a sound. The dead fisherman was caught on something, and one pale hand beat helplessly at the rising and falling water. A pair of crabs were locked onto the head and were busily dining on putrid flesh.

"That's fucking nasty, Chief," one of the seamen in the launch said, aiming his rifle.

Chick pushed the barrel aside. "Don't waste the round. Let the sea have him." He looked under the pier to the right and pointed. "You think *that's* nasty?"

The others peered into the shadows to where the chief was pointing. Wedged between a piling and a concrete retaining wall was the white carcass of an adult sea lion, also bobbing in the ebb and flow. It was covered in bites, and as they watched, gray arms broke the surface, hooked fingers digging into the rotting meat and pulling, heads and shoulders emerging as teeth chewed into the animal before sliding back down.

The four men with Chick stared in revulsion, then looked at the surface of the water all around their launch. Chick laughed. "Keep your hands and feet inside the ride at all times," he said, then looked past his men, and his smile faded. Out at the marina to their north was a rough pier of earth and stone, separating it from the river. Chick saw no fewer than a dozen pale creatures trying to claw their way out of the water, hands unable to find a purchase on the slime-coated rocks, slipping and sinking only to emerge and try again.

He looked at the water. *How many are down there? Is that why this place looks so empty? They're not really gone, they're just below us.* He pictured hundreds of town residents at the bottom of the harbor, trudging through silt and stumbling over mossy stones, tangled in a century's worth of fishing line and long-forgotten lobster pots as fish and crabs picked them slowly apart.

Chick gave an involuntary shudder, then ordered his men out of the launch and onto the wooden walkway. He organized a more relaxed line than the ordered stack Amy was using and led his men up the stairs.

The rain arrived, casting a murky pall over the harbor as the team reached the top of the pier and moved along its length, looking down at their launch from above. A conveyor belt hung over the water like a long arm, something that could have been lowered to fishermen, who would feed their catch up the belt to be deposited in bins. Netting with orange and yellow floats was strung high on drying racks, and even months after the fishing had stopped, the odor of the place's former industry clung to it.

The warehouse facing the dock had two high garage doors, both capable of handling forklifts, both of them closed. A metal door, also closed, stood between them. Chick took the team to the end of the dock where a ramp descended to a boardwalk, which in turn ran the length of one side of the southern marina. Rows of canopies, some tattered by weather, lined the boardwalk, and colorful banners sagged overhead. Paintings and sculptures, racks of souvenir T-shirts, and tables covered in crafts stood out in the rain, and the planks were littered with dropped bicycles, straw hats, and canvas shoulder bags. One of the banners read, *Welcome! Brookings Art Festival, August 11–18.* Moored at the edge of the boardwalk and accessible by a gangplank was a replica of an eighteenth-century two-mast schooner. An arch over the walkway was decorated with the image of a parrot and the words *Captain Scupper's Party Cruises.* Nothing was moving down on the ship's deck, or along the length of the boardwalk.

"Seven-five-four, Team Two," Chick said into his radio, rainwater dripping from the bill of his ball cap. "We've reached the commercial dock, no contact. Going inside."

The single door between the garage bays was unlocked, and they went in single file, Chick in the lead with a small flashlight clicked into a holder beneath his rifle's muzzle. The smell hit them at once, making everyone recoil. Two months' worth of rancid snapper, crab, tuna, and shrimp assaulted their noses, and the men fought to keep from retching. One failed, and Chick had to clench his teeth to keep from doing the same. If there were Whiskey-Deltas in here, he thought, they'd never smell them over the spoiled fish.

"Spread out, lights on," he ordered, and the men fanned out to either side of the chief, switching on their own rifle-mounted flashlights and advancing slowly.

The structure turned out to be three smaller warehouses connected one behind the other, with a small cannery at the back. They found loading bays and worktables, rows of hooks holding yellow overalls and jackets, coils of hose and grinders for fish waste. Rows of ice makers stood empty and silent. Chick spotted some warehouse racking stacked with pallets of cardboard boxes and led them to it. A quick inspection unveiled a stockpile of canned tuna, crab, and sardines.

"Jackpot," Chick said, grinning. He looked at his men and nodded, and they immediately began stuffing cans into cargo pockets. Chick peeled open a can of sardines, sucked the oil from one fish, and then began chewing greedily. Again he nodded at his men, who tore into cans of their own, stuffing their mouths and making happy groaning and smacking noises. A month and a half at half rations made this feel like a feast, and the senior chief, considered a heartless bastard at sea, was instantly elevated to hero status. Charlie watched them eat for a bit, grinning, then got them back online.

Moving deeper into the warehouse, they came upon a creature in shorts and a T-shirt, bent over a rolling tub at the waist, its upper body inside shoving putrid fish heads and tails into its mouth. It was making a grunting sound similar to his men as they had feasted on canned fish. Charlie reached his rifle into the tub and tapped the barrel against its head. When the creature looked up with milky eyes and into the muzzle opening, Charlie pulled the trigger.

He keyed his mic. "Team Two, contact. One Whiskey-Delta down, continuing sweep."

Now that he knew the opposition fed not only on the living but carrion as well, Charlie realized that this place would be a magnet for the dead. He cautioned his men to be extra watchful and was glad he did. They shot down three more corpses, all feeding on one thing or another, as they completed their sweep of the building. With each kill, his men seemed more confident, and Charlie did nothing to shatter their illusion or jar their short memories. That confidence was useful. He didn't want to remind them how quickly they would be fucked if they got hit by a swarm, like the one at Port Angeles. Let them enjoy the moment, he thought.

At the very back of the building was a row of offices, the only place left to investigate. Charlie split them up in order to check the offices quickly, taking the door to the far right. He found it locked, so he shouldered it in and brought his light up fast, just as something in the room let out a frightened squeal.

His light showed four of them in here: a big bearded man holding a cleaver, a ratty-looking woman in a dirty yellow fleece, and a narrow, bald man in a gray T-shirt that read *Oregon State*. A two-year-old boy sat on the floor next to the bigger man, a filthy street urchin of a child with a rope tied around his neck. The big man was gripping the other end.

Chick panned the light across them. "Show me your hands," he ordered. "And you drop that cleaver right now."

It hit the cement floor with a clatter. A pair of backpacks and a pillowcase were on the floor as well, cans of fish spilling from within.

"Doing a little shopping, I see," said Chick. "Who are you people?"

"I'm Ava," the woman said, starting to stand but stopping when Charlie waved her back down with the rifle barrel. The child didn't answer, and the big man just grunted, "Robbie."

Chick looked at the rope around the boy's neck, then at the man holding it. "What the fuck, Robbie?" he said. "You think he's a dog, or are you saving him for a snack in case the food runs out? Take that fucking thing off him right now."

Robbie complied, not looking at the chief.

"Very, very bad," Chick whispered.

The thin, bald man cleared his throat. "I'm Henry Blake, from Eugene. I'm an English professor."

Chick stared at him. "You're a teacher? Really?" He pointed his M4 and shot Henry Blake in the face, the bullet flinging the body against a wall. Robbie made a panicked noise and lunged for his dropped cleaver. Chick rotated at the hips and shot him in the head too.

Boots and flashlights raced for the office from outside, and his crewmen crowded into the doorway, weapons raised.

"Hostile Limas," Chick told his men, then looked at the woman. "United States Coast Guard, we're here to help you." His rifle barrel tracked toward her, and Charlie began to grin. "Are you hostile too, Ava?"

She shook her head and looked in his eyes. "No, sir. I'm friendly."

Two hours later, deciding there were no armed camps in the immediate area that might pose a threat to her ship, Liz gave the order for *Joshua James* to come about. The 418-foot cutter then reversed slowly into the mouth of the Chetco, the commercial docks to its stern, the Coast Guard station to port, and the bow pointed out to sea before it dropped anchor. From here the vessel and its fifty-seven-millimeter gun commanded a dominant view of the small coastal town.

Brookings, Oregon, had a new master.

EIGHTEEN

By midmonth, the crew of *Joshua James* was settling into its new home. Inventory from the cannery went a long way toward replenishing their food supplies, and this was supplemented by clearing out the Coast Guard station's mess pantry. A food services truck was located near a marina restaurant and emptied, providing a little variety beyond canned fish. The boatyards at the far end of the south marina held some useful machine parts and lubricants, and both the diesel and gas tanks that had once served marina craft were pumped dry to fill the cutter's fuel bunkers. During a patrol, Amy Liggett found an ambulance and drove it back to the Coast Guard station, much to the delight of their rescue swimmer, Castellano, who, although he was an enlisted man, was named ship's medical officer.

Water remained a problem. The three remaining contractors were able to get the desalinization system working again, but only for a single afternoon before it failed once more. Mr. Leary, the older electrician and the unofficial leader of the contractors, reported to the captain that he didn't think it would run again until numerous mechanical and electrical parts were replaced, pieces very specific to the system. The brief time it did run provided them with a quarter tank of drinking water, but despite the filtering system, it tasted vaguely oily. Rain collection buckets were set out, and several fire hydrants on shore were opened only to find there was no pressure, and no water to be had.

In the weeks since their arrival, refugees hiding in Brookings had seen and made their way to the big white ship anchored at the mouth of the harbor, some approaching by small boats but most coming in overland. There was a trickle at first, but that quickly swelled to more than three dozen. Liz put Ensign Liggett in charge of shoreside security and gave her a four-man detachment. The young ensign was responsible for disarming refugees—most had one type of weapon or another, mostly for hand-to-hand combat— inspecting them for bites (none were bitten), and settling them into quarters at the Coast Guard station. The captain also ordered her to screen the new arrivals for useful skills and assign them to work parties.

"So far we don't have much," Amy told her commanding officer during an afternoon meeting aboard ship. "A lot of motel and restaurant workers, retail and shop employees, office clerks, a couple of painters and construction workers. At least a third are children. There's a pair of fishermen, a kid who was an auxiliary sheriff's deputy, and a fish and game warden."

Liz had looked at Amy's list. "We're a nation of baristas and video game designers." Then she looked at her XO. "Everyone works, Amy, or they can't stay. Anyone can collect water and wash laundry and dishes, and you have a few skilled laborers here. Find them jobs. Incorporate the deputy and the fish and game officer into your security detail. If you get pushback from anyone—"

"I can handle them," Amy said.

Liz smiled at her. "You're turning into a capable and dependable officer, Miss Liggett. Keep up the good work." Amy had smiled and doubled her efforts, just as Liz intended.

Having both the opportunity to go ashore and something of a

home improved morale immediately, and the atmosphere of quiet reserve in the wake of John Henry's hanging appeared to have passed. It was also no longer necessary to restrict the crew from monitoring the radio. Two months after the outbreak, the airwaves were eerily silent.

Although the Coast Guard Cutter *Dorado* was stationed only twenty-six miles to the south on the California coast, it never appeared, and Liz decided the other cutter's captain would have more important worries of his own. Even if it had shown up looking for trouble, Liz was confident that she would have easily outgunned the much smaller vessel, but she had no wish to fire on her own and was glad not to have to give the order.

The dead were an ongoing problem.

Amy Liggett's shoreside security was regularly tested. Corpses from the nearby RV park were drawn by the activity at the Coast Guard station. There were more than the young officer had expected, and her team was forced to expend more ammunition than she wanted to stop their approach, often coming in waves like a tide. In response, she organized a team of refugees armed with hatchets, axes, and improvised stabbing weapons to meet the oncoming dead. It worked; the dead were slow, and she had enough manpower among the civilians to put them down without wasting bullets.

She also created a pair of shooting platforms on the station's lawn, parking a pair of dump trucks on the grass forty yards apart, and posting round-the-clock, rotating sentries armed with M14s up in the beds. Whiskey-Deltas that slipped past her skirmishers were engaged from there. Refugee work parties collected the bodies, dragged them out to a breakwater, and burned them.

"I'm concerned," Amy told her captain. "The shooting incidents are increasing because the numbers of the dead seem to be climbing, and sometimes it's too much for the people on the ground." So far her team of civilians had avoided being bitten, but there were some close calls.

"By now the RV park is probably empty," Amy said, "but I think they're starting to come from those hotel and seaside condo complexes farther south. I'd like to lead a clearing operation."

Liz denied the request. There simply wasn't enough manpower or ammunition, the same reasons the scavenging parties couldn't go exploring much beyond the immediate marina areas. A residential area to the east could provide them with much-needed supplies, and the town itself on the other side of the river would be a real boon, but—at least for now, she conceded—they couldn't risk the losses.

Still, there were three losses in as many weeks. Fortunately, to Liz's thinking, only one had been a coastie while the other two were refugees on work details. Those deaths weren't as significant as trained crew. Including the two surviving men from *Klondike*, and the pair of airmen they had picked up in Port Angeles, *Joshua James* was down to a total of eighteen serving Coast Guardsmen.

Charlie knocked at his sister's door, and she let him in. He was wearing a black knit watch cap and a dark gray fleece pullover under his combat vest. In addition to the grooming standard, Liz had loosened the uniform regs, in part to conserve water used for laundry, but also to boost crew morale. The chief wore his sidearm as well as a machete-like blade he'd found on a fishing boat, and his M4 was slung on his back. He brought coffee.

Liz smiled in appreciation and took the cup, waving him into a chair. She was able to drink without wincing now, the knife wound to her face less painful and healing in a ragged pink scar, just as Castellano said it would. This had become a routine for them, some quiet time in her quarters late in the evening before third watch began. She asked the same question she did every night.

"How's the crew?" Since their time at sea, her brother had changed, making a real effort to win over the crew, eliminating the derogatory sea slang from his vocabulary (terms such as *deck ape* and *bilge rat*) and treating the young men and women as human beings. As a result, and as the only chief on board now, he had become something of a father figure and big brother seeing to their needs, keeping them positive, encouraging them when they were low. He now had both the respect and pulse of the crew, and that was important to any captain.

Chick eased into a chair. "They're holding it together. Keeping busy helps, and so do regular meals. Having the civvies handle some of the workload is a big relief. Getting the chance to kill a Whiskey-Delta *really* helps some of them, helps with their anger and fear."

She nodded. "Any problems?"

He gave a shrug. "Homesickness. Questions about their families, worry about being infected. Nothing too serious; I'm dealing with it. No one is speaking against you."

"And my officers?" Liz knew Charlie watched and listened and would give her the straight story, a very valuable asset.

"The girl is too busy to gripe. She's trying really hard, and she listens when I talk to her." In the Coast Guard, it was the chiefs who typically trained and looked after junior officers. "She'll be okay. Lt. Riggs was a little bent out of shape when you wouldn't let him recon the airport down south, but he's over it. It would be great to get him a helicopter."

"And I'd love to get him one. It would change everything for us," Liz said.

"Otherwise he's a fair leader and a good watch-stander," said Charlie. "He's just itching to fly."

The captain nodded. She hadn't been speaking lightly. A working helicopter would open up all sorts of doors: improved recon, extended scavenging efforts, and the ability to send out longer ground patrols that could depend on air support and medevac if needed.

"Hey, I got you something today," Charlie said, and pulled a black square of folded cloth from a pouch on his combat harness. "I found it on that booze cruise schooner in the marina." He opened it for her to see.

She looked at it and shook her head. "You have a sick sense of humor, Chick."

He laughed and tucked it away.

She leaned back in the chair and sipped her coffee. "How are you holding up?"

The patented Charlie Kidd grin appeared. "Never better."

He looked it too, but that hadn't always been the case. Charlie had forever been rough around the edges, and he'd had his share of problems. In school there had been truancy, underage drinking, and fighting. Lots of fighting. He didn't get along well with other kids, and not being as large as most of them, he was often picked on. Charlie compensated by going on the offensive, taking on boys much bigger than he was and taking his share of beatings in the process. In time, when kids realized the small but scrappy boy wasn't afraid to fight back—sometimes by ambush in a school hallway followed by a ruthless pummeling—they left him alone. In high school Charlie discovered the weight room, put on mass and muscle, and became a real threat that people avoided.

He used his new size to settle old grudges, and was expelled several times. Teachers began to label him a *bad kid*.

Liz's mother and father, both professionals working in Boston, grew increasingly worried that their son was headed down a road that ended in either prison or self-destruction. It was Liz who persuaded Charlie, after he'd kicked around aimlessly after high school for a few years, to join the Coast Guard, where he would be provided with much-needed focus and discipline. Charlie consented and quickly began to thrive in the structured world of the military.

He faced obstacles and setbacks, however. Learning to play well with others didn't come easily to him, and there was still the occasional fight. These were almost always off-duty with alcohol involved, but he'd once gotten into a confrontation aboard ship with a larger man who outranked him, but who said the wrong thing to Charlie.

I said step lively, short stuff. And what the hell are you smiling about?

The senior man ended up with four missing teeth and Chick landed in the brig, minus one stripe.

Surprisingly, Charlie had come back from the incident and worked to improve himself, changing his attitude and committing to a career in the service. Liz was proud of him for that. A lot of people would have used the setback as an excuse for self-pity, choosing failure over hard work, but not him. He was still rough-around-the-edges Charlie, and he still struggled with relationships. He had never had a woman in his life who was more than a fling, although recently Liz had noticed he was spending time with a refugee named Ava, and in his case she looked the other way regarding fraternization. He had made something of himself, rising to the rank of senior chief. A comfortable retirement would have been in his future.

A retirement where he could go out on his boat and murder drug traffickers. She tried to push that aside.

Despite his many improvements, Liz knew her brother better than anyone, and she could tell that inside, he hadn't changed all that much from the little boy always on the alert for attack, prepared to meet it with a disproportionate level of violence. It seemed that something was always simmering just beneath Charlie's surface, a darkness behind those smiling eyes.

Liz knew where it came from.

"I finally heard that one of the civvies you shot was a teacher," Liz said, her voice soft as she watched him.

Chick looked right back at her. "I heard that too."

. . .

*M*om and Dad are getting sick of this, Chick," Liz said. *They were in her 1980 sky-blue Mustang, two years old now but new to her. All her friends thought it was cool that she had a car at sixteen, and Liz was in love with the sleek, powerful machine. And maybe in love with Scott Darby too, a boy one year older than her, though she was less sure of that. Eight-year-old Charlie rode in the Mustang's passenger seat.*

"It's bad enough you get held for detention almost every day," she continued, "but now Saturdays too?" *She lit a cigarette. Mom and Dad didn't know she smoked, but she wasn't worried about lighting up in front of her brother. If there was one thing the little turd did well, it was keeping his mouth shut.*

Like he was doing right now. Charlie rode in silence, hands clasped in his lap, looking at his Keds.

Liz held the cigarette below the door as they stopped at a traffic light. Lexington, Massachusetts, wasn't that big a town, and she didn't want someone who might know her mother to see her smoking and make a phone call.

"Why can't you just be normal?" *Liz demanded.*

Charlie said nothing.

Liz went to the public high school, but Charlie was still in elementary school, and the teachers didn't care for her little brother's foul language, lackluster schoolwork, and playground scuffles. He was held after class as punishment all the time now, and it was Liz who had to break away from whatever she was doing—as if she were being punished for having a life!—to collect him at the end of the day. Mr. Drummond, the athletics coach, finally announced that what the boy needed was the disciplines of sports and physical exercise, and he took on Charlie's correction personally, forcing him into four hours of Saturday detention every week.

And Liz was expected to drop him off and pick him up. It was embarrassing. This was the fourth Saturday in a row, and it wasn't fair. Why should she suffer because Chick was a little snot bag?

"I've had it too," she said, flicking her butt out the window a full block before they reached the school. "You better cut the shit, Chickie."

He said nothing as the Mustang rumbled to a stop at the side door to the elementary school, and made no move to reach for the door handle.

"Well? Get out."

Charlie looked at her, and when he did there were tears in his eyes. "Don't make me go, Sis," he said, his clasped hands coming up. "Please just take me home."

"What are you doing, you little creep?" she said. "Mom and Dad will beat your ass. This wouldn't be happening if you didn't act like—"

The boy seized her arm in both hands, tears running down his cheeks. "Please."

Liz pulled her arm free. "Why?"

Chick just shook his head.

"Fine." She reached across him and opened his door. "Get out right now. And you better be here when I come back at three o'clock."

He looked at her for a long moment, then climbed out of the car. Liz watched the eight-year-old walk slowly toward the school, his head down as he wiped at his eyes. Mr. Drummond stood in the doorway smiling, and waved to Liz as she drove away.

She hadn't learned about what had been happening until many years later, right after Charlie graduated from his Coast Guard basic training in New Jersey. Liz, a young officer by then, had gone to the ceremony dressed in her whites, glowing with pride for her little brother and the service branch they now both shared. Their parents had passed several years earlier, and Liz was all Charlie had left.

In a quiet moment under a tree on base, Charlie finally told her about Mr. Drummond, and in a voice devoid of emotion he described what the man had done. There had been no sexual molestation, he assured her, but the physical abuse was something else entirely. Drummond made him run endless basketball drills, and when he was too slow or lost his grip on the ball, he was forced to drop his gym shorts while the man beat his bare buttocks with a leather belt. Drummond assured him that if he told anyone, Charlie would not be believed, and then Drummond would creep into his bedroom one night and strangle him. Sometimes Charlie was forced to drink glasses of water until he could no longer swallow, then had to stand on the court's foul line until he peed himself.

"He did other things," Charlie had said. "All in the name of discipline. All of it hurt. And sometimes he caught small animals, pets mostly, and made me watch while he killed them in the gymnasium basement." He didn't add that eventually *he* was made to do the killing. Charlie went on to describe a menu of abusive acts perpetrated by the man. After that moment in his sister's car, right up until now, Charlie had never spoken of it. He endured.

Liz felt like she might be sick, cried, and held her brother before becoming angry and demanding justice. All that passed quickly as guilt hit her like a bullet.

"You tried to tell me, Chick," she had cried. "Oh, God, I'm sorry."

Charlie didn't know why he waited until what should have been a happy moment to break the news. He didn't blame her, but he also never said as much, and wasn't able to explain that, either. He told his sister she was to do nothing, and had never spoken of it again, to her or anyone. Mr. Drummond was never revealed for what he was, and if the school knew, they covered it up quietly.

Now, as Charlie Kidd sat drinking coffee across from his sister, he examined her lean face, the lines around her eyes, and realized how very long ago that had been. He waited to see if she would press the issue about the man he'd killed in the cannery. The fact that he'd been a teacher was purely coincidental, and Charlie had been more bothered by the fact that the man was allowing a child to be held like cattle for a future meal. Not much, however, for Charlie Kidd knew he was no crusader. It had been more for the sport.

Liz said nothing more. Charlie knew his sister continued to carry the guilt for what had happened, that she had tried so hard in the years following to look after him. Though it might have helped her feel better, Charlie never felt the need to talk to her about it. He supposed it was too painful. He had, however, found an outlet for that pain.

Nearly a dozen murders in twenty-one years. Henry Blake was nothing, merely the latest.

The Coast Guard had taken him to ports all across America and the Caribbean, and he'd always waited until the need was truly upon him before taking a nocturnal trip off the ship to find someone worth killing. They were usually men, though two had been women. He didn't act impulsively, careful to cover his tracks. There was nothing sexual about it, no ritualism or bloody messages. And he never spoke to his victims, gave no explanations as they watched him screw a silencer onto the end of his pistol, some pleading, others praying.

It was a release, and it was fun. The words *serial killer* never entered his thoughts.

He would never talk about that part of his life with his big sister, either.

As October drew to a close, Liz faced a steadily growing list of problems. Fresh water remained a constant issue, and despite the supplies from the cannery, feeding more than fifty people every day was becoming a real drain on their resources. The scavenging parties were forced to travel farther beyond the ship's sphere of control. One such run resulted in two civilians being killed outright, and the fish and game warden returning freshly bitten.

Charlie quietly took care of him that very night.

Liz decided that the extended raids must have stirred up the dead, because the rifle positions at Amy's two defensive dump trucks fired much more regularly as the dead drifted in, costing precious ammo. They were starting to slip past at night too, and one Whiskey-Delta even got into the Coast Guard station itself and killed a twelve-year-old girl. Generator-powered lights were set up on the lawn, allowing the sentries to spot and stop the dead as they came out of the night, but generators used fuel. More resources being depleted.

The Guardian Ethos of the Coast Guard was a code by which Liz had lived her entire adult life. Part of it stated, *I serve the citizens of the United States. I will protect them. I will defend them. I will save them. I am their shield.* But Elizabeth was finding it increasingly difficult to view these refugees—especially those who appeared to make little in the way of contribution—as the people she was supposed to be protecting. More and more they felt like a burden, and their losses no longer mattered to her beyond the resulting change in logistics.

In the span of two days there was an incident of rape in the Coast Guard station's barracks and an attempted theft of weapons and supplies as a man tried to escape into the night. Both offenders were civilian refugees.

Liz had them both hanged, not even bothering to attend. Amy Liggett was ordered to preside over the executions.

Charlie Kidd handled the rope.

NINETEEN

Rosa was cold, and the thin scrubs, now soaked to the waist, did little to protect her. Her sneakers slid across a metal deck two feet below the surface of waters that were only a few degrees north of freezing, and her teeth chattered behind clenched jaws. Rosa's medical knowledge told her that hypothermia wouldn't be far off if she didn't find a way to get out of this water and warm up.

But there was no time.

Michael was down here somewhere, and he would be cold too. Would he be smart enough—would he be *able*—to get himself out of the water? A baritone gurgle came from the darkness somewhere ahead, and she knew that *Nimitz* was not only taking on water but also moving. She felt the motion in her body, a subtle tremble and the vaguest of rocking. When she put her light on the corridor she saw the surface canted slightly to the left, in line with the ship's list, and as the ruptured hull took on more of the bay, every space in that direction would flood more quickly than those to starboard. When she reached an intersection, she headed to the right. Hopefully Michael would have done the same.

A new stench filled the air, and her light revealed a blanket of trash covering the water's surface. With each step the odor sharpened, making her wrinkle her nose. This wasn't a dead smell, it was something else.

Two open hatches faced one another across the passageway, and she aimed her light and pistol into each. On the right was a small compartment filled with pipes and valves, and a heavy-duty stainless steel washer and dryer. Plastic bottles of bleach and detergent as well as a few shirts had collected in the corner where the list was greatest. When she looked through the hatch on the left, she recoiled at the vile odor inside. The lid to a trash disposal unit was raised against the far wall, and the opening beneath it—as well as whatever foul depths the trash chute led to—was flooded and overflowing into the compartment, the waste from below floating up and out.

As she quickly moved away, she couldn't help but wonder if somewhere down in that black hell, a dead crewman clawed at filth-streaked walls.

There was a long, deep metallic groan that seemed to come from everywhere, and she stopped, still shin-deep in putrid, freezing seawater. It was not a sound the dead made, she decided. It was the ship. The subtle, rocking sensation intensified slightly, and deep here in the lightless bow she had a moment of disconnection, her sense of direction gone. She was lost in a dank, frigid purgatory where the dead hunted the living and the living were doomed to wander until they froze to death or were devoured.

That's panic you're feeling. Stop it.

Only the angle of the water showed her port versus starboard, and though she knew the carrier was moving, she didn't know if it was floating in the direction of its list, turning in a circle, or even drifting backward.

The deep gurgle, like the breathing of a fearsome, mythological beast deep in its cave, had her worried about one direction the ship *might* be heading. Down. *Could an aircraft carrier sink? Of course, any ship could sink. But were those tears in the hull enough to do it?*

There was nothing she could do about it, so she shook her head and tried to focus, fighting the urge to simply start running, trying to think about what she was doing and trying *not* to think about the cold. And yet the cold *was* the immediate problem, as well as finding Michael.

I'm getting scattered.

A throaty snarl from behind her reminded Rosa that those weren't the only immediate problems, and she turned with her light to see the passageway crowded with three flabby and bloated creatures coming toward her from just beyond the hatches to the laundry and the trash disposal. Seawater dripped from bluish lips, and white eyes stared out of pale, swollen faces. Two were in uniform; one was naked.

Rosa raised her pistol. *Fifteen yards, poor lighting.* She lowered the weapon as she couldn't risk missing and wasting rounds, couldn't chance attracting even more attention with the echoing noise of shots. Instead she turned back and kept moving up the passage, slogging through the water and looking for a better place to make her stand.

The flashlight eventually picked out a T intersection ahead with a closed hatch set in the wall facing her, and she waded into it. To her left and right were short hallways leading to open hatches, the murky shapes of stacked bunks and lockers beyond each. *Crew berthing.* Splashing came from the one to her right, and she almost turned away before thinking, *What if that's Michael in there? What if it's not, and I trap myself in a space with no way out?*

The bloated trio trudged through the floating trash behind her, the naked one in the lead and making a wet snuffling noise as it got closer.

"Michael!" Rosa yelled, her voice carrying.

No response.

"Michael, can you hear me?" The sound of her voice caused the bloated trio to move faster, and the splashes neared the entrance to the berthing compartment. Rosa kept the light on it, hoping to see . . .

A young woman's face appeared in the light, pasty-skinned with cloudy gray eyes, wet hair plastered to her face. She growled and started through the hatch. Shadowy figures moved behind her. Ripples of disturbed water washed against the backs of Rosa's knees, and now the rancid odor of the bloated trio cut through the reek of backed-up garbage, making her gag.

The hatch in the wall before her had the words *ENLISTED REC* stenciled in white letters across it. Rosa hadn't taken the time to listen at the door to check if anything was moving on the other side. The bloated trio was closing, and the pasty woman with her shadowy companions was moving in from the right. No time.

Without knowing what awaited her, Rosa threw the hatch handle, pushed it open, and went in.

He had once been Machinist's Mate Sam Englewood of Flagstaff, Arizona. At eighteen he'd fled small-town life at the edge of the Grand Canyon to find adventure in the Navy, eager to be away from the parched, high desert so he could experience the vastness of wind and sea. His every expectation had been surpassed, and he'd fallen in love with the Navy.

Last summer his ship was overwhelmed by the multiplying dead, and Sam died at the hands—and teeth—of his own shipmates. His death was a bad one, caught halfway through a partially closed hatch, both legs chewed away at the knees. Since then he'd dragged himself through the lonely, flooded corridors, submerged from the chest down and pulling himself along on stiffened arms. Months in the water had turned him a bluish-white, his decomposing tissue heavy with seawater. There was no pain, no concept of the passage of time, only the driving hunger he had no way of satisfying.

Until now.

Food had suddenly appeared with a creak of metal and a burst of white light. This was followed by the sound of breathing, a sudden presence of warmth and movement. The gnawing hunger flared in his dead and diseased brain.

With a wet gasp, the former Sam Englewood started pulling himself through the water of the partially flooded compartment, his face barely held above the surface as milky eyes hunted in the dim light.

Rosa shoved the hatch closed behind her, pushing hard against the resistance of water flowing over the knee knocker, and dogged the handle tightly. She knew the dead would open it when they arrived at the other side, so she swung her light around looking for a way to jam the handle.

It was a recreation center. One of the recent earthquakes, or possibly a combination of the ship's collisions and the resulting water, had flung couches and chairs at skewed angles, tipping over a television and dropping a soda machine on its face. A Ping-Pong table had slid into a far bulkhead, one end collapsed, and shelves that once held books and games were shaken empty. The surface of the dark water was adrift with swollen paperbacks and magazines, Ping-Pong balls, and plastic video game controllers. The room stank of decay and stagnant water.

Something heavy thumped against the hatch behind her, and Rosa put her weight on top of the handle, holding it down.

Swinging the light around again, she saw an open hatch on the far side of the room with a passageway beyond, and she could see nothing moving down there. *My exit.* She panned left, still holding the handle down with her gun hand—something was making it wiggle—and saw the overturned television and floating game controllers. They were of an older style that connected to the unit, not the newer, wireless versions.

The cables. I'll tie the handle down. But that would mean letting go and crossing the room. She'd never get back before the creatures on the other side—

A cold hand gripped her at the knee and she screamed, swinging the light down out of instinct. It grazed the head of Sam Englewood, propped up in the water at her feet. In the beam she saw a rotting boy in blue coveralls grabbing her leg with his other hand now, hauling himself out of the water, mouth gaping.

Rosa tried to jerk away, then released her hold on the handle and shoved the muzzle of her Glock down against the crown of the corpse's head, pulling the trigger twice. There was an explosion of soggy brain matter, and she screamed at a hot burst of pain in her foot. The dead boy's grip loosened and the body slid down her leg, slipping beneath the surface with a head shattered by contact gunshot wounds. The hatch handle flipped up and the weight of hungry corpses on the other side propelled it open, the steel banging hard into Rosa and causing her to stagger sideways.

Her foot burned and throbbed. *Not a bite. Ricochet.* Then the bloated trio was stumbling into the compartment, only feet away from her. The pasty girl and her shadowy bunkmates were snarling behind them, pushing against soft flesh in their hurry to get at the food.

The medic shot the naked corpse in the side of the head. It fell, and its fellows were forced to shove the limp figure to the side, buying Rosa precious seconds. She headed across the room, limping now as she waded, still holding on to both the flashlight and the pistol. Moans filled the room, accompanied by heavy splashing. Her foot hurt *so* much, and she wondered how much damage the bullet had done.

Rosa stumbled through the next hatch and into yet another unexplored passageway, leaving a trail of blood in the water.

Michael opened his eyes to absolute darkness.

He was drifting, his body sliding across something hard and unyielding until his back struck something equally hard, stopping him. There was movement around him, something tugging at his leg and ribs, but no pain. He reached for the movement, fingertips brushing against something soft, and the sensation in both places stopped immediately.

The boy gripped a vertical pipe along the wall to pull himself to a standing position, his movements slow, feeling resistance all around him, eyes wide and seeing nothing. The movement he'd sensed earlier was going away from him, and he followed, each step an effort. A sound came from somewhere ahead, a thumping, muffled and distant. He headed toward it.

Michael's reaching hands touched something soft again, and his fingers closed on it. The something moved, and just as quickly he released it, continuing to follow the movement in a darkness that seemed to push back at him.

He was hungry. Oh, so hungry.

There was something that felt like a red spark going off in his brain, but Michael could articulate neither the color nor the organ in which the reaction was occurring; his was a world of sensation, not words. The redness flared again, and for the briefest of instances Michael's eyes saw what was before him as if through a red-and-black lens: a flooded passageway where two others like him, completely submerged, were moving slowly through the water, heading for an ascending metal stairway. Then the flash was gone, and Michael was returned to the darkness. Hungry. Following.

The movement ahead of him started upward, and Michael's

awkward feet found the steps, knees bending stiffly as he climbed. He could see the shadowy figures above him now, for there was a soft, gray light somewhere above.

Hungry. His teeth clicked slowly together.

The boy's head broke the surface as he trudged up and out of the same stairwell opening through which he'd been pulled, his feet finding the flooded deck. A light resting under the water off to one side created a gray sphere in the room. In that light he saw the two that had preceded him shuffling toward an opening. To his right stood a third, a woman who stared at him for a moment before turning away slowly.

The boy's gnawed-upon thigh and open rib cage drooled pink fluid mixed with seawater, and his eyes were clouded over constricted pupils. He opened his mouth to make a sound, and water bubbled out. Behind his teeth, his tongue was rapidly turning black.

Another red flash, the world seen in red-and-black tones, and Michael felt a ripple pass through his body. The hunger was worse now, but he didn't follow the others, even though he knew it might mean food. He was feeling a different pull, and instead he moved through the partially flooded compartment, past coils of rope and racks of chain, finding a dark corner. The boy lowered himself into the water, the surface nearly covering him, and curled into a fetal position. The red flashes in his brain accelerated, sparks firing one after the other in a crackling sensation that began to travel down through all the muscles of his body.

Michael's black tongue moved, and he gurgled under the water.

Then his body began to convulse as the transformation came on.

TWENTY

There were corpses in the cars, and they were moving.

Evan walked under the shelter of the elevated freeway, out of the rain, passing a mountain of automobiles that had spilled from the ruined structure above. Below in the shadows of the highway, Evan's boots crunched through weeds turned black and brittle. Groans and thumping came from the spill of tipped-over and angled cars, gray arms reaching through shattered windows and dead faces snapping their teeth, still strapped into their seats. Trapped on the freeway high above, these drifters had avoided the worst of the fire, and he could still make out their features.

Evan decided the burned ones were better. They looked less human. He turned away and kept moving, his broken wrist still slung against his chest.

The remains of a chain-link fence crossed his path up ahead, but when he reached it he found it peeled back by heat in many places, sooty and melted, and he passed through without difficulty. Boots kicking through cinders, he emerged from the shadows of I-580 and back into the rain. Here, the downpour kept the ground from turning into black dust as he walked. Evan's eyes swept back and forth across the terrain, searching for movement, waiting to see those deadly shapes rising from the cinders.

He saw none. He was alone.

Wishful thinking.

The rain made a gentle pattering sound all around him. The sky above was a slowly turning mass of dark clouds that promised no end to the cold rain, and Evan decided the temperature had slipped below fifty degrees. The downpour made it worse, and though he was thankful for the layers of his jacket and flight suit, he had no protection for his exposed head and neck. He shivered.

The vest has a signal mirror, a whistle, and even sunscreen. No goddamn hat. Perfect.

He moved past a field of burned trees and stopped, looking at what lay before him. From the air, the terrain had seemed like just another scene of destruction, quickly flown over and easily forgotten. Things were more real here on the ground.

It was a neighborhood, or had been before petrochemical fires swept through here, and likely an affluent one. Gently curving streets wound through the charred shells of megahomes, roasted trees and skeletal shrubbery standing amid ashy lawns once groomed and immaculate. Stone and brick walls marked the boundaries of larger properties, the remains of sprawling houses set well back behind them. Garages had collapsed onto Bentleys and Range Rovers, and the black hulk of a Lexus SUV rested on its rims not far from where Evan stood. The place looked like black-and-white footage on the History Channel depicting scenes of destruction caused by German planes during the Blitz.

Evan saw that he had emerged at the neighborhood's midway point; to the right the streets descended in tiers to the water's edge, and on the left the roads and shattered homes climbed in levels up a hillside. He couldn't imagine what these places must have once cost, or even the kinds of jobs and incomes people would have needed to afford them and the toys that went with such a lifestyle.

At the curve of a street not far away, Evan saw what looked like a burned-out police car but decided it was too small for that. A private security company? That would fit.

The rain and the lengthening afternoon cut visibility to the point that he couldn't see much into the bay, only a soft, dove-gray curtain that thickened as it stretched across the water. Similarly, the neighborhood spreading to the south grew ghostly and then disappeared behind a veil of rain and mist. He shivered, wished again for a hat, and walked into the road.

Silence hung about him. Nothing was moving, but he eyed the burned structures warily. There were lots of places for drifters to hide, and they were surely out there. He had no choice but to keep moving.

A spasm of coughing racked him then, one that left him seeing little white floaters in his vision, and he took several long pulls from the oxygen bottle. The pressure gauge showed that it now held only a quarter of its original content, and he wondered again at the vile particles he must have been breathing in as he crossed the destroyed refinery fields. He decided he was grateful for the rain, as it suppressed the ash and made it easier to breathe.

Evan climbed onto the roof of the Lexus, his weight making it creak, and pulled the small pair of binoculars from his vest. The streets held only debris, blackened vehicles, and downed trees. There were a few charcoal bodies on the asphalt, but they weren't moving. *Shooting victims during the outbreak? Drifters who'd had their brains fried during the firestorm? Or the walking dead, still virulent and waiting for some stimuli to get them up and moving?*

He turned his binoculars down the hillside toward the water's edge. Surf slid up and back against the rocks and the occasional stone pier, and he caught sight of movement. Focusing, he saw a family of otters out at the end of a pier, slipping into the water and then hopping back out. It made him smile. Something had survived, and they couldn't care less about the fate of the human world.

A gust of wind drove the rain hard at him for a moment, and he hunched into his vest and jacket, turning his back. *Probably closer to forty degrees.* When he looked again, the otters were gone. Evan checked his map. He was in an area labeled as Point Richmond, and to the south, beyond the affluent, hillside neighborhood, the map showed a stretch of green space, a park or preserve of some kind. Beyond that was Brickyard Cove, a place with more big houses, marinas, and yacht clubs. He remembered flying over it.

Thirst began to pull at him, and simply tilting his head back and opening his mouth wasn't getting it done. He searched his survival vest but found nothing capable of collecting water. Maybe he could find something in the ruins of these houses, but the thought gave him pause. Was he thirsty enough to risk encountering the dead within those tangles of broken walls and fallen beams? Not quite, but he knew he would be soon.

Evan wanted to keep moving south toward where he knew the carrier to be, but he stopped himself. Did he really think he was going to walk out of here? Walk the shoreline down through El Cerrito and into Oakland, and not be eaten? Did he think he would find a boat south of his position in Brickyard Cove? He'd flown over that too, and already knew there were no boats. He was being stupid. He could walk out of here, but only into another hell. At least here it was quiet.

What would Vlad do? First, he wouldn't have gotten himself shot down, and even if he had, the Russian would probably be halfway to Nimitz *by now.* But Evan was still alive and still moving, so he congratulated himself for that small victory. How long he remained alive would depend on straight thinking and a good measure of luck.

High ground. He thought about the locator beacon with its rubber antenna sticking out of his pocket. Vlad said it used satellites, like a GPS unit, so high ground wouldn't matter, would it? Evan knew from his time aboard *Nimitz* and his conversations with the handful of Navy men that there were precious few of them left functioning. Would the beacon even do him any good? And the unit's battery would have a limited life span . . . eight hours, Vlad had said? He didn't dare count on it. No, it had to be high ground, where he might have success using his flares.

Evan headed up the curving street, walking down the center, watching the ruins to either side. The silence was palpable, and he wondered at the absence of crows. Everywhere he'd been since this nightmare began, there had been crows, a dominant, surviving species shrieking and squabbling over carrion. Not here. Had they been burned out of the sky, or was the air too poisonous even for them? He shook his head. *You think too much.*

The rain made sooty puddles on the asphalt, backing up in the cement gutters along the curb where drains were choked with debris. Around him, blackened trees stood behind soot-covered walls, their limbs reaching for the sky like skeleton hands, and the wind rattling through those fingers carried the scent of meat left too long on the grill. His boots scuffed along the street, his eyes constantly searching.

At an intersection he came upon what had been a landscaping truck, and a quick inspection yielded nothing of use. He turned left, taking a street that curved up past an enormous house missing its roof, a shell of walls and windows missing glass, fallen beams visible beyond.

The street climbed past several more big homes, then curved left again. Ahead of him, a Porsche Cayenne had broadsided a '67 Camaro—someone's pampered toy—and pinned it against a curbside electrical box. Both vehicles were burned down to their rims, and as Evan discovered upon looking inside, any evacuation supplies the vehicles might have carried had gone up as well.

The lump of charcoal pinned behind the Camaro's melted steering wheel made a wheezing sound and tried to turn its head. Evan ignored it and went to the trunk, kicking at the lid until it popped a bit and he could work his fingers under the lip, heaving it up with a loud squeal. The spare was a congealed mass wrapped around a rim, but the jack and, more importantly, the tire iron were still screwed down on top of it. *Thank God for good old-fashioned Detroit iron. New cars only had that crappy swivel wrench thing.* He left the crash behind, now carrying the jack handle instead of the pistol.

Still nothing came at him from the burned houses, and at the top of the curve the street climbed again, cutting back onto a higher tier. Evan followed the incline, seeing that there were no more houses higher than the ones on this street. He'd reached the top of the hill. Rainwater tumbled down a curb gutter on his left, and he crouched to let it flow across one hand, tasting it. Then he cupped his palms and swallowed more. It didn't taste particularly good, but it also didn't have a metallic flavor, so he drank his fill.

There's probably a dead thing in this gutter just up the street. Fuck it.

As he squatted beside the curb, he caught movement in his peripheral vision and jumped to his feet, gripping the tire iron once more. The thing was moving slowly, coming through an opening where a driveway passed through a decorative brick wall. Iron gates stood open to either side, one hanging on a single hinge. The thing—male or female, he couldn't tell—was missing an arm and walking with its torso bent to the left, moving in a crooked, halting gait. It was slow, clumsy, but it was still coming at him.

Evan strode to it and swung the jack handle, coming at the head from the side, like a kid aiming at a T-ball. The head disintegrated in a puff of black dust, burned black chunks, and gray sludge. The body collapsed with a cracking sound, and Evan stood over it, looking at the sluglike brain matter.

How the hell is that making it possible for this thing to move and kill? And for him, that was the single most frustrating aspect to the entire goddamn apocalypse. *How?* He shook his head and gave the sludge a stomp for good measure.

Ahead, he saw a house that looked like it would do. It had no wall around it and was fairly close to the street, but it was tall, set into the hillside behind it in a series of climbing floors, perched highest among its neighbors. It must have been an impressive thing once, he thought, a boxy, modern design of stucco-faced concrete and expansive windows. The glass was gone now, and the stucco was baked black and encircled the base of the walls in a ring, but the concrete remained intact. As Evan walked up the short driveway, he saw that three of its four garage doors were open and empty. Holding his small flashlight between the fingers of his slung hand, Evan readied the jack handle and went into the garage.

Fire had swept through here as well; piles of ash were heaped in the corners and the remains of a long workbench and cabinets stood against the far wall, the stainless steel doors warped from the heat. To his left, in the remaining, closed garage bay, Evan saw something that broke his heart. The former biker recognized the twisted motorcycle's shape at once; a 1947 Indian Chief. It would have had big curving fenders, whitewalls, a fringed seat, and acres of chrome. Evan wondered if it had been red. Now it was black and warped, someone's thirty-thousand-dollar vintage toy reduced to scrap metal.

The interior of the house was as expected; every room on every level was scorched and blackened lumps were all that remained of top-end furniture and electronics. The concrete stairs between each floor remained intact, and the roof had managed to hold up in places. Evan continued his tour of the home, finding nothing of interest but, more importantly, ensuring that he was alone.

A pair of curled-up, charcoal bodies lay in a pile of ashes that might have been a king-sized bed, but they were long dead and harmless. The oily remains of a pistol dangled from one skeletal finger. *Murder-suicide.* Evan turned away, suddenly ashamed for having mourned the loss of a motorcycle.

Satisfied that he was alone, he returned to the kitchen and poked through the debris until he found a stainless steel mixing bowl that wasn't too badly warped. He figured it could hold rainwater and carried his prize upstairs to the highest room, which featured a balcony that looked out over the neighborhood and the misty bay beyond. He set the metal bowl outside.

For a while he stood in the balcony opening, staring out at the grim afternoon. It was after six o'clock, and the weather would help bring on an early night. Should he find a way up to the roof and use one of his flares? If someone was tracking in on his beacon, it would pinpoint his position. If anyone was close enough to see it. If anyone was coming.

And what else might the flare attract?

He decided the weather would cut visibility to the point that using a flare now would be a waste. He would wait until morning, and hopefully it would clear. For now he needed rest.

He'd have to take his chances, as there was no way to barricade the place, nothing he could use to warn him if a drifter entered the house. Evan sat and settled his back against a wall, trying to make his wrist comfortable and wishing for some Advil. Pistol in his right hand and resting in his lap, he closed his eyes and listened to the rain peppering the metal bowl, doubting sleep would come. He was cold, and he never slept well when he was . . .

Evan dreamed of running, holding Maya's hand as the two of them fled from something they could not see, something that wanted to hurt them, wanted the baby. As he dreamed and night fell on the Bay Area, the long, black silhouette of a ship slid silently past Richmond, heading south.

TWENTY-ONE

Chief Liebs stood in what had once been a *Nimitz* classroom, where crewmen learned everything from first aid to the repair protocols for broken catapult equipment. It had since been transformed into a school, and twelve children sat at the tables, half of them orphans. They were doing work that ranged from junior high mathematics to the coloring and pasting of kindergarteners.

The young girl named Wind was hugging Miss Sophia's leg, telling her about what happened in the bow, and about Michael. The chief filled her in on what he knew.

"You said Doc Rosa sent Denny back here?" Sophia asked the girl.

"He was scared to go back there," she said, "so she told him to come find you."

Sophia, one of the survivors whom Angie West had rescued at the firehouse, and who had taken up housekeeping with their pilot Vladimir, looked at the chief and shook her head. "We haven't seen him." She glanced nervously at Ben, the three-year-old orphan she and Vladimir had adopted. He was sitting with some of the other children, coloring a cow Sophia had drawn for him.

The gunner's mate shook his head. *Another missing kid?* "We've got problems with Evan's flight. I can't go look for Denny right now."

Sophia was about to say something when the room began to vibrate, the shaking growing in intensity. Children began to cry out and then scream as markers and toys rattled off tables and a free-standing whiteboard tipped over with a crash. The bigger kids held on to the smaller ones, huddled on the floor as the shaking made table legs jitter and the steel walls of the room seemed to rumble with the voice of some monstrous beast.

Then it was over. The adults moved through the room, checking to see that no one was hurt. A minute later a speaker mounted to the ceiling hummed with a voice they all knew.

"This is Father Xavier, speaking to all *Nimitz* residents. We have been boarded by a group of dangerous people who mean us harm. They are loose on the ship, and we are working to find them. Everyone is to lock down someplace safe, and make sure you are armed." There was a pause, and then, "Be prepared to defend your-selves."

Sophia looked at the chief, then at the only other adult in the room, a woman named Kay who was part of Calvin's extended fam-ily, and who had two of her own children in this room. Calvin's other son and two daughters were here as well. Kay saw the look and nodded toward a pair of shotguns that had been leaning in a corner and were now lying on the floor.

"I can't stay," said Liebs, running for the hatch. "Lock down and don't come out until it's over," he called, ducking through and slam-ming it closed behind him.

Sophia walked to Kay and spoke quietly. "Let's keep them all in here, and keep them calm," Sophia said. The younger ones were already picking up fallen papers and crayons, but the older children were watching the adults.

Kay nodded. "We can use metal chair legs to wedge the handles. They should hold, and we have the shotguns."

Sophia walked Kay to the corner and picked up one of the weapons, holding it close against her leg so the children wouldn't notice, still speaking softly. "Denny has to be somewhere between here and sick bay. I'm going after him."

Kay put a hand on her friend's arm. "Xavier told us to—"

"I heard the announcement. We can't leave him out there."

Kay hugged her. "Be careful."

"Lock up behind me. I won't be long." A moment later Sophia was in the passageway, and the hatch to the school thumped closed behind her, followed by a metallic rattle as Kay jammed the handle.

Sophia took a deep breath, racked the shotgun, and headed out.

The gunner's mate was still in his full battle gear from when they'd brought the refugees on board and escorted them to the officer's mess, and so now he jogged down a passageway with his M4 up and ready. Xavier's announcement—the equivalent of a general quarters alarm—hadn't given any details, but it was easy enough to put together what had happened. Liebs cursed himself. This had been their greatest fear, and he'd let his guard down. Stronger even than the self-recriminations was anger. Hostiles had breached his security and were roaming his ship. He was going to goddamn well put them down.

He ducked into an office that at one time belonged to a team of flight deck officers and snatched the phone off the wall, punching in an extension.

"Communications, Petty Officer Katcher," said a voice.

"PK, it's the chief."

"Hey, Guns," the man started, "what the—"

Liebs cut him off. "Listen up, PK. You heard the skipper's announcement. We've been boarded, nine adult hostiles. I don't know how they're armed. You packing?"

"Affirmative, I've got a sidearm."

"Good," said Liebs. "Make sure Banks is up to speed, and button up the bridge. Any luck with Evan's beacon?"

"That's a negative, Guns. I'm scanning the frequencies, but no contact yet."

The gunner's mate blew out a breath. "Okay. We can't try a rescue right now, anyway. Keep trying, and call me if that situation changes."

"Aye-aye, Chief."

"And PK, report any sightings or contact with boarders. Don't leave the bridge, don't try to engage."

"But Chief, if I get a shot—"

"You heard me, Petty Officer," Liebs said.

"Copy that. And by the way, the ship is adrift."

"I know, I can feel it," said the chief, clicking off. He spoke into the mic for the Hydra radio attached to the shoulder of his combat vest. "Stone, it's Guns, come in."

The boy responded at once. "I heard the announcement, Chief. Where do you need me?"

"Meet me at the armory. If you can find anyone along the way, bring them with you."

"Copy that."

"And Stone," Liebs said, "if you see someone you don't recognize, open fire. No hesitation."

"No problem." Stone clicked off.

Liebs headed back into the passageway, jogging once more. He keyed the mic again. "Xavier, it's Liebs."

Xavier and Calvin faced one another across the officer's mess; Mercy lay dead on the floor by an entrance, and Big Jerry lay near the galley doors with a butcher's knife sticking out of his chest. The two men were without words, looking at their lost friends, both consumed by a torrent of grief and guilt. Tommy went to the crying toddler still sitting on the deck, trying to comfort the boy as he watched the other men.

Xavier spoke first, his voice low. "We have to find them, Cal. We have to stop them before they hurt anyone else."

Calvin's eyes flashed, his face that of a wounded animal. "I'm going to find Michael."

"No," said Xavier, and Calvin took a step toward him, one hand still clenched around the knife he'd used to make sure Mercy didn't come back.

"Stop me," the hippie leader said.

Xavier walked toward him slowly, meeting his eyes. "Rosa is already looking for him."

"I'm taking this little guy to the school," Tommy said, "and then I'm going after Michael and Rosa."

The priest nodded, and the orderly lifted the abandoned toddler into his arms and pushed through the mess hall's doors, leaving the two men alone. "It's the best we can do for Michael," Xavier said. "For now."

Calvin said nothing.

"They'll find him, they'll bring him back." Xavier stood before his friend now. "And telling Maya about Evan will have to wait. If he's still alive, we'll find him too, but not right now."

"Everything you do gets people killed," Calvin said.

The words were a slap. He couldn't deny it, but there was no time to indulge in self-pity. Neither could his friend. The priest's expression remained hard, unchanged. "We need to find them," Xavier said. "Nothing is more important than that right now."

"My son—" Calvin started.

"There are other people who need protecting besides Michael," Xavier said, his voice sharp. "Your other kids, among them."

Tears sprang to Calvin's eyes. "You're a bastard," he whispered.

I know. The priest stepped close to the man. "I need you to toughen up, Calvin. Yes, I said to let them in and it was a mistake. Hate me later. It doesn't change the fact that they're here, and they're killing people." Xavier's eyes were cold. "The only way to save our people is to hunt these murderers down. You *have* to do this, and right now." *Oh, he was such a poor excuse for a friend and a priest.*

Chief Liebs called him on the Hydra then, and Xavier filled the gunner's mate in on what had happened with the refugees, and what he wanted from the chief. Then he clicked off and looked back at his friend.

The hippie stared at the ceiling, tears on his cheeks, thinking of his son wandering lost and afraid; of the young pilot and writer who had become a son to him, missing as well; and of his eldest daughter, who had now lost as much as Calvin. He thought of all the other faces aboard *Nimitz*, people he'd known for years and new friends he'd made. Other faces looked back at him, the people he'd failed, ever-present spirits haunting him.

"I'll go," Calvin said quietly, but then he pointed a finger at the priest. "But understand something, Father. If you come with *me*, then it's a manhunt and nothing less. No negotiating, no forgiveness, no mercy. You leave God behind for this."

A silence stretched between them, and then Xavier unslung the shotgun from his shoulder. "Let's go hunting."

S ophia padded down the corridor in sock feet, her shoes left behind at the school's hatch. The shotgun held eight shells, and other than blue sweatpants with *NAVY* down one leg in yellow letters and a zip-up sweater, it was all she had.

According to Wind, Doc Rosa had told Denny to go straight down to the classroom from sick bay. That left a lot of space in between; the medical center was on the 03 Gallery Deck just below the flight deck, along the central line of the vessel, just forward of amidships, and the classroom was slightly to starboard of the center line, but located on Second Deck, four levels below. For those who knew the layout, it was really a simple matter of descending the right stairway. Denny knew it as well as any of them, but he was young, and he'd been frightened.

Needle in a haystack.

Sophia headed up the starboard side toward the berthing compartment the orphans shared with some of the surviving adults, thinking he might have gone to a familiar place. When she turned a corner, her sock feet slid to a halt. The hatchway to the berthing compartment was open, and a man's arm was protruding from it, limp on the floor. She crept forward, the shotgun held before her and trembling.

She peered around the edge of the bulkhead. Lying on the floor with his throat cut was one of Calvin's people, a man called Pablo. She didn't know if that was his real name. The man's face wore a wide-eyed, surprised expression, and the blood was still pooling about him. His killers were close.

Not long dead, and that meant . . .

Pablo's eyes clouded over, and his fingers twitched.

Sophia wanted to scream, and she almost turned to run but then forced herself to stop. She couldn't let him get up and start roaming, and couldn't risk the sound a shotgun blast would make in these quiet passageways, alerting the man's killers. There was nothing nearby she could use, and she had no other weapons.

Biting her bottom lip and holding back a whimper, Sophia reversed the shotgun, aimed the butt at those cloudy, rolling eyes, and started smashing. Each blow shot a spatter of red across the walls, her sweatpants, and her face, and the thing on the floor grunted, flailing its arms. Three blows, five, six, and it was done. Sophia looked at the damage to make sure Pablo wouldn't be getting back up—the shotgun butt had done a thorough job—then sagged against a bulkhead and threw up.

After blotting her mouth on a sleeve and wiping the worst of the gore off the weapon on Pablo's pants leg, she entered the berthing compartment. Sophia had been here many times, looking in on all her orphans, ensuring that they had clothing and warm bedding and were brushing their teeth. Four adults lived here too, but right now everyone was out doing their jobs on the ship. Denny wasn't here.

Neither were any of the weapons the adults kept near their beds.

Sophia moved back into the corridor, stepping over the man's remains without looking down, and pressed on.

With Pablo gone, how many of Calvin's adults did that leave? Ten? She ran through the names in her head. *Yes, ten adults including Calvin and Maya, Mercy, Stone, and Kay. Evan made eleven. How many left from the firehouse? Herself, Big Jerry . . . God, were they the only ones left from there besides the kids? Rosa, Xavier, the four Navy guys . . . Not many people to fight off intrud-ers.* There had seemed to be so many of them back at the hangar on Alameda.

A cough and low voices echoed from somewhere up ahead, and Sophia ducked through a hatch marked *SONAR ACCESS 1.* She found herself in a compartment crammed with computer towers and walls of electronic circuitry, a single light bar glowing overhead. She eased the hatch until it was nearly closed, leaving a crack of space, and held her breath. The shotgun barrel pointed at the slender opening. If anyone decided to come through the hatch, they would get a surprise.

Boots thumped past the opening, and through the crack she had an instant's view of two bearded men in ratty sweaters, one carrying a rifle, the other a fire axe and a handgun. Neither man belonged on the carrier. They went by without slowing, speaking quietly to one another, and Sophia counted to thirty before looking out into the passageway once more. They were gone.

Her sock feet whispered over the steel decking as she continued toward sick bay, feeling as if her entire body were trembling. She kept her finger off the shotgun's trigger for fear that she might pull it by accident. At another intersection she turned left—checking first to be sure it was empty—and hurried up this new passage.

Had she been wearing shoes, her footsteps might have masked the faint sound on her right. Instead she slid to a halt and listened. It came again, a soft whimper from inside an enlisted berthing space on her right. Sophia entered slowly, the shotgun ready and her finger now curled around the trigger, advancing between triple stacks of racks, peering around banks of lockers.

"Denny," she called in a stage whisper. "Is that you?"

There was a cry and a blur of movement as something shot out from under a bottom rack. Sophia spun, nearly firing. Denny sobbed and ran to her, and Sophia dropped to her knees and took the boy in her arms. "Shh, it's okay, you're safe," she whispered. The boy shuddered, his tears soaking into her sweater. "I've got you, Denny, you're safe." *Needle one, haystack zero.*

"M-M-Michael . . ." he started.

Sophia stroked his hair. "I know, sweetie, I know. Wind told us."

"I'm s-s-sorry," he cried.

She hugged him tight. "You didn't do anything wrong." Then she held him at arm's length. "We have to hurry back to the school, okay? And I need you to be as quiet as a ninja. Can you do that?"

Denny nodded, wiping at his eyes.

"Okay, kick off your shoes. Grab my pocket and don't let go." She stood and took the weapon in two hands again. Denny slipped out of his sneakers and clung to her, his other hand clamped over his mouth, body trembling.

Sophia paused at the entrance to the berthing space, got her bearings, and headed down the passageway, turning left at the next available intersection. She thought they were now in the corridor everyone called Broadway, a main route that ran from bow to stern and traveled almost the length of the ship, passing through wider-than-normal knee knockers every so often. They padded along quickly as Sophia calculated how long it would take to get back to the classroom. Minutes only on a direct route. Denny had made more progress down through the ship than she had a right to expect, and for that she was grateful.

Another turn and she was headed starboard again, picking up the pace. Denny kept up without protest. Thirty feet to go.

"Hey!" a voice shouted behind her, and Sophia started to run, grabbing Denny by one hand and pulling him after her. A rifle fired and both woman and child let out a scream, the bullet whining off a nearby bulkhead. The sound of more than one pair of running feet pounded down the passageway behind them, followed by the crack of a pistol. Another bullet *pinged* off a pipe three feet from Denny's head, kicking up sparks.

Sophia reached the hatch to the classroom and started pounding on it with her fist. "Kay! It's Sophia, open up, hurry!" A glance to the right showed her the two bearded men she had seen before, both running at her.

"Kay, hurry!" she yelled, as Denny began to cry.

The man with the pistol stopped and aimed. The weapon barked, and a second later a bullet whispered past Sophia's head close enough to make her hair move. A metallic rattle from inside then, and the hatch opened, Kay standing there looking afraid and holding her own shotgun. Sophia shoved Denny through and leaped over the knee knocker behind him as another bullet sparked off the hatch frame.

The two women slammed the steel oval closed, and Sophia held the handle down while Kay jammed a chair leg against it. Most of the kids in the classroom behind them were crying now, huddling together at the far side of the room.

Fists began banging on the outside of the hatch, accompanied by muffled curses.

.   .   .

U p on *Nimitz*'s flight deck, Maya walked alone on the port side edge, staring into the misting rain to the north, night falling rapidly. She wore a gray hooded rain poncho and wrapped her arms across her chest for warmth. The earthquake had forced her to crouch and plant both hands on the deck to keep from falling, but it passed quickly. Now, especially since her life was one of sensation, she could feel the carrier moving. It wasn't much, but it was no longer stationary, and in the mist and gloom she couldn't *really* tell how fast the ship was traveling.

She wanted the diversion, wanted to think about what that would mean, their sanctuary no longer safely rooted to one spot, but she couldn't focus. All she could think about was that Evan was out there somewhere. Before the shaking started, Banks, the Navy operations specialist, had found her walking the deck. Using a notepad, he told her they'd lost contact with Evan and were trying to find him. He said he was sorry and went back into the superstructure.

Maya's face was wet from rain and tears. She wiped at it, then slid her hands to her stomach. *Be okay, Evan. We need you to be okay.*

It hadn't occurred to anyone that Maya would be unable to hear Father Xavier's warning over the PA.

TWENTY-TWO

"That was intense," Charlie said, grinning and climbing to his feet. He and the six others with him had been moving down a passageway when the tremor struck, and it threw them to the deck.

Of the nine people in his boarding party, Charlie had sent two of the men off on their own to wreak havoc, keeping the ship's defenders moving in different directions without time to organize. At the right moment he would break off another two, who would try to find weapons before starting trouble of their own. The remaining four would stay with him as an assault group, and this smaller team was already armed. The woman whose throat Ava slit provided them with a rifle and handgun, and they'd found their own weapons in a compartment not far from the mess hall. *Should have secured those in the armory, Chief,* Charlie thought. And of course Ava had her straight razor.

The woman had no reservations about first using the toddler and then leaving him behind. He wasn't hers, and she'd confessed to Charlie weeks after he'd found them all hiding in that cannery that she and the big man with the beard *had* been planning to eat him if supplies ran short.

Charlie didn't like that, but he liked the attitude behind it. He could use someone like this, and they'd been sexual as well for some time now. Ava seemed to enjoy their time together.

"Keep moving," he ordered once everyone was on their feet, and the group set out once more.

Walking point and carrying an M4 was the young auxiliary deputy they had picked up in Oregon. He was eager to prove himself, and Charlie liked that. It would make it easier to use *him* too. The other two were civilians as well, as the decision had been made that trained crew were too valuable to risk on the first assault. Chick was the only coastie in the entire boarding party, as he had to lead the team. The next one would be different.

Charlie didn't mind. He'd personally selected his team not only for their potential as boarders, but for their personalities. All were well on their way to disentangling themselves from the morality and restrictions of living in a civilized society, and they were desperate to survive at any cost. Charlie had found that promising to alleviate that desperation was a powerful leadership tool. It hadn't taken much for Chick to transform these ragged refugees into killers, convincing them that seizing this ship was their only chance at salvation.

Good pirates, all, he thought.

They came to a place where corridors intersected near a set of ladderways that climbed up to the Hangar Deck and descended to Third Deck, according to the stenciling on the wall. Chick motioned to two of the women on his team, who moved down the left passageway. They would make their way through the unfamiliar passageways in an attempt to circle back to flank and ambush the pursuers who would surely come after Charlie and his band.

"Up," Chick said, and the young deputy started up the ladderway, Ava and the others following, Charlie coming up last. For now only he and the deputy carried rifles, but he was confident that would change soon. The people aboard this ship had grown lazy and careless, confident in the knowledge that they were safe out here on their island, with no reason to secure weapons.

They emerged in a passage that looked like every other one Chick had seen since coming aboard. He had no schematic, had never been on a carrier in his life, and had seen them only at a distance, moored in various ports he'd visited. *The mighty carrier,* he thought. *The most powerful ship in the fleet, and the most vulnerable.*

Chick didn't need a map. His mission was one of mayhem, the destruction of every soul he encountered. If they came across a prize like the armory, all the better, but their mission was death. For Chick, that meant one person in particular. *And oh, they had been so close!* The time hadn't been right, though. It would be soon.

They followed the corridor until it led them to an open hatch, and stepped through into the drafty openness of the main hangar.

A nother thump on the hatch, and a muffled voice on the other side called, "Open up, we won't hurt you."

Kay stood at the hatch with her shotgun. "You shot at us!"

"I promise we won't hurt you," the voice said.

Behind Kay, Sophia was moving the children out the hatch at the other side of the room, taking a head count as they passed and whispering to each to take off their shoes. Calvin's older girl, age thirteen, led them.

"How do I know you're telling the truth?" Kay shouted, glancing back. Only a few kids left. There was no answer from the other side, and she looked at Sophia, shaking her head. Sophia motioned for Kay to join them, and the woman ran across the classroom.

"Go to the head of the line," Sophia whispered. "We need to get to a berthing space. One way in and out, and there'll be water and a bathroom."

Kay nodded and ducked through the hatch, running past the line of frightened children, holding a finger to her lips as she passed. She reached Calvin's older girl. "Have everyone hold hands," she whispered, then led off with the shotgun pointed ahead of her. One by one the children linked hands, hurrying after her. At the rear, Sophia closed the classroom hatch and put the shotgun's stock to her shoulder, aiming it down the passageway as she started walking backward.

The boarders would find a way around from the other locked hatch, she knew, and were probably already on the move. Even during all that time at the firehouse, Sophia had never gone on a supply run, had never fired a weapon at anyone, living or dead. Chief Liebs taught them all how to shoot during their time aboard *Nimitz*, but that was target practice. Could she shoot another person?

The whimpering shapes scurrying behind her were helpless, harmless children who had done nothing wrong. Little Ben was among them. Sophia knew the answer was yes.

Try me, you bastards.

The two women moved along the passageway, one carrying a shotgun, the other a pistol. They wore dirty flannel, jeans, and hiking boots. The woman with the handgun was more of a girl, a high school dropout who'd been working as a part-time cashier in a Brookings supermarket. The older woman was stout, her hair worn in a short brush cut, a former logging truck driver who preferred football and drinking with the boys to book clubs and cooking shows. She liked the cashier, and not just for her looks. A short while ago the girl had slit a man's throat with a kitchen knife, allowing the two of them to pick up these weapons from the sleeping area he'd been exiting.

As they came to a choice of corridors, left or straight ahead, the truck driver motioned for the girl to keep moving past hatch after hatch. The closeness of the low ceiling covered in pipes and cables made the older woman a bit claustrophobic. At the next intersection the trucker put a hand on the girl's shoulder to stop her, and they both listened.

Footsteps, down to the left.

The truck driver patted the girl's back and pointed to the left, then continued ahead on her own.

The cashier crept down the left corridor, raising her pistol.

Xavier and Calvin moved one ahead of the other, Calvin leading with his assault rifle to his shoulder, Xavier with the shotgun up and ready, turning frequently to watch their backs. Both tried to step carefully and quietly, and Xavier clenched his teeth as the grenade fragment deep in his thigh tissue shifted, touching a nerve. For the priest, the hunt brought back bloody memories of patrols as a young Marine in Mogadishu. For Calvin, there was only the area in front of his rifle muzzle, and a seething rage.

They were moving aft, just to starboard of the center line of the ship. The passageway seemed to have more cross corridors and hatches than ever before, so many places for a threat to hide. They would approach a hatch, Xavier would turn the handle and push, and Calvin would go in with the rifle. Each compartment got only a cursory inspection before they moved on. It was a slow process, but they didn't dare leave an unexplored space behind them, just as they hadn't while hunting zombies in this maze.

As they came to a point where yet another passageway crossed, Calvin pointed to himself and then the right, then at Xavier and to the left. The priest nodded, and both men moved.

She was only ten feet away, Xavier saw, startled at her presence, a girl with greasy hair tied back in a ponytail, wearing layers of thermal and flannel. She was crouched against the wall and might have been cowering and hiding except for the pistol she was aiming, and Xavier's finger touched the shotgun's trigger.

The supermarket cashier fired twice, and the priest felt a pair of hammer blows to the chest that knocked him flat and stole his breath. Before he went down he saw the girl pause in surprise and, through his pain, Xavier had the thought that the girl had never shot anyone before.

Calvin triggered a full-auto burst, the heavy 7.62-millimeter rounds shredding the girl from chest to hairline in a haze of pink and gray. The hippie pivoted in the intersection, checking each hallway as he stood over his friend, rifle muzzle searching. The priest was gasping for air, and Calvin grabbed the man's ammo vest and hauled him into the hallway opposite the dead girl.

Xavier wheezed as Calvin helped him to sit, propping him against a wall.

"Hurts, doesn't it?" Calvin asked.

It was close to a minute before the other man regained enough breath to whisper, "Yes." His hands slid across his armor, fingertips finding two flattened slugs lodged in the Kevlar.

"Lucky she didn't have a rifle," said Calvin, peering back into the intersection to see if any of her companions had been drawn by the gunfire. "At that range it would have punched through your armor, and you'd be talking to God now."

Xavier was still drawing tight, shaky breaths. "Left him . . . behind . . . remember?"

Calvin nodded. "Good. Then it's up to *you* to be faster on the trigger next time." The hippie collected the dead girl's handgun and handed it to the priest, helping him stand. "You okay?"

Xavier nodded.

"One down," said Calvin, leading them back into the corridor.

. . .

K ay took the line of sock-footed children down a hallway, paused when it came to a T, looked both ways, and led them left. Aside from the whimpering of the younger ones, the kids were wide-eyed and quiet. The older children whispered encouragement to the most frightened among them. Near the middle of the line, three-year-old Ben kept whispering, "Papa."

Sophia kept her eyes to their rear, still moving backward, glancing behind her to see the linked chain of children making a turn into another passageway. *We're so exposed out here,* she thought, *and moving so slowly.* She looked back in time to see a bearded man with an axe and a pistol walk out into the same passageway she was watching. He saw her and stopped, startled.

Making a noise that was half scream and half snarl, Sophia fired, the shotgun kicking hard into her shoulder. The bearded man let out a howl and fell on his ass, then scrambled back out of sight.

"Bitch!" came a cry from down the hallway.

Behind her, the children reacted to the shotgun blast with cries of their own, moving faster. Sophia racked another shell and stayed at the corner, aiming at the place where the bearded man had retreated.

Your life is precious, my love, she heard Vladimir say in her head. *Sell it dearly.*

A second bearded face poked out from the distant corner, and Sophia fired again, the stock slipping out of position a bit, the kick making her cry out as the weapon nearly dislocated her shoulder. Down at the corner, buckshot sparked off the bulkhead just above the man's head, and the face disappeared behind a scream. Then Sophia moved, pumping the weapon with some difficulty—her right arm felt numb and it hurt to move it. She ran after the fleeing children.

Kay made one more turn, and then she was hurrying the children through a hatch, telling them to find a place to hide and stay quiet. Sophia joined her a moment later, both women happy to see one another. They followed the kids inside and slammed the hatch, Kay holding the handle down while Sophia did a quick search and returned with a power cord ripped from the back of a TV. They wound it between the handle and a large hinge, pulling it snug, then used a bedsheet as a rope to tighten it further.

Calvin's girl and Kay got the kids settled into racks out of sight at the back of the compartment, sending them to the toilet in groups. Sophia picked up the handset of a wall-mounted phone and looked at it. The device had no PA features, and right now she couldn't remember a single extension to where anyone might be. Frustrated, she slammed the receiver back into its cradle, then pressed an ear to the hatch.

Nothing.

She tested the handle once more, then pulled a folding chair up to sit in front of the hatch. Sophia pointed her weapon at the only way into the compartment and waited.

I t was almost dark, and the temperature was dropping as the rain fell harder. Maya remained on the flight deck, hoping Banks had somehow been wrong, searching the sky for blinking red-and-white lights. Rain plastered strands of hair against her face, and she shivered. Was Evan cold too? Was he hurt? She couldn't let herself think about the alternative.

Maya saw that the drifting aircraft carrier was gliding toward the Bay Bridge at an oblique angle, something unnatural for a ship. It looked as if it would pass directly under the span without coming near the supports. What would happen then?

The wind drove wet, gray curtains across the flight deck, and Maya hunched into her poncho, unable to endure it any longer.

She headed back toward the superstructure. Pat Katcher ran communications, and he would be able to tell her more about Evan. Maya went through the wide hatch and started the climb up the tower.

Had she stayed on deck, she might have seen the ghostly silhouette of a ship gliding toward *Nimitz* out of the coming night. She might also have seen the mass of drifters that were gathering at the edge of the bridge high above, climbing over the railing as the flat, wide deck of the aircraft carrier began moving below them.

U p in the superstructure's comm center, Pat Katcher sat at his station wearing headphones, glancing on occasion at the empty sweep of the air search radar, and scanning through radio frequencies.

"*Nimitz* calling Navy zero-two, come in." He drummed his fingers on the console. Either Evan or Gourd should have answered by now, with either the Seahawk's radio or their personal survival units. Seeing nothing in the air and getting no response from either man wasn't a good sign. The fact that he wasn't picking up any rescue beacons was even more grim.

"*Nimitz* calling Navy zero-two. Evan, Gourd, can you hear me?"

Still nothing.

Suddenly there was a squeal from one of the frequencies he kept tuned and recording at all times after both he and Father Xavier had heard talking and the word *Reno*. Now that channel was alive with garbled transmissions, voices he couldn't quite make out, but definitely more than one, talking to one another. Then the signal dropped to a line of dead static.

"Shit!" Katcher said, reaching for the playback controls.

Just then another voice came over the military-only Guard channel, a strong, clear signal. Pat Katcher's eyes widened as he heard a woman's voice.

"USS *Nimitz*, you are ordered to surrender your vessel. Muster your crew on deck in fifteen minutes or we will fire upon you."

Then the electronics tech heard a deep boom from somewhere beyond the superstructure's steel walls, followed almost immediately by the scream of a fifty-seven-millimeter shell sailing across the flight deck.

"That was your first and only warning," the woman's voice said over the radio. "Fifteen minutes only. This is *Adventure Galley*, out."

TWENTY-THREE

November—Brookings, Oregon

"Ensign, did you just use the word *extortion*?" Liz asked, looking up from a plotting table. They were down in the cutter's combat center, the room filled with mostly nonoperational equipment and lit by dim, red overhead lights. Petty Officer Vargas, the operations specialist and weapons section head, was sleeping on a narrow mattress in the corner of the room.

Ensign Liggett, standing opposite her captain with the plotting table between them, cleared her throat. "That isn't what I meant to say, ma'am."

"Mm-hmm," Liz murmured, looking back down at a map of the Oregon-California coastline. Although both women still wore blue uniform trousers bloused into combat boots, Amy now wore several thermal shirts with a hooded *University of Oregon* jacket over the top of them. Liz wore a once-white Irish cable-knit sweater with a turtleneck. Her cap was still pulled over her eyes at regulation distance above the bridge of her nose. Both wore sidearms.

"I meant that it could be perceived as that," Amy said. "By the civilians. They're the ones doing the work and taking the risks."

Liz made a notation on the map with a red marker and didn't look up. "And they're living here under *our* protection," she said, "receiving medical care from *our* Petty Officer Castellano and using *our* ammunition."

"Yes," said Amy, "but they're finding their own weapons and ammo now. During the scavenging runs."

"Confiscate them," Liz said, using a ruler to measure distance, then converting inches to miles in her head.

"But—"

"Confiscate them," Liz repeated. She looked up at her XO. "We can't allow a force that outnumbers us to have uncontrolled access to weapons, especially a potentially hostile force this close to the ship."

"Hostile? Captain, those are civilians looking to us for safety. They're not hostile."

"No?" said Liz. "We disagree on that."

Amy thought Kidd's eyes looked red in the shadows beneath the bill of her cap. It was the combat center lighting, she knew, but it was still unsettling.

"Weapons are for the sentry positions only," the captain said, "and are to be issued to those going on runs, on a limited basis. They are to be collected immediately upon the group's return, and all ammunition accounted for." Liz went back to her map.

"Some of them are going on runs without telling anyone," Amy said. "There's close to four dozen of them now, and only one of me. It's impossible to keep track of them at all times."

Liz sighed and straightened. "It sounds to me as if you're not in control of your command, Miss Liggett. The shoreside station and the refugees are your responsibility. I need to know if you're up to the task."

Amy stiffened. "Of course. It's not an easy task, though, and like I said, I'm the only—"

"Enough," Liz said, pinching the bridge of her nose and closing her eyes. "You know how I feel about whining."

Amy's face reddened, and not from embarrassment, but the change was lost in the light.

"I'm hearing about refugee issues from other sources," Liz said, "when I should be hearing them from you."

"I *am* reporting to you, Captain," Amy said.

"Yes, I hear about water collection efforts, ammunition expenditure, I hear about who is sick and who needs medicine. I hear you complain about how difficult it is to keep the Whiskey-Deltas back." Liz leaned forward on the table. "What I'm not hearing from you are reports that the civilian scavenging parties have begun raiding into the town, and that they're having some success."

"They're also experiencing losses," said Amy.

"Which concerns me not a bit," Liz replied. "I'm hearing about runs on nearly untouched grocery stores and pharmacies, on sporting goods shops and even a police station. I hear about wheelbarrows full of kerosene cans and bottled water, cases of booze, and yes, even firearms. Either you don't know about this," Liz said, looking at the younger woman, "or you haven't thought it was important enough to tell me. Either answer is unacceptable."

Amy looked down. The statement was a trap, and anything she said would be wrong.

Liz let her stew for a moment, then said, "I don't want to hear the word *extortion* again, do you understand? Nothing is free in this world, certainly not safety and security. Call it *rent* if you have to call it something, but these people *will* contribute to the welfare of the ship and crew that keeps them out of harm's way, or they'll be expelled to fend for themselves out there."

Out of harm's way. Amy managed to keep the disgusted look off her face. Close to fifty civilian refugees were living in the Coast Guard station now, squatters sleeping where they could, using patched-together kitchens only feet away from toilet buckets. They stood their own watches to guard against the dead, and risked their lives venturing into unsecured parts of Brookings in hopes of finding enough food to keep them and their families alive. Coast Guardsmen no longer manned the sentry positions in front of the station, and participated in none of the raids.

The only time the crew left *Joshua James* was for coastie-only raids, carefully planned in advance and only to locations that could be reached in the launches. Only Amy Liggett went ashore to the station, now more of a liaison than anything else. And Chief Kidd, of course, who had a lady friend there, a situation the captain was pointedly ignoring.

In the three months since the outbreak, Amy discovered that not only had she come out of the Academy filled with the unrealistic rhetoric of things like *duty, honor, and others before self,* but she'd been blind as well. Elizabeth Kidd once seemed larger than life, a career female officer who would mentor and guide Amy through an honorable profession, dedicated to her crew and to saving lives. Now Amy knew that only one thing drove her captain: hanging on to her precious command at any cost and justifying her agenda with words like *responsibility.* The young officer wondered just how far Kidd would go to keep what she had.

"My order stands," said Liz. "Half of everything they collect. Half the food and water, half the fuel and camping supplies, half of what they take from pharmacies. In fact, they are to surrender *all* medication. Petty Officer Castellano will continue to oversee their medical care. We can't have them wasting resources by self-medicating." She went back to her maps.

"Yes, ma'am."

"I want all alcohol dumped in the harbor," Liz said without looking up. "We don't need the kind of trouble it can bring. And you are to confiscate all firearms and ammunition, parceling it out for sentries and raids only. I want a daily accounting of that."

"Captain," Amy said, "without actually conducting a search, I don't see how we can keep them from hiding weapons."

Liz looked up again in annoyance. "Make it clear that anyone holding out on us will be hanged."

Amy stared at her, unsure of what to say. Part of her earlier question about how far the captain would go had just been answered, though.

"You still cannot appreciate the weight of my responsibility, can you?" Liz sighed and shook her head. "You're inexperienced, I know, and perhaps I need to set a better example for you. Having a command means making hard decisions, Amy. Sometimes those choices are unpleasant, but the ability to lead depends upon making them."

Amy nodded slowly, looking at a woman she realized she didn't really know at all. "And if they refuse to pay *rent*, Captain?" she said. "What then?"

Liz made another marker notation on her map. "I'm sure you can imagine what this ship's weapons systems would do to that Coast Guard station at this range. If they protest, make sure they can imagine it too." Liz stood and straightened, twisting her back with a crack and yawning. "That will be all, Miss Liggett. You're dismissed."

A week after Liz and Amy's talk in the combat center, an early winter storm barreled in off the ocean, hitting the coast with terrifying force. Heavy rain pounded the Pacific Northwest, and in Brookings, sustained winds of sixty miles per hour—with gusts as high as ninety miles per hour—lashed the seaside community. Trees were knocked flat, power lines fell, and in several places roofs were torn completely away, the walls beneath them collapsing. The worst of it hit at night, sealing *Joshua James* in a black envelope of screaming darkness, waves surging into the river's mouth and crashing against the bow, lifting the cutter and dropping it back down so that it strained against its anchor.

On shore, the civilian refugees huddled in the Coast Guard station, eyes turned upward and listening as the roof groaned and popped. They watched the doors as well. Weather didn't bother the dead, and it was too dangerous to put out the normal sentries.

Joshua James was designed for storms like this, and the ship rode it out, battened down tightly. The night watch stayed safe and dry within the warm protection of the bridge, gripping handles and consoles while the ship rose and fell, watching as rain hammered the glass. Lightning forked out over the Pacific.

Liz and Charlie were in the captain's cabin for their late-night coffee, both of them long at ease with the roll and swell of a ship in a storm. Blackbeard was curled on Liz's bunk, half sleeping and peering at them through slitted eyes. A half-eaten bowl of cat food sat on the deck nearby, and several dozen more cans were tucked in a cabinet. One of the crew had found a few cases of the stuff during a rare excursion into a water's-edge area of Brookings, along with several bags of cat litter. Liz gave him twenty-four hours off-duty time as a reward.

Brother and sister held their mugs and drank without spilling. They'd been talking about the day's events, what the refugees had been doing, and how Amy Liggett was performing. So far she'd carried out Liz's orders, and the refugees were cooperating, surrendering their firearms (all the captain knew about, anyway) and making their fifty percent tithing.

"They're sure not doing it because of her personality or leadership qualities," Charlie said. "It's because they know you're not afraid to use the rope."

Liz smiled thinly. The old-time sea captains had it right all along. The modern world had grown soft, conditioning everyone to expect special treatment and to be spoken to in language that wouldn't hurt their feelings. Along the way, true discipline became fuzzy. The old ways worked the best, she'd decided.

They were quiet for a while, lost in their thoughts as the storm sea lifted and rolled the ship. Then Liz looked up. "Chick, the FBI said you murdered three people during a drug deal. Is it true?"

Charlie sipped and looked at her over the rim of his cup. "Does it matter now?"

"Not to our situation," Liz said, "or to what was my career, not anymore. But I want to know."

"I thought it was four people," he said without a change to his expression. "One got away, huh? That guy that tried to make a swim for it. I guess he got to shore." He shook his head. "Damn, I was positive I hit him."

Liz set her cup down, still holding it so it wouldn't slide. She stared at her brother. "Drugs, Chick? How long have . . . why . . . ?"

He smiled. "It wasn't really a drug deal. Well, *they* thought it was."

"Make sense," she said.

A shrug. "I met a guy in Seattle who knew some cartel guys, and I told him I had a quarter million to invest in coke. After that it was really just setting up time and place."

"Where the hell did you get a quarter million dollars?" Liz demanded.

He laughed. "I didn't. I just told them that, and brought a bag with a couple of phone books in it. Those guys were so cocky and comfortable that they didn't check until it was too late. They couldn't imagine someone would cross them."

She shook her head again. "Coke? Chick, what were you thinking? Do you *use* coke? How long have you been selling it?"

"No, I don't use it and I wasn't going to sell it. When it was over I dumped the shit in the Pacific."

"Then why?"

He sipped his coffee. "I did it for Leo."

Liz sat back in her chair. Her brother had known Chief Leonard Massey since he joined the Coast Guard. The two of them had come up through the ranks together, served together aboard ship several times, and even made chief the same year as one another. He was Charlie's best friend, and as far as Liz knew, his *only* friend.

Two years ago, Chief Massey was stationed in Miami and led a boarding party onto a megayacht suspected of being used by some cocaine cowboys. There was a close-range gunfight, and Leo caught a bullet. He died right there on the yacht. The man who shot him surrendered at once and was later convicted of homicide in connection with drug trafficking. In exchange for providing federal agents with information about the cartel, however, Leo Massey's killer had his sentence commuted from death to life without parole. Losing one of their own during drug operations was every coastie's fear, and seeing the chief's murderer go unpunished—anything less than lethal injection wasn't enough, as far as they were concerned—was a bitter pill. Charlie had never spoken of it, other than to acknowledge that his friend was gone.

"Chick," she said, leaning forward, "the man who killed Leo . . . these people weren't him."

"Nope," he said, "but they were cartel, and I paid them back with interest."

"But it wasn't *him*," she insisted.

The corner of Charlie's mouth turned up. "Sis, assholes are assholes, and they're all just as satisfying."

"But . . . how could you risk everything like that? Your life, your career . . . *our* careers."

He laughed again. "I didn't think I'd get caught. We were all on the boat, the four of them and me, all real friendly." He made his finger and thumb into a gun and pointed it at his sister. "And then I popped them. One jumped over the side, and I fired, thought I popped him too, but it was dark. He must have gotten away and told someone, otherwise I wouldn't have been taken off my ship in irons, and they wouldn't have tried to take your command away." He shook his head. "I really am sorry about that. I know how much your ship means to you."

"You're *sorry*? Chick, if all this hadn't happened, we—"

"But it did happen, Sis," he said, finishing his coffee. "And good thing too, or we'd have been in some hot water." He shook his head. "Sloppy mistake on my part."

"Chick, you murdered three men to avenge Leo? That's . . . that's *crazy*." The last word came out in a whisper, as if Liz were afraid to speak it.

"Maybe," he said, eyes dancing.

Liz looked at the man across the table, the *killer* across the table. How had he become this person without her seeing it? How much of it was her fault for failing him when he'd been little, failing to protect him from a monster like Mr. Drummond? Drug dealers gunned down, federal agents blown out of the sky, refugees shot in the back room of a cannery. None of it seemed to bother him at all. What else had he done that she didn't know about?

They sat there without speaking, the swells making them rock in their chairs. Charlie frowned at his empty coffee mug, while Liz's sat untouched on the table in front of her as she looked at a man she realized she really didn't know at all. An overhead speaker broke the silence.

"Captain to the bridge. Radar contact."

Mr. Waite pointed to the radar scope, Liz standing beside him. Amy Liggett and their helicopter pilot, Lt. Riggs, peered over their shoulders. "It's a ship, no question about it," said the quartermaster. "Ten miles out and closing."

"The *Dorado*?" Liz wondered aloud, thinking of the cutter stationed to their south.

Waite shook his head. "Too big. Could be a tanker, or maybe military."

"Any radio traffic?"

"Negative, the channels are clear."

Liz peered at the scope. The blue-green blob indicated a ship moving almost imperceptibly across the screen. "I want to know what it is before it catches us anchored in a goddamn river. Senior Chief?"

Charlie moved to her side.

"Ready for storm duty?" she asked.

"Always, Captain."

"I want you and another crewman to launch the MLB," Liz said. "Put eyes on that contact and report back as soon as it's identified."

"Aye-aye," he said, and disappeared down the bridge ladderway.

Liz looked at her XO. "Sound general quarters."

Charlie and a bosun's mate sat in the bucket seats of the cockpit-style control room, the senior chief driving the motorized lifeboat with a pair of joysticks. Wiper blades slapped furiously at the cockpit windows, doing little to hold back the driving rain and spray. They made no difference, for it was black outside and they were operating on instruments alone. Beyond the heated interior, the storm attacked the forty-seven-foot launch as if enraged that any man would dare put to sea in such a tempest.

"Contact bearing to starboard, zero-four-zero," said the bosun's mate, holding on to a rubberized grip mounted over the right seat radar scope.

"Here comes a big one," Charlie said, and then the bow of the launch slammed into something unyielding, climbing, climbing as Charlie applied power. They were nearly vertical for an instant, engines howling back against the wind, and suddenly there was a moment of weightlessness. The bow tipped forward again, and the launch, airborne a full fifteen feet above the surface, crashed back down on the other side of the swell.

Beyond the windshield was a charcoal wall shot through with green and streaks of foam, and within seconds the launch was climbing again. The hull shuddered, and as the bow appeared to point directly into the black sky, the bosun's mate let out a wail and closed his eyes. "We're going over backward!" he shouted. Charlie rammed the joystick forward for maximum power and bared his teeth.

The launch cleared the swell, trailing foam, and slammed once more into the trench on the other side. The bow of the small vessel knifed through the dark water and climbed another wave, repeating the process several more times, each climb growing slightly less steep as the craft moved out from the roughest of the surf. A mile away from shore, the waves were no less towering but were farther apart, rolling swells that the MLB handled easily. Wind and rain continued their incessant hammering.

"Give me a bearing," Charlie ordered.

The bosun's mate opened his eyes and in a shaking voice reported, "Contact bearing to starboard, zero-four-four. Eight miles."

Charlie steered the launch to an intercept heading, taking the dark waves on an oblique angle, powering across the surface as seawater crashed across the deck. The bosun's mate gave him regular updates on the contact's position and distance, the miles between them closing. When they were within one mile, Charlie switched off the cockpit lights, leaving only the glow of the instrument panel. He powered back to twelve knots, careful to keep the launch angled into the swells so as not to take them broadside, something that could easily tip them over.

"It should be right there," the bosun's mate said, pointing. "I don't see any lights."

Neither did Charlie. There should have been something by now, even if only the contact's red and green navigation lights. The radio frequencies held nothing but dead air.

At half a mile, Charlie said, "Hit the spots."

The man in the right seat switched on the high-intensity lights mounted atop the cockpit and antenna cluster, then took hold of his own joystick to maneuver a powerful spotlight. As Charlie slowed further, the white beam tracked right to left across the darkness. Rain slashed across it like a curtain, impossible to penetrate.

"It's right *there*," the bosun's mate growled. The radar scope showed the contact—a huge shape—as just off their starboard bow, but the storm hid it from sight. Seconds later, it was the storm that finally revealed it as a string of dazzling lightning strikes split the sky, searing the image in an instant of flashbulb white that trumped the masking rain.

"Fuck *me*," Charlie whispered.

It was a cruise ship, completely without lights and power, adrift at the mercy of the sea. And it was heeled over to port at what Charlie judged to be a thirty- or thirty-five-degree angle, waves washing over the railings of its upper decks, surging around the supports of water slides and crashing against the hollows of steeply angled swimming pools. Its bow was pointed south, but the vessel was broadside to the sea, being pushed toward land with every wave.

"Why hasn't she foundered?" the bosun's mate said, finally putting the spotlight on it, the beam crawling across its hull in a circle of white, all that could be seen now that darkness had once again replaced the lightning. The angle of the ship reminded both men of news footage they'd seen about the *Costa Concordia*, the cruise ship run aground off the Italian coast years ago by a reckless captain, capsizing and ending up mostly on its side within swimming distance of a beach. The pitch to this ship wasn't quite as severe, but it was close, and the sight of it was unsettling to anyone who spent their life at sea.

Charlie powered the MLB around it, keeping a safe distance for fear a wave would throw them against her side, and motored along the seaward, starboard side that was tipped up toward a violent sky. The ship was massive, 960 feet, nearly the length of an aircraft carrier, eleven decks high and eighty-three thousand tons. It had a dark blue hull and a white superstructure with two red stacks climbing above. On the side of each stack was an iconic silhouette known the world over.

"This is the sickest," the bosun's mate muttered, working his joystick.

The spotlight revealed that about half the lifeboats were missing on this side, one still dangling partway down the hull, hanging crooked on its cables. When the light settled on the boat, a gray arm stretched from within a side hatch, its hand pawing at the yellow fiberglass.

Charlie used the launch's powerful engine to fight the waves and motored around to the stern, seeing the ship's name in elegant, yellow script. They continued back around to port, the direction of the tilt, and the spotlight inched across portholes and glass balcony doors. Many were smashed, the sea flowing in and out at will, but others remained intact, and behind many of them were gray corpses dressed in shorts and tank tops, sundresses and flowered shirts. They pressed against the glass, mouths open in silent moans.

Charlie suddenly realized he had been aboard this ship, not as a passenger but with the Coast Guard, during a safety inspection ten years ago in San Diego. He remembered the gilded atrium, the rich décor and attention to detail, a thousand feet of fun and luxury. *How many guests and crew aboard? Three or four thousand?*

It was probably making a summer run from Vancouver to Alaska, he thought, or south to San Diego. Summertime . . . it would have been filled to capacity, half of them kids. Charlie could picture thousands of corpses crawling along tilted passageways in the dark, stumbling past statues of princesses and cartoon animals, feet shuffling through drifts of broken plates and glass. Some would be trapped in staterooms, others wandering restaurants and shops and theaters, still more caught in flooded, lower decks. All of them in the dark, all of them hungry. He imagined the moans that would echo through those carpeted, steeply angled corridors, and shuddered.

"That, shipmate," Charlie said, "is a ghost ship."

The bosun's mate simply moved his head up and down without speaking.

Charlie checked the cruise ship's position and calculated the movement of the sea. "It's going to be on the rocks by morning," he said, then turned the launch back toward Brookings and applied power. He lifted the radio mic. "Seven-five-four, this is Recon Launch One. Contact identified."

The storm blew out around six the next morning. While Amy Liggett went ashore to see how the refugees had fared in the night, Liz, Charlie, and several others went back out in the motorized lifeboat. Although the sky still churned with hues of black and gray and a light rain continued, the seas had calmed considerably, and they were all able to stand on the vessel's top control deck, facing the spray in foul-weather ponchos.

As Charlie predicted, the cruise ship had indeed reached the rocks during the night, and came to rest in the shallows a hundred yards west of where the town of Brookings sloped down to meet the Pacific. In the light of morning, the scene was even more chilling and awe-inspiring. The ship, upon grounding amid the rocks and shoals, had been pushed even farther to port and now tilted toward shore at an even forty-five-degree angle. Surf curled about its hull, but decks that had once been kept awash by the sea were now able to drain. Dozens of separate waterfalls gushed from points along the length of the ship, seawater pouring out through smashed windows and over balconies, carrying with them a tide of flotsam: luggage, couch cushions and bedding, plastic cups and stuffed animals . . .

And corpses.

Decayed bodies flowed through these openings as well, plunging into the shallows with pinwheeling arms. After a number of minutes, heads broke the surface as those same corpses trudged across the sandy bottom and emerged at the shore, crawling onto dry land. Some floundered against slick rocks, but most climbed steadily toward a road that ran along the water's edge, a place lined with shops and sidewalk benches. Back at the ship, other creatures didn't wait to be washed out like floating garbage. They clawed their way up tilted stairways and through hatches, following one another over the railing, hitting the water, and then slowly making their way toward the beach.

Liz lowered her binoculars. To no one in particular she said, "This is going to be a problem."

TWENTY-FOUR

The newly arrived dead were a problem that seemed to compound with each passing day. By December, thousands of corpses had relentlessly made their way out of the grounded luxury liner and through the shallows up into the town. There was no way to stop them.

Before the ship beached itself and discharged its rotten cargo, the dead in Brookings had seemed manageable. They were scattered and, at least around the marina, could be engaged at a distance. Now they traveled in packs and herds, more than could be controlled with the diminishing supply of ammunition. The influx affected the scavenging parties most of all.

Until now, the refugee bands out gathering supplies were growing more confident, traveling farther into both the residential and commercial parts of town, coming back with impressive scores. The dead they encountered could usually be taken out with handheld weapons. Now, a raiding party of six or eight might find themselves confronted with a hundred or more zombies coming at them as a mob in the street, with dozens more angling in from yards and doorways to their flanks and rear. Human losses were climbing, and it seemed that no group going out returned with its original number.

One entire party of ten headed into town, and never came back.

That one was especially hurtful to Liz. Ten adults capable of scavenging and serving on work details gone, weapons and ammunition lost, and ten more bodies rising to join the infestation. She wished she'd met the cruise ship at sea before it made landfall. She would have used the gun mounted on the foredeck to send it to the bottom.

The number of runs decreased, and so did the fifty percent tribute Liz demanded. That meant less food for her crew, and Liz knew that if the situation continued, she would have to go back to rationing, which would be a serious blow to morale. Not that morale was high to begin with.

An atmosphere of malaise was settling over the cutter, the crew unhappy with sporadic bathing in the cold falling rain, monotonous duty without the hope of shore leave, and illness. The ship was rife with poor nutrition, deplorable hygiene, and a worsening state of sanitary conditions. The pumps that operated the heads and flushed out the bilge had failed, and the crew was reduced to using plastic buckets for toilets, just like the refugees on shore. The ship reeked of feces and unwashed bodies, and Mr. Leary and the other contractors reported that, like the water desalinization unit, unique, military-spec parts would be needed to get the pump system running again.

It made Liz feel like screaming.

Amy Liggett made her way down the cutter's central passageway, headed for the bridge. She'd just returned from shore where a kind woman with two children had slipped her a deodorant stick, a razor, and a travel-sized shaving cream in exchange for getting out of a corpse-burning detail. After a moment's hesitation, Amy accepted the bribe and returned to conceal the items in her quarters aboard ship. Now she was due to give the captain her daily briefing, something she'd come to dread.

Her route took her through the ship's mess, and as she approached she heard low voices and the clink of silverware. When she entered the compartment, the four enlisted Coast Guardsmen seated at a table fell silent. She came to a stop.

"Good afternoon," she said.

The crew looked at her, then at each other. The petty officer third class who oversaw the propulsion system, her mentor since the day Amy had reported to *Joshua James*, nodded slowly and said, "Ma'am." The others said nothing.

Amy looked at them, and most looked away. "Enjoying your meal?" she asked. *God, that sounded stupid.* The crew looked at their trays, then at each other.

"Is there something we can do for you, Ensign?" the petty officer asked.

Amy was shocked. The two of them had always been on a first-name basis, the older man taking her under his wing and teaching her the skills she needed with patience and kindness. She'd never heard him speak so formally.

"Negative," she mumbled, moving through the mess and into the passage beyond. Behind her, the murmuring of voices resumed.

Elizabeth sat in her captain's chair, legs crossed and looking at a map of Brookings. Sightings and incidents of contact with the dead were marked with circles in red pencil, along with notes of estimated strength. There were a lot of circles. Blackbeard was stretched out in a sunbeam, his body pressed against a forward bridge window, sprawling across a navigation console. The cat now had free run of the ship.

Boots trotted up the ladderway to the bridge, and Liz heard her XO say, "Captain?" She motioned the younger woman forward and folded away the map. "Are you here to tell me about the fishing boat, Miss Liggett?"

"I just found out about it myself," Amy said. "I spoke to the parties involved and talked them out of it." While touring the Coast Guard station, Amy learned that a handful of refugees were planning to leave Brookings, taking the big, deepwater commercial fishing vessel lying at anchor in the marina. Alarmed, she immediately spoke with the group's leader, himself a fisherman, and made the case that it was safer to stay in the company and safety of others here in Brookings. There was argument: complaints about mistreatment, about the increasing activity of the dead and, of course, about the fifty percent tribute they were compelled to make. Amy narrowly won the argument by pointing out the many dangers and unknowns awaiting them in an uncertain and overrun world. It had given them pause, for now.

"It's a good thing for them that you did, Amy," Liz said, looking at her from beneath the bill of her ball cap. "Because if they tried to leave, I would have let them clear the mouth of the river and then sunk them with the forward gun."

The surprise must have registered on the girl's face, because the captain shook her head.

"I'm concerned that it shocks you," Liz said. "You *do* see the security risk something like that would pose, don't you? They might tell someone we're here, and then we'd be dealing with bandits instead of just untrustworthy refugees and the walking dead."

Amy managed to mutter, "Yes, ma'am."

"Good," said Liz. "When we're done here, put a small crew together and bring that fishing boat alongside. See that its diesel tanks are pumped into our own bunkers. Then tow it back into the mouth of the south marina and scuttle it. That should prevent anyone from getting a similar idea."

The younger woman nodded slowly, frustrated that the captain always seemed to know what was going on ashore before she did. It wasn't too surprising, though. Charlie Kidd was friendly with that refugee woman Ava, had leave to go ashore wherever and whenever he liked, and met privately with the captain every day.

"Proceed with your report, please," said Liz.

Amy went through her usual list of topics: food and water status; results of a small, short-range raid that netted little; ammunition expenditure; and a body count of the dead eliminated by the shoreside sentries over the twenty-four hours since her last report. When she started to talk about morale among the civilians, the captain waved her off.

"I have my own problems aboard, Ensign."

Amy knew it, and the behavior she'd just witnessed in the mess was only one more indicator. It seemed her commanding officer was holding Captain's Mast several times per week now, mostly for incidents of malingering, the punishment for which was added duties or assignment to a work party. Once, however, Chick overheard a crewman saying that he was simply going to slip off the ship and take his chances in the forest one night, maybe find a cabin and hunt for his meals. Simply for suggesting it, the captain locked the crewman in the maintenance closet for five days on quarter rations.

Better than the alternative, Amy thought. Senior Chief Kidd, in his unrestricted wanderings, had found a long, supple leather strap somewhere and presented it to his sister. "Just in case you decide to bring back the custom of lashes for offenses," he said, smiling.

There had been no lashings, but the captain also didn't refuse the gift.

Amy concluded her report, then left to assemble a crew. She had a fishing boat to sink.

. . .

Chick leaned against the railing of the cutter's stern, the SRP launch ramp below, the empty helicopter pad above and behind. Lt. Riggs stood beside him. Riggs looked around, then unzipped a chest pocket of his flight suit and passed a small silver flask to Charlie. The chief grinned, took a drink, and handed it back.

"That's some good hooch, el-tee."

The lieutenant nipped at the flask and passed it over. "I have a few bottles stashed in my quarters. I might have an extra one."

"Perfect," Charlie said. "I have an empty flask in my quarters. It's lonely."

"We'll have to fix that," said Riggs.

Charlie sipped. "You're okay for an asshole officer, you know?"

The helicopter pilot smiled and took a pull. "And you're not bad for a mad dog killer, Senior Chief."

"You'll have to be more specific," said the burly, older man.

Riggs laughed. "The DEA bird you shot down in Seattle. The crew told me all about it."

Charlie drank and said nothing, giving him a sidelong look. The lieutenant saw it and shook his head. "Don't get me wrong. It was the right thing to do. They would have taken away the ship, and the ship means survival." The officer stared out at the harbor. "It's all about survival now."

The chief nodded. He liked the lieutenant, not because he was willing to be a real person and have a drink with an enlisted man, but because of his attitude. He'd never flinched or raised an objection about the need to fully utilize the refugees and maintain ship security, and not once had he griped about the fact that a girl he outranked was the ship's executive officer. Riggs supported Charlie's sister without question, and that made him okay by Charlie.

They passed the flask back and forth for a while in comfortable silence, looking out at the water and deserted buildings. Then Chick straightened and unslung his rifle.

"You gotta be *fucking* kidding me," he said.

"What?" Riggs asked, looking around.

Charlie pointed. "Ten o'clock, over on the bridge." He raised his rifle and looked through the combat sight. "Now I've seen everything," he said with a chuckle. He passed the rifle to the officer, who sighted where Charlie was pointing.

"Is that . . . ?"

A corpse was shuffling across the US 101 bridge that linked the harbor with the main town. The thing was heading in the direction of the marina, and fifty yards behind it, a pack of half a dozen corpses followed, all dressed in vacation clothing, several of them kids. The corpse out front, the one that had caught Chick's attention, was wearing the kind of character costume seen in theme parks. The costume looked like it might have been a big, silly dog, but its torn and gore-matted condition made identification difficult. Its head had fallen off, the decaying skull of a woman poking out through the opening.

"That is wrong on so many levels," the pilot said, handing the rifle back to Chick.

"Any guesses where it came from?" the chief said. "Any of them?" One of the dead little girls was dressed like a princess. *They've found us,* Chick thought, *and now they're going to keep on coming.* He elbowed the officer. "What do you want to bet I can put one in the cartoon character's head from here?"

Riggs snorted. "That's got to be five hundred meters, Chief. No way."

"Then you'll win your bet," Chick said. "What do you say?"

"I'll give you *two* bottles for a shot like that. What do I get when you lose?"

The chief smiled. "My lady friend on shore knows another young lady who might be interested in spending time with a fine young officer such as yourself. Especially if he could bring her a bar of soap and maybe some toothpaste. I can make the introductions."

The lieutenant bobbed his head. "That sounds *good.*"

Charlie took a breath, steadied his aim, and released it in a hiss as he pulled the trigger. A second later the costumed woman's head rocked to the left, and down she went.

"Damn," Riggs gasped, then looked at the chief. "Mad dog killer."

Charlie smiled at him and slung the rifle. "I'm gonna enjoy that hooch, el-tee."

TWENTY-FIVE

Amy Liggett tried to make Christmas festive for the crew, hoping it would help with morale. She risked the dead on shore and chopped down a tiny pine at the edge of the RV park, bringing it back to the ship. Then she used a pair of tin snips to cut simple ornaments from empty metal cans to decorate the tree, and tried to get the crew to sing some carols. Every effort fell flat. The holidays were making her shipmates heartsick for home and lost loved ones, and people were too concerned with scratching unwashed skin and the stench from the plastic toilet buckets to care much about "Jingle Bells." The captain hadn't even acknowledged the time of year.

The crew was hungry after being put back on half rations. Now that thousands of walking corpses roamed Brookings—with more finding their way out of the grounded cruise ship every day—the scavenging runs had stopped completely. The civilian refugees bunkered down in the Coast Guard station and didn't venture out, because in the past week hundreds of corpses had poured across the US 101 bridge and found their way around the marina, and they were now walking through the nearby RV park. This activity caught the attention of the dead gathered around the motels and condos to the south, and they began to move as well, adding their numbers to the horde.

Military-grade weapons were no longer issued to the refugees for defense, and the ammunition for the hunting weapons and shotguns their sentries were permitted to use was almost gone.

Two Coast Guardsmen deserted Christmas night: the crewman locked up for five days, and the petty officer third class who'd been Amy's mentor, the man so reserved with her in the mess. During the night, they slipped away with weapons and sea bags of supplies, and the captain could risk no one to go look for them. Their absence cut the engine room team by half.

Liz wanted to lash the petty officer on watch for not spotting or stopping the desertion. Instead she made him stand on the foredeck for eight hours in a cold, misting rain dressed only in a pair of boxer shorts. Chick made a trip out into the rain and whispered in the shivering man's ear, telling him he was getting off easy. If the decision had been his, Charlie said, he'd have seen the petty officer keel-hauled.

Charlie Kidd headed south in the motorized lifeboat, driving from the top deck and enjoying the wind and sting of spray. Lt. Riggs stood beside him in a foul-weather poncho, gripping the rail, excited to be off the ship for a while. It was the day after Christmas, and the sky was a palette of shale, beginning to break up enough for some rare sun to fall upon the coast. The launch was two miles offshore, powering through easy seas at twenty knots.

"Our position is untenable," Liz said before sending them south. They had been ordered to recon the coastal California town of Crescent City, putting eyes on the airport, harbor, and small Coast Guard station located there. The captain reasoned that the town had to have fewer of the walking dead than Brookings, and if it looked good, *Joshua James* would relocate.

The trip took just under an hour in the MLB, and as they drew closer, Charlie slowed and angled in toward shore. The sea rolled over rocks at the base of a low cliff, stunted pines climbing the hillside above. Ahead of them, near what would be the harbor entrance, the two men saw the red-and-white shape of the Battery Point Lighthouse.

Charlie glanced up at the cliffs to his left. Somewhere beyond the trees, he knew, was Pelican Bay, a supermax prison built to house California's "worst of the worst," a place of long-term confinement and simmering violence. If the dead within those walls had somehow gotten out, then Crescent City would be completely uninhabitable.

Lt. Riggs looked at a map. "We should see the airport coming up on the left."

Charlie kept an eye on the rocks as he took the forty-seven-foot craft as close as he dared toward shore and powered back to a cruising speed. Riggs used a pair of binoculars and pointed. "Right there, I can see a hangar." Evaluating the condition of the airport was the reason Liz sent the man on this mission.

The Del Norte County Airport was spread across a low, flat stretch of land close to the shore, large enough to handle commuter express planes for a trip to San Francisco, but nothing bigger. A minute was all it took to see that the airport was a complete loss. The few buildings still standing were burned-out shells, and the hangar Riggs had seen was gutted and empty. Out on the field sat the black and broken remains of a twin-prop SkyWest Express. Crows lifted off from the fuselage, winging into the morning sky.

Riggs made a distressed noise and looked away.

The launch continued south, and the town itself came into view. Much like Brookings, Crescent City extended almost to the water's edge, and at its south end, man-made breakwaters formed a sheltered harbor for commercial fishing and a few pleasure craft.

"There's our answer," Chick said. Beside him, Riggs only stared.

Crescent City had burned. Block after block of charred homes and businesses marched back from the shore, streets choked with abandoned cars and downed power lines, all of it black. As they neared the harbor, the reason became immediately clear. A fuel supertanker had come in from the Pacific and run up onto the narrow stone jetty that framed one side of the town's little sheltered bay. Its hull and holds had ruptured, dumping millions of gallons of gasoline into the harbor.

"Probably came in with that storm," said Chick. "This place got a tanker instead of a cruise ship."

"A single lightning strike would have set it off," said the helicopter pilot.

The supertanker was burned down to its waterline, and the fire had ripped across the harbor, sinking anything still afloat. From there it spread, consuming the docks, the town, and part of the surrounding forest. Even a month later, sea winds hadn't completely erased the smell of fire.

Charlie continued around to where the tiny Coast Guard station was positioned on a knuckle of land framing the other side of the harbor. Neither man needed binoculars to see that the small buildings that made up the station were burned flat; the skeletons of two school buses were parked out front.

"I'll be damned," Charlie said. "It's been here the whole time."

At the pier behind the little station, the bridge windows and antenna array of the USCGC *Dorado* protruded from the surface of the water. The rest of the eighty-seven-foot cutter was submerged, its keel resting on the bottom.

"This place has had it," said Riggs.

"Let's go tell the skipper," Charlie said, turning the launch north.

We're out of options," Liz said. She, her two officers, and her brother were gathered in the small working space one deck below the bridge, the door closed. "We can't stay."

Heads nodded around the table.

"I've been working on this for a while," Liz continued, "anticipating this would happen eventually. I'd hoped we could stay until spring or even beyond, but issues with the cutter's system are making life aboard next to impossible, and we didn't expect a ship full of corpses to make it so we can't scavenge anymore. I have a plan."

She unfolded a map covered in red notations and spread it across the table. The others leaned in as Liz put a slender index finger on the page. "There are four other operational Legend Class cutters in service, each identical to *Joshua James*. The *Hamilton* is based in Charleston, South Carolina." She tapped her finger. "But the cutters *Bertholf*, *Waesche*, and *Stratton* are all stationed at Coast Guard Island, Alameda, in the San Francisco Bay."

Looks were exchanged as they imagined what such a city must be like now.

Liz went on. "I'm not naïve enough to think that any of those cutters are still there. Even if they were, they'd probably be in the same condition as the *Dorado*." She nodded at Charlie and the lieutenant. "But the base supports three national security cutters, and that means their warehouses and machine shops will have all the parts and equipment we need to get this vessel running properly again. If we're *very* lucky, we might find that the armory hasn't been completely raided, and there could be food stores and fuel as well."

Amy and Lt. Riggs were starting to smile. Liz nodded. It was the reaction she was hoping for and the same one she would want to see from the crew; hope, and having a goal upon which they could focus, was a powerful motivator. "This is going to mean a lot of work, and there are still hard decisions to be made."

Amy looked at her captain for elaboration, but the other woman went on.

"San Francisco and the surrounding area is heavily populated, and it's going to be crawling. Far worse than Seattle, worse than we can imagine. We don't know if there's a military presence there, whether refugee clusters—if any—will be hostile, and we don't know the condition of Coast Guard Island. It could look just like Crescent City."

The smiles began to falter at that point, but Liz went on quickly. "That's why we're going to make a detailed plan and conduct some reconnaissance." She looked at the pilot. "Mr. Riggs, you're going to get the chance to fly."

This isn't what I had in mind," Riggs said. He was seated in front of a console down in the cutter's combat center, a colorful array of lights and switches before him. At his left and right hands were rubberized joysticks. Mr. Vargas, the operations specialist, sat beside him, and Liz stood behind his chair.

"Stow your complaints, mister," she said, poking him in the shoulder. "This beats other duties I could invent."

Riggs laughed. "Roger that, Captain."

It was late morning on the day after their meeting belowdecks, and Liz had ordered the anchor raised, taking *Joshua James* several miles offshore and putting the stern into the wind. Riggs, Charlie, and a work party of six had been prepping since daybreak, and now the unmanned drone was ready.

The MQ-1 Predator was an older, earlier-model UAV, smaller than the MQ-9 Reapers used in Afghanistan, though still capable of carrying the AGM Hellfire missile. No such weapons had been delivered to *Joshua James*, and in fact the Predators had been aboard only because the cutter was due to test the close-in weapons system mounted aft of the superstructure. They were to have been the subject of target practice, and new drones for regular operations would have been delivered just prior to commissioning. These older birds were still sophisticated units capable of conducting detailed, aerial reconnaissance, sending back real-time digital video. They also carried an infrared camera with digitally enhanced zoom capabilities that could identify the heat signature of a human body from an altitude of ten thousand feet.

The drone could fly 460 miles to a target, loiter overhead for fourteen hours, and then return. It was just less than 360 miles to the San Francisco Bay, so Riggs would have more than enough time to conduct a detailed recon.

Normally, the MQ-1 required 125 feet of hard surface runway to take off. The Coast Guard variant, however, was adapted for launch from a rail-and-catapult system that could be assembled across the length of the helicopter flight pad and out over the stern. The drawback to this process was that since the drone needed an equal length of runway in order to land, the cutter could not recover its own drones. Normal procedures called for the Predator, upon completion of a mission, to be flown to a military airfield to await later pickup. In this case, Riggs would bring the drone back to Brookings and attempt to land it on the access road approaching the Coast Guard station.

"Ready for takeoff," Riggs said, flexing his hands around the joysticks.

Mr. Vargas spoke into a microphone. "Drone launch, drone launch. All personnel clear the flight deck."

Once video cameras showed the helicopter pad empty except for the drone and its launch rail, Liz said, "Launch when ready, Mr. Riggs."

The lieutenant checked the speed and direction of the wind, glanced at a barometer, and looked at the bird's video feed one last time. It gave him a view directly off the drone's nose, currently a shot of the rail stretching beyond the stern and out over open water. There were other video angles he could switch to once he was airborne.

"Firing," he said, depressing a button on the console. The video image began vibrating slightly as the UAV's propeller spun up to power. "Launch," he said, punching another button.

Assisted by the miniature catapult built into the rail, the Predator shot off the deck with a howl, skimming a few meters above the waves for a moment before climbing. It rose sharply into the morning sky, the hum of its propeller fading. Although it was capable of flying as high as twenty-five thousand feet, the UAV obeyed its pilot's controls and leveled off at twelve thousand.

The northern Pacific coast slid beneath it as the Predator headed south.

C oming up in about two minutes," Riggs said. Liz had taken over the seat beside her pilot while Mr. Vargas made another coffee run to the galley. Flight time so far was just over three hours. Above them on the bridge, Amy Liggett and their quartermaster slowly backed the cutter once more into its anchorage at the mouth of the river.

On-screen before them, in addition to the pilot's frontal view, was a color, look-down video from ten thousand feet, the drone flying much slower now than it had been. The Bay Area was overcast, but the Predator was flying just beneath the cloud cover, its gray skin making it almost invisible.

"Will anyone hear it?" Liz asked.

"I doubt it," said Riggs. "And even if someone hears the hum and thinks to look up, they won't see it." The bridge and city came into view, and Riggs's voice dropped to a whisper. "There's no one *left* to see it."

The Predator passed over the Golden Gate, and then the city itself. Mr. Vargas returned with three cups of coffee to find the two officers leaning into the images on screen. He nearly dropped his tray when he saw what they were looking at.

"It's dead," Vargas said softly.

Liz and Riggs could only nod. Some of the city had burned, other parts had toppled, and the streets were choked with debris.

The lieutenant zoomed the camera, and the dead came into view. They were everywhere.

The captain shook off a chill. "Let's take a look at the island," she said. The lieutenant flew the drone across the bay and quickly reached Alameda, loitering overhead and zooming in once again.

"It's infested," the pilot said.

"But it looks intact," Liz countered, taking control of one of the cameras and tracking it slowly across Coast Guard Island. As expected, there were no ships in port—certainly no Legend Class cutters—but it didn't look as if the place had burned, which was a good sign. Riggs was right, however. The station was swarming with thousands of the walking dead.

"We'll work it out," she said.

Lt. Riggs kept his face expressionless as he listened to her words and took in what he was seeing. *Work it out?* That little dustup at Port Angeles had been *nothing* compared to what awaited them down there. A battalion of Marines with heavy weapons would have trouble taking this place. *They* were going to seize it with a couple dozen coasties using light arms?

He saw a blip on a radar scope to his left. "Airborne contact," the pilot said, tapping the scope. He began tracking the look-down camera on the contact as he steered the drone toward the Bay Bridge. Below them was a slow-moving, haze-gray Navy helicopter.

"They're going to pick us up on their air search radar," Vargas said from behind them.

"Maybe," Riggs muttered, keeping the camera on the bird. It was headed for an aircraft carrier sitting motionless off western Oakland, just south of the Bay Bridge. He zoomed in and saw a Black Hawk parked alone on the deck. "No fighter aircraft . . . I got movement on deck." He zoomed again and saw a few people walking normally, not with the stiff-legged movements of corpses. As he watched, one of the aircraft elevators rose, delivering a low-slung fuel truck that moved across the deck toward the Black Hawk.

Liz said, "Are they military?"

"Can't tell from up here. I can fly lower, but then we run the risk of detection."

"Negative," said Liz. "Hold at this altitude and we'll watch for a bit."

They did just that for the next six hours, Mr. Vargas continuing to shuttle back and forth between the galley and the combat center with fresh coffee. They watched the Navy bird make an awkward landing, saw that the Black Hawk, although fueled, never left the deck, and eventually watched both aircraft ride the elevator to be stored below. The Predator digitally recorded every moment. At the end of those six hours, Liz and her pilot were convinced of several things: the ship was grounded and listing to port, there was a skeleton crew mostly composed of civilians, and the supercarrier—now identified as the *Nimitz*—was still under nuclear power. As evening fell, the two officers watched lights come on in the bridge and from within the hangar deck.

"Can you fly one of those birds?" Liz asked.

Riggs laughed. "You bet your . . . ah, yes, ma'am."

She stared at the carrier's image on the screen. Power, aircraft, fuel, stores, and a desalinization system that no doubt worked. It was a prize the likes of which William Kidd could never even dream.

"Bring your bird home, Lieutenant," she said, standing and stretching. "I want you, Miss Liggett, and the senior chief assembled in my quarters at seventeen hundred hours."

Riggs did as ordered, and several hours later he brought the Predator in for a landing on the intended access road. A zombie wearing a fast-food uniform blundered into its path as it touched down and was cut in half by the fast-moving UAV. The Predator fragmented into spinning pieces from the impact.

The surveillance flight was a success.

.   .   .

Liz passed around a photograph showing *Nimitz* resting at a tilt to the west of Oakland. Blackbeard was crouched under the bed, watching Charlie, tail flicking.

"This is our new objective," Liz said. "It has everything we need and poses less risk than the hordes on Coast Guard Island."

Amy was jubilant. "This changes everything! There'll be more than enough room and resources to take on our crew and all the refugees on shore."

The captain had no comment and only rubbed slowly at the ugly scar running down one side of her face, now beginning to turn white.

"They'll be willing to share it with us, don't you think?" Amy said. "If we show them we don't mean them harm."

Charlie and Lt. Riggs exchanged glances.

"Perhaps," the captain offered. "Amy, I want you to conduct a detailed inventory of all our supplies, including arms and ammunition. Will you do that right away, please?"

The young woman left smiling. Charlie closed the door behind her and turned to his sister. "You don't plan on sharing anything, do you?"

"That is not my intention."

Riggs frowned. "Captain, no disrespect, but what about an attempt at negotiations, or perhaps even using our military status to bully our way into control of that ship?"

"I understand your point, Mr. Riggs," Liz said. "However, both options leave us exposed. If things didn't go the way we wanted, we'd be vulnerable and lose the advantage of surprise." She tapped a finger at the photo of *Nimitz*. "Better to strike under our terms instead of reacting."

"Of course, Captain," he said.

She looked at her brother. "We'll need crew for this. I want you to conduct some discreet screening of the refugees. Look for people who will make good combatants, men or women without families.

I don't want anyone pressed into service, only those who are ready to fight for the right to survive, no deadweight. Do you take my meaning?"

"I know just the types we need," said Charlie.

"And I want to reemphasize the word *discreet*. The other refugees cannot hear about this, and Miss Liggett is not to be involved." She shook her head. "I'm afraid she's grown too close with the civilians, lost her objectivity."

Liz looked again at the photo of the aircraft carrier. "Senior Chief, if I gave you an armed team, do you think you could get through the dead, then in and out of those boatyard warehouses on the south end of the marina? Bring back some supplies?"

"No sweat."

"Good." She slapped a hand against a white metal bulkhead. "Bring back all the paint you can find. I want you to turn this cutter black."

It took a week with all hands participating to paint *Joshua James*. When the black ran out, dark blue was used. It wasn't pretty, but now the frigate-sized ship would no longer stand out like a white beacon. At night, it would be nearly invisible.

Liz mustered her skeleton crew and told them they would be heading south, sold them on the promises that *Nimitz* held for their survival and future. She spoke about hot food, hot showers, fresh water, and working heads. The crew was ecstatic, but their captain cautioned them that if those currently holding the carrier became aggressive, *Joshua James* would be forced to defend itself. There was no protest. The crew was with her.

During that same week, Charlie identified eighteen refugees (most of them male, but a few women included) who had neither families nor any reservations about killing in order to stay alive. They were told to stay quiet until summoned.

Amy was quick to notice that conversations she was not involved with were taking place, which she perceived as an intentional attempt to keep her out of the loop. When she brought her concerns to the captain, she was given a sharp rebuke.

"I don't have time to entertain your hurt feelings, Miss Liggett, nor do I care to hear your theories on conspiracy. Follow your orders. I will worry about what is and is not happening aboard my ship. Are we clear, lady?"

Amy hadn't brought it up again, and kept her head down. But she watched, and worried. Most of all she worried about the captain's statement about aggression from the people on *Nimitz*, and that the crew of the cutter might have to defend themselves. She didn't want to risk another tongue lashing, however, and remained silent.

On the morning of January 2, Charlie Kidd collected Ava, the little boy she was found with wearing a rope leash, and his would-be pirates from the Coast Guard station, bringing them aboard along with whatever food and water supplies the rest of the refugees had been able to save. The rest of the civilians protested, and one man tried to grab a cardboard tray of bottled water out of the chief's hands. Charlie shot him in the head, and the rest of the refugees scattered.

Within twenty minutes of the shooting, *Joshua James* raised anchor and steamed out of the mouth of the Chetco River, bow pointed at the Pacific. On shore, refugees ran from the station and lined the water's edge, families and children, the elderly and injured, all crying out and waving their arms, shouting at the departing vessel.

Shocked and enraged, Amy Liggett stormed onto the bridge, yelling that those were innocent, helpless people being left behind, reminding her captain that the Coast Guard mission was to *protect* them, not abandon them. There were tears in her eyes as she demanded that Liz turn the cutter around and take them aboard.

Liz nodded at her brother, who relieved the ensign of her side-arm and locked her in the maintenance closet they'd turned into a cell. The cutter put to sea, towing the forty-seven-foot MLB in its wake, then turned south. Back on land, hordes of the dead tracked in on the cries of anguish coming from the water's edge, and moved on the Coast Guard station in a hungry surge.

BLACK FLAG

TWENTY-SIX

January 12—Nimitz

Maya reached the superstructure's bridge level, feeling the climb in her thigh muscles. She was young and fit, but it was still nearly an eight-story climb. Doc Rosa said exercise was good for the baby now that she was out of her first trimester, when the risk of miscarriage was at its highest. She walked the short distance to the hatch. The Navy guys climbed these stairs all day long, and most were older than her, so she couldn't complain. Besides, the stairs would keep her backside toned. Evan would appreciate that.

If he's not dead.

She tried to push the hateful thought away. It didn't want to leave. At the hatch, she gave the handle a tug, but it was unmoving. She tried several times with the same result. Locked? Since when? She banged a fist against the steel.

Banks and PK heard the thumping at the bridge hatch, and Banks moved to it. "Who's there?" he called. There was no answer, so he asked again. More thumping, and more insistent.

"I'll be back," he told Katcher, jacking a round into his sidearm before moving outside onto the bridge catwalk. He would circle around, go through another hatch, and come up behind whoever was trying to get in. If it wasn't someone he knew, they were going to get some new holes in them.

I t was still raining as *Nimitz* passed beneath the Bay Bridge. Corpses in soiled and tattered clothing that were lining the edge in droves crawled over the bridge's railing and flung themselves into space. In seconds they were smashing onto the flight deck, bones snapping and insides bursting through split flesh. Some landed head down and were destroyed instantly. Others were crippled so badly they could only flop about on the deck, but most either crawled or dragged their fractured bodies into grotesque standing positions and started moving.

Several drifters threw themselves off the bridge just as the aircraft carrier's conning tower passed beneath them.

F rustrated, Maya turned from the bridge and backtracked to where a side hatch opened onto the outside catwalk. She would bang on the outside of the bridge windows until someone let her in.

A gust of cold, wet air hit her as she pushed the hatch open and stepped onto the steel grating, one hand gripping the slick rail. The drop-off to water was to her left as she moved forward, the bridge lights glowing ahead on the right. The sky was full dark now and the clouds masked both moon and stars. The catwalk shuddered briefly under her feet, then twice more.

The bridge hatch ahead of her opened suddenly, an oval of light spilling out as Mr. Banks emerged. Maya raised a hand as he turned toward her, and then something dark dropped from the sky, slamming onto the catwalk between them. Another fell behind the operations specialist, hitting the railing and slithering bonelessly over the side for the long drop to the waters below. Another landed on the steel grate and started to stand.

The shape that had fallen between them lifted its head and bared its teeth at the young woman.

Maya saw Banks spin, saw the flash of his pistol, and she unzipped the hip pocket of her coveralls. Her hand found the checkered grip of the little .380 automatic Evan had given her, and which Chief Liebs had then taught her to use properly. She worked the slide and shot the thing on the deck, then saw Banks aiming at her and yelling something.

She dropped to the catwalk as Banks's pistol flashed silently with three quick shots. Maya pivoted in a crouch to see a trio of limping ghouls on the catwalk behind her. Two went down, but the third soaked up the gunfire with its chest and lunged for her. She threw herself on her back and fired upward between her knees, the bullet catching the creature under the chin and blowing out the top of its head. It collapsed onto her legs, and she kicked free.

Then Banks had her by the arm, hauling her up and pulling her back to the open hatch. More dark shapes were plunging through the night, some missing the ship completely and falling into the sea, others smashing through the radar and antenna clusters atop the conning tower. Banks pulled Maya through the hatch, slamming and securing it behind them.

PK stood on the bridge wearing a startled look and holding a pistol. "Raining zombies?" he said. "How messed up is that?"

Father Xavier, contact the bridge immediately," PK said through the intercom, his voice carrying throughout the ship. He'd been calling and getting no response since someone fired a shot across their bow. Now that Maya and Banks were safe on the bridge, he was back at it.

Banks was standing with Maya near the bridge windows overlooking the flight deck. More than a hundred shapes dropped out of the sky and smacked onto the deck before the carrier cleared the Bay Bridge on the other side.

Maya took a legal pad and pen from a bridge console, and they began scribbling back and forth, Banks catching her up.

Still no word on Evan, sorry, Banks wrote.

Are you still looking?

Yes, scanning all frequencies. Xavier has us on lockdown. Refugees that came on board are hostile. Being hunted down now.

Maya scribbled questions back at him. *Who is hunting? How many refugees? Where are they?*

Banks answered what he could, emphasizing that she was to stay here with them, safe on the bridge. After a moment's hesitation, she nodded agreement. Then Banks told her about the radio contact from a ship called *Adventure Galley*.

Fired a shot across our bow, he wrote. *Demanding we surrender.*

Banks didn't need to be a trained lip reader to see Maya mouth the words *Fuck that.*

Xavier wished Pat Katcher would shut up. The demands that he call the bridge *right now*, however, not only persisted but were sounding more urgent. His voice echoed through the passageways. *Why didn't the bridge have a Hydra radio?* Neither he nor Calvin could take the time to find a phone right now. They were hunting—or being hunted—and shots had already been fired. Calvin had a buckshot pellet in the meat of his left thigh to prove it.

Minutes ago a big woman with short hair and a flannel shirt popped out into the passageway behind them and fired a shotgun. It was a hasty, unaimed shot, and most of the blast blew apart a cluster of electrical conduit running up one wall. The two men spun to return fire, catching a glimpse of the woman as she ducked back out of sight. Now they were advancing slowly with their weapons to their shoulders.

The empty hull of her shotgun shell was lying on the deck at an intersection, and they swung their weapons in every direction. Corridors, hatches, ladderways, but no woman.

"She could be anywhere," Xavier breathed.

Calvin nodded and started right, easing up to a hatch. He gripped the handle and pushed, both men staying out of the opening for a moment, and then Xavier went in low with his shotgun. A pair of fluorescent bars illuminated a planning room of some kind, filled with tables and chairs, several whiteboards, and a projector. There was no one inside.

"Father Xavier, call the bridge *immediately*." Pat Katcher's voice had an annoyed tone as it came from an overhead speaker.

"Take it," said Calvin, crouching in the open hatch and watching the hallway. Xavier picked up a wall phone and punched in the bridge extension. The electronics tech answered at once.

"Skipper, Jesus . . . I mean, what have—"

"Talk to me, PK," Xavier said.

The young man paused. "Father, a shitload of drifters dropped onto the ship when it passed under the Bay Bridge. A bunch are still moving. We also got a radio transmission from a ship calling itself *Adventure Galley*. It sounds familiar, but I don't know why, and they're demanding we surrender and muster everyone on deck. They just fired a warning shot across our bow."

The priest digested the message. *Compounding problems.* "Any other transmissions?"

"No, sir."

"Okay, don't respond to them. Is anyone with you?"

"Banks and Maya are here. They had a close call with some drifters out on the catwalk, but everyone's okay. We're locked in the bridge."

"Good," said Xavier. "Stay there. See if you and Banks can get some surface radar working so we can see where this other ship is, and where *Nimitz* is going."

Katcher said he would try, and clicked off.

Xavier turned to his friend. "Maya's on the bridge, and she's safe," he assured him before filling him in on the rest.

Calvin kept his eyes on the corridor. "Go. You deal with that. I'll get this bitch, then hunt down the rest of them."

Xavier had shamed and bullied his friend into this hunt, and now he was supposed to run out on the man? They couldn't permit these boarders to have free run of the ship, but they suddenly had new problems. He keyed the mic on his Hydra. "Chief Liebs, it's Xavier."

A moment later the chief's voice said, "Go ahead."

Xavier updated the gunner's mate on what was happening belowdecks, and now topside with both the dead and the appearance of a hostile ship.

"Copy," said Liebs. "Stone is with me; we're leaving the armory, fully loaded. Meet us on the port side catwalk amidships, right below the flight deck. We have to be ready to mount a defense."

Xavier acknowledged and turned to his friend, who was standing at the hatch now. Before the priest could speak, Calvin repeated, "Go."

Xavier unsnapped the Hydra radio from his combat vest and handed it to the other man, smacking his shoulder. "Watch your ass." Then he slipped through the hatch and jogged to the right, shotgun held low in front of him.

Calvin watched him go. When he was sure the priest was safely away, he unlaced and kicked off his boots, turned the radio volume down as far as it would go, and ghosted left up the passageway.

TWENTY-SEVEN

They found something to pry up the handle, Sophia thought. There was a metallic groan at the hatch, the lever inching upward and stretching the television cord and sheets they'd used to lash it down. She and Kay stood back from the door, watching the lever move.

The children were all the way at the back of the berthing compartment, hiding under bottom racks or in the head and showers, trying to stay quiet. The lever creaked and rose another inch.

"It's not going to hold," Kay said, her voice on the edge of panic.

"And they're going to come in shooting," said Sophia. She looked around, seeing nothing else that could wedge the handle, nothing that would make a difference. She looked at the other woman. "Go back into the compartment. If they get through me, you'll have to take them." She didn't have to tell her what would happen to the children if both adults fell.

Kay was pale and looked ready to cry, but she bit her lip and nodded, disappearing back into the room. Sophia moved behind a triple stack of bunks facing the hatch and knelt behind them, resting the shotgun across the mattress, aiming at the door. It was poor cover, she knew, but it might buy her time for an extra shot.

Another creak, and the TV cords snapped, the knotted sheets beginning to tear as the handle went up. Sophia tensed.

Stay right here, buddy," Tommy said, setting the toddler on the deck. The little boy had one hand over his eyes and was sucking a thumb furiously, his small body trembling as it had been since the orderly took him from the officer's mess after Mercy and Jerry were murdered by the boarding team. He hadn't fought or squirmed as Tommy carried him through the passageways, and for that the man was thankful, but the boy hadn't spoken, either.

Not surprising. He's seen so much horror just since coming aboard. What had he seen during his time with these killers?

Tommy had been heading toward the room Sophia and Kay used as a school when he heard the gunfire echoing through the corridors. It made him stop, and the child began to whimper. He wished he were holding the rifle slung around his neck, but he couldn't grip that and carry the boy at the same time, so he'd settled for the pistol. Another brief exchange of gunfire followed the first and he moved toward it. The boy started whining, and Tommy briefly wondered how responsible it was to be heading into trouble while carrying a child. But gunfire meant *his* people were in trouble, and so he went.

Things were quiet for a while, and he slowed to a creep as he lost the direction of the shooting. Then he heard a scraping of metal, a creaking noise, and low curses coming from around a corner.

"I'll be right back," he whispered to the toddler. The boy sat on the deck and covered his face with his hands, his chest hitching. The sight of this terrified child made him angry: not at the boy, but at those who had dragged him along on their brutal mission. Tommy shoved the pistol into its holster, bringing up the rifle.

. . .

Almost . . . got it . . ." the bearded man said, his face purpling as he heaved on the heavy pry bar he had taken from a nearby fire-fighting station, forcing the handle upward. His fire axe and pistol were on the deck beside the hatch and his bearded partner stood behind him, rifle pointed and ready.

"Almost . . ." There was a pop and the handle flew up, the man dropping to his knees and letting go of the pry bar. "Yes!"

A long rattle of 5.56-millimeter bullets cut the two men down.

The one who'd been using the pry bar was on his back, blood in his mouth as he struggled to breathe. He saw someone wearing green medical scrubs and an orange backpack run up to stand over him, pointing a rifle down and to his left, firing a single shot into his partner's head. Then the muzzle swung back toward him, aiming at his face.

The bearded man tried to say, "No," but it came out as a gurgle. The muzzle flashed.

Sophia listened to a long silence after the initial burst of gunfire followed by two shots. Then came the muffled sound of a child crying in the corridor. Someone banged on the hatch. "It's Tommy," said a voice outside. "Who's in there?"

"Be ready, Kay," Sophia called, approaching the hatch with the shotgun to her shoulder, finger on the trigger. The lever had been forced up, the hatch standing slightly ajar, and she eased it open with the toe of a sneaker, aiming. The passageway outside was blood-splattered, two dead men crumpled on the deck with neat bullet holes in their foreheads to go with their other wounds. A child was crying somewhere to the right.

"It's Tommy," the orderly called. He'd moved back from the hatch, not wanting to become collateral damage.

Sophia peeked into the corridor and saw him. He approached her and held out the little boy. She set down the shotgun at once and took him into her arms.

"You have the kids?" Tommy asked.

"All of them," she replied, passing the toddler to Kay, who had come up behind her.

The orderly nodded and quickly collected the dead men's weapons, carrying them into the berthing compartment and dumping them on a rack. Then he brought in the heavy pry bar.

"Who is this?" Kay asked, rubbing the toddler's back and swaying with him. The child was crying behind his hands.

"They brought him along as some kind of diversion," Tommy said with an edge to his voice. "I don't know his name." He looked at the toddler, who popped his thumb into his mouth and looked away, shaking his head. Tommy sighed and handed the pry bar to Sophia. "Use this to jam the handle. It should hold."

She took it, felt the weight, and knew he was right. Tommy went back into the corridor, rifle to his shoulder. "I'm going after Rosa."

Sophia closed the hatch behind him and jammed the pry bar against the handle.

The compartment was cold and black with two feet of seawater covering the floor. Rosa had no power, no phone, and no radio, just her flashlight, and found herself wondering how long the batteries would last.

It was a small space containing quarters for two men that doubled as a tiny office. She figured they had to be chiefs or senior petty officers, as low-ranking enlisted men didn't get private quarters like this, and no commissioned officer would be quartered down here in the bowels of the vessel. The racks, stacked one atop the other against one wall, lifted up to reveal bed-sized storage compartments beneath. The lower rack was flooded out, but the upper one still held the neatly folded clothing and personal items of its former occupant. Rosa was able to put on dry—though slightly large—clothes and layer up with extra T-shirts and socks. A bulky sweater went over the top of it all.

While she went through the contents of the storage space, she was careful not to look at the photos of the man's family, set carefully to one side.

After she had run from the bloated and pasty corpses in the recreation room, Rosa had made a series of turns, dodging down passageways and through black compartments, wading through the knee-deep water. Groans echoed through the maze of flooded corridors, joined on occasion by the deeper creak and rumble of the torn hull taking on water. She could feel that the ship was on a sharper tilt now.

The flashlight's beam revealed bloodless faces and yellow eyes in almost every direction, and she had shot at them until she had emptied her magazine and replaced it with a fresh one—her last. More shots left her with only six rounds, but she didn't regret firing. It had kept her alive and held them back, allowing her the time and space needed to duck into this compartment unseen. A privacy bolt beside the hatch handle ensured it would remain closed.

Now, lying on the top bunk and wrapped in a wool blanket, Rosa looked down at the leftovers of a medical patch job floating on the water's surface in the room: paper from bandage packaging, bloody gauze, and a plastic hypodermic for antibiotics. Her sneakers, one torn and bloody on one side from where the bullet had entered, rested at the end of the bunk next to her medical pack. Under the blanket, her right foot was bandaged and throbbing.

Thank God it was only a ricochet. A direct shot into her foot would be crippling, and the dead would've been on her in seconds. As it was, the flattened slug had lodged in the meat behind her little toe, and Rosa was forced to scream into a pillow as she plucked it out with a pair of forceps. There was Demerol in her kit, though it remained unused. She needed a clear head, so over-the-counter pain relievers would have to suffice, but they weren't doing much.

The blanket and layers of dry clothes warmed her, and although she wanted to be out there looking for Michael, she knew she'd be of no help to him if she shut down from hypothermia and became an easy meal for the former crew. Warmth and rest. She had no choice.

Michael. Lying curled up with her head on the pillow, pistol close to her hand, she stared out at the small room, thinking about the boy. *Some rescuer I am. I hope you've been smarter than me.* She shut off the flashlight to conserve the battery. *Hang in there, kid. I'm still coming.*

Rosa slept.

Lying mostly submerged in the blackness of the gear handling compartment, Michael's body, still in a fetal position, jerked and convulsed. The corpse of a female sailor approached and briefly inspected the figure, decided it wasn't food, and shuffled away.

Muscles rippled beneath Michael's tightening skin, while firecracker strings of red electrical pulses made his brain jump. Eyes moved quickly behind closed lids as if the boy were not dead, but deep in REM sleep. His body ejected blackish fluids into the water.

Primal, violent urges flashed in his mutating brain as Michael's flesh began darkening to a deep crimson.

TWENTY-EIGHT

Five pirates, Charlie Kidd and his four civilian recruits, moved along the starboard side of the hangar deck. The young auxiliary deputy was in the lead, following Charlie's whispered directions and commands. They stayed close to the high steel wall, advancing quickly, weapons trained out into the big space. Forklifts and low-slung motorized carts sat on the rubberized decking, along with pallets of crates and the shadowy outlines of five helicopters parked at the end of the bay, hinged tail booms neatly folded against their sides.

Ahead of the group, near an aircraft elevator in a space open to the sea and the night, someone had built a square of sandbags, stacked to form a low wall. The interior was filled with soil and rows of crops. Charlie found it bizarre to see a garden growing in this place of cold steel, green leaves fluttering in the sea breeze.

Sudden movement whipped them all left, and they saw a man with long hair, cutoffs, and sandals dart from behind a pallet of crates, running for an open hatch on the port side. He was carrying a rifle but wasn't pointing it, only running away.

.   .   .

Charlie aimed his M4 and shot him down. The group immediately ran to the fallen body, and Ava slit the hippie's throat just to be sure he was dead.

"Where were you going?" Charlie mused, crouching and relieving the dead man of a canvas flight deck vest, its pockets stuffed with six heavy magazines of rifle ammunition. Then he collected the rifle itself, grinning. It was an M14, the 7.62-millimeter assault rifle of the early 1960s, originally produced with a wood stock and grips. This was the newer version used by naval services, prisons, and Special Forces: blued steel and a dense, black plastic composition. A lethal weapon, and Charlie knew it well.

"Hello, baby," Charlie said, running his fingers over the weapon.

The deputy kicked the body. "This one's gonna be up in a minute." He pointed the muzzle of his rifle at the head.

"Don't," Chick said. "Save the bullet. He'll make things interesting for the folks aboard once he's up and walking."

"He might attack us," the kid said.

"And then you may shoot him," Chick said, as if speaking to a five-year-old. The chief handed his assault rifle to Ava, shrugging into the canvas vest full of magazines. The others quickly moved away from the corpse as Charlie took his time to ensure that the M14 had a full magazine, flicking off the safety. Then he followed his people as they continued through the hangar.

Chick looked around at hatches and ladderways climbing to interior catwalks. Once he was inside and stirring things up, his mission was to make certain it was safe for the second boarding party—the one that would be heavily armed with three times the original boarding group's numbers—to reach and enter the ship. The carrier's defenders would try to stop them, and Charlie knew they had only two ways to do that: put a helicopter into the air armed with an anti-ship torpedo (which they couldn't do, not while he controlled the hangar bay) or mount fifty-calibers to the catwalk rails.

U.S. aircraft carriers were mighty things, but it was the ship's aircraft that allowed the carrier to visit earth-shaking destruction on an enemy, as they both served as offensive weapons and provided for the ship's defense. Without them, the ship was extremely vulnerable, relying on an entire battle group of screening ships including destroyers, guided missile cruisers, frigates, and subs to protect it from attack long before a threat could reach striking distance.

Nimitz, like all supercarriers, had minimal defenses of its own: a few Phalanx close-in weapon systems with Gatling-gun-style barrels to chop inbound missiles out of the air, and several batteries of surface-to-air missiles (SAMs) to shoot down aircraft. Neither system could protect the carrier from a surface threat. It had no gun batteries, only the fifty-cals to guard against small craft and suicide bombers in speed boats. If Charlie and his team could secure the catwalks where those guns would be mounted, the carrier would be helpless when the second boarding party came at them.

Chick was about to order two of his group to stay and watch the choppers while he and the others headed up to the catwalks when another flash of movement appeared down near the helicopters and he spotted a man running. Charlie saw the muscular upper body, the short haircut, and the brown face with its cruel scar.

The priest!

Charlie opened up with the M14 at once, the powerful *cracks* ringing though the hangar. Bullets sparked off metal and the priest suddenly stopped and dodged, throwing himself behind the nose of a Navy Seahawk. The auxiliary deputy sent three-round bursts into the bird, peppering its thin skin with holes.

From beneath the helicopter's fuselage came the flash of shotgun fire, the air around Charlie and his pirates buzzing with angry hornets, a nearby wooden crate splintering. They went for cover.

"I'll watch the front," Charlie yelled at the deputy. "You watch the tail. Don't let him out."

The boy knelt at the right end of the crates and sighted on the rear of the helicopter while Charlie targeted the nose. The shotgun crashed from under the chopper's belly, splintering the crate again.

"The rest of you get to the catwalks like we planned," Charlie said to the others, then looked at Ava. "You know what to do." He aimed back at the helicopter and fired three heavy-caliber bullets at the place where he'd seen the shotgun flash. "This fucker is *mine*."

You just hide there, Father, Charlie thought, searching for movement. *I can afford to be patient.*

Adventure Galley

Aboard the cutter, now renamed by the captain after her infamous ancestor's ship, Elizabeth Kidd stood in the combat center looking over her operations specialist's shoulder. She had admitted to herself that her team had stopped being Coast Guard a long time ago, and might as well call the ship what it was. On a video screen, one of the cutter's exterior infrared cameras was zoomed in on the drifting aircraft carrier, showing her images in varying shades of green. It was the same system they'd used to surveil the vessel across the long distance of the bay, from their position of concealment behind the Richmond–San Rafael Bridge.

The cutter had slipped into the San Francisco Bay five nights ago, invisible as it hugged the northern coastline and dropped anchor behind the bridge. Then they had watched, and planned and trained. By the time Liz decided to strike, her boarders were eager and pep talks sprinkled with rhetoric about taking what was rightfully theirs urged them on. For Liz's part, the time spent watching gave her a good idea of just how thin the crew aboard *Nimitz* was, as well as the comfortable, unsuspecting patterns into which they'd fallen. She'd been pleased when the Black Hawk lifted off the deck yesterday without any torpedoes aboard and hadn't returned.

The appearance of the Navy helicopter was unexpected, but the way it flew carelessly into their air defense envelope told her it was accidental; her ship remained undetected. Shooting it down was an easy decision and left the carrier vulnerable. One bird was down and the other missing. How many pilots could they have?

On the bridge two decks above, Mr. Waite was now conning the ship in a slow, distant circle around the crippled aircraft carrier, permitting Liz to use the exterior camera to get a view of her prize from all angles. Since her warning shot, there had been no sign that the occupants were mustering on deck as ordered. This wasn't particularly surprising; they were mostly civilians as far as she'd seen, disorganized refugees who'd lucked into an island fortress. That fact made her angry, considering how hard she'd fought—and what she'd lost—just to reach a point where her people were barely holding on. She'd used this in her speeches to the crew as well.

"Why should *they* have it so easy when *you've* had it so hard? What did *they* do to deserve such a sanctuary?" It worked, and her crew was now bloodthirsty.

No, the carrier's occupants hadn't complied, and Liz didn't expect they would. She'd given Chick six hours to create as much chaos and destruction as possible before sending in the second team—and now that *Nimitz* had passed under the Bay Bridge, the walking dead were aboard as well. Even if they could coordinate a surrender, the flight deck wasn't an inviting place to assemble.

Liz had no intention of firing on the carrier again unless there was no alternative. She wanted it intact, and the shot across the bow was a bluff. That, combined with the terror of Charlie Kidd belowdecks, would soften them up nicely for the second wave.

Lieutenant Riggs would command the motorized lifeboat they'd towed here with them, leading a group of the remaining ten civilians Charlie had recruited and most of her Coast Guard crew. Their numbers would easily overwhelm whoever remained aboard after her brother ripped through them. Although Riggs was a pilot and not a true seaman, he accepted the assignment eagerly. He'd also welcomed the promotion to executive officer, after Ensign Liggett put on that mutinous display as they left Brookings, Oregon.

Liz would hang the girl at her leisure.

Amy had lost track of time. Was it possible she'd been locked in this maintenance closet for a week? She thought it was. The captain had ordered the room's lightbulb removed, so the only illumination came from the narrow crack at the base of the door. Once a day the door opened about six inches (prevented from opening further by someone's boot braced against the other side—she'd tested it) for a handful of crackers to be tossed inside, along with a plastic bottle of water. She didn't get fresh water until she'd handed out the empty. Twice, a bowl of half-eaten cat food was pushed inside. After resisting for a day, Amy gave in and devoured it. The stuff tasted as bad as it smelled, and she decided that cats probably didn't care, considering they licked their own rear ends. Amy had a bucket for a toilet, and it was never emptied. The closet was foul. She was hungry, dirtier than she could ever remember, and her bones and muscles ached from sleeping on the cold steel deck.

Footsteps or voices would pass in the corridor outside, but no one stopped to speak to her. When she pounded on the door or yelled, she was ignored.

The young woman had no illusions that anything awaited her other than the rope, but she decided she wouldn't have done anything differently. Well, instead of simply yelling and demanding the captain turn back for the Brookings refugees, she could have taken the bridge at gunpoint.

Here in the dark she could see their faces clearly, the families struggling to survive, looking at Amy with trust even as she burdened them with more and more of the captain's restrictions. She saw the children, and for days their images brought tears. She was all cried out now, though.

They're all dead. All of them, even the kids. They'd been left with no way to defend themselves against the oncoming horde, and there was nowhere to run. *I own that. I should have seen what that bitch was planning.* Amy would have liked to blame it on the fact that she was young and inexperienced, that she was only following orders. How convenient it would be to tell herself she'd been seduced by all the lofty concepts she'd learned about command and duty and obedience to those appointed above her. And how simple to rationalize that she'd been overwhelmed by her captain's reputation and charisma.

Right. Lie to yourself the way you lied to those people. Will that save you from the rope? She knew it wouldn't, but she no longer cared about being hanged on deck while the crew looked on. Amy decided she deserved punishment, for she'd betrayed those people just as assuredly as the madwoman commanding this ship.

When she heard the fifty-seven-millimeter gunfire on the foredeck, felt the dull vibration in the steel beneath her, Amy knew that Elizabeth Kidd was now inflicting her terror on yet another group of refugees. It made the young woman clench her teeth until her jaws ached and make fists so tight the nails left marks in her palms.

No amount of forgiveness could undo the role she'd played in Brookings, she knew that. As she sat alone in the dark, awaiting her fate, she wondered if she might find *some* small measure of absolution. Not for the defenseless people she'd left to their fates, but for herself.

TWENTY-NINE

January 12—Richmond

A sound awoke Evan, and at first he thought it was because the rain had stopped. He no longer heard the steady patter in his water-collecting bowl, so he crawled through the dark on hands and knees out to the balcony, where indeed the rain was no longer falling. Evan cupped his working hand into the bowl and took several small drinks. He wished for pain relievers to go with the water; the fractured wrist was aching. *What time was it? Ten? Eleven?* He hadn't put on his watch today.

The sound came again and he froze. *Not the rain.* It was a thump, and it came from inside the house somewhere. A chill ran across his skin as Evan realized he had a visitor, probably the dead kind.

A look outside revealed little. Although the rain had stopped, it was still overcast, and darkness blanketed the empty neighborhood. He strained to see down onto the burned lawn, the driveway, the street beyond. If anything was moving down there, he couldn't tell.

Because it's already inside.

Evan gathered his few possessions and tucked them into the pockets of his survival vest, then considered: knife or pistol? He would prefer to engage at a distance, but it was even darker inside the multilevel concrete house, and he couldn't be sure he would hit the mark. Then there was the sound, and what that would attract. Reluctantly, he holstered the Sig Calvin had given him last summer and pulled the survival knife.

A scraping noise floated through the house, and Evan crept to the bedroom doorway, holding his breath and listening. Another scraping, followed by the scuff of a footstep. *Coming up the stairs. But which floor?* The gutted house was an echo factory, making it difficult to judge the distance and location of sounds.

How many in the house? How many already on this floor? He could picture them, burned corpses standing in the shadows with clicking teeth, sensing for movement. He imagined the hallway outside his room filled with them, just waiting for him to step out so they could rush him with claws and jaws open, incinerated nightmares screeching and—

Stop that shit! His writer's imagination was trying to unhorse him. But now the nightmares were real, weren't they? Evan clenched his teeth and stepped into the hall, the survival knife raised and ready to plunge into a blackened head. The hallway was empty.

The sound of something rough sliding against a concrete wall came from the darkness ahead. Evan wished for one of those pistol attachments that permitted a small flashlight to be snapped in place under the barrel, but he had seen no need for one while he was choosing his equipment. He was a pilot, there were no zombies in the sky, and because of his rare and newly acquired skill, he was not permitted to go into the unsecured areas of the carrier with the hunting parties. He supposed he'd never considered actually surviving a crash, and he regretted the decision now.

A mournful, broken wail came from the darkness, closer than he expected, a cracking sound that reverberated through the house and gave him another chill. It was answered a moment later by a chorus of similar cries coming from beyond the balcony.

They're on the lawn too. Are they communicating? Jesus, they don't do that!

Evan forced his imagination into neutral. Why he'd never tried writing fiction was beyond him. *Okay, less storyteller, more Vladimir.*

That thought propelled him down the hallway, knife pointed ahead of him now. He remembered a landing that overlooked switchback stairs from his daytime tour of the house, and a hallway that continued on toward the bedroom where he'd found the remains of the murder-suicide. Evan stopped at the edge of the landing and looked over the solid banister.

It took a moment to focus, for his eyes to distinguish the grays from the blacks. Where blue-tinted windows once climbed the face of the house at the central staircase were now only empty frames, and what outside light there was resolved the grays into walls and stairs. A darker shape, black against the gray, was past the turn at the switchback and halfway up the stairs to Evan's level. It was one of the burned things, and as it climbed, its right shoulder scraped against the wall, leaving a sooty smear on the concrete.

Evan risked a look down and saw no others but wasn't reassured. There could be more on the floor below him, just out of sight. Most certainly *would* be more.

A dry croak from below confirmed his fear.

The thing on the stairs let out another parched wail and scraped the wall again, nearly at the top. *More Vladimir.* Evan waited until it set a foot on the uppermost hallway floor, then stepped in and swung the survival knife overhand, driving the blade into its forehead. There was a cracking sound, and the charcoal orb split in two, spilling cold wet sludge onto his knife hand as the body collapsed. It rolled down to the switchback, a brittle arm snapping off in the process.

A groan from below came again, but this time as a pair.

Evan held back a cry of disgust as he wiped the sticky hand violently on the leg of his flight suit. He wanted to run, forced himself to stand still. How far would he get in the dark? The street could be full of them, and *they* didn't need light in order to find him.

Should he figure out a way up to the roof, use one of his two flares? He'd seen no stairs leading up from this level, and anyone wanting to get onto the house's roof would need a ladder. *Perfect! He would be safe up there; the dead couldn't climb.*

The throbbing in his left wrist reminded him that neither could he, not one-handed.

Shit. What was he going to do, stand here all night and take each one as it reached the top of the stairs? And then what? Morning would be no different. And what would happen the one time he missed, or when his arm grew too tired to swing?

Evan saw another black figure climbing toward the switchback below, followed closely by a second. Their moans came out as a dry wheeze, and more scrapes and thumping could be heard from somewhere downstairs.

What would Vladimir do?

He'd tell you you're fucked, Evanovich.

Taking a deep breath, Evan readied himself to meet the next creature.

January 12—San Francisco Bay

South of Richmond, USS *Nimitz* was drifting steadily into the centermost point of the East Bay, still on an oblique with its port side facing northeast. The Bay Bridge was a dark silhouette behind it.

Stone handed a heavy belt of fifty-caliber ammunition to Chief Liebs, and the older man finished loading the left side of the twin-barreled heavy machine gun he and his younger partner had fitted into the gun mount on the port catwalk beneath the flight deck. They repeated the process for the right side of the weapon. The fifty's position was approximately a third of the way up this side of the ship from the stern. They couldn't mount any weapons farther back; when *Nimitz* rubbed the Bay Bridge's massive concrete supports last summer, the collision had torn away not only a Phalanx gun system and a battery of surface-to-air missiles, but that stretch of catwalk as well. The walkway ended at a twist of steel and a ninety-foot drop not far from where the two men were working.

"That one's ready," said the chief, slapping the large weapon. "The next position is amidships, under the port side catapults." He pointed forward.

Stone nodded, then in a flat tone said, "Be careful," pointing above and behind the chief. A broken corpse, its ribs jutting out of a narrow chest, was tangled in the flight deck's safety netting over their heads, a system designed to prevent crewmen from being blown overboard by jet blast. The thing reached a twisted arm down through the netting, kicking with legs bent at odd angles, and gnashed its teeth. Dark liquid drooled from its mouth and fell to the catwalk.

Chief Liebs shot it in the head with his M4, and the creature stopped moving. It continued to drip.

"How many of those dropped on us when we went under the bridge, do you think?" said Stone.

"No idea," growled the chief. "Too many. Hopefully they're too fucked up from the fall to be able to get around much. But then, *hope* is not a strategy."

"I've heard that before. Who said that?"

The chief led them forward along the catwalk, careful to avoid the dripping fluid. "I'm not sure. Probably a Republican. The officers used to wear that phrase out on us."

"Makes sense."

"Yes it does," said the older man.

Liebs used the Hydra to call Xavier, wanting to inform him that the first fifty-cal was loaded and in position, and to report they had seen nothing of the mystery ship that fired on them. There was no answer on the radio. Liebs thought that maybe the priest and Calvin would be waiting for them at the next gun position, as discussed.

Liebs was walking toward a short stairwell that led from the flight deck down to the catwalk when a corpse staggered down the stairs and crashed into the railing. It wore the remains of a business suit, and its neck was broken so that its head hung to the side. The rest of it was intact, and it lurched toward them with a growl.

Liebs fired, dropping the dead businessman just as two others, a black woman and a teenage boy, both withered and drawn, stomped down the stairway behind it. Stone's M4 came up and he dispatched those two. A rotting soldier in camouflage followed, its left arm and side crushed from the impact with the deck, creamy eyes glaring at them. Liebs took it out.

When no more appeared, the two men approached the stairs slowly and checked them. Empty. They hurried past.

"They're even nastier when they're broken like that," said Stone.

"As bad as your greenies?" Liebs was referring to the nickname Stone had coined for the color and condition of the ones that were especially bloated and juicy, like balloons filled with spinach dip. The boy had also come up with the term *wet ones* for the seawater-bloated corpses in the bow.

"No, nothing's as bad as those."

The chief smiled. "Keep an eye on our six, shipmate." He led them down the catwalk to the next fifty-caliber position.

THIRTY

Calvin had been hunting for hours, entering and clearing compartments, sweeping back and forth across second deck. There was no sign of his prey, and she'd had numerous opportunities to climb to an upper deck or drop to a lower one, but he sensed she was still here. There were so many places to hide.

Now he heard boots running on steel up ahead, and as Calvin came to an intersection he didn't hesitate, coming around the corner with the rifle up, trigger finger tensed. The corridor was empty, and the sounds of running had stopped. The hippie padded back the way he'd come, passing wardrooms and briefing compartments, storage lockers and heads for both men and women. In minutes he was back at Broadway and moving forward, his rifle muzzle trained on the corridor ahead.

Distant gunfire had sounded in this direction quite a while ago, brief and violent, followed by silence. Calvin was tracking the noise when the sound of running drew him away. Now he was back on target.

The stocky woman wearing a flannel shirt, who had shot at them and put a buckshot pellet in Calvin's thigh, suddenly darted across the passage up ahead. Calvin triggered a three-round burst that sparked off steel and ruptured a vertical pipe. The hiss of steam filled the intersection ahead, and the hallway was quickly obscured by mist.

Calvin crouched and duckwalked forward. The moment he did, a shotgun fired from inside the steam, pellets whining over his head. He put two bursts into the mist, walking the bullets from floor to ceiling where he thought the corner was. If she was there, this would finish her.

There was no cry, no sound of a body hitting the deck, and the shotgun didn't fire again. When Calvin reached the intersection he found an empty, red twelve-gauge hull on the deck, warm to the touch. The sound of running boots came again, from the right this time. The woman had crossed back the way she'd come, concealed in the steam.

That, or there was someone else down here with him.

The hippie moved right, into the starboard side of the ship. A grunt and a rattle came from an open hatch up ahead, and Calvin followed his rifle inside, sweeping it left and right. It was a compartment filled with helmets and boots, racks of vests and shelves of flight deck gear. At the far end was an open hatch, and a cluster of float coats was swinging from hangers where someone had stumbled into them. He moved into the next compartment, a ready room of some kind with rows of benches facing a lectern and projection screen. Hatches stood open to the left and right, and he caught a blur of movement on his left.

Calvin dove to the floor just as a shotgun blast blew apart a wooden bench beside him. He crawled backward, and a second blast destroyed the bench he'd been hiding behind a second ago. Calvin kept crawling until his sock feet connected with a bulkhead. There was nowhere left to go.

The clicking of shotgun shells being fed up a tube came from the left, and Calvin rose to his knees, swinging the assault rifle in that direction, his thumb coming up in the same instant to move the selector switch from semi to auto. Ten rounds ripped from the muzzle in an instant of white flashes, sparking off steel, blowing out a light, and tearing apart conduit. There was a scream, followed by more running boot steps.

Calvin leaped over the splintered benches and reached the hatch, finding that it led to a short corridor with a sudden turn. There was a splash of red on the wall, and a blood trail on the deck. He changed magazines while still behind cover before following.

Numerous turns and a multitude of hatches in these tight spaces might have easily thrown off a pursuer, but the blood trail and her boots thumping as she ran gave the woman away. The blood soaked into the hippie's socks as he followed, and he noticed how dark it was. *Hit in the liver. Won't get far.* The man slowed and checked before passing an opening or turning a corner, following the growing pools of blood.

The trail took him past a scattering of shell casings and a pair of bodies lying in the passageway, both torn up by automatic rifle fire, each with a safety shot to the forehead. They were bearded, dirty, and not part of the *Nimitz* family. Calvin moved past, following the trail.

On the other side of the hatch where the bodies lay, Sophia never heard the man go by.

Calvin came upon a shotgun lying on the deck, the grip and stock slick with blood. Staggering, bloody boot prints led away from it down a right-hand corridor. A red palm print on the steel showed him where the woman had kept herself from falling.

Soon, now. He kept going.

Chief Liebs's watch said it was approaching midnight, and neither Xavier nor Calvin had appeared. He and Stone completed the mounting and loading of the twin fifties both amidships and at the bow, this last one done on a catwalk tilting toward the water at an uncomfortable angle with the ship's list. Liebs noticed it was more pronounced than earlier.

"I think I see it," Stone said, pointing. He was looking into the darkness to the west, the carrier still drifting north on the oblique.

Chief Liebs stood beside him, peering into the night. The two of them were back at the gun mount amidships, still thinking the priest and hippie might show up. "I don't see anything."

"Right there," the younger man said. "See the wake?"

The chief stared, then thought he saw a strip of white against the black background. As his eyes adjusted, he could make out a black shape ahead of the wake, the sleek silhouette of a warship several miles out.

"Damn, your eyes are good."

"It's out of range, isn't it?" asked Stone, resting a hand on the twin heavy machine guns.

"It might as well be. Remember what I taught you about these?" The chief indicated the heavy weapon. "Effective range is just over a mile. It *can* hit targets out to four miles, but that's just praying and spraying, and you have to be willing to expend a serious amount of ammo while you try to work out the range. That gives your opponent plenty of time to zero in on your muzzle flashes and use his own weapons to put you to sleep forever." He shook his head. "Our aggressor is well beyond effective range, and that's not by accident. If he *does* have a deck gun aboard, and he must since PK said he put a round across our bow, you can bet we're within *his* effective range. He doesn't have to get closer than he is right now to chop us up."

Stone looked at the Navy man. "Could something this big *get* chopped up? This thing's a monster."

Liebs stared out at the wake in the distance. The vessel appeared to be circling, moving around to their stern now. "It's a ship, and it needs to float. You put enough shells into her waterline and she'll go to the bottom. Water comes in through the holes and"—he snapped his fingers—"the sea does the rest. Shell hits also cause fires, and that will sink a ship just as quickly."

"Why would they want to do that?" Stone asked. "Aren't they going to try to take us?"

"Probably." Liebs watched the black ship slip from sight behind the carrier. Thinking about what he'd told the boy about range made him wonder if they should even bother to mount the fifties on the starboard side, whether it would even matter. Then something Stone said made him pause, thinking . . .

"We need to move," the gunner's mate said.

A bullet sparked off the bulkhead next to Stone's face, making him cry out and drop. Liebs went down too, crouched and looking both ways down the catwalk. More bullets buzzed past, cutting the air like lethal, flying insects or ricocheting off steel. He saw the muzzle flashes, about a hundred feet down the catwalk toward the stern by the ruined section.

Before either man could bring up his rifle, one of those muzzle flashes went full auto, turning into a stuttering white spark. Liebs and Stone went flat and hugged the gridwork of metal as snaps and hisses cut the air around them and more bullets caused sparks and dings as they found the catwalk railing and the flight deck overhang above. It was wild, unaimed fire, but there was a lot of it.

Liebs felt something punch through the top of his right boot. "I'm hit," he grunted. Another round plowed a red gash down his arm, and a third creased his scalp. Stone let out a hiss as a bullet punched in and out of the meat in his upper arm, narrowly missing the bone.

The gunner's mate pushed his rifle ahead of him, but before he could fire, a bullet smashed into the muzzle, bending the steel opening. A fragment of lead tore a chunk out of his left eyebrow.

"Fuck this," Stone snarled, leaping to his feet and charging, M4 to his shoulder and squeezing off three-round bursts as he ran. The staccato of full automatic stopped and was replaced by pistol fire. A hot buzz kissed the boy's ear, and then four slugs hit him center mass, dropping him to his knees. Fighting for breath, Stone put his green combat sights on the shapes behind the muzzle flash and squeezed, squeezed, squeezed until the firing pin clicked on an empty magazine. He let the rifle drop against his chest on its strap as he struggled to stand, jerking his nine-millimeter pistol from its holster and stumbling toward the now-motionless shapes.

The firefight had ruined his night vision, but moonlight was now beginning to poke through breaks in the cloud cover as the storm front dissipated, and the boy crouched over the bodies. Two men and a woman lay on the deck in a pile, all of them refugees he'd seen coming in on the boat earlier today. They were torn up, and for a moment he thought that under the moon, the blood looked like motor oil.

The injured woman snarled and sat up, slashing at his face with a straight razor. Stone jerked away, the blade missing by millimeters, and sprang to his feet. Without a conscious decision he lashed out with his right boot, kicking sideways, catching her under the chin. There was a sharp CRACK and her head lolled bonelessly to the side, her eyes open.

Stone used his Beretta and put a round in each of their heads.

"You okay?" Liebs asked. He'd come up behind the young man, and waited until Stone finished his work.

The younger man ran a hand over his body armor, finding the pistol slugs. "That hurt like a bastard."

"Well what did you expect, John Wayne? Did you think you were storming Normandy?" The chief shook his head. "You're going to bruise up nicely. Anything else?"

"A round went through my arm, but it still works." He looked at the other man's boot, and the red line across his scalp. "How about you?"

"I've been better," said Liebs, "and I'm limping, so I'll be slow. Can you keep moving?"

Stone snorted. "I'm good to go, Chief. Where to?"

The chief dropped his damaged M4 and replaced it with the identical rifle lying beside the dead woman, then kicked the rest of the pirate weapons over the side. It was too dangerous to leave them where others boarders might find them. He led them back to the short stairway leading to the flight deck, and both stopped to reload before going up.

"Remember," the gunner's mate said, "there's going to be dead things up there left over from the Bay Bridge. Just drop them when you see them; don't worry about making noise. The sneaky part of this mission is over."

"Where are we going?"

"The stern," said Liebs. "You said it, they want to take us, and you don't do that with a deck gun." He started up. "They're going to launch another boarding party, and they'll head for the swimmer's platform."

When they reached topside, the two men stopped and stared. A hundred corpses were standing on the flight deck, but none of them were moving. All were facing southeast with their heads tilted.

Xavier was stretched out flat on the rubberized deck, his body pointed straight back and away from the Seahawk's right tire, trying to keep himself as narrow as his cover. The tire was shredded from gunfire, but the rim and the landing gear strut—though bullet scarred—had kept him safe for the hours he'd been hiding here, pinned down and unable to move in either direction. Ten feet behind him was a sheer bulkhead with no exits, and nothing to hide behind. To his left was fifty feet of open space he'd never be able to make it across before he'd reach the cover of a forklift, and to his right was a twenty-foot gap between this and another parked helicopter. He didn't know if there were any exit hatches in that direction, either.

Every time he tried to move, rifles cracked, bullets tearing up the decking around him, banging into the tire rim or hitting the helicopter above. They knew where he was but didn't dare advance; there was too much open ground between the crate behind which they were hiding and Xavier's position. They also knew he wasn't afraid to shoot back. Empty twelve-gauge hulls littered the deck around him. He didn't know if he'd hit anyone.

He couldn't move, they couldn't move. A stalemate. But Xavier didn't have time to wait them out. Every hour that slid by meant the other boarders were moving deeper through the ship, causing more destruction, taking more lives. He had to do something.

They're counting on that, aren't they? Waiting for you to do something stupid. He forced himself to remain still, peeking around the edge of what remained of the tire, concealed in the shadows under the helicopter's belly. The hangar bay was well lit, and he had a good view of the splintered crate that was their hiding place. Every now and then a face would poke out from one side or the other, then duck back out of sight, nothing at which he could shoot. Xavier was certain one of those faces belonged to the man who'd introduced himself as Charlie.

This had gone on far longer than Charlie expected; hours, in fact. The son of a bitch was patient. During that time, the hippie he'd killed earlier turned and rose, but instead of wandering off to make trouble for other people, it had come straight for Charlie. He'd had to finish it with a head shot.

Now he checked his watch. *Almost showtime.* Charlie looked at the auxiliary deputy. "Kid, listen up. I want you to make a run at him."

The young man's eyes widened.

Chick gave him an encouraging smile. "Don't be scared. I'm going to lay down so much cover fire he won't dare lift his head. You swing wide, haul ass for that forklift. Then we'll have him flanked, and we'll finish it."

The deputy looked at the distance, the wide open space, then back at Charlie.

Charlie game him a charming grin. "Trust me."

A moment later, Chick popped up and started squeezing off bursts at the tire where the priest was hiding, the heavy bullets tearing apart rubber and decking and blowing metal panels off the side of the chopper's cockpit. The deputy bolted from behind the crates and started running.

Xavier cut him down with a shotgun blast that opened the boy's chest.

"Dammit," Charlie growled, firing his magazine dry, then dropping back down and quickly inserting another one. *Patient son of a bitch.*

THIRTY-ONE

The red numbers of a digital clock mounted above the cutter's bridge windows read 23:55:03. Elizabeth keyed the mic on her handheld radio. "Boarding Two, this is Command."

"Go, Command," Lt. Riggs answered.

"Five minutes to launch." Liz received a double click as acknowledgment. Right now Riggs would have his team fully loaded aboard the motorized lifeboat, still tethered to the stern and waiting to cast off. On her command, Liz's second boarding party would begin their run at the carrier. The prize had now drifted vaguely northwest, with land positioned an almost equal distance around it in every direction.

When they departed, Liz would be left with Mr. Waite and a helmsman, Mr. Vargas in the combat center, Castellano the rescue swimmer, two men in the engine room, and the civilian contractors. Everyone else would be en route with the assault group. It was an all-or-nothing gamble as she couldn't possibly operate the cutter for any length of time with only eleven people, but she was confident they would prevail.

Liz would have preferred if the cloud cover held instead of breaking up. An assault in darkness was better, but now the moonlight was illuminating the bay, the carrier, and her cutter, and would reveal her assault craft. No matter, she thought, lifting binoculars. They were past the point of no return, and the odds were heavily in her favor. A little over three miles away, the lopsided shape of *Nimitz* drifted across choppy waters. It looked like a weary, wounded elephant. She and her crew were the lions that would bring it down.

Liz had briefly considered striking the American flag flying on the radar mast high above and replacing it with the skull and crossbones Charlie had found on the booze cruise ship in Brookings. She'd rejected the idea as a bit over the top, but that didn't change who she was. Watching her prize in the distance, Liz decided that of the two versions of William Kidd's life—the unlucky man of honor trying to clear his name while others betrayed him, and the ruthless, clever buccaneer who'd buried fortunes still hunted for in modern times—she preferred the latter. It was stronger, more fitting of the Kidd name. *Her* name.

"Prepare to be boarded," she whispered. Liz turned to her quartermaster. "Mr. Waite, report."

The man didn't look up from his scope. "Our heading is one-four-five at seven knots. Target's position is at three-one-five on a five-knot current, three and a quarter miles to port. Surface winds at eleven knots, south-southeast."

"Very well." She picked up the handset beside the helmsman. "Mr. Vargas, how does our air look?"

"The system comes and goes," he said, "but the skies look clear, Captain."

Good, she thought. The missing Black Hawk was a concern, and she certainly didn't need it showing up and complicating her attack. "Air defense status?"

"System is in the green," Vargas reported.

Liz nodded. The close-in weapon system would ruin that Black Hawk's day if it showed up, just as it had with the Navy bird up in Richmond. The digital bridge clock ticked over to midnight, and the captain keyed her handheld radio.

"Boarding Two, Command. Launch. Launch."

Lt. Riggs acknowledged, and Liz looked out the windows until she saw the motorized lifeboat pulling away from the cutter, leaving a wake of white chop behind it. "Mr. Vargas," she said, calling the combat center. "Stand by to provide cover for the boarding party." Then to her quartermaster she said, "Mr. Waite, bring us bow-on to target."

As the cutter wheeled to port, turning until it faced the aircraft carrier, the remote-operated fifty-seven-millimeter Bofors deck gun whined into position. The barrel stopped moving once it was centered on the wounded flattop.

"Steady now," Liz said, standing beside the young helmsman. She wasn't sure if the words were intended for him or herself. As she watched the MLB race toward the prize, Elizabeth wondered about her brother and whether he was still alive. She pushed the thought roughly aside. *No time for that.* Right now there was only the deadly business of surface warfare.

Lt. Riggs stood beside the helmsman who was running the launch fast at the sheer wall that was the carrier's stern. Every deck surface around him, as well as the MLB's belowdecks, was packed beyond capacity with bodies and equipment. Everyone had a rifle and a sidearm; each was laden with bags and bandoliers of magazines. All of them carried either coils of rope with hooks fashioned in the cutter's machine shop, pry bars, or acetylene torches for locked hatches.

They were terribly overloaded, almost thirty people aboard,

traveling on a choppy night sea at high speed. Completely unsafe. It was a short ride, Riggs told himself, and besides, this was combat. The normal rules didn't apply. His heart was pumping fast at the prospect of battle, not with fear but with exhilaration. *He and his crew were going to storm an aircraft carrier! How many men in history could claim to have done that?*

Only minutes to go now.

As the mass of USS *Nimitz* loomed before them, Lt. Riggs stood a little taller and started to grin.

THIRTY-TWO

It was a long-feared nightmare and the subject of scientific speculation and Hollywood fantasy: a 10.0-plus magnitude earthquake along one of California's many fault lines. A killer of epic proportions. Many wondered, but few could imagine the destructive power contained within a megaquake of this size.

In the seismology world, the notion was derided almost completely. Experts thought the energy release would be the equivalent of detonating one trillion tons of TNT, and the earth simply couldn't produce that type of energy. While a few claimed that it was not only possible but inevitable, others stated with confidence that there were no known fault lines long enough to even be capable of producing a 10.0 magnitude event.

The Pacific and North American plates, grinding together deep beneath the earth's crust, cared nothing for scientific speculation about what they could and could not do. They were, and had been for some time, hung up on one another under the Hayward Fault, able to expel small bits of energy, but unable to truly "clear their throat."

The fault was longer than it appeared as it connected to a network of lesser faults in the Hayward group and merged with the Calaveras Fault in the south. These connections multiplied its destructive potential well beyond any existing predictive model. With the exception of the small tremors last fall and the foreshock only hours ago, the Hayward Fault had gone through a long "quiet period" of inactivity. This was especially ominous to seismologists, who had—correctly—interpreted this as a time of steadily building pressure.

They were right about the pressure.

They were wrong about how bad it would be.

The San Francisco earthquake of 1989, the Loma Prieta earthquake, originated sixty miles south-southeast of the city. It lasted from eight to fifteen seconds and registered a maximum intensity of 7.1. It was a truly terrifying and destructive monster.

By comparison, the Alameda earthquake that struck on January 13 at five minutes past midnight was a 10.6 magnitude event that lasted four full minutes. Its epicenter was beneath the former naval air station at Alameda, right in the middle of the Bay Area.

The trigger was much like a finger snap and when enough stress was applied, there was a sudden movement, a release of energy, and a *snap*. As the stress finally built to intolerable levels under Alameda, the Pacific and North American plates experienced their own finger snap, letting off a burst of energy the planet hadn't experienced in millions of years.

Seismic waves traveled outward from the point of origin in expanding, concentric rings, creating S-waves that caused repeating, oscillating ripples in the earth similar to snapping a bedsheet over and over. In this case, the bedsheet would be made of glass, rigid and fragile—like the thin surface of the earth. What came next was the stuff of bad dreams.

. . .

S everal places around the Bay Area were built upon soft mud fill
and silt beds, including the island of Alameda, the industrial and
petrochemical areas of Richmond, and Treasure Island, a former
Navy base turned trendy community and the location of the Bay
Bridge's central support. The intensity and duration of the shaking
liquefied the mud and silt beds within a minute. Much of waterfront
Richmond and all of Alameda immediately sank, the bay rushing in
at once to cover structures and communities. Ten thousand of the
walking dead on Alameda were consumed in a broiling cauldron of
mud, seawater, and masonry.

Treasure Island sank as well, dropping the Bay Bridge's central
support. The span was already bucking and hurling sections of
roadway into the bay, and now the plunging central support pulled
both the east and west stretches down with it amid an endless
screech of twisting steel. Abandoned automobiles and thousands of
walking corpses tumbled into the churning water with it. After the
initial fall, all that remained was the land-side approaches at the San
Francisco and Oakland ends, frayed ends of metal and asphalt poking out over the water.

They wouldn't be there for long.

As the earth's surface rippled and jumped, the massive cables of
the Golden Gate Bridge snapped and the framework went next,
twisting and falling away, deforming the towering red supports at
each end. The southern tower crashed into the Pacific. At the north,
only the Sausalito support would survive, with its approach roadway leading to it and then abruptly dropping away to nothing.

U nder the bay, the oscillation of S-waves caused the buried BART
tubes to burst through the earth, wriggling like wet pasta. In
moments they fractured, flooded, and disintegrated. Corpses that

once stalked these dark tubes, shambling past stranded trains that last summer echoed with the screams of trapped commuters, now whirled through the deep waters of the bay by the thousands. Had anyone been able to see them, they would have looked like vast clouds of underwater gnats.

In every community, any masonry structure not built of steel-reinforced concrete was instantly destroyed; homes, apartment complexes, warehouses, and historical landmarks were reduced to rubble in seconds, dust rising into the night in vast clouds. Buildings designed to resist earthquakes had never been intended to survive violence of this magnitude and followed soon after. Skyscrapers leaned and toppled, or dropped straight down into billowing clouds.

The city of Oakland, so close to the epicenter at Alameda, was shaken flat, leaving only skeletons of soot-covered I-beams among the rubble. Even that would soon be gone.

Even as the city above toppled, the bedrock that made up San Francisco's peninsula rolled and vibrated until it shattered like a china plate. From Daly City north, the peninsula gave a great heave upward, then crashed back down below sea level in fragments.

The Pacific reacted at once to fill the void, rolling in as a frothing beast, the city's remains beneath its surging waves. Only the Transamerica Pyramid survived, a white spear jutting a mere fifty feet above the ocean's surface, waves crashing against its sides. It lingered through several more S-waves, then sank.

Not far away, the buildings of Alcatraz were shaken into gravel. Like San Francisco, the bedrock here shattered as well, and the island vanished.

. . .

A ct Two began ninety seconds into the quake.

A t not quite seven minutes past midnight, the earth started crack-ing, a fast-moving and violent event, creating a fissure running the entire length of the Hayward Fault. In thirty seconds, every city in the fissure's path shattered, from Richmond down to San Jose.

The planet seemed to growl as, with a terrestrial thunder, the fis-sure became a crevasse, the earth's crust yawning open along the fault's length. The waters of the San Francisco Bay poured into this opening, the charging Pacific following.

USNS *Comfort*, the former supertanker turned hospital ship, and the vessel that had lured Calvin's Family and Evan to the Bay Area, was no longer tethered to a pier. Oakland Middle Harbor was beneath the waves now. The long white ship, still teeming with hun-dreds of the undead, executed three-quarters of a rotation before tipping over the edge of the crevasse and disappearing.

On the bay, where swells were now climbing to thirty feet and more, the Pacific was being sucked east into the crevasse, moving fast and with unthinkable force. A black Coast Guard cutter went to flank speed and took the waves with its razored bow, pointing west and fighting to keep from being pulled back into a void that was swallowing sea and land alike. A listing aircraft carrier, without propulsion or a way to steer itself, helplessly rode the wild sea as it was drawn inexorably toward the plunge.

A forty-seven-foot motorized lifeboat, loaded beyond safe capac-ity, was caught by a thirty-five-foot-high wall of water and flung end over end through the night. Bodies spun away into the sea, and those belowdecks were battered against steel bulkheads. Most of the boarding party trapped below were already dead when the tiny craft was sucked over the falls and plunged into the abyss.

Nimitz turned broadside to the angry Pacific and was instantly punished for it, the surging water tipping it on a forty-five-degree angle and pushing it closer to the edge of the crevasse. By now, the eastern side of the San Francisco Bay had taken on the look of the white waters approaching the drop-off at Niagara Falls, except this waterfall was more than fifty miles long. The aircraft carrier righted itself for a moment as the sea surged beneath its keel. The next wave would push it into oblivion.

The nightmare's third act occurred at three minutes and thirty seconds into the event. In a terrifying demonstration of the planet's power and brutality, the earth's crust west of the crevasse heaved upward for an instant, then crashed back down, sinking an additional fifty feet lower than the previous sea bottom, creating a vast, momentary water pocket. Simultaneously, the land east of the crevasse was thrust up in a hundred-foot-high, gray-black wall of rock running the length of the fault.

This geological drop and thrust pinched the new crevasse shut, and the sudden offset in the ocean floor created a massive displacement in the water. The roaring Pacific filling the water pocket now hurled itself against this new cliff face and was thrown back toward the open sea in waves climbing as high as fifty feet.

A sleek black warship attempted to come about as the deadly tide reversed itself and was lost behind a towering wave.

A wounded aircraft carrier, listing dangerously forward and to port, spun in the churning sea, white water crashing across its flight deck and sweeping away the few drifters remaining there. The vessel climbed a wave that came at its stern, hovered at the crest for a moment like an enormous teeter-totter board, then slid down the steep back side and out of sight.

The megaquake subsided at nine minutes past midnight. In its wake it left a landscape so raw and broken that it could have been a scene from the planet's violent birth.

The cauldron of the new bay surged with the debris of mankind: fragments of buildings, railroad boxcars, bits of aircraft and cap-sized ships, tractor-trailers and roofs of houses. And with every surge of the Pacific current, thousands of bodies were forced to the surface.

They reached.

They groaned.

And they were pulled beneath the waves once more.

THIRTY-THREE

January 13—Richmond

On the uppermost stairway landing of the concrete house, Evan was getting tired, just as he'd predicted. The charred fragments of twenty corpses littered the steps below him, victims of his survival knife, and more climbed slowly toward him, crunching their fellows underfoot as raspy groans filled the house. Evan had long since switched on his flashlight and stood it upright on the concrete banister so he could see what he was fighting. Stealth no longer mattered; they knew he was here.

His good arm ached from swinging and stabbing, and his broken wrist cried out from all the exertion. Some broke apart as he kicked them down the steps; others merely tumbled down to the switchback. More took their place. Evan lost track of time.

Then came a moment when the moaning abruptly ceased. The half-dozen burned drifters on the stairs stopped climbing and instead shuffled until they all faced in the same direction, then cocked their heads and stood silently. Evan had seen this behavior before, during his run through the charred petrochemical fields. He couldn't tell how bad the quake would be so he stood his ground, chest heaving, blade still held ready. Several seconds later the shaking started, pitching his flashlight over the side of the banister. The house bucked beneath his feet, and he was thrown to the floor. There was a sound of concrete cracking, and he scrambled back down the hall just as the central stairs and the landing where he had just been standing collapsed into the house.

Worse. Much, much worse.

Back in the bedroom, Evan could see out beyond the balcony, scattered moonlight beginning to reveal the rooftops of the houses below. They seemed to ripple for an instant, then detonated in an explosion of brick, glass, and wood fragments. Within seconds, the residential blocks nearest the water dropped into the sea, and the bay surged forward, consuming the neighborhood.

Evan moved out onto the shaking balcony, thinking he would climb onto the iron railing and somehow pull himself up to the roof. Then the house came apart around him and he was falling, tensing for impact, expecting to be impaled on a twisted piece of rebar. Instead, the sea charged in and he was caught by the water, swept up and over the spot where the concrete house had been only seconds ago, thrown hard against the hillside behind it just as this ground too shook apart and fell beneath the foamy surface.

Like the float coats used by *Nimitz* deck crews, Evan's survival vest featured a water-activated pellet that triggered an internal gas canister and inflated the vest with a sudden *whoosh*. A second pellet automatically activated the small white strobe at the vest's collar, and Evan found himself floating in savage waves.

His body felt as if it were flung in every direction as the water rose and fell, his left arm slipping free of its sling, and the air was filled with a cracking sound so loud and so close that he thought it would make his heart stop. Evan washed up sharply against something hard and metallic, and he instinctively wrapped an arm and his legs around it, realizing it was the base of a shuddering radio tower. In the moonlight he could see the earth yawn open to his left with a massive rumble, a black maw stretching in two directions and widening by the second. Seawater and shattered houses roared over its far edge in a waterfall.

From somewhere beyond the crevasse came the long, metallic scream of the Richmond–San Rafael Bridge coming apart, but there was little time to think about it. The radio tower was leaping and shuddering, trying to pull loose from the deep anchors holding it to the earth, threatening to shake him off and back into the swirling waters. Evan locked both elbows around the metal strut and tightened the hold with his legs. The tide that pushed him here had now poured back into the still-widening crevasse, and he found that he and the radio tower's base were less than twenty feet from the chasm's crumbling western edge.

The tower gave out a long groan and leaned toward the abyss. Evan screamed and hung on.

There was an abrupt vacuum then, an instant where sound and air vanished as the expanse of the bay beyond the crevasse suddenly *dropped*, and he thought of the surface of a not-quite-baked cake falling. The silence was broken as the roaring sea rushed into the sudden depression with a fury Evan knew he could not look upon and keep his sanity.

At that moment, the ground let out a roar of its own and heaved upward. A towering wall of rock shot skyward, spitting truck-sized boulders into the sea as if they were pebbles, rock slabs the size of buildings calving away like Arctic ice. The radio tower fell to the left, smashing onto the edge of the crevasse, its top snapping away and vanishing into the depths just before the rising angle of the newly risen cliff pinched the crevasse shut. Clinging to the tower's remains with his arms and legs, looking like a sloth hanging upside down, Evan saw that the base was lodged in a vertical crack that split the face of the wall, trapped there, prevented from slipping into a sea that was now surging against what had become an ocean cliff.

The sea.

Evan's radio tower, now a forty-foot, horizontal tangle of red-and-white steel, was hit by a wave that completely submerged him, the force nearly tearing him free. He held his breath, and when the water fell back he came up choking. The choppy surface was only a few feet beneath him when the wave went out, but he was submerged again when the next surge pushed against the cliff.

The shaking and monstrous rumble of tortured stone continued, frightening on a level that pierced Evan through some primitive core, and he screamed back at it. The quake was still trying to shake him loose, and his arms and legs were ready to give out. When the next wave washed over him, he swallowed seawater.

The water dipped back, and Evan vomited, coughing and gasping. *Can't stay like this.* Ignoring the pain in his fractured wrist, he forced himself to crawl up the side of the shaking tower. It took two cycles of waves to complete the move, and each time he held a deep breath and squeezed his eyes tightly shut, hanging on. At last he was on the top of the tower—at least it was the side facing up—and although the waves still crashed against him, they didn't cover him, only washed around his body. He was able to breathe. The survival vest, now inflated and even bulkier, threatened to pull him off with the water when the waves struck, however. He still had to hang on to the steel to keep it from floating him off his perch. Evan reached for the snaps to cut it loose, when Vladimir's voice barked at him.

"You will never *take it off."*

Right, not until my boots are back on the deck of the carrier. If it's not already at the bottom of the bay. That thought brought an image of Maya holding her belly with both hands, and Evan wanted to scream. Instead he forced himself to crawl down the radio tower to where its base was jammed into a split in the rock. Surf still rising and falling around him, the earth still vibrating the tower and dropping bits of stone from the cliff above, Evan carefully reversed until his back was to the rock, planting his boots against a steel strut and gripping another with his good hand.

A wave rose against him, then retreated. He had a solid hold.

Evan felt the shaking stop, and at once the tortured sounds of cracking rock quieted. The sea remained, crashing against the high cliff that stood roughly where downtown Richmond had been, but at least for now, the earthquake was over.

Unbroken water stretched before him in the moonlight. He saw no land masses, nothing protruding from the surface, and only unrecognizable debris riding the high swells. By his last calculations, he should've been able to look west to see the hilly fingers of land where both Tiburon and San Quentin poked into the bay, but there was nothing. If anything remained of the rest of Marin County, it was either hidden behind the darkness or beneath the Pacific.

Before him now was an alien sea, and he was afraid of it. Looking around revealed only cliff face to his left and right, more cliff face above, none of it climbable. Even if it was, and he managed to pull himself a hundred feet up its sheer face and over the top—using only one hand—what new devastation would be waiting?

His personal locator beacon, the yellow cell-phone-sized device he'd activated and stuck in a pocket, was gone. So was the Sig Sauer handgun, jarred from its holster by one impact or another. And now he realized he'd dropped his survival knife when the concrete house came apart and the water took him. The two cylindrical flare grenades were still clipped to his vest, but they'd spent a lot of time in the water, and Evan wondered if they would even work.

Let's find out. The flashing strobe on his vest gave off some light, but it was also killing his night vision to the point that in between the flashes he was completely blind. He clenched the flare between his knees and pulled the pin, letting the spoon fly. There was a pink sputter, then nothing.

Shit.

Another pink spark, a stutter, and then the top of the cylinder erupted with a fluorescent pink light too bright to look at. It heated up fast, he discovered, so he plucked it from between his knees and wedged it into a crack in the rock wall.

No one will see it. No one is left *to see it. It's there to make me feel better.* For a moment, it did. Then he looked down the forty feet of mangled radio tower stretching out just above the surf. In the shimmering pink of the flare he saw that a wave had washed something else up onto his perch.

It was dead.

And it was crawling toward him.

THIRTY-FOUR

Nimitz

The wave threw Rosa off the top rack and into the frigid water. Tilting like a funhouse room, the small berthing compartment slammed her against a fold-down desk and she went under. Her injured foot banged against something and she let out a scream that came out as a burst of bubbles. Then the room tilted in the other direction as the carrier was swept up by another wave.

Rosa reached frantically, caught hold of a pipe, and pulled herself out of the water, gasping and bracing against the roll of the ship. Her warm, dry clothes were now soaked, and the medic shivered in the darkness, fighting to clear her head. *Was the ship going down? No, but it was caught in phenomenal waves, enough to toss around a carrier. How was that possible in the San Francisco Bay?*

The medical backpack washed against her legs as the room leaned and the water—at her knees—sloshed to the other side of the room. She grabbed the pack and pulled it on. It was heavy, the contents saturated.

Flashlight. She pawed at the water, found the sneaker torn apart by the bullet, and threw it aside. Below the surface, her bandage was soggy and unraveling. *It's a Maglite, it won't float.* She waited a moment until the room tipped left, then took a breath and went under, hands probing into the only place it could go: under the lower rack. Her fingers quickly closed on the flashlight's long metal barrel, and she popped out of the water, shaking her head as the compartment tipped to the right.

Please work, please work. . . .

A cool white beam lit the compartment and Rosa sighed in relief. Bedding and personal items floated on the surface around her as she timed the tipping, took another breath and submerged. This time she came up with her Glock.

Rosa didn't know how long she'd slept, couldn't guess what was happening to the ship. Michael was still out there, though, so her mission was unchanged. He would be terrified, maybe even crying out. That might help her find him, but it would help other things too. She tried not to think about that.

Gripping the Maglite and pistol, Rosa threw the privacy bolt and hauled the hatch open, letting in a surge of water. It was thigh-deep now, and so very cold. She went out, keeping a wide stance and anticipating the severe roll now, staying on her feet. The passageway was clear of the dead for the moment, her light revealing a flooding, sloshing corridor stretching far to the right and left. *Which way?*

Then she *did* hear a scream.

It wasn't human.

It couldn't remember being Michael, had no concept of a mother who'd loved him, a father who fretted about his childhood diabetes, of a life before or after the plague. That was gone. Dead. No longer Michael. So much more, now.

The newly born Hobgoblin stood in the darkness of the gear handling compartment, legs in a wide stance as the floor tilted back and forth. It needed no light, for its eyes viewed the world in variant shades of red, gray, and black, even in absolute blackness. The creature looked at its hands, its body, and the smooth crimson flesh pulled taut over new muscle. It still tingled all over, and the electrical activity firing in its brain—sensed as flickers of red light behind its eyes—had subsided but not entirely dissipated.

It felt no pain, no cold. There was hunger, a burning sensation that must be sated, but there was another, even more powerful drive. The Hobgoblin wanted to kill, to rend flesh with its hands and teeth, to cause pain . . . and fear. It wanted to hear screams, and these combined desires were so powerful that the creature trembled.

Across the room, a dead woman struggled to stand near an equipment locker, the motion of the room repeatedly throwing her back into the water before she climbed once more to her feet. The Hobgoblin instinctively knew it was neither threat nor of any consequence, it just *was*. Something to be quickly dismissed.

More sensations came at the creature, images of violence and new perceptions. Without the words or need to describe them, the young Hobgoblin knew the importance of speed and stealth, understood it was strong, what its hands could do, how they would do it . . . ripping, crushing, tearing. . . . It suddenly understood *prey*, and its flesh tingled at the image, red pulses going off in rapid fire within its brain. It pictured prey in many forms and in seconds realized that *this* was what would satiate its hunger for fear and violence. Prey. Stalking. Killing.

The ten-year-old's new, mutated incarnation shuddered at the prospect, and it threw back its head, emitting a piercing, inhuman shriek of lust.

Then it caught a scent, nostrils flaring, and its eyes narrowed as lips pulled back from its teeth. *Prey*.

The Hobgoblin started moving.

. . .

The scream froze Rosa in place and made her skin crawl with a chill that had nothing to do with the freezing water. There was madness in that scream, a sound no human could make, and it terrified her, tapping something feral in her primordial brain.

When she was fourteen, Rosa spent a week at a Wisconsin lake with a girlfriend and her parents. One night she'd been awakened by the most diabolical yowling and shrieking right outside the cabin, and both she and her girlfriend had run screaming to the girl's parents. In the morning, the girl's father told them it had been raccoons, either fighting or mating. Rosa decided right then that if a demon rose from hell, *that* was how it would sound.

Until now.

It came a second time, echoing through dark steel tunnels, and Rosa couldn't tell if it was coming from the left or right, or how far away. *It's close. And the dead don't make that sort of noise. Nothing does.*

Swinging the flashlight in both directions, she expected to see some demonic horror waiting to pounce, but the passageway remained empty. Rosa knew she'd come from the left, so she waded right, staggering from bulkhead to bulkhead as the ship rode whatever unimaginable sea event it was now experiencing. She couldn't picture the waves required to make this behemoth move like this, tried to envision the storm (*it* had *to be a storm, right?*) that was assaulting the ship. Her worst images of hurricanes didn't seem sufficient.

Yet Rosa knew she would gladly endure whatever howling tempest awaited on the flight deck if it meant escaping these black corridors of the dead. The dead and . . . something else.

A heavy sloshing came from up ahead, and she jabbed the flashlight beam forward. Flung through an open hatch by the ship's movement, a pale and pasty thing in khakis had collided with the left bulkhead only ten feet away. Its milky eyes found her, and it groaned.

Rosa shot it in the face, and it collapsed. *Five rounds left.*

The gunshot still ringing in her ears, Rosa heard the inhuman scream come again, definitely behind her now . . . she thought.

And it was very near.

A primitive instinct caused the Hobgoblin to screech in rage and delight at the echo of the single gunshot. It was newborn and had yet to learn restraint. But its body tensed as its new brain said that *this* was something that could hurt it, and instinctually understood caution, the ways of stalking, and then gave the creature a strong sense of direction and distance to the shot. The Hobgoblin moved that way, down a narrow passage, the flooding waist-deep on a creature that occupied the frame of what had been a ten-year-old boy. Then it began angling, no longer heading straight in the direction of the sound.

Wet clothing and clumsy shoes were irritating, and the creature tore off the shirt and pants, ripped at undergarments and clawed at sneakers until they came away. Then it was bare, hands smoothing across its crimson skin, feeling the powerful muscles underneath, touching the fatal wounds on its body, the ragged edges already toughening like leather. Better.

It must be fast. It must be quiet. It knew these things, but it also felt the hunger, the need to rip and bite, feel hot blood on its skin. *That* particular image was maddening. It must have *control*. Be quick. Be clever. Resist the urges.

But above all, it had to kill.

R osa didn't know this part of the ship at all. After the initial attack, her time had been spent mostly between the mess and common areas on Second Deck and the medical spaces on the 03 Gallery Deck. In those areas, it seemed there were ladderways at every turn, numerous opportunities to climb to higher decks. It was not so down here, and she was disoriented as well. Was she heading forward or aft? On the starboard side or to port? She thought she was on Third Deck but could be as deep as Fourth Deck. Could she be all the way down on the Engine Room level?

She noticed that the ship's violent pitching had slowed to a more predictable roll. The seas must have calmed.

There was very little stenciling on walls or hatches down here, only an occasional incomprehensible abbreviation or string of numbers and letters. Rosa supposed that crewmen assigned to these areas quickly figured out where they were and how to get around, and anyone who didn't had no business being down here.

She pressed on, reaching a point where she could continue down the passage or take a new corridor that branched to the right.

I'm going in circles.

Moaning came from the darkness ahead, and her flashlight revealed several crooked silhouettes at the edge of her light, moving toward her through the water. Too far to risk wasting a bullet, and she couldn't bear hearing that ghastly screech again when the *thing* heard her fire. Rosa moved right, passing several unmarked hatches, finding no ladderways.

The medic realized she *was* looking for a way up and out of this place. Did that mean she was giving up on Michael? She wanted to deny it, but she was scared, and she wanted out. The guilt of leaving him behind warred with her fear, and she wanted to cry. How could she abandon a child like that? How could she stay down here another minute?

Rosa knew what kind of person would leave a ten-year-old boy to his fate in a place like this, and the fact that Michael had sacrificed himself so that Wind and Denny could escape made her feel smaller still. She was weak, a fraud who claimed she wanted only to help people, but then ran when she was needed most. Michael would now join the ranks of the others she'd betrayed with her cowardice; her partner Jimmy, her mom, anyone she'd hurt because she was only *pretending* to be a doctor. This realization was like acid in her mouth, yet not powerful enough to turn her back. She kept looking for a way out.

The passageway ended at a single hatch marked *ACCESS-JP5 BKR 01-PRESCONT.* The hatch was closed, and someone had jammed a long steel pry bar between the handle and the door.

"No," she whispered, resting a palm on the hatch. It was damp and cold. There were no openings to the right or left, only the way back, and moaning and splashing was coming from there. *No, I can't face them. No more.* She was freezing and tired, her foot was sending arrows of pain up her leg, and all she wanted to do was sit down, let the water and the cold take her someplace quiet and safe. It would be so easy. . . .

Figures appeared at the back of the hallway, dead faces with black eyes. Two, half a dozen, more pressing in from behind.

"No!" she shouted, firing the pistol, the muzzle flash blinding as the bullet blew off a jaw. She shoved the weapon into its holster and jerked the pry bar free with a squeal of metal. Without caring what was on the other side she was through the hatch, water pouring over the knee knocker, and then she was shoving it closed. Rosa nearly dropped her flashlight as she jammed the pry bar home against the handle on this side, just as something began beating at the steel.

The medic drew the pistol and panned the Maglite around, ready to fire one of her four remaining bullets. It was a high, echoing room, perhaps two decks high. She realized she was standing on a metal catwalk that encircled the compartment, and the space beyond the railing dropped yet another deck; the place was a tube, and the water from beyond the hatch had simply spilled through the gridwork. This place was dry, free of the flooding.

The center of the chamber was filled with a forest of vertical purple pipes of many different sizes. Valve wheels and gauges bristled from the pipes as they rose in cornfield rows through the high room, and there was a sharp odor in the air that made her nostrils burn.

She suddenly understood the meaning behind the hatch's cryptic message; this was a pressure control room for the JP-5 jet fuel stored in bunker number zero-one.

Her eyes watered. *Was it leaking?* No, she'd encountered a genuine leak before, and this didn't compare. *And if it was leaking, then the fumes would take her out soon enough and none of this shit would even matter anymore.*

Rosa moved right, following a curving steel wall, passing tool lockers and boards displaying piping schematics, the wet bandage trailing behind her. She'd traveled perhaps a quarter of the circle when her light picked out a ladder bolted to the curving wall. Panning up, she saw that it rose to a small metal platform with a hatch set in the wall behind it.

Freedom.

Then she stopped. Why had this room been barred from the outside? Ahead and behind was only empty catwalk. She stepped to the railing that overlooked the pipe-filled center and pointed her light downward.

Fifty dead faces peered back up at her, and the groaning rose like a hellish choir. Through the pipes she could see a metal stairway that curved from this catwalk down into that space. The dead turned as one and began crowding up the stairs.

Rosa started for the ladder, then stopped when she heard a hatch creak open beyond the forest of pipes. The footsteps that stepped through the hatch and moved along the catwalk were slow but didn't drag or stumble. Cautious movement? She put her light in that direction.

"Michael?" she whispered, hoping.

It was.

THIRTY-FIVE

Stone opened his eyes. He was almost certain he'd stopped throwing up—there couldn't possibly be anything left inside him—and along with his stomach, the world had stopped heaving, trying to spin him away into the cataclysm. His hands were raw from where he'd been gripping the nylon rope, his body entangled in the safety netting just off the port side of the carrier's flight deck. The boy's eyes burned from salt water, and he was shivering.

Now I know what a drowned rat feels like.

The aircraft carrier was still riding high seas, but the waves were more widely spaced now, no longer driving the massive vessel into the air and then dropping it into impossible trenches. He couldn't remember being hit by the wave, but he'd seen it, a towering wall of blue-gray capped with white that came at the ship from the stern and starboard. Then there'd been a spinning sensation, his hands groping for something that might stop him, his lungs burning from lack of air. Stone was sure he would drown, or be crushed against some unyielding piece of the ship.

Instead, one hand caught the safety netting and locked on, and the boy had pulled himself into it, riding out the nightmare of rising and plunging seas, shaking in the netting.

Stone remembered seeing the dead, motionless on the flight deck just moments before the world tried to rip itself apart. Now, as the cloud cover scudded east, moonlight blanketed the bay and he could see that he wasn't alone in the netting. Half a dozen broken and moaning corpses had been washed over and were tangled as he was, snapping their teeth and trying to crawl free. The closest was only ten feet from him, an elderly woman who looked as if her fall from the Bay Bridge had dropped her on her face, flattening her features and skull. She croaked behind a compressed jaw and shattered teeth.

He couldn't see Liebs in the netting. The man was standing right beside him when the monster wave appeared.

"Guns?" he called, his voice sounding like the croaking dead woman.

No response.

He called louder. "Guns? Chief, answer me!"

The gunner's mate didn't answer, and the old woman croaked at him again, trying to disentangle herself from the netting. Stone thought about his friend, washed overboard into the night. The boy lowered his head against the netting and the tears came.

The dead woman croaked again.

Baring his teeth, Stone unsnapped the automatic in his shoulder holster and shot the drifter in the forehead. "Be quiet," he whispered.

"A head shot at ten feet with a stationary target. Should I be impressed?"

Stone looked up at the voice to see Chief Liebs standing above him on the flight deck, smiling. The man lay down and reached out. "Give me your hand."

A moment later Stone was standing on the flight deck. The boy looked at the gunner's mate for a moment, then gave him a ferocious hug. "You're alive," he said, his voice cracking.

Startled, Liebs suddenly smiled and hugged the boy back. "Good to see you too, shipmate."

They laughed, talked about the wave and being hung up in the netting, then looked out at the moonlit bay. It awed them to silence. Everything looked different; a great cliff was to the east, Oakland was gone, and so was the Bay Bridge. To the west, the Golden Gate had vanished except for a lone support at its north end. Where San Francisco had been was only the Pacific, rolling into the bay unchecked. There was no sign of the black ship.

"We're heading west," Liebs said, "at a good clip too."

"And we're listing a lot more to port," said Stone, gesturing at the increased tilt to the flight deck. They were the only ones here. The dead had been either washed into the safety netting or swept away by the sea.

"Chief Liebs, Calvin. Do you copy?"

Upon hearing the voice, the two men stared at each other in surprise, then at the radio still clipped to the gunner's mate's combat vest. Stone's had been torn away at some point.

"I can't believe it still works," said the younger man.

The chief shook his head. "I can't believe it was made by a government contractor and still works." He keyed the mic. "Go ahead, Cal. I'm on the flight deck with Stone."

"I'll meet you there," Calvin said.

s everyone okay?" Petty Officer Banks called. There wasn't much that could be thrown around on the bridge; it was all bolted down. The people were another matter, and they'd been bounced around plenty. Warships weren't known for their soft, forgiving surfaces.

PK stuck his head out of the communications room and gave the man a thumbs-up, then went back to where Maya was sitting propped against a comm console, lightly touching her fingertips to a gash in her forehead.

The electronics tech crouched in front of her. "Are-you-okay?" he asked, exaggerating the words. Maya laughed at the face he was making as he spoke, and nodded. The man patted her leg and went in search of a first-aid kit.

Maya's hands went to her belly. *Are* you *okay?*

He'd thought the radical tipping of the deck would flip the Navy helicopter right over on top of him. Xavier had been thrown hard against the bulkhead to his rear, then just as quickly sent rolling back into the chopper's landing gear. He'd lost his cover and expected the man behind the crates—Charlie, the man who'd led killers into their home—to shoot him, before he realized his opponent was being tossed about just as he was.

The helicopter might indeed have fallen over on him had it not been chained to the deck. Even though *Nimitz* was grounded and going nowhere, Vladimir always insisted that every safety precaution be followed when it came to aircraft.

Thank you, Vladimir.

At some point when the ship was rising and falling, spinning and tilting, Xavier had lost his grip on the shotgun. Now that he was once again lying on his stomach, hidden behind the helicopter tire and unsure of where the other man was, he could see it resting on the rubberized hangar deck floor, out in the open, twenty feet away.

Not a chance. That just smells *like an ambush waiting to happen.* Instead he drew the pistol Calvin had given him, the one taken from the girl who'd shot him in the body armor. A quick inspection revealed he had seven rounds. There were plenty of shotgun shells in his combat vest, but there was no way he was going out there to retrieve the weapon.

Where was this guy?

. . .

In over twenty years at sea, Charlie Kidd had never experienced anything even approaching what they'd just been through. Knowing ships and storms, he calculated it would have taken fifty-foot waves at least to toss an aircraft carrier about, and concluded that there would be little or nothing left of the urban sprawl encircling the bay. The Pacific had exerted its authority, and he counted himself lucky to be alive.

But you're alive too, aren't you, priest?

The crate behind which Chick had been hiding was sent tumbling away in the tempest, and he'd found himself sliding across the deck as it tilted at a sickening angle. Then the forklift by the far bulkhead shifted and began to slide, coming at him. Chick scrambled and dove as the heavy piece of equipment tipped and crashed onto its side.

That was where he was now, crouched behind its bulk, peering at the shot-up helicopter from a new angle. The M14 was still in his hands—he wasn't sure how he'd managed to hold on to it—and he scanned the shadows beneath the helicopter for something to use it on.

The kid deputy killed by the priest had turned just as the cataclysm started, staggering across the deck, thrown flat and then crawling on hands and knees. He'd crawled too close to one of the open aircraft elevator shafts when a monster wave hit the ship, the impact flinging the dead kid out into the sea.

Where . . . are . . . you?

The priest's shotgun was lying out in the open. Would the man be reckless enough to make a grab for it? Up until now, he'd shown patience and proven he wasn't stupid. Would the man get desperate and *do* something stupid?

Chick ached to get the man in his gun sights. His hands flexed around the rifle. *Come out, come out . . .*

The senior chief no longer cared about the others who had come aboard with him, or about the mission. Only a fool would believe his sister and her ship had survived that. It was over. But *this* wasn't. The priest was their leader, and he'd dared to stand against Chick and his sister. His death was the only mission that counted now.

Come out, come out . . .

Xavier couldn't stay any longer, couldn't keep hiding. People would be hurt, frightened, and he couldn't help them while hiding behind this tire. In a single movement the former boxer propelled himself to his feet and sprinted to the right, across the twenty-five feet of open space between this and the next chained-down helicopter. Halfway across, he saw the hatch in the far bulkhead, partially hidden by shadows, a way out he couldn't see from his former hiding place.

He poured on the speed.

A rifle cracked and a bullet hummed past his head.

Then he was behind the chopper and at the hatch, hauling it open, going through. From the hangar deck behind him came a loud curse, followed by the sound of running boots.

Calvin was sitting on the cold deck, back pressed against a bulkhead, wrists draped over his drawn-up knees. His assault rifle rested beside him in a clutter of spent shell casings.

He'd followed the blood trail and found the woman. She attacked from an open hatch on the left, just as the aircraft carrier began heaving in the monstrous waves. She was mortally wounded, her flannel shirt and jeans soaked red from where his earlier rifle bullet punched through her lower side. The wound *had* been mortal, and death claimed her while Calvin was still hunting.

A snarl of hunger was the only warning the hippie got as the logging truck driver burst from the hatch, on him in an instant with clawing fingers and snapping teeth. The two of them locked together, Calvin trying to fend her off with the rifle as a barrier while the ship threw them down the passageway and back again.

Calvin head-butted her to no effect. He shoved and she hung on, still snapping, a fingernail clawing a red stripe down his neck. And then *Nimitz* bucked hard to the right and threw her clear. Calvin swung the rifle muzzle around and sprayed her with 7.62-millimeter bullets, emptying the clip, ensuring that he not only hit the head but *blew it apart.*

The woman went down, little more than bone fragments and jam from the neck up.

Now Calvin rested against the bulkhead, feeling the turbulent sea subsiding to a rhythm the ship handled easily. He pulled the Hydra radio from his combat vest and turned up the volume, keying the mic.

"Chief Liebs, Calvin. Do you copy?"

After a moment the gunner's mate responded. "Go ahead, Cal. I'm on the flight deck with Stone."

"I'll meet you there." Then the aging hippie put the radio away and lifted his wrist from where it rested on his knee, the denim there dark and wet. Calvin looked at the torn flesh where the woman had bitten him, then rested the damaged hand in his lap.

He thought about Maya and Michael, about his other children and a grandchild he would never see. He thought about those already lost. Then Calvin lowered his head and allowed himself to weep silently.

THIRTY-SIX

Adventure Galley

The cutter's night-vision camera captured the image of the motorized lifeboat carrying Lt. Riggs and most of Liz's crew being hurled through the air by a towering wave, only to be sucked into the crevasse as soon as it hit the water again. Moments later, the earth thrust upward, sealing the crevasse and creating a towering cliff against which the sea crashed and was thrown back.

Gone.

There was no time for rage or grief, because the sea was trying to kill her. Terrifying swells capped with white raced in from the Pacific, sweeping away all traces of civilization and threatening to send the cutter to the bottom. She'd ordered the helm to turn straight into it, calling the two remaining men in the engine room and ordering flank speed, then joined the frightened young helmsman to help him hold course.

The 418-foot vessel climbed, crested and dove, and at the bottom of the trench between the waves, the sleek bow cut the water and knifed under, the sea surging up against the bridge windows. Liz gripped an overhead handhold and watched in terror, thinking the ship would simply keep going, arrowing to the bottom like a crash-diving submarine. Each time, however, the bow burst from the surface and began climbing the next swell. At the crest, the cutter's propellers cleared the water as the vessel tipped forward, blades whining like airplane props before biting in once more.

Liz had never experienced a sea like this. What the earth had done was unimaginable, and the resulting destruction—to both cities and terrain—demonstrated both the power and brutality of nature. But this was a geological event, not a storm, and it ended relatively quickly. The sea soon came into balance with the larger, deeper bay, finding new shores to surge against, and the land ceased its movement, seemingly satisfied with its new form.

Ocean waves pushed in from the Pacific, but now they were thrown back into a powerful new current, one that entered the bay, then curved like a horseshoe to rush back out. Liz was forced to turn and point the cutter east, maintaining forward propulsion to keep from being pulled out into the Pacific.

Nimitz had no such propulsion. Liz saw the flattop on her surface radar, several miles away. It had passed them at some point during the event and was now running bow-on toward the northern edge of the newly widened San Francisco Bay at ten knots. If it didn't run aground somewhere, Liz knew, it would be dragged out into open water. The vessel's severe list and inability to maneuver told her it would not last long out there.

Now that her ship was no longer in peril, fury began building in her, reddening her neck. Riggs and her crew were lost, and any chance of taking the carrier was lost with them. Charlie and his team were likely dead as well. And still *Nimitz* eluded her.

Not for long.

Liz snatched up a handset. "Combat center, bridge. Are you still alive, Mr. Vargas?" She had to call twice before getting a response.

"Vargas here, Captain." He sounded dazed.

"Clear your head, mister," Liz snapped. "How many rounds left in the forward gun?"

A pause. "Nineteen, ma'am. Armor-piercing and high-explosive mixed."

"Very well," she said. "Light up your target acquisition system and prepare for surface action." She clicked off and lifted her binoculars, finding *Nimitz* in the moonlight. "Mr. Waite," she called to her quartermaster, "set an intercept course for that carrier. Flank speed."

Did she have a concussion? Amy wasn't sure. Her head hurt, and her body felt like a punching bag after being thrown about the maintenance closet. Other than some brief training maneuvers, she'd never been to sea or experienced a storm. She could only imagine this had been just that, but so fierce and sudden? And then to end just as quickly? It was like nothing she'd ever heard about.

She sat on the deck and ran her hands over her body. Nothing broken, nothing cut—wait, her ear was bleeding, but not badly, and there was a lump on her head. She felt the rolling motion of the sea, so they were still afloat.

With a groan she got to her feet, holding on to a shelf as sudden dizziness threatened to put her back on the floor. Then there was a shadow in the light at the bottom of the door, a rattle of keys as the deadbolt was unlocked. The door opened and Amy shielded her eyes, blinking in the sudden light. Mr. Leary, the older civilian contractor, was standing there. He looked pale.

"Are you all right?" he asked.

Amy stared at him for a moment, then nodded.

"Come out of there." He extended a hand.

She saw that he was alone and allowed him to guide her out into the passage. "Why . . . ?"

Leary shook his head. "It was wrong leaving those people behind in Oregon," he said. "It was murder. We're all dead anyway, Miss Liggett. No one should die locked in a closet." He dropped his ring of master keys on the deck and walked away, his head down.

Amy watched him go, then checked the passage. It was empty, and the ship was quiet, lacking the normal sounds of people moving and talking and working.

Dead anyway.

She snatched up the keys and started running.

Alone in the cutter's combat center, Mr. Vargas sat in a chair facing the fire control system. His left arm was broken after slamming against a vertical water pipe and now hung limp in his lap. Although the pain would spike with excruciating bursts, it was bearable as long as he didn't move around a lot, and it wouldn't interfere with his duties. He could do this one-handed.

On a screen to his left was the infrared image of *Nimitz*, three miles out. The camera watching it was locked on and held the target, pivoting as the cutter executed a 180-degree turn and headed west at flank speed. Vargas switched on the targeting system for the forward gun and punched in a code to slave the video image to the fire control computer.

A small square with crosshairs at its center appeared on the image, and with a fingertip pressed to the screen he dragged the square until it was centered on the carrier. The fifty-seven-millimeter Bofors gun had an effective direct range of 9,300 yards—double that if arcing shells at a forty-five-degree angle—and the carrier was well within its reach. It could fire 220 rounds per minute, but at that rate his nineteen remaining shells would be depleted in 3.6 seconds. With a tap of the screen he set the firing selector to *single*, then tapped the word *lock* nearby.

Out on the bow, the radome mounted over the deck gun's barrel locked on target, and with a hydraulic whine, the gun turret rotated slightly and the barrel elevated a half inch. The weapon's gyro-stabilized sights would now make continuous corrections, holding the deck gun on target despite the rise, fall, and roll of the sea.

"Target is locked," Vargas reported.

Liz watched the carrier through her binoculars, the cutter closing fast and keeping well off its port side, just in case someone was foolish enough to try using the same fifty-caliber heavy machine gun she carried on her own ship. She knew that weapon's capability and kept out of its range.

Elizabeth Kidd knew she was finished. They couldn't take the carrier, couldn't look to it for the life support it once offered. Nor could she and her handful of crewmen continue operating the cutter; there simply weren't enough of them. She could drop anchor and use her remaining launch to send a shore party in search of supplies, but that was no longer an option. The earth and sea had eradicated all traces of civilization; there would be nothing to scavenge. And even if she managed to get the cutter back out to the coastline and somehow found another harbor, she didn't have the manpower to take and hold it. The food and water aboard would run out, and the fuel tanks would run dry. She'd gambled on seizing *Nimitz*, and lost.

I'm sorry, Chick. I failed you again. But if we don't get to live, then neither do they.

"Mr. Vargas," she said into the mic, "make your first target the carrier's bridge, second line of windows down from the top of the superstructure. One round of HE. Fire when ready."

Vargas tapped the targeting screen to enhance until the windows and catwalks of the superstructure's decks filled the screen. Then he found the level the captain wanted and used his thumb and forefinger to pinch his targeting square, tightening it on the new objective. He centered the crosshairs on a window, then pulled up the battery menu and tapped an icon reading *HE*, for high explosive.

A light turned green, and Vargas depressed a red firing button with one finger.

The deck gun roared, its muzzle flash a white tongue that leaped across the cutter's forward deck. There was a brief, high-pitched scream, and then the bridge of USS *Nimitz* erupted in a flash of red and white, glass and burning debris raining onto the flight deck.

The captain's voice came over his headset. "Adjust your target to *Nimitz*'s port side bow, at the waterline. Make every shot count, Mr. Vargas. You may exhaust your magazine."

The man's right hand danced across the touch screen. It was an awful thing he was doing, he knew that; there were civilians aboard, and they'd made not a single aggressive move against the cutter. But orders were orders. And besides, *he* was going to get to sink an *aircraft carrier*! The thrill of that quickly swept aside any moral reservations he might have had.

THIRTY-SEVEN

Nimitz

Michael was about fifty feet away from her, with only the curving catwalk between them. Only it wasn't Michael anymore. It was . . . something else.

In the glow of the flashlight beam, Rosa could tell by the wounds on his naked body—and the creamy glaze of his eyes—that he was dead. The shock she felt in knowing that the child she'd come to rescue was lost to the dead was replaced by her horror at the changes he had undergone. His flesh was a maroon shade, and new muscle rippled across his chest, arms, and legs, far more than nature had ever allotted to a ten-year-old boy. She thought she saw the muscles shiver beneath the taut skin. Michael had grown no taller, and his powerful upper body joined with the small stature reminded her of baboons and pit bulls. He bared his teeth.

A word floated up from her memories of catechism class: *demon*.

Mutation was the next word. Although the medic had a quick and capable mind, she had trouble wrapping her head around the idea that a genetic mutation could do that, and so quickly. It wasn't possible.

The impossible creature hunched and curled its fingers into claws, then let out the crazed, inhuman screech Rosa had heard earlier. The medic recoiled at the sound, her bladder nearly releasing in the same primitive reaction as prey in the wild when confronted by a predator's cry. The thing moved at her then, fast and low, powerful leg muscles driving it forward.

Rosa jerked the pistol up and fired twice. The first bullet hit the meat of a pectoral muscle, and it didn't flinch. The second bullet hummed through empty space, because the creature was no longer there. With a grunt it leaped sideways, flinging itself over the railing, out into the center of the room with its forest of pipes.

There was no thud as it hit bottom, because it didn't land. Rosa caught a glimpse of it hanging from a large valve wheel by one hand, then swinging its body out of sight behind a cluster of pipes. She hunted for it with the light, shadows flickering between the vertical steel tubes. Rosa tracked the pistol along with the moving flashlight.

There was a *clang*, a series of thumps, and another *clang*.

It's moving through the pipes, leaping from one to another.

The primordial screech came from somewhere within the steel forest, and Rosa fought the urge to bolt. Neither did she dare to freeze as she knew it was still moving in there, no doubt getting closer, trying to flank her.

Rosa's eyes went up as she raised the flashlight higher, to where the pipes stretched upward another deck. Maybe it was climbing above her and preparing to drop while her eyes looked for it at this level. She snapped the light back down and caught a flash of dark red skin as it leaped between pipes, ten feet in and six or seven feet higher. She almost squeezed off a shot, but then it was gone.

The moans of the dead horde in the pipe shaft echoed off the walls, and her flashlight showed her that the first of the corpses had completed the climb up the stairwell. A *Nimitz* crewman in blue coveralls with most of his face bitten away stumbled along the catwalk, the others close behind it.

She had to move but was afraid that if she turned her back, Michael would be on her. Where could she go? Climb the nearby ladder to the little platform and hatch above? The dead couldn't climb ladders. That thing could, though. Then she decided it wouldn't even need to go up the ladder. It could scale the pipes and then leap across space, landing on her back as she climbed. Her panic and indecisiveness had her paralyzed.

The screeching howl came again, perhaps from the center of the pipe forest, perhaps from above. She couldn't tell and kept probing with the light, desperate to find it so she could kill it.

It's different from the others. Can it be killed?

Groans from the left, closer now. She snapped the light over and saw ten of them, rotting in their uniforms and work coveralls, surging down the curve of the catwalk toward her.

Can't stay! Two bullets left, can't face them. Move!

Rosa moved, running to the right around the curve, away from the horde. The sounds of thumping against metal came from the pipe forest as the thing moved with her, possibly above her now. Michael had come through a hatch on this side. It was her way out. And there it was, set in the wall on the opposite side of the room from where she'd entered, standing open and . . .

Corpses were pushing through from the other side, one after another, tripping over the knee knocker and then pulling themselves upright, eyes reflecting the flashlight beam. They snarled and moved toward her, their noises echoed by the hungry figures behind her.

The bone-chilling screech came again from the pipe forest.

With a roar, Charlie Kidd leaped through the hatch from the hangar deck, triggering a burst from his M14 at waist level. The priest was thirty or forty feet away, pistol raised and facing him in a long passageway. Among Coast Guard boarding parties, and in all law enforcement circles, hallways were known as *fatal funnels*; there was simply no place to go once the shooting started, and when there was a shooter at each end, the one slower on the trigger usually died.

Charlie and Xavier fired at the same time.

The big black man went down with at least one hit to the chest. In the same instant, the senior chief felt the side of his head struck as if by a hot, iron fireplace poker. He grunted and collapsed against the left wall.

Xavier was flat on his back. The 7.62-millimeter rifle bullet had hit him in the right side of his chest like a train, and he couldn't remember falling or banging the back of his head on the steel deck. He couldn't breathe and felt like an elephant was standing on him as he fought to draw in air. The pistol was no longer in his hand, and he clutched at his chest through the armholes of his body armor. The fingertips came away slick and red.

Have . . . to . . . breathe . . .

Xavier couldn't move, simply lay on the deck like a fish out of its bowl, sucking at nothing. His vision grayed at the edges.

Head wound. Chick's mind struggled as if moving through mud, fuzzy and blinded with a white, pulsing light he couldn't escape by closing his eyes. He was lying on one hip, sagged against a bulkhead, and the world's nastiest headache had his brain in a vise. Something warm and wet was running down his neck.

Fucker shot me in the head. He was amazed. He wasn't supposed to get hit! One hand rose to the side of his head, fingertips shaking, and he touched ragged flesh where his right ear had been, finding only a bloody channel plowed along the side of his skull by a bullet and ragged pieces of meat that had been his ear. He stifled a cry, tears running from his eyes as he squeezed them shut, trying to block out the glare of white pain in his head. He wanted to be sick. His hand fluttered and fell to the deck with a thump.

Sleep. I'll sleep, and then I'll feel better.

Chick's body relaxed and slid further down the wall, and the pain seemed to subside just a little bit. *That works. Sleep . . . I'll just . . .* A groan from down the corridor made him open his eyes. The priest was rolling onto his side, trying to get to his hands and knees.

No! Charlie fought to rise, felt the passageway spin, saw the black man fall to his stomach, then grip the frame of an open hatch and pull his body through. The chief bit down on his lip hard enough to draw blood, the pain widening his eyes. He grabbed the M14 from the floor beside him, forcing himself to stand as he leaned on one wall.

Then he was staggering down the corridor and fighting double vision, intent on the hatch, as he left the handgun and a blood trail behind him on the deck.

The smallest of breaths caught in his lungs, and Xavier gasped, trying to pull in another. He was still on his hands and knees, blood was dripping from one side of his body armor and onto the deck, and his chest hurt so much that he wondered if this was what a heart attack felt like. He was sluggish, wanted only to lie down until he could breathe again. Another short breath, and Xavier fought to draw air as he grabbed the side of a metal locker and used it to help himself stand.

It was a large storage room, filled with rows of equipment lockers. Yellow oxygen tanks with hoses and masks hung on one wall, and filling the center he could see long racks of yellow coats and pants, rows of boots and lines of helmets. Firefighter gear. A steel ladderway on the left climbed one wall to the deck above, but the thought of dragging himself up those steep stairs made him gasp harder.

He pulled a long, wheezing breath, still holding on to the locker and wanting to lie down. Was his right arm going numb? It felt unresponsive, but that might just have been a reaction to the pain in his chest. Another small breath. If only he could rest for a few minutes.

He heard bootsteps in the passageway beyond the hatch. *Where my pistol is.* Xavier clenched his teeth against the pain and plunged into the racks of coats and gear.

Stone and Chief Liebs ran across the flight deck, looking for cover as the carrier's bridge rained fiery debris from above. The blare of a fire klaxon filled the air. They found a depression on the starboard side and jumped down into it, a rectangular pocket in the deck where launch controllers had once gathered to manage flight operations, protected here from the waist down. Pieces of twisted, smoking metal clattered to the deck around them.

Liebs looked up at the shattered bridge level, billowing smoke in the moonlight. *Banks . . . PK and Maya . . .*

"Out there!" Stone shouted suddenly, pointing across the water.

Liebs could feel the carrier moving, but without the landmarks of San Francisco and Alcatraz—both had vanished beneath the surface—it was hard to judge direction. He thought they were moving west, and a glance forward showed him the hills of Tiburon, the northern support of the Golden Gate Bridge coming up on the right. Yes, it was west, with the black Pacific beyond.

The gunner's mate looked to where the younger man was pointing. In the clear lunar glow, the low-slung, black silhouette of the enemy warship could be seen pacing them several miles to starboard. And then the shape was obscured behind a red-and-white flash.

"Incoming!" he yelled, pulling Stone down into the flight controller's pocket. A shell screamed in, and then there was a blast, the aircraft carrier shuddering as the *BOOM* of a deck gun rolled across the water. Another high-pitched whine then, another *BOOM*, and a second impact shook *Nimitz*.

Liebs lifted his head and risked a look. The superstructure had taken no new hits, and the flight deck was clear. *The hull. They're going to sink us.* A third shell detonated against the aircraft carrier's port side.

Stone was standing up beside him now and had come to the same conclusion. "What can we do?" he shouted.

Liebs shook his head. "Not a goddamn thing."

Calvin grabbed the railing of the starboard catwalk and hung on as a third shell punched into the other side of the ship, then started moving again. Bodies littered the grid of steel underfoot, freshly killed humans as well as the dead put down a second time, and his boots pounded among them as he ran for the short stairway leading to the flight deck.

The shriek of an inbound fifty-seven-millimeter shell came a second before another blast and rumble. He climbed to the flight deck, saw the smoking bridge high above, and saw the enemy ship steaming parallel to them miles away.

"Liebs! Stone!"

"Over here!" the gunner's mate shouted, and Calvin spotted the two men. He ran to them and jumped down into their hole.

The deck gun put another high-explosive round into the carrier's savaged hull.

"Can we shoot back?" Calvin asked.

The gunner's mate shook his head. "We've got nothing but the fifties. And even if we put a fifty-cal on the port rail, they're out of range. It wouldn't do much if we *could* hit them. That's a goddamn warship out there."

The hippie leader's mind raced through everything he knew about *Nimitz*, everything he had seen, then stopped when his mind came to a single image. "Chief, can you put one of those RIB boats into the water?"

"Look, if we abandon ship—" he started.

Now Calvin shook his head. "Can you do it?"

"Yeah, sure."

The older man told him what he wanted, and the gunner's mate looked at him with cool, appraising eyes for a long moment, then nodded. "It might work, Cal," he said. "But it's a long shot."

"Cal, no way!" Stone shouted. "That's insane!"

Calvin smiled at the boy, squeezed his shoulder, then showed them both the bite wound. Stone cursed and looked away. Chief Liebs looked at the torn flesh that was a death sentence and said, "We have to hurry."

THIRTY-EIGHT

Richmond

Where cities once rose from the eastern shore of the San Francisco Bay, an angry planet had thrust a fifty-four-mile-long wall of bedrock high into the air, a cliff climbing a hundred feet above the crashing shore. In what had been Richmond, a fragment of red-and-white radio tower jutted horizontally over the water, wedged into a crack at the base of the cliff.

Evan, his back pressed against the rock and his boots braced on a steel crossbar, sat atop the remains of the tower, his useless left wrist in his lap. Death was coming for him in the form of a rotting, middle-aged woman wearing scraps of a red dress, strands of wet hair plastered to her pale face. Waxy blue eyes stared at him, and teeth clicked together as the corpse dragged itself down the length of the tower.

In the distance there was an occasional red flash in the night, a hollow boom, but Evan's attention was locked on the drifter. If the dead had been more coordinated, he knew, it would be on him already, but it moved slowly, gripping the steel and pulling itself forward. A wave surged up from below, and for a moment the tower was awash, the dead woman lost from sight beneath churning foam. Perhaps it would wash her off? But then the water receded, and she was still there, hanging on and inching forward.

The flare sputtered out, leaving them in the black-and-white of the strobe blinking on his vest. Evan popped his remaining canister, jamming it into the rock face, able to see her once more in the dazzling pink light. The drifter made a croaking noise deep in its throat. Ten feet to go.

Another wave pushed up onto the tower, and for an instant a pair of bodies was tangling in the broken steel at the far end, arms flailing. The tide carried them away before they could catch hold.

How many of the dead in the Bay Area? Evan did the math. *Eight million? Most of them would be in the sea now, churning with the current like vast schools of fish. How long before more washed up onto the tower?*

The dead woman croaked again and pulled herself closer, closer, one hand reaching out to touch his right boot. Evan pulled his legs in. She advanced, and reached again, clawing for his ankle.

Evan kicked out savagely, his heel connecting with the bridge of her nose and rocking her head back. He kicked again, feeling bone give way beneath rotting flesh, and the dead woman pawed at the boot hitting her face, letting go of the steel. Another kick sent her off the tower and into the sea.

"Yes!" he cried. "Drown, bitch!"

The next wave brought another pair of drifters against the twisted radio tower, and this time both creatures managed to hang on. They clawed their way to the top and started pulling themselves toward him.

Evan thought of the woman he loved, the child he would never see, and his despair turned into a sob.

THIRTY-NINE

Adventure Galley

In the combat center, Vargas cursed and slammed his fist into the console as the lights on his control panel flickered and the image on his targeting screen went fuzzy. *Goddamn system! The quake must have knocked something loose.* He flicked a row of switches, powering down the deck gun and the targeting computer, then flicked them up again. The console hummed.

"Mr. Vargas," the captain's voice said into his headset, "why have you stopped firing?"

He cursed again. "The fire control system is acting up, Captain. I'm trying to reboot it now."

"I want that gun up and firing, mister."

No shit. "Yes, ma'am. I'm working on it." The infrared video feed on his left still showed the carrier, drifting west. He'd been able to put a nice cluster of shells together at its forward port waterline, and the ship was tilting harder than it had been. Of course that might just be wishful thinking, he conceded. It was difficult to tell at this distance, and harder still with such a big target.

"Operate the gun manually," the captain's voice ordered.

Yes, I know. What the fuck do you think I'm trying to do? "Yes, ma'am. A few more minutes and I should have it." *Maybe.*

"Snap to it, mister."

The screen in front of him jumped, and the image slaved from the exterior camera appeared, *Nimitz* at the center. There was no targeting square or crosshairs. Vargas checked his board and saw that the gun's radome and gyro-stabilizers both glowed red, signaling that they were offline. He pounded the console again, but that only made the video image jump back to a field of white-and-green static.

Vargas took a deep breath. *Stop hitting the electronics.* He powered down again. If he could get the video feed to come back, then he might be able to switch from the automated fire control to manual, operating the deck gun with a joystick. It would lack the precision accuracy he'd enjoyed before—it would be *real* shooting, aiming a pip on screen and judging range in his head—but at least he'd be able to fire.

The magazine counter read thirteen fifty-seven-millimeter shells remaining.

Vargas let out a long breath and forced himself to wait while the system rebooted once more.

Amy Liggett reached the captain's cabin without encountering another crewman. Where was everyone? The cutter shuddered from what could only be the deck gun firing. She didn't have to speculate about the target, and that caused a renewed anger to boil inside her.

The cabin was empty as she'd expected, except for Blackbeard, who meowed loudly from his perch on the captain's bunk.

"I'm sorry your mommy is such a bitch," Amy told the cat, crossing the room as another shot boomed from the deck gun.

Blackbeard watched her, then licked at a front paw.

Since it sometimes contained codes and classified orders, the combination for the captain's wall safe was shared with the executive officer. Amy was betting Kidd hadn't changed it since locking her former XO in a maintenance closet.

The handle clicked and the safe door opened.

The deck gun boomed again.

FORTY

Nimitz

Charlie went through the hatch to the firefighting gear room more carefully than the last, pausing to listen, then entering with his rifle barrel leading. He was still seeing double, still nauseated, and blood from his head wound was saturating the right side of his sweater.

The other man's blood trail was easy to follow.

Lockers, shelves, and long racks of gear extended out into the compartment, row upon row of firefighting coats and pants, lines of boots and yellow helmets, oxygen tanks and hand tools. He leaned against a steel locker and aimed his rifle down the aisles, searching for movement. The blood trail led up the center aisle.

A bang came from off to the left, something heavy falling against hollow metal. Charlie swung the M14 in that direction and fired off a burst, bullets tearing through fire-resistant coats, punching holes in helmets and sparking off steel.

Time's up, Father.

. . .

A bullet punched into the sheet metal of an equipment locker six inches over his head, and Xavier jerked left, away from it, stumbling down an aisle where brass hose fittings and nozzles hung from pegs in ordered rows. Tanks of foam with handheld spray hoses were lined up on the opposite side. It was still painful to breathe, and his chest was filled with a burning sensation, but he was starting to pull in more air with every gasp. It made him wheeze, and he tried to suppress the noise.

Xavier's vision was still gray at the edges, and the deck behind him was streaked with a staggering blood trail and red boot prints.

He stumbled over a bench and crashed against a rack of silver hazmat suits, falling to the floor, making the gear swing. Another burst of rifle fire tore blindly through the compartment, tearing up several of the hazmat suits behind where he'd been standing a moment before.

Maybe he'll run out of bullets. Xavier crawled on his hands and knees to keep low. From behind him in the compartment came the clatter of an empty magazine hitting the floor, the click and snap of a fresh one being loaded into a rifle. *Too much to hope for.*

Xavier tried to crawl faster, looking for a way out, and came to the bulkhead running along the back of the compartment.

There was no hatch.

The dead were closing on Rosa from both sides of the catwalk, the horde of crewmen that had come up from the pit on her left, a half-dozen more in rotting uniforms moving through the hatch ahead of her, all of them surging toward their meal. She aimed the flashlight and shot the closest one in the head, and the crumpling body was immediately pushed aside by the others.

One bullet left. That one's for me.

•   •   •

The Hobgoblin's brain flared with red light at the pistol shot, violent urges driving it into a frenzy. It scrambled hand-over-hand up a pipe, then jumped across open space to another, hands catching hold of a valve wheel and bare feet planting against smooth steel, ending up where the pipe forest edged closest to the catwalk.

The scent of prey was overpowering, and it looked down through its red-and-black world to see the bright glow of the thing it needed to destroy. To both sides were others that were like him, yet different, and they wanted the same thing. The Hobgoblin would not be denied its prize.

Michael's muscles tensed, and then he let out an ungodly shriek and leaped.

Rosa made a move for the ladder that climbed to a hatch above, dropping her flashlight as she gripped a rung. It rolled to the edge of the catwalk and stopped, throwing its beam on a crowd of shuffling bodies coming in from the right. Snarls rose behind her, and she knew she was seconds away from being torn apart.

Then the thing in the pipe forest shrieked. Rosa looked up to see a dark mass dropping toward her, arms outstretched and roaring with mad lust.

She screamed and fell to the catwalk, shoving her pistol upward and pulling the trigger.

Then the Hobgoblin was on her.

FORTY-ONE

Nimitz

The crippled aircraft carrier moved west on a ten-knot current, the port side hull shredded by armor-piercing and high-explosive rounds. The firing fell off for a while, but the damaged section had now slipped below the surface and was taking on water at an alarming rate.

Nimitz drifted along the land mass on the north side of the bay, an area where Sausalito had crumbled into ruins. Ahead was the remaining support tower of the Golden Gate Bridge, its red steel climbing into the night sky, the approaching roadway still intact and leading up to the support, then dropping away into space in a gnarl of broken asphalt, bent red steel, and twisted cables.

Water churned about the tower's base, and on its present course, the current would carry the flattop straight into it. High above, the roadway approach was packed with the dead, crowding together right up to the drop-off. Several noticed the approaching carrier and tried to walk toward it, stepping off the side and tumbling down into the sea.

The rest simply stood in a shifting crowd, staring at and thinking about nothing, while the wide, flat deck of the ship drew closer.

Rosa was flat on her back, the creature's weight atop her, the maroon face staring into hers with its mouth open in a snarl. Michael's expression was frozen in a rictus of fury, but the waxy eyes saw nothing. A neat bullet hole was punched through the center of his forehead.

The groans of the dead came at her from both sides, and Rosa shoved the body off, scrambling to her feet. A sailor galloped at her from the left, and she threw her empty pistol at it, leaping for the ladder that climbed one wall of the tubelike room.

Hands caught at her backpack and she shrugged out of it, climbing in bare feet. Each time her bullet-damaged foot pushed off a rung, she let out a scream of pain. More hands tore at her legs, nails ripping through the fabric of her oversized pants. Another hand caught the bloody bandage trailing from her right foot, pulling her back down. Rosa screamed again and tore it free, still climbing.

Then she was above them, a crowd of reeking drifters pressing at the base of the ladder, reaching upward. She looked down, out of reach now, seeing the mass of agitated shadows in the glow of the flashlight still on the catwalk. Wincing and crying out from the pain in her foot, she reached the tiny platform at the top of the ladder, a single, closed hatch waiting in the wall beyond.

What if someone wedged this one closed from the other side, just like the hatch below? If that was the case, she was finished. The dead would keep her trapped up here on this platform until she died of thirst or decided she could no longer take it and flung herself out into the three-deck shaft of vertical pipes. Either way, she would join their ranks.

Her hand touched the handle. *It's locked.*

But then the handle moved on its own, the steel oval swinging away from her. She cried out as a hand shot out to grab her arm.

"Oh my God, Doc!"

Tommy stood on the other side holding a flashlight, his assault rifle hung around his neck on a sling. He pulled her through the hatch. "I heard the shots! I've been looking for you, are you okay?"

Rosa sobbed and fell against him, her body trembling.

The orderly held her close. "Michael?" he asked.

The medic shook her head, face buried in his chest.

Tommy put an arm around her waist. "Let's get you out of here."

Charlie Kidd stalked up an aisle between firefighting suits, rifle to his shoulder, following the blood trail. His vision continued to sway into double images and back again, and he still felt like throwing up but forced down the urge. He was leaving his own trail now, losing blood from the head wound. Soon he would pass out and drop, he knew, and there would be no one to give him medical attention. Death was close.

So be it. You first, Father.

The aisle ended at a wall with another aisle crossing right to left, the rear of the compartment. On the deck before him, boot prints and bloody smears went in both directions. *Right or left?* His finger tensed on the trigger and he leaped out, swinging right, squeezing a long burst from the M14.

The bar was iron, six feet long and capable of prying open cockpits and helicopter doors. Xavier gripped it in two hands and let out a primitive cry, thrusting it like a spear and driving it into the man's back.

Charlie grunted as three feet of bloody iron erupted from the center of his chest. He dropped the rifle, eyes blinking and mouth moving wordlessly. Then there was only darkness.

Xavier let the impaled man fall, the bar running him through clattering on the deck. "You should have gone left," the priest whispered. Then he stripped the dead man of his spare magazines and picked up his rifle. Xavier looked at the figure on the floor, trying not to hate him for all he had done, struggling to muster feelings of forgiveness and mercy.

Xavier shot Charlie Kidd in the head. It was all the mercy he could summon.

FORTY-TWO

Adventure Galley

Twenty-five minutes! The twitchy fire control system had Vargas in fits, blinking on for a moment before crackling back into a wash of static. Console lights flickered green and then glowed red once more. The captain's strident demands in his ears had finally caused him to rip off the headset and throw it across the combat center.

He had it now, though. The video image was steady on both the camera feed and the gun screen. Auto-targeting and gyro-stabilization were both offline, but the operations specialist had managed to bring up the manual controls for the deck gun. A white circle was centered on-screen, rising above and then falling below the image of the aircraft carrier as the cutter rode the seas approaching the mouth of the Pacific. He used a joystick to keep the pip on target, able to use only one hand and forced to release the stick so he could press the fire button.

The deck gun boomed, and on-screen a splash plumed from the water a hundred yards short of the carrier. Vargas adjusted the pip and fired again, then once more, starting to walk the splashes into the target.

The magazine counter read ten shells remaining.

He twitched the joystick, fired the deck gun, and then laughed out loud when a white bloom appeared on the green-and-black screen, right at the carrier's waterline.

"All mine now," he said to the empty combat center, timing his next shot with the rise and fall of the ship. He fired again. Another hit.

Elizabeth Kidd stood at the starboard bridge windows with her binoculars, watching the impacts, relieved that Vargas was firing once more and had found his range. She was keeping track of the rounds in her head, deducting each shot from the count she knew they had on board. Now that Vargas was on target, there would be enough shells to send the carrier to the bottom.

Her back was turned to the ladderway leading up to the bridge, and she didn't see a haggard-looking Amy Liggett creep up through the opening with Special Agent Ramsey's Sig Sauer in her hand. The sound of the floor hatch being dropped and dogged shut made her turn.

Amy stood with the pistol pointed at her captain. "Cease fire. Now," she said.

"Ensign," Liz started, "you don't—"

"*Now!*" Amy pointed the pistol at Liz's face. "They did nothing to you, nothing to deserve this."

Liz shook her head slowly. "You haven't seen—"

Amy cut her off again. "I've seen plenty. You're a monster, and this stops right now."

Over at the navigation station, Mr. Waite moved toward her suddenly. Amy pivoted and shot him in the chest. The young helmsman charged her too, but he hesitated, and Amy spun back, firing again, hitting the boy and sending him to the deck.

Liz's sidearm was in her hand then, and she blasted six rounds into the young woman across the compartment. Amy fell, the pistol dropping from lifeless fingers. Liz strode through the bridge and fired three more shots, one for the head of each corpse lying on the deck. She wasn't about to let them get up and prevent her from finishing what she'd started.

The deck gun boomed again, but she was away from the bridge windows now, unable to tell whether the shell had connected. She took the helm, keeping the cutter on course.

Let's complete the mission.

FORTY-THREE

San Francisco Bay

Salt spray and wind stung Calvin's cheeks as he raced the gray RIB boat across the bay, moonlight illuminating the black shape of the warship ahead of him. The gun on the vessel's bow fired, blooming red in the night, and a shell streaked through the air overhead, hitting the carrier behind him.

Calvin gripped the craft's wheel tightly as it pounded over the waves, slowed by its cargo but still closing the distance rapidly with the throttle thrown all the way forward. He knew that he would be spotted at any moment—either on radar or by a lookout—and that the gun would turn on him. Calvin didn't hesitate. The deck gun roared again, trying to kill his family, his friends.

He would protect them.

Strapped to both sides of the launch and protruding forward past the rubberized bow were MK-54 torpedoes, armed for contact detonation by Chief Liebs just before he and Stone lowered the boat into the water. Each of the two 608-pound weapons was eight

feet long, and their 97-pound warheads carried a combined equivalent of 476 pounds of TNT.

The deck gun did not turn on the small launch, and the cutter
held its course.

The warship's shape grew before him, and in the moonlight Calvin could see the vessel's mast, an American flag snapping in the
wind.

Calvin's last thought was of his children as he drove the RIB
boat into the cutter's side at over forty knots.

The blast was a spectacular white flash as both warheads connected with the vessel right at amidships.

Returning from the RIB boat launch bay to the flight deck, Chief
Liebs and Stone had watched the launch's wake as it crossed the
water, ducking each time a shell from the deck gun slammed into
the carrier's side, but refusing to take their eyes off their friend.

Ship-killing was exactly what the MK-54s had been designed to
do, and the blast shattered the side of the other vessel, breaking its
keel. The cutter's bow and stern leaped skyward in a V as the center
folded.

In seconds, both ends of the broken warship slid beneath the
waves.

FORTY-FOUR

Adventure Galley

The bow, bridge, and broken remains of the cutter's radar mast—everything forward of the torpedo blast—spiraled down through the black waters in a plume of oil, bubbles, and debris. It went down backward, the sleek bow pointed toward the surface for a bit, eventually pushed over by the current until it turned upside down. When it impacted with the bottom of the bay, the ship sent up a cloud of silt and steel fragments. Pieces of deck rail, black hull panels, and a splintered radar dish bloomed around it before sinking slowly to the sea floor. The bodies of the rescue swimmer, Mr. Vargas, and Leary the contractor billowed out as well, then joined the sinking debris.

Radar masts crumpled as the forward half of the ship settled, kicking up more silt, and the broken cutter came to rest completely inverted. A quarter mile away, the severed stern ended up on its side, bursts of air exploding from ruptured compartments and open hatches churning the silt cloud around it.

Red emergency lights glowed dimly on the cutter's bridge, though all other instrumentation had gone dark. The sealed hatch to the ladderway leading to lower decks created a pocket of air; none of the bridge windows had ruptured, and the inverted compartment was intact, pressure holding back the black waters outside.

Lying on what had been the ceiling, or *overhead*, of the bridge, Elizabeth Kidd opened her eyes to find herself entangled with the corpse of her quartermaster. Everything hurt. The blast had thrown her over the helm, across the compartment to slam into the navigation console. With difficulty she pulled herself out from under the dead man, a blast of raw pain informing her that her right leg, bent beneath her at an unnatural angle, was broken in several places.

She touched her jaw tenderly and winced. That was broken too, and her tongue discovered she'd lost several teeth. Liz tried to spit, but the broken jaw made it too painful, so she only managed to let blood trickle down her chin. Looking at the windows, at the water beyond, she knew her beloved ship was no more.

How had they done it? Without planes, carriers had no real offensive weapons.

It didn't matter. As bitter as the loss of her brother and her crew was, Liz took comfort in the knowledge that her deck gun had done so much damage to *Nimitz* that the carrier was already with her on the bottom, or well on its way.

One last piece of business.

There was a thump to her right, and Liz painfully turned to see a face pressed against the outside of the bridge window. Another soon joined it, a pair of pale, decaying things with cloudy eyes, hair drifting in the current. They looked in at her and beat the glass slowly with their fists.

More pounding came from the opposite side of the bridge, and in the red emergency lights Liz saw faces over there as well. Still more pressed against the glass, figures standing on the bottom of the bay and ringing the bridge, peering in at the lone woman and pounding, frustrated by their inability to reach her. Liz thought one of those faces might be Mr. Vargas.

She began crawling across the steel, biting her lip as she dragged her fractured leg behind her, eyes scanning. There, a pistol lying ten feet away, either hers or Amy's.

"Sorry," she said to the ghouls beyond the glass, pulling herself toward the handgun. "I won't be joining you. *I* make the decisions on *my* ship."

The pistol was still six feet out of reach when a deep cracking started at the front of the bridge, a four-foot, jagged line splintering the glass. Fists beat at the fracture from outside, and the cracking turned into a squeal.

Liz lunged for the pistol as the window imploded, glass and corpses pushed violently in by the sea, flinging Liz back against a bulkhead as the bridge quickly filled with icy water and death. Her eyes stung from the salt, and she choked on seawater as she saw hands and teeth coming at her in the muted red light.

Elizabeth Kidd's final sensation was pain.

In the end, a woman who had worked her entire life to rise above others, to stand out, give commands, and have her orders obeyed, joined the thoughtless millions shuffling across the sea floor.

Just another face in the crowd.

FORTY-FIVE

January 13—Nimitz

The aircraft carrier did not strike the remaining support for the Golden Gate Bridge, and the survivors aboard were spared a rain of the walking dead falling from the sky. Instead, *Nimitz*'s keel, too close to the shore, ground over a ridge of submerged rock extending into the bay from the Sausalito land mass, bringing the vessel to a halt half a mile from the remains of the bridge. The current still pushed at it from behind, and the underwater ridge would not hold the vessel back forever, but for the moment it had come to rest.

Breaches in the hull on the port side, first from the carrier's collisions last summer and now as a result of concentrated fire from the cutter's deck gun, were substantial. Water flowed in steadily, and the ship's pumps struggled to maintain neutral buoyancy. It was a battle they were slowly losing.

By the time the sun rose over the craggy new cliff face to the east that morning, *Nimitz*'s survivors began emerging from below and assembled on the flight deck. Chief Liebs, Stone, and Xavier came together first and were waiting when the handful of surviving hippies started appearing alone or in pairs, finally deciding it was safe to venture out after hiding as the priest had instructed. There weren't many left.

Sophia, Kay, and the children of *Nimitz* appeared at the starboard side, everyone holding hands as they crossed the deck. Sophia was carrying the toddler abandoned by the pirates, and little Ben walked alongside, his small hand in hers.

Rosa and Tommy found their way topside, the orderly now carrying the petite medic on his back as if she were a pack. Tommy set her down—her right foot was freshly bandaged—and the two of them immediately started looking the group over, tending to their assorted injuries, beginning with Xavier. Rosa ordered him to sit and strip off his body armor, then knelt beside him.

The priest rested a hand on her shoulder. "Michael?"

Fresh tears sprang into her eyes, and she shook her head.

"Is there any chance . . . ?" the priest started.

"No," she said, her voice cracking. "He . . . he turned into . . . he turned."

Xavier nodded and squeezed her shoulder. Rosa pushed his hand away, her brusque doctor's voice falling into place. "Be still so I can look at you."

Tommy crouched on her other side. "Listen to the doc, Father. Arguing just pisses her off. I know."

Xavier gave in and let the two medics examine him. The body armor had absorbed most of the bullet's energy, but a 7.62-millimeter round moved at extremely high velocity, and this one had penetrated the Kevlar a bit. Rosa informed the priest that all his work in the gym and hitting the bags had built up nice, dense muscle in his pectorals, catching what energy remained in the bullet and preventing it from going deep enough to damage something vital. The doctor was able to pluck the flattened round from the hole in his chest with a pair of long forceps. Then, using liberal amounts of alcohol, she stitched his chest closed right there on the flight deck.

Tommy gave the priest a towel into which he could scream during the procedure. Heavy bandaging completed the task as Tommy moved on to treat Stone and Chief Liebs, each with his own bullet wounds.

"What a fuc . . . what a mess we all are," said Rosa.

Xavier wiped the tears from his eyes, wincing as his chest muscles moved. "What you said, Doc."

The double-wide hatch at the base of the superstructure creaked open, and two figures emerged, both tattered and bloody, both darkened by smoke. Maya helped PK limp across the deck toward the group, struggling to walk on her own. The others ran to them and swept them both up. PK was in bad shape from the blast, and the medics went to work on him at once.

Maya found herself encircled by Xavier, Chief Liebs, and Stone. She signed to them that Banks had been killed in the blast, then looked around the deck. She signed the word "Daddy?"

The men shook their heads slowly, and Maya's hands went to her mouth.

"Michael is gone too," Xavier said, making sure she could see him speaking.

The tears began, and she wiped them away. "Evan?"

The gunner's mate took her hands. "I'm sorry."

Maya began to cry, and Stone led her toward Sophia and the children. Her sisters and surviving brother would need to be told about their father, and it was only right that the news come from Maya.

Xavier's fists clenched at the senselessness of it all. The walking dead were what they were, an affliction put upon the earth either by God or nature, as present in all their lives now as weather and sunrises. But would mankind *never* stop preying upon one another? The priest let out a long breath. Sadly, there was no one left upon whom to place the blame for all this death.

Except for you.

Xavier hung his head. He would wrestle with that thought another time.

Chief Liebs rested a hand on his shoulder and pointed at the sharp tilt to the deck, then at the nearby fragments of the iconic bridge where legions of the dead waited to fall on them. "We're not going to be able to stay here," the gunner's mate said. "Either the weight of the flooding causes the ship to roll over, or the current pushes us loose and into the bridge. We don't have the manpower to deal with what would spill onto this deck."

The priest nodded. "How many RIB boats are left?"

"Two," said Liebs. "Not enough to handle us all. Not in one trip, anyway."

"Where would we go?" Xavier wasn't really asking the Navy man for an answer as he turned in a circle. To the south, where San Francisco had been, was now only rolling ocean, and the Pacific waited to the west beyond the bridge. North was the hills of Sausalito. Perhaps they could trek overland, find an intact community somewhere to the north where they might find shelter and supplies. But if the horde waiting at the nearby bridge was any indication, the ruins in Sausalito would be crawling with the walking dead. He imagined leading a line of frightened children and wounded adults through there and shook his head. To their east was a towering, impassable cliff that extended both north and south as far as he could see.

But the chief was right. They couldn't stay here. Nothing but bad options.

Xavier sighed, feeling the pain of his wounds and the weight of years well beyond his own. "Let's use what time we have to gather weapons and supplies, then prep the boats. We'll stay as long as we can, but then some of us will have to remain behind while the rest abandon ship. You can come back for us if you find safe landfall."

The gunner's mate shook his head slowly. "Where are we going?"

The priest looked out at the hostile world. "I have no idea."

FORTY-SIX

January 13—Groundhog-7

Nimitz was not responding to radio calls, and as they flew southwest, the view below began providing an explanation. The earthquake they'd felt up in Chico must have originated in the Bay Area, because the closer they got, the more devastation could be seen below. Entire communities lay in shattered ruins; roadways had buckled and bridges were down. Landslides had swept aside highways, rail lines, and towns.

The dead moved across the landscape, the ever-present inheritors of the earth.

The sun was beneath the horizon, purples and oranges streaking the western sky as evening fell. The Black Hawk cruised along at four thousand feet, Angie West sitting in the co-pilot's seat with Vladimir across from her, both wearing helmets with radio headsets. In the back, Halsey crouched behind the starboard door gun, clipped into a safety harness and struck silent by the destruction passing below. Angie's husband, Dean, slept strapped into a rear bench seat, wrapped in a blanket, his bandages slowly turning red from his many wounds. He was in bad shape, and Angie was worried about him.

She looked back into the troop compartment. Her three-year-old Leah was buckled in beside her daddy, also under a blanket, asleep and leaning against him. Had it only been a few hours ago that Angie and Dean rescued her from a gang of murderous bikers and engaged in a long, running gunfight? Angie's heart ached at how much she'd missed them, and soared at the fact that Dean had kept the two of them alive over the long months of hardship and separation. It had come at a cost; dear friends lost and the discovery that Angie's parents were dead. But her husband and child were alive, and she wasn't ashamed to admit to herself that reuniting with them was worth the price.

"*Nimitz*, Groundhog-Seven, we are inbound to your position," Vladimir called over the radio. "Acknowledge."

There was nothing.

Angie looked down as twilight settled over fields of destruction. "Looks like it was the big one," she said.

"Yes," the Russian replied, "I have seen this in the movies. An earthquake to break California off into the ocean, although that does not appear to be entirely the case."

"Everyone thought it would be L.A.," Angie said.

"Mother Nature has fooled us yet again," Vladimir said. "How very crafty of her not to do what people expected."

Angie watched through the windscreen as the helicopter moved over the hills of Napa, then crossed Vallejo, identified as such only because of a map and their position. Now the city lay in ruins, flattened as if by a thousand tornadoes.

"It appears we have a new geological formation ahead," the pilot said as the Black Hawk approached the upheaval that had created a new line of coastal cliffs on the Pacific. Fragments of superhighway and square miles of shattered brick, wood, and steel were all that remained of the population centers that once stood where the cliff now existed. Vladimir descended to one thousand feet and brought the helicopter into a hover above the cliff's precipice, facing west.

No one spoke.

It was like discovering the edge of the world. The megaquake had utterly transformed the built-up and heavily populated Bay Area into a massive, primitive cove where the Pacific rolled in across seemingly endless space. The San Francisco peninsula was gone. There were no cities, no bridges, and no aircraft carrier; only the rolling sea backlit by a winter sunset. The magnitude of it all shocked them to silence, leaving only the beat of rotor blades above them.

Vladimir checked his fuel status and muttered a curse. He'd been counting on a safe landing zone, and now it was gone. Alternative options were all unpleasant.

"Vlad," Halsey called over his headset, "I got something low on the starboard side. Looks like a flashing light."

The Russian rotated the aircraft to face north, and Angie lifted a pair of binoculars. "I see it too. Two miles out, maybe less."

Vladimir spotted the blinking light and immediately accelerated to full military power, descending rapidly. It took only moments to cross the distance, and the Russian dropped the aircraft until it was a mere fifty feet above the surf, the towering cliff wall to their right. Angie and Halsey saw the remains of a radio tower jutting from the cliff, several motionless bodies piled at one end, clothing whipping in the rotor wash. One of the bodies wore flight gear, a vest-mounted strobe light winking in the falling light.

"It's Evan!" Angie shouted.

"Is he alive?" Vladimir demanded, his voice tight.

She looked. There was no movement. Three corpses were draped across the tower struts at his feet, each with its head kicked flat.

The body in the flight suit lifted a hand, but Angie couldn't tell if it was the simple reaching of a mindless corpse. Then the hand curled into a thumbs-up.

"He's alive!" Angie shouted.

"Door gunner," Vladimir called in his stern, commander's voice, "prepare to recover a downed pilot."

Angie looked at the nearness of the cliff, at the blur of blades as Vladimir brought them lower and closer. "Can you get close enough?" she asked, thinking about her daughter asleep in the back.

Vladimir's eyes were hard and focused. "We are going in," was his only response.

Evan Tucker was strapped into the co-pilot's seat, shivering beneath a blanket. Angie had moved into the back to make room for him and gave Halsey a big hug from behind, yelling over the wind that she had never seen such an act of bravery. While the helicopter hovered at one end, the ranch hand removed his safety harness, climbed down onto the wobbling, creaking radio tower, and crawled to Evan. Then he walked them both back down the shaking structure to the chopper doors, surf rushing about their legs and wind threatening to blow them off as the blades spun overhead, close enough to the cliff to kick loose stone free with their downdraft.

Halsey blushed and smiled.

Vladimir had the Black Hawk back at one thousand feet now and ordered Angie and his gunner to begin looking for the aircraft carrier's wreckage as he began a slow circuit of the new bay.

"You crashed," Vladimir said.

"I was shot down," Evan replied.

The Russian grunted. "And how did you enjoy autorotation?"

"You mean crashing? It sucked."

Vladimir muttered the Russian word for *amateur* and shook his head with a deep sigh. "Sadly, I am quite certain it will not be the last time."

Evan made a face. "Sorry, I'm not the great Vladimir Yurish, Lord of the Skies."

The Russian's face split into a homely grin. "I *like* this name. Use it whenever you please. And for your information, Evanovich, I have crashed my birds four times during my career. Not one incident was my fault, of course, and we were discussing *your* incompetence, not my innocent misfortune."

Evan laughed. "Good to see you too, Vlad."

The Russian nodded. "Welcome back, *tovarich*."

C ontact, zero-one-zero," Evan called, leaning forward in his seat and looking through binoculars. "Looks like the carrier."

The Russian adjusted course to the new heading, quickly spotting what Evan had seen. In the last of the light he could make out the dark rectangle of the carrier, sitting motionless just off the bay's northern shoreline, about a half mile from the remains of the Golden Gate. The ship was listing to port at a dangerous angle, far worse than it had been when they flew off its deck only days ago.

As they closed, Evan thought the ship looked dead, an empty derelict. One more piece of humanity's remains in a world that had moved on without them.

Vladimir approached from the stern, switching on his landing lights as he descended toward the lightless deck. Evan didn't bother to ask if his friend could safely set down on such a steep angle. He'd decided that there was no feat with an aircraft so crazy that the Russian wouldn't immediately attempt it, and likely succeed on the first try.

Crouched between the seats and wearing a headset, Angie watched as the dark ship filled their windscreen. Her heart fell. *They're gone.*

And then flares began to light off in a rough square across the flight deck.

FORTY-SEVEN

Nimitz

Maya raced at Evan as he climbed from the chopper. She saw that he was injured, and so she resisted the urge to leap into his arms and wrap her legs around him, instead simply holding him tight and covering his face in kisses. Then she held his cheeks and stared at him as if he might not be real. Evan laughed and held her, feeling no pain, never wanting to let go.

Sophia and Ben were there to meet Vladimir, and after hugging his lady and kissing her deeply, the towering Russian lifted his boy into the air and spun him in a circle.

"Papa!" Ben cried.

Xavier hugged everyone and told the Russian that the ship's deck lights and communications were knocked out during the attack. Vlad thanked him for the flares, and told him he would have landed even if the carrier had been belly-up.

The priest crouched and introduced himself to a suddenly shy Leah West. She hesitated, eyes wide as she stared at the big black man whose face had been so marred by brutality. With a tiny finger she traced the line of the scar that ran from his hairline to his chin, then kissed him on the cheek. "Kisses make it better," she said.

Rosa and Tommy organized a stretcher team to take Dean down to medical, as Halsey introduced himself to those gathered on deck. Xavier walked with Angie, their arms around one another, the priest gritting his teeth against both the pain of the fresh wound in his chest and the older grenade fragment in his thigh.

"You did it," he said. "Your family's safe."

Angie nodded. "Carney died. Skye too, I think. We couldn't find her."

The priest thought about the girl, a troubled soul if ever he'd encountered one. Then he told Angie about the boarders, the earthquake, the shelling from the pirate vessel. He listed those lost, ending with Calvin's sacrifice. There was an emotional moment, and they both cried for a time.

Chief Liebs joined them, and Angie looked at his bandages and the weariness on his face. "Must have been a hell of a fight," she said.

The gunner's mate nodded. "We're not done yet." He pointed to the bridge remains not far away. "There's a whole bunch of bad news that's going to drop on us when this ship breaks free from whatever's holding it back. Good thing you showed up when you did. We were going to abandon ship in the morning."

"And go where?" the woman asked.

He shrugged. "The father and I haven't come up with a good answer for that."

Aboard aircraft carriers, there is a constant, subtle vibration so unobtrusive it is generally not even noticed until it is absent. At that moment, the gentle vibration in *Nimitz* ceased. All three of them felt the change and looked at one another.

"What was that?" Xavier asked the Navy man.

"I don't know," said Liebs, "I've never felt that before."

Several minutes later, a tall, thin young man in Navy coveralls appeared at the top of a catwalk ladderway on the edge of the flight deck. He looked around, then sprinted toward the trio.

"Holy shit!" Chief Liebs exclaimed, recognizing his nuc, the young nuclear engineer rescued with him from the dry-goods locker so many months ago. In the Navy, nucs belonged to their own odd little tribe, keeping to themselves and only emerging from the deep for a quick meal before vanishing again. This boy had been no different, usually unseen. "I figured you were dead," the chief said.

The boy ignored the remark, his eyes intense. "The reactors shut themselves down. Did you feel it?"

That was the missing vibration, Xavier thought. "Why?" He noticed the boy was soaking wet.

"Because of the flooding. All power is out now."

"Can you get it restarted?" Angie asked.

The nuc shook his head impatiently. "You can't just flip a switch and turn on a nuclear reactor. Besides, they're underwater by now."

"Can't we pump them dry?" Xavier said, looking at the chief.

The man was pale. "No power," he said, "means no pumps. There's nothing to keep the sea out."

Nimitz gave a long groan and shifted, the current pushing its keel free from the submerged ridge of rock. At once, the deck made a great creaking sound and tilted several more degrees to port. Slowly, the aircraft carrier began to move again.

"We're going to sink fast," the gunner's mate said, then looked west, up at the remains of the Golden Gate Bridge. In the darkness above, the dead grew agitated, many stepping off the side as they noticed the ship drifting toward them. Thousands more were packed on the high roadway.

"But first," Liebs said, "we're going to have company."